Killing Trot

Book 3 of the *Unlikely Heroes* series

Written by

Aileen Chorley

A Terrible Mistake

Waves crashed on the shore. The three of them stared at the empty sky, glaringly empty now the two craft had gone.

"It'll be months before I can get to Marios Prime," Graham said, distantly.

"Weeks before I can get to Lixia," Brash murmured.

Jenna grabbed her hair, staring at the sand. "I might never see Flint again."

Brash turned to her. "Jenna, I..."

"I know. We made a terrible mistake."

"I thought it was you I wanted but..."

She raised her head. "No time for that. We'll head to Lixia. You'll make up with Allessa. I hope to God Flint's still there. Come on."

"I need to break it off with Yasnay first," Graham said.

They turned to him. "You've not done that?" Jenna asked, staring at him.

"No. I had this blinding epiphany when I woke up. I rushed straight over here."

"Fucks sake," Brash said.

"Make it quick," Jenna told him. "And... be gentle."

*

Brash and Jenna perched on a low white wall outside the apartment, waiting for Graham to break up with his Saffria girlfriend.

Jenna looked around. She would miss Draztis, the city of Hercillen quite beautiful with its white buildings and coastal location. But they had done what they came here to do. They had abolished slavery.

The rest of their crew had just left, heading to Marios Prime. Except Flint. He was taking Allessa to Lixia, the Sentier's home planet. Jenna and Brash had stayed on for some alone time, but the kiss on the beach brought everything into perspective. The romantic feelings had gone. Jenna knew now she'd been clinging to him, clinging to the past, clinging to her first love. But that love was spent. She glanced at Brash, taking in his tall, lean form, his loose dark hair. As handsome as he was, he was no longer what she wanted. She wanted Flint, the man she had thrown over for him. If she didn't catch up

1

with Flint on Lixia, she might never see him again. Flint wasn't sure he would *go* to Marios Prime.

Brash chewed his lip, hoping Allessa would forgive him. So, the Sentier had tentacles that protruded from her fingertips? At the moment, they seemed irrelevant. He'd been conflicted in his feelings, and the tentacles had swung things... in the wrong direction. What a jerk. He glanced at Jenna. Her shoulder-length blonde hair shone in the daylight. She was slim, beautiful, perfect... but he craved long dark hair, silvery skin, and alluring grey eyes. Hell, he even craved six fingers with retracting tentacles.

The sound of wailing drew their attention. Jenna and Brash looked at each other. The wailing became shouting and they cringed.

Graham emerged, shell-shocked. A vase flew after him, missing his head by inches. Jenna and Brash dodged out of its way.

"Come on," Graham said, "let's go."

Jenna ran after him. "You OK?" A shattering crash exploded behind them. Jenna glanced around. Yasnay's lilac face had turned purple.

"That was the hardest thing I've ever had to do."

Picking up their pace, they raced through the sun-drenched streets, lanky Bortten bowing in reverent submission. The whole city knew who they were. Gods. It was an unfortunate side-effect of their mission, and one they could do little about now.

They headed for the rear of the city, to the army airbase. Located in a shallow valley, the gates of the base opened for them immediately. The Bortten manning the gates bent his spindly body, his sunken face and aubergine eyes fixed on the ground. Neither Brash, Graham, nor Jenna spoke Bortten, but as Jenna could read and transfer thoughts, she had no trouble communicating with the ghoulish-looking soldier. She instructed him to rise. He did, his bottomless eyes gazing at the odd shapes her mouth made when she spoke. She told him they'd come to collect the craft Flint had arranged for them.

The soldier walked off, returning with two more lanky, zombie-looking figures, their cropped black tops showing off gross, grey-ribbed bellies. They carried bags of provisions, six each, which they managed easily with their six arms. Jenna stared at the bags, marvelling at Flint's thoughtfulness. A churning wave of sickness rose up in her.

The soldiers took them to a tortoise-shaped, brown craft. One of them pressed a square pad on the side, and a short gangway lowered. The crew followed them into a dismal loading area. The Bortten placed the provisions down carefully, and Jenna thanked them. Bowing graciously, they left. Graham hit a pad, and the gangway rose.

"Come on," Jenna said, running to the flight deck. "We need to get moving."

The basic flight deck had a small cockpit area with two seats, and two seats set further back. Brash studied the controls.

"You're OK flying this thing?" Jenna asked.

"Yeah, should be straight forward," he said. "Flint's labelled everything in English."

Again, she marvelled at Flint's thoughtfulness.

"Strap in," Brash said.

Jenna and Graham sat in the back two seats, the six armrests getting in their way. The craft shook as it fired up, the technology as basic as it looked. As they took off, the craft lurched from side to side. Exchanging a worried glance, Jenna and Graham strapped in. Pressed into their seats, they blasted out of the atmosphere, the ride becoming smoother.

"Sorry about that," Brash called back. "These armrests got in the way. Do they need all six?"

Jenna looked at Graham. "You OK?" He nodded, mutely. "You're sure you've made the right decision?" A stupid question because no way were they turning back.

He nodded, things becoming clearer to him. "I care about Yasnay but it wasn't what I had with Daria."

"You're just realising this?"

"I've been an idiot... It was always Daria. How could I have been so blind...?"

Jenna fumbled for an answer. She'd been blind too.

Graham raked a hand through his dark hair. "I don't know... Maybe I was... punishing her. She hurt me. A lot." Blowing out a strained breath, he shook his head. "How could I do that to her?"

Jenna touched his arm. "Don't feel too bad. Johnson had a lot to face up to. There were... issues with her mother, and maybe you helped her see them."

Graham looked at her. "No, I mean, how could I do that to Yasnay?"

"Oh. Err... well, you didn't realise what you were doing, did you?"

He rubbed his forehead. "A lot can happen in a few months. What if I get there and Daria doesn't want me anymore?"

"You can't think like that. I'm sure she'll want you."

Jenna stared out at space, wondering if Flint would still want her. At one time, she couldn't have imagined feeling this way about Flint. When they'd left him with Cornelius and the Erithians, he was a distant, tortured soul, but when they came back, he'd changed. Muscles replaced those weedy arms. Life

3

possessed that once vacant face, a face more noticeably good-looking, and framed by a halo of ice-blonde hair. Over the past months, he'd constantly surprised them. He could fight like a ninja warrior, he had more strength of spirit than any of them, and she had come to admire his integrity. The crew had shoved the role of captain onto him because they wanted to have fun, but he had proved himself more than capable of the job, outshining their old captain, Lucas Brash.

Jenna shifted, restlessly. If only they had their own craft. It had the Super Mega Hyperdrive, could make enormous leaps through space, was capable of traveling huge distances in no time. The craft had been one of SLOB's, built in the Spearos galaxy. Nothing in this region compared to it. It had allowed them to get back to this galaxy after killing SLOB. To get to the Spearos Galaxy initially, the Erithians had opened a portal using the power. She pondered that. The Erithians had directed the power... She could direct the power...

She shook her head. The Erithians were beings from another dimension.

"I could never pick up on cues," Graham mumbled.

"What...?"

He glanced at her. "You're supposed to know what they're thinking, aren't you, even when you don't?"

"What who's thinking?"

"Women."

"Ah." Jenna smiled. "I think that's called sensitivity."

"Maybe, but it would help if she'd just come straight out with stuff."

Jenna chewed her lip. "Being honest is... scary, I suppose."

"So, what was that about her mother?"

"Oh. Well, I don't know how much you know about Johnson's mother, but she was... ruthlessly hard. I don't think Johnson ever measured up. Her mother taught her not to rely on others, especially men, despised that weakness. When you proposed, it sort of stoked things up. You know, subconscious stuff."

"Really?"

"Her mother sounded bloody awful. She never bought Johnson birthday presents."

"Birthday presents?" A twinge of guilt stabbed his chest.

"Flint helped her see things more clearly."

Graham frowned. "Flint?"

She nodded.

He shook his head. "I'm beginning to think that man can do anything." He glanced at Brash, and lowered his voice. "So, you fucked Flint and Allessa off, and now you're trying to get them back?"

"Well, I wouldn't put it like that but that's exactly how it is."

He shook his head again. "How is it you can want someone and not even know?"

"I suppose we're experts at self-deception."

"Yeah..." He leaned back, his gaze becoming distant. "It was her eyes, you know..."

"What...?"

"Daria's eyes that first attracted me to her. Those mesmerising, unusual grey eyes... I mean, she was pretty intimidating at first, but those grey eyes drew me in."

Jenna nodded, thoughtfully. Johnson's eyes *were* striking. When considered objectively, Johnson presented an appealing package, yet it was easy to overlook this, focusing instead on her muscular arms, and very scary presence. The woman wouldn't take shit from anyone. Jenna appraised Graham. Pleasingly handsome and easy going, she bet he'd taken tons of shit from Johnson.

She rested her head back, thinking of what they had achieved on Draztis, absorbing the scope of everything they'd done over the past three years. This crew had been through a lot, and most still in their twenties. At twenty-four, she was the youngest but she was no longer the girl she'd been.

"How old is Flint?" she absently asked.

"Twenty-nine, I think. You don't know?"

"I never asked him..."

Violent pounding knocked them around in their seats.

"We're experiencing buffeting," Brash called back.

"No shit," Graham said, getting up and stumbling forward. "What's out there?"

"Nothing."

"We're experiencing turbulence in space?" Jenna asked, holding onto the armrests.

The buffeting stopped abruptly.

"What *was* that?" Jenna asked, looking out.

"I don't know," Brash said, studying his instruments. "No other ships on the scanner. Everything looks fine..."

"I'll check things over," Graham said, walking out.

Jenna moved forward. Negotiating the armrests, she sat in the seat beside Brash. "If there's something wrong with the ship, we might not get there in time." She tried to keep a lid on her panic.

"Don't worry, we'll get there," Brash said, checking his instruments again.

"And what if we do and they tell us to sod off?"

He turned to her. "Flint won't tell you to sod off. The man's besotted with you."

"Well, maybe he's not now."

"I don't think he's the type to hold grudges."

She breathed in then out, her gaze returning to Brash. "We well and truly screwed things up, didn't we?"

He nodded, reflectively.

Graham returned twenty minutes later. "The engine room's a rust bucket but I couldn't find any faults."

"So, what was that?" Jenna asked.

"Whatever it was," Brash said, looking out, "we're through it now."

Jenna stood. "I need a drink."

Walking into the loading bay, she riffled through the bags, grabbing a bottle of water. Taking a swig, she looked around the hollow, featureless space. Throwing back the rest of the drink, she slung the bottle down, and moved over to rusty ladder steps. The steps went down to the engine room but she climbed up, entering a dimly-lit metal corridor. Compact cabins branched off to the right. Two contained bunks, one a tiny medical facility, and one an even tinier kitchen. The craft had been built for transporting small numbers of troops, and officers would have made use of these rooms. The layout reminded her of one of SLOB's small craft they had stolen. That craft had a weapons deck. Opening another door, she found two basic guns. Not much to stave off an attack, especially if the attack came from the other side of the ship. The craft was woefully inadequate.

At the end of the corridor, a rusty ladder led up to an escape hatch.

The buffeting hit again. She grabbed hold of the ladder, the lights in the corridor blinking on and off, a high pitch whine making her eyes widen.

The noise and buffeting stopped. The lights came back. She ran down the corridor, climbing down the steps, Graham descending beneath her.

"What's happening?" she called to him. "Are the engines shot?"

"I don't know," he flustered.

She joined Brash on the flight deck. "That sounded like the engine was about to blow."

Brash raked a hand through his hair. "The readings are fine. Nothing on the scanner. I don't know what the hell this is. Stay here, I'm going down there."

Jenna kept her eyes on space as she waited.

"Well?" she asked when they returned.

Graham scratched his neck. "Everything's fine."

"So, what was that?"

"Some weird space phenomenon," he said with a shrug.

"That's it? That's all you've got?"

He frowned. "You got anything better?"

She had nothing. Nothing but an unsettled feeling.

Goodbye, Buddy

Newark stopped and stared at the building, squinting in the blinding orange daylight. The luxurious, sprawling residence, made of wood and glass, was unusual in Kaledia. The acres of scrubby grassland surrounding it served as countryside here.

"You're living in Daka's old gaff?" he asked Cornelius.

The white-haired man turned to him. "Yes, Mr Newark. After you left, the Hefruk asked if I wanted to acquire the building at a knock down price."

"A knock down price?"

"Seemed no-one wanted to purchase it. Many fear more enemies of the former drug lord will return."

"Oh. How did you pay for it?""

"I felt it incumbent on me to visit a casino."

Newark raised his eyebrows. "You used to frown at Trot for fleecing those places."

"Yes, well, Takeza deserves a grand place to live after the past she's had." The part-human, part-Kaledian old man smiled at his part-human, part-Kaledian, ex-prostitute girlfriend.

Newark stared at Cornelius then shook his head with a smile. "You've succumbed like they all do."

Cornelius raised his eyebrows in a question mark. Newark held up a hand, not bothering to explain. How could he tell this man, who had lived secluded with the Erithians all his life, and who up until recently had been a virgin, that women made men daft. It hadn't happened to him, of course, but he'd seen good men fall. Newark liked Cornelius's bird, Takeza, and she'd had a shit life locked up in one of Daka's whorehouses, but she'd turned Cornelius, their wise old mentor, into a schmuck. Newark glanced at Skinner, who gave him a knowing look.

Johnson didn't hear a word. She looked around, absently. Fraza stared into nowhere. The orange-haired, pot-bellied Kaledian missed Jenna terribly.

"Shall we go in?" Cornelius suggested.

They entered one vast, hollow space. A wide staircase faced them. A kitchen area lay far over to the left, a living area to the right. Though the place had some new furniture, it appeared as bare and unhomely as a shuttle terminal. It had been emptied and cleaned since they'd last seen it. Newark stood there with fond memories, picturing the dung-smeared walls, the pond-puke floors, and all the other inventive ways they'd trashed the drug lord's house before they'd taken him down. If Daka was alive, he'd regret the day he trussed them in ropes.

"I'm thinking of putting walls in," Cornelius remarked, looking around. "Now, there are ample bedrooms. Please don't take ours but help yourselves to the others."

"Do they have beds?" Johnson asked.

"Yes."

As the crew wandered upstairs, Cornelius turned to Takeza. "You're sure you don't mind them staying?"

She nodded. "I like them. Are you going to tell them now?"

"Yes. After the meal."

*

Cornelius and Takeza prepared an evening meal. The crew stared at Cornelius chopping vegetables in the kitchen. It was a far cry from the martial arts expert who had trained them in his dojo. Newark didn't know what to make of this domesticated man.

"You're using a knife?" Newark asked, humorously. "Can't you use your magic shit?"

"I can direct the power in many ways," Cornelius said, "but there is something wholesome about chopping vegetables."

"If you say so."

"What are you making?" Johnson asked, wandering over.

"A taygor stew," Cornelius said.

"Taygor?"

"It's a small rodent."

Her face fell. "Great."

"The rodent, apparently, is a delicacy here."

Newark glanced at the pot. "Hope you've shoved a ton of them in there. I'm starving." After all the strange shit he'd eaten these past months, rodent didn't sound too bad.

Skinner ambled around, looking in nooks and crannies. Cornelius glanced at him. The man seemed to be holding it together. Fraza, however, stood staring at the black sightless window.

"Would you like to help, Fraza?" Cornelius called.

Fraza turned and moved over, staring at the knife Cornelius offered him.

10

"You look like you haven't used a knife before," Cornelius remarked with a smile.

The Kaledian's eyes raised to him. "My parents wouldn't let me near knives. They thought them too dangerous for me."

Cornelius stared at him. "Ah. Well, I'm sure you can be trusted with it."

Fraza took the knife and began chopping. When he sliced into his finger, Newark laughed. Cornelius took the knife back, healed Fraza's finger, then instructed him to sit at the table.

The Taygor stew tasted good. Newark had second helpings. Fraza wasn't hungry, so Newark polished his off too.

After dinner, they migrated to the lounge on the far side of the building.

"Got any beer, Cornelius?" Newark asked.

"Yes." Newark, Johnson, and Skinner's faces lit up. "It's in the kitchen. In the long cupboard."

Newark and Skinner retrieved a keg and glasses.

As they poured the beer, Cornelius studied the group. They looked lost without a captain. Cornelius had managed to retrieve Skinner's braver self following his meltdown, and though the skinny, brown-haired man appeared together again, he seemed aimless at the moment. Cornelius could do nothing to improve Skinner's limp sense of humour but everyone had limits. Newark, as always, was himself, endearingly objectionable, his light brown hair messy as ever, his well-built body hiding the fact a child lived inside. Johnson still appeared heart-broken over losing Graham. Indeed, it would be a wrench for all of them, leaving Graham behind. Fraza was the one who concerned him most, though. The Kaledian wasn't functioning without Jenna. Somehow, he had to remove the crutch that was Jenna Trot. Fraza had to find that crutch within himself. It was a taxing problem for Cornelius.

Beers in hand, the crew settled back.

"Now," Cornelius said, "I have wonderful news." The crew stared at him, expectantly. "Takeza is going to have our baby."

Newark spat out his beer. The rest gawked at the older man.

Cornelius gave it time to sink in, and the crew's attention transferred to Takeza's belly. Could it *get* any bigger?

"You seem taken aback," Cornelius said to them.

Johnson shook her head. "No, that's... great news."

"How pregnant is she?" Skinner asked, still staring at the belly.

Cornelius looked at him. "The doctor on Draztis wasn't too sure. Our anatomy is much different to theirs. At a guess, three months."

"So, what's the gestation length?" Johnson asked.

11

Cornelius scratched his temple. "Well, as we are the only two part-human, part-Kaledians we know of, I'm afraid that is unclear."

"What's the Kaledian gestation length?"

"Thirteen months," Takeza said.

"So, split the difference. Eleven months."

"I'm not sure that adds up," Cornelius said.

"It adds up to me."

"Can I be a god-father?" Newark asked. "What do they do?"

Cornelius turned to him. "They look after the child if the parents die."

"Oh. I'll get back to you on that."

"You know," Skinner put in, thoughtfully, "children can split up the best of relationships. Sleepless nights, pressure, the endless demands... Drives sane people crazy."

Cornelius and Takeza stared at him.

"'Course," Newark offered, "you could direct the power to shut the brat up."

"Are you calling our child a brat?" Cornelius asked.

"Hey, keep your hair on. I'm not the one keeping you up all night."

"Don't have a girl," Johnson contributed. "You'll fuck them up and screw any chance they have of keeping a relationship."

"Don't have a boy," Newark countered, "he'll have bright orange hair like Fraza."

"Takeza has orange hair," Cornelius pointed out.

"Yeah, but she's a girl. A boy would look like a fuck-wit."

"Are you saying Kaledian men look like fuck-wits?"

"Duh."

Cornelius glanced at Takeza. "I think I'm ready to retire. How about you?" She nodded.

"Hey," Newark said, "how come Takeza can speak English but you have to transfer thoughts. You had a human dad, didn't you?"

Cornelius stared at Newark. Bright thoughts did occasionally pop into his head. "Well spotted," he said. "My father would have spoken English to me but he died when I was young. I was brought up with my mother's tongue. When she died, I had to use thought transference all the time to communicate with the Erithians."

"Good job you could pull that shit off then," Johnson remarked.

"Yes, I had been learning from an early age."

"Why did your parents stay with the Erithians?" she asked, curiously.

"Well, they liked it there and... being told your son is instrumental in saving the universe is a pretty compelling reason."

"Yeah... Hey, maybe Takeza could teach you English, if you can be arsed to learn."

"She has been doing. Is has been a shared interest for us."

Yeah, Newark thought, but not as shared as all the screwing they'd been doing.

"So, you *can* speak English?" Johnson asked. Cornelius nodded. "Well, why don't you?"

"When you receive my thoughts, you block out my voice. I'm virtually whispering anyway but if you actually listened to it, it might be... disconcerting."

"Oh, come on, Cornelius," Newark said. "Give us a bit of English."

"Very well."

Cornelius spoke to them in English, and it freaked the hell out of them. He sounded like somebody else.

"Bloody hell, Cornelius," Newark said, "you don't sound like that at all."

"Actually, I do. The thing is, the voice you hear in your head is based on your own preconceptions of how I should sound. Wise old father figure, perhaps? Whatever your preconceptions are. In fact, you'll each hear me differently."

"That's fucked up."

"Still want me to speak in English?"

The crew shook their heads.

"Well, it's been a tiring day," Cornelius said, getting up. "We will bid you good night."

Newark watched them go. "Tired, my arse. We all know what he's skedaddling off for?"

"Well," Johnson mused, "he might as well get it in now before her belly gets any bigger."

"Don't their bellies get in the way anyway?" Skinner pondered.

Newark and Johnson pondered this too. Their eyes moved to Fraza, who stared at the wall in a world of his own.

*

The crew lounged around the next day. And the day after that. By day three, boredom and restlessness set in. They missed having a purpose and, though they'd never admit it, they missed having someone tell them what to do.

13

Cornelius sat them down for a chat. "Jenna and Mr Brash will not be back for months," he said. "Mr Flint, likewise, if he comes back at all. In the meantime, you need to find yourselves a purpose."

"Like what?" Johnson asked.

"Well, it could be anything. There must be some good causes you could apply yourselves to in this city. In fact, that could be your first purpose. Finding one."

"What are we?" Newark asked. "Good Samaritans?"

"Yes, Mr Newark. You saved the universe, you abolished slavery in a whole region of the galaxy. Did anybody pay you for this?" Newark shook his head, feeling slightly miffed. "Then good Samaritans is exactly what you are."

"OK, but kicking butt isn't the same as... what...? Collecting for charity or something? We've already wiped Daka out. What's left to do here?"

"Oh, I'm sure you'll sniff out corruption or abuse if you look hard enough. Jakensk is a big city. There's always some unsavoury characters up to no good."

"So, we're not good Samaritans," Skinner remarked, humorously. "We're batman."

Nobody laughed.

"OK," Johnson said, nodding. "We'll scope the place out. I'm bored as shit sitting around here."

As they got up, Cornelius touched Fraza's arm. "Fraza, could you stay behind, please?"

Newark turned. "Have you got any dosh, Cornelius? We're skint." Cornelius threw him a purse of Kaledian coin. "That mind-reading shit comes in handy."

"That wasn't mind-reading. Well, it was, but it wasn't." Newark stared at him, puzzled. "Please don't use it to get drunk."

"Sure."

As the crew left, Cornelius turned to Fraza. "I'd like to speak to you," he said.

Fraza scratched his ears.

Cornelius assessed him. "Your OCD is still a problem for you, I see."

Fraza nodded then jerked his head three times.

"Well, seeing you with OCD is much better than seeing you disappear," Cornelius said, gently. "You've had a rough few months, haven't you? You fell apart when Jenna lost her memory. Then the two of you got separated by slave traders."

Fraza looked at him, intently. "She forgot who I was."

14

"I believe so. The point is, Fraza, you have immense power inside you. Jenna gave you confidence. Somehow, she managed to free you from the strangle-hold of your mind. But you can't rely on Jenna any longer. You have to learn to rely on yourself."

Fraza scratched his ears. "If I knew how to do that, I would."

"Something about Jenna spoke to you. She believed in you in a way no-one else had. I'll admit the girl *is* pretty amazing," he said, shaking his head. "But my point is, she initiated your own belief in yourself. And that is what *you* need to do now."

"How?"

"Take a yact. Go exploring on your own, get to know yourself, rely on yourself."

Fraza stared at him. "Much of the planet is unexplored wasteland."

"You took a yact once before, remember, when you found me and the Erithians?"

"I had no choice, and I was lucky to find you."

"Perhaps you'll surprise yourself."

Fraza shook his head, vigorously. "I can't do that again. When we escaped the plantation on Juyra, Newark said I was dead weight. He said he nearly got eaten by a plant because of me. I don't think he's forgiven me for it." Fraza scratched his ears.

"Knowing Newark, he would have got himself eaten by a plant anyway."

"He said I stood there and did nothing."

"You don't remember?"

Fraza shook his head.

Cornelius rubbed a hand over his mouth. "You had them to protect you on Juyra, to do it all for you. But what if you didn't? What if you had to do it for yourself? You can direct the power, Fraza. I once said the power was weak in you. I was wrong to say that. It is as strong as your mind allows. According to Jenna, you have done far more than I ever have. You need to learn to get out of your own way but you'll not do that here."

Fraza looked at him, fearfully. "What if I die out there?"

"What if you live as if you were dead for the rest of your life."

Fraza's eyes widened.

"Remember," Cornelius said, "you have your own Jenna inside you, and his name is Fraza."

*

15

Newark, Johnson, and Skinner walked through the city streets, wearing shades. The bright orange sunlight only dazzled humans. Jakensk was a bustling hive of activity, the main streets wide to accommodate the paddling-pool-shaped hover craft, called yacts. They flew several feet above the ground. Off the main streets, a labyrinth of narrow alleyways held the underbelly of the city.

Though Kaledians were the indigenous species, green Guthrins, blue Stilgens, and beefcake Revlans also lived here. Humans could be seen all over the place but few settled. Marios Prime, the human name for the planet of Kaledia, lay on a trading route, which was why the crew had arrived here in the first place. They'd been taking shore leave. If it hadn't been for Daka, they'd still be aboard Osiris. When Daka tied them in ropes, that's when their real adventures began.

Johnson stopped and looked in a window. The shop sold human attire. She stared at a short blue dress. Graham's new bird, the lilac-skinned Saffria, wore dresses all the time. Did he prefer women in dresses? She looked down at herself - boots, tight-fitted black jeans, and a sleeveless grey t-shirt.

"You thinking of buying a dress, Johnson?" Newark asked, unnerved.

Johnson turned to him. "Don't be fucking stupid. Come on, let's go for a drink."

"Thought we were being batman?" Skinner said.

"Batman can wait."

They passed eating houses, where pot-bellied Kaledians tipped their heads back, and wolfed down wriggling, tentacled creatures. Newark shuddered. He still hadn't got used to the sight of that. He stared at Johnson as she entered a classier drinking establishment.

"What are you doing?" he asked. "They'll never let us in there. Come on, let's go to our local." Their local, a scruffy joint in a run-down part of the city, had no admission criteria, and served cheap beer.

Johnson ignored him. Newark and Skinner looked at each other. Reluctantly, they followed after her.

For Kaledia, the place was class but the bright orange walls and dazzling lighting did nothing for the ambience.

A Kaledian man stepped up to them and looked them over. Johnson gave him a 'fuck off' glare and he backed away slightly, his eyes widening as he recognised who they were. The humans that had saved the city from Daka. Their pictures had been all over the news. He ushered them forward, moving customers out of their seats. Newark grinned, sticking his thumbs up to Skinner.

16

Without Flint or Fraza to translate, they couldn't place their orders but they didn't need to. A selection of free drinks was brought to them straight away.

"Being a good Samaritan has its perks," Newark said, leaning back and taking a long swig of beer.

"Still think this was a bad idea?" Johnson asked, looking around. The well-dressed clientele was varied in species.

As the drinks kept coming, the three of them settled in for the day. And night.

Pot-bellied Kaledians slow-danced in the centre of the room. It may have been slow but it wasn't exactly close. Those bellies really did get in the way. Again, Newark pondered the mechanics of Kaledian procreation.

"There are humans over there," Skinner observed, pointing with his chin.

In the far corner, a large group of dressed-up humans, probably shore-leavers, enjoyed a night out. The women wore dresses, and Johnson watched the men flirt with them.

"They're not from Osiris, are they?" Newark asked, having a disturbing thought. If the Admiral ever found them, they'd be hauled back aboard. He doubted the tight-fisted old git would buy their saving the universe story, and he'd also want to know where his daughter was. Newark had the feeling Trot wouldn't want to see her dad. She'd made no effort to contact him.

"Don't recognise any of them," Johnson said.

"Good."

Johnson watched the humans get up to dance. She seldom danced. The last time had been on Draztis, when she'd drunk tea that was more than tea, and they'd been trying to get on good terms with corrupt slave traffickers. That was a great party, she reflected.

"D'you want to dance, Newark?" she asked.

Newark spat out his drink. "Dance?"

"I'll dance," Skinner offered.

Johnson glared at him. "Fuck off, Skinner. You'd cop a feel, you fucking creep."

Skinner stared at his drink.

"I just want to dance," she said to Newark. "I don't fucking fancy you, so don't get any ideas."

Newark rose from his seat as if in a dream. Walking to the centre of the room, he gingerly put his hands on her, and they moved from side to side.

"So, what's with the dancing?" he asked, staring at her, oddly.

She shrugged.

As she danced, Johnson studied the other humans as if they were a new species. Her eyes landed on a strong, lean man, sitting back in his chair, observing her under loose dark hair. He had an exotic flavour, undeniably attractive. His dark eyes never left her, as if she was a new species too. Johnson held his stare. Nobody stared her down. After a time, he stood and walked her way. Johnson kept her eyes on him as he came closer.

"Could I have this dance?" he asked, the slight Spanish accent as compelling as his dark eyes.

"Fuck off," Newark said.

Johnson disentangled herself from Newark and took the man's hand.

Newark stared at her before wandering back to Skinner. "She fucking dumped me."

Skinner laughed, watching the dancing pair. They moved together closely, the man's hands wandering down her back.

"She's going to get laid tonight," Newark remarked with envy.

"I'm not sure," Skinner said. "Look at the woman in the blue dress. She doesn't look too happy."

"So?"

"She looks like a steaming pressure pot, and she's glaring at Johnson."

Newark's eyes honed in on a blonde-haired woman. Her tight face and blazing eyes told Newark she was a fuse about to blow. "What's *her* problem?"

"Johnson, it would seem."

Oblivious to the woman, the Spaniard leaned in to Johnson. "What's your name," he breathed in her ear.

"Daria," she said, her lips brushing his neck. "What's yours?"

"Emilio. You are very beautiful."

Nobody had ever called her beautiful before. She knew he was feeding her bullshit but she went along with it anyway.

The steaming pressure pot lurched to her feet. Newark moved to get a better view. The blonde lunged forward, grabbing Johnson's arm, pulling her off the Spaniard. Johnson turned, punching the woman in the face, flooring her at once. As Johnson went in for the kill, two men grabbed her arms but she back-punched one, bursting his nose, before spinning around to lay into the other.

Emilio stood there, staring at Johnson, entranced. The woman was incredible. As more joined in, he went to her defence, battling his own side. Skinner and Newark steamed in too. Tables got trashed. Clientele backed away.

18

A group of hired Revlans charged over and split up the fight. The humans got thrown out into the street, all except Johnson, Skinner, and Newark, who were heroes here and the gloss hadn't worn off Daka's demise.

Johnson plonked herself in her seat and took a deep swig of beer.

"Think she was his girlfriend?" Newark asked, feeling buoyant from the exercise.

"I don't fucking care," Johnson said.

"Bitch stopped you getting laid."

"Stopped us all getting laid," Skinner remarked, looking at the door.

"There's more fish and all that," Johnson threw out.

Newark looked around. "Not here, there's not. Let's try somewhere else."

*

Cornelius stared at their bruised faces. "What happened?" he asked.

"Ask the jealous bitch who attacked me," Johnson said.

He looked to Skinner for more. Skinner explained.

"You spent the whole day in a bar?" Cornelius asked.

"Yep," Newark said. "They kept bringing us free drinks."

"You have my money then?"

"Err... No. We spent that in the next place."

"So, you basically wasted my money and the whole day."

"What are you?" Johnson asked. "Our father?"

Cornelius's face took on a hard quality. "No, I'm your landlord. So, if you want to stay here, you'll find something worthwhile to do, and that doesn't involve squandering my money in bars."

She sniffed. "OK, if you won't sub us, we'll get Fraza to hit the tables."

"Fraza has gone."

"Gone? Where?"

"He has taken a yact, and gone off to find himself."

"Is he mad?" Newark asked, staring at the man. "Fraza's a fucked-up mess. He'll never survive out there."

The three of them stared at Cornelius, concerned.

"He'll be fine," Cornelius said with a wave of his hand.

Their stares transferred to the waving hand. They'd seen it too many times before.

"We have to go after him," Johnson said, walking to the door.

"No," Cornelius said with authority. "Fraza has to learn to look after himself." He let out a breath. "It's touching you all care about him, but he needs to learn to care for himself."

"This is bullshit," Johnson said, opening the door.

The door slammed shut. As she tried to open it again, an invisible force knocked her on her arse.

She looked at Cornelius, defeated.

Newark flopped in a chair. *Goodbye, buddy.*

A New Adventure

Johnson, Newark, and Skinner applied themselves more thoroughly to their assigned batman role. They scoped the city, avoiding the bars - Cornelius had refused to give them any more money.

"Hello again," a voice said from behind, and the three of them turned to face the Spaniard from last night. He took off his shades, his exotic eyes lingering on Johnson. "I enjoyed our dance," he said in his appealing accent. "I'm sorry it got interrupted."

Newark looked around for the mad bitch.

"Was that your girlfriend?" Johnson asked, lifting her shades too, soaking in those dark engaging eyes.

Emilio scratched his neck. "No. The woman has had an unhealthy obsession with me since a recent... one-night stand."

"Unhealthy? Perhaps you should knock her lights out. Give her a healthy dose of reality."

The Spaniard couldn't ascertain if she was joking or not. He smiled, regardless. "Well, that might get me fired."

"Fired?" she asked, confused. "You aren't in the space corps?"

"No, I work for a well-known oil company. We've recently opened a site near Kelparz." The crew looked at him, nonplussed. "It's the second largest city on Kaledia. Anyway, we've been given permission to drill, and work began recently. I'm heading over there in the morning."

"Oh," Johnson said, hiding her disappointment.

"The Kaledians are letting you take their oil?" Newark asked, confounded.

Emilio looked at Newark, studying him properly for the first time. "In exchange for a healthy percentage of the profit, which they call a land fee, and an extortionate amount of taxes. The Kaledians don't have the expertise or equipment we have. Unfortunately, though, we've been experiencing a lot of trouble."

"Trouble?" Johnson asked.

"Somebody has been sabotaging our equipment. A compound has been built around the rig but now they're resorting to violence."

"Don't you have muscle?"

"The company has hired security but they haven't managed to stop it, nor have they found the source of the trouble." His eyes focused in on her. "Anyway, as I said, I'll be heading out tomorrow. Shame," he said, regretfully.

"Your company needs muscle and brains," Johnson asserted. "That's us."

"It is?" the Spaniard asked, glancing at Newark.

"It's what we do," she said but he chewed the inside of his lip, uncertainly. "We are the ones that took out the former drug lord here. Daka? You might have heard of him?" Johnson neglected to mention Trot's involvement.

"That was you...?"

"So, if your company wants to pay us, we'll get the job done." She turned to Skinner and Newark. "You're up for this, aren't you?"

"Hell, yeah," Newark said.

Skinner nodded.

"You're the ones that took out Daka...?" Emilio stared at her, entranced. Stories of Daka's demise had become legend in this place.

"Yep," Johnson said, nodding.

"Right... Well, I'll have a word with my boss then." A smile possessed the Spaniard's god-like face. "Maybe this isn't goodbye, after all. Have you got some way I can contact you?"

Johnson gave him their current address.

"I'll be in touch," he said, looking at her meaningfully.

She nodded, watching as he walked away, taking in his well-proportioned frame, the calm confidence of his stride. Emilio glanced around briefly, and their eyes locked.

"You *so* fancy him," Newark said.

She shrugged. "What's not to fancy?"

"Cornelius will be pleased with us," he said, pleased himself. A new city to explore, money in their pockets, and new butt to kick. Life was looking up.

*

Cornelius did not look pleased.

"I thought you wanted us to find a purpose?" Newark said.

"I do, but I was thinking along the lines of helping the weak, not multi-million-pound corporations."

Newark shook his head. "There's no satisfying some people," he said under his breath.

"We *are* helping the weak," Skinner put in, humorously. "Johnson has a weakness for the man."

"Shut the fuck up, Skinner," Johnson said. "Look, it's a way to earn money and something to do for a few months."

"Or *someone* to do," Newark joked.

22

Johnson turned and punched Newark in the face.

"Fucking hell, lighten up," Newark said, holding his cheek, staring at her in askance. "Least my joke was funny."

"I don't chase any man, got that. From now on, they chase me."

"OK, let's all calm down," Cornelius said. "Very well, if this is what you want to do, fine. Takeza could use some peace and quiet in her condition."

"We'll be back before the baby comes."

"Wonderful," Cornelius replied with a strained smile. He loved these people but one baby would be enough to deal with.

"Could you bung us some dosh to tide us over," Newark asked with a purposefully cheeky grin.

"Fine."

"And, by the way, if Fraza does ever come back, tell him good job for not getting himself killed."

A sudden thought popped into Newark's head. What did Kaledian coffins look like?

*

Fraza travelled on a brand new yact with tons of spare fuel rods to keep him going. As yet, he hadn't got far. He'd stopped outside Jakensk, and sat by a murky green river with his head in his hands, contemplating the upcoming ordeal. Kaledia was a big planet, much of it unexplored. He had the power and this should have made him feel better but it didn't. He just didn't trust himself out there. Yet, if he could do this, what would that say about him?

After hours of struggle, he got in the yact and took off.

S.O.S

The strange phenomena hadn't happened again. It had been two weeks since they'd left Draztis, and the time dragged. They weren't used to travelling so slowly, and the ship was confining. It would be another three weeks before they reached Lixia.

Graham and Brash took turns in the cockpit. Jenna spent the time running up and down the loading bay to keep active. Sometimes, she'd spar with Graham. For the most part, Flint occupied her thoughts. Would he still be there when they arrived on Lixia?

Dropping into the back seat on the flightdeck, she let out a big sigh. Graham sat beside her. "Miss our ship?"

"Miss the bar too. I could do with a drink." She glanced at Brash. "How about I learn to fly this-"

Buffeting rocked the ship, far worse than before.

"What is this?" Jenna called out, alarmed, as Graham staggered to the front.

"I don't know." Brash struggled to control the craft. It wasn't stopping this time. "I'm going to set down on that planet," he shouted over the din. "We can't fly through this."

"But that'll add time to our journey," Jenna shouted back.

"If we don't get the ship out of this, we might not get *anywhere!*"

Brash altered course. Through the maddening turbulence, Jenna stared out at the purple planet. They didn't have time for detours.

The ride became smooth as they approached the planet, descending through a cloudless atmosphere. They landed on bare grey rock. A pale purple sky hung over them. The barren rock stretched off into the distance in all directions.

"According to the guidance map," Brash said, "this planet is called Gate." He checked the readings. "The air's thin but breathable."

Graham leaned over. "He's programmed English in there too?"

"Is it inhabited?" Jenna asked.

"No," Brash told her.

"So, what now?"

"Now, we check the ship over, and hope whatever that was has passed when we take off again."

"If this keeps happening, we won't have enough fuel to reach Lixia," she said, concerned.

"Why *is* this happening, though?" Graham asked. "What could cause it? A disturbance in space..."

He came up with nothing.

"Well, let's hope the ship's OK," Brash said, looking around the grey wilderness. "Because, if we're stuck here, we're screwed."

As Brash and Graham gave the craft a thorough check, Jenna walked around outside. Nothing broke the skyline. The deathly silence rang in her ears, the stillness disorientating. The thin air made her dizzy. She returned to the craft and lay on the floor of the loading bay for a few minutes.

Brash and Graham came up from the engine room.

"You OK?" Brash asked her.

She sat up. "Fine. So?"

"There's nothing wrong with the craft," he told her. "I'm going to take a different trajectory out of here in case the anomaly is still going on."

It was a smooth ride out, and continued to be smooth for the next few days, the crew certain the strange phenomena had passed. When it happened again, Jenna's disbelief turned to fury. "No!" she yelled, punching the seat.

"Jenna, calm down," Brash called back.

"Are we going to have to stop again?"

"If it doesn't end soon. It's sending the instruments haywire. It could damage the craft."

It didn't stop and they were forced to land on the nearest planet, the ship descending through dense cloud. Visibility low, they referred to the read-outs, which showed forested terrain. Brash picked up on a clear patch, and headed for it.

Breaking the cloud, the craft got pelted with rain, visibility still low. Coming in to land, they touched down. In a boggy swamp.

"Get us out!" Jenna yelled.

Brash desperately tried to lift the craft. "I can't get it up! Whatever this is, it's sucking us down!"

"Are you freaking kidding me!"

"What the fuck *is* this stuff?" Graham flustered.

They were sinking at an alarming rate. Brash gave up. "There's rocks," he said, pointing. "We can make it out on them. Grab some provisions." He and Graham sprang into action.

"What about the ship?" Jenna pleaded.

"The ship's gone, Jenna."

And so was any hope of catching up with Flint.

Brash and Graham charged into the loading bay, grabbing bags of provisions. Jenna stared out in a daze.

"Jenna, come on!" Brash yelled.

Running out, she grabbed a bag, and followed them up the ladder. Brash forced open the escape hatch. Exiting onto the roof, they jumped onto flat, protruding rock, rain pelting them mercilessly, the warm air oppressively humid. Moving from rock to rock, they made solid ground.

Turning, they watched in a daze as their ship sank from view. The plop of a bubble absorbed their attention.

A heavy silence followed.

Graham raked a hand through his wet hair, and looked around. A mass of twisting branches and enormous dark-green leaves surrounded the swamp. "The information profile reported life here," he said, "but it didn't specify how intelligent."

"If they're not intelligent," Brash said, concerned, "that means no transport, and no way of getting off this planet."

"Which way?" Graham asked.

Brash shrugged, helplessly. "Come on," he said, leading them into the trees.

Jenna remained rooted to the spot, staring at where their ship had been, her hopes and dreams sunken with it. It was over...

Brash turned to her. "Come on, Jenna," he said, gently. "We need to move."

Lost, she followed after them.

They trudged through forest, the pounding rain a constant backdrop, their wet clothes weighing them down. Brash kept his eyes peeled. He didn't trust alien forests. The last one he'd entered had nearly claimed Newark's life.

Hours passed. The forest stretched on endlessly. So, too, did the rain. They pressed on, quiet and morose, lost in their own worlds, holding onto the shred of hope they'd find civilisation.

As darkness fell, they camped in the hollow of an enormous tree that shielded them from the rain. Brash dug out a blanket, which the three of them shared. None of them spoke as they drifted into an uncomfortable sleep.

Another day brought more rain, but eventually, the rain let up, the pelting becoming lazy droplets dripping from leaves. Shrieking birdsong put them on high alert. Until they got used to it. Steaming humidity sucked air from their lungs. Moisture clung to their skin. Brash and Graham took their shirts off, tying them around their waists. The sky above turned from cloudy to the palest turquoise. When the end of the forest came in sight, hope soared.

Breaking free, they walked forward to find themselves on a high plateau. Miles of dark-green, empty grassland stretched ahead of them.

"It could take weeks to find anyone…" Jenna murmured, distantly.

Brash and Graham stared ahead, her words ringing with truth.

Pressure built inside Jenna. "Why did you have to land on this damn planet," she threw at Brash.

"Jenna, stop complaining," Brash said, harshly. "That's not going to help."

"It's alright for you to say. You know where Allessa's going to be."

"I don't know that for sure. You know Sentiers travel around."

"By the time I reach Johnson," Graham murmured, despondently, "she'll have moved on with her life…"

"Look," Brash said, raking a hand through his hair, "the most pressing matter now is to stay alive and find civilisation."

"It wouldn't be," Jenna shot, "if you hadn't pitched down in a bloody bog."

"It was impossible to see anything. The readings showed flat land. Should I have landed in the trees?"

"You should have flown around until we got out of the cloud!"

"Stupid Bortten junk-craft!" Graham threw out, kicking the air with his foot.

"I didn't know it was bog," Brash levelled at her.

"Exactly."

"You're acting like a brat," he said in a hard voice.

"That's because I made a huge mistake and I can't believe I *did* that."

"I made a huge mistake too. I can't believe I fell for it."

"Fell for it? As if I was reeling you in with batting eyelashes? You were the one charming me with nostalgic memories and those toying dark eyes. I can't believe *I* fell for it. You come sniffing around me when you'd slept with Allessa…?"

"I wouldn't have slept with her if you hadn't kissed Flint."

"Well, that's a matter of debate, isn't it? And a kiss isn't the same as sleeping with someone."

"Maybe you would have slept with Flint if I hadn't caught you."

"Maybe you would have slept with Allessa if I hadn't kissed Flint."

"No, because you wouldn't have taken that drug and forgotten who the hell you were. We'd never have ended up on Juyra in the first place."

"You even slept with someone in Cankar."

"That was a shape-shifting prostitute I thought was you!"

Graham turned, his eyes bulging. *That* was what happened?

Jenna sniffed. She couldn't call him out on that.

Brash gave her a hard look. "You laughed at me when I told you, remember?"

She sniffed again.

28

Gaze lingering on Brash, Graham drew in a collecting breath. "Look, we need to focus," he said, injecting some common sense.

"Focus on what?" Jenna threw out. "We're stuck here, and our ship's stuck in a bog." She shot Brash another look.

"Well, if you're so clever," Brash retaliated, "why didn't you use the power to try to raise the sh..."

Brash stared at her. Jenna stared back at him. Why *didn't* she try to raise the ship?

"I could try to raise the ship," she said with a spark of hope.

"Is no good," Graham told her. "By now, everything will be goosed."

Jenna turned to him. "Not necessarily."

"We left the hatch open."

"Shit." Gazing at him, she dropped to the ground, holding her head in her hands. "Oh my God, I'm so stupid..."

Brash sniffed now.

She looked up at him. "You could have thought of it too."

"Hey, you're the one with the power."

"Typical of you, isn't it? Absolve yourself of all responsibility."

"What the hell are you talking about now...?"

"You blamed Flint for Draztis being attacked but you had years of experience on him."

"OK, enough," Graham said, tersely. He blew out a breath. He was stuck on a planet with a couple of ex's bickering like hell. And he couldn't see it getting better as the days went on. "Look, stop talking to each other, the pair of you. It's getting us nowhere."

They stopped talking but resentment lingered. Brash walked around, trying to dispel the tension. He shouldn't have allowed himself to get dragged into that. Would he ever be the captain Flint had become?

As Jenna stared at the ground, something else occurred to her. She looked up at them. "I really *am* stupid..."

"You're not stupid," Brash said, relenting. "We're all fraught."

"No, I am. Why didn't I think of it before? I can mind-link with Allessa. Tell her we're in trouble."

Brash and Graham stared at her. "You can do that over distance?" Brash asked, amazed.

"I spoke to Cornelius from Venulas. And Juyra," she told them.

"Holy crap," Graham said, bringing a hand to his mouth.

She frowned. "Didn't Cornelius tell you? I directed him to Iprian."

"He said he had a feeling."

"How...?" Brash asked her. "How can you do that?"

"Minds can bridge distance," she said.

"Is there anything you can't do...?" Graham asked, staring at her in wonder.

She looked at him. "I can't remember to do shit when I need to."

"Wait," Brash said, "do we know where we are?"

Graham nodded. "I looked at the map while you landed. This planet is called, Shyrah."

"But where the hell on the planet are we? How would they find us?"

"According to the map, there's a large crater about thirty miles due west of here. Maybe that's our best hope."

"You took all that in?" Jenna asked him.

"Structures fascinate me," Graham said with a shrug.

"That's right. You wanted to be an architect, didn't you?"

Glancing away, he nodded.

"OK," Jenna said, "go and entertain yourselves. This might take time."

She lay on the grass and closed her eyes, getting into a relaxed, empty state. She thought of the Sentier, opening a channel to her.

*

Flint and Allessa were two weeks from Lixia. They had not experienced any strange buffeting, nor were they restless. Both had been absorbing the fact that the ones they wanted didn't want them.

For so long, Flint thought Jenna would pick him, but he had witnessed her reconnecting with Brash. He'd accepted her decision with grace, yet the woman had affected him deeply. His feelings for her had taken him by surprise at first, given they'd warred with each other constantly. She was strong-willed, argumentative, and insubordinate, nothing like the girl he had first met. Although, he saw moments when that kind-hearted, caring girl re-appeared. Following their kiss, and maybe because Brash caught them, she had taken that drug and lost her memory. Then she became the girl he remembered but he wanted both sides of her. Since she'd got her memory back, she had become all of herself. She was a many-faceted young woman and he loved every aspect of her.

Allessa still couldn't believe Lucas had made his decision without telling her. She supposed she had done the same, leaving the plantation on Juyra without telling him. Yet, she had left because she had feelings for him. He obviously didn't. She had never done relationships before. Sex, yes, but not relationships... until Lucas. One thing she was clear about now, she would not allow her equilibrium to be disturbed again.

They sat in the cock-pit, talking about the crew.

"I will miss them all," Allessa said. "Humans are a... curious species."

"Even Newark?" Flint asked with an amused smile.

She smiled back. "He is most curious of all. The Sentier are... thoughtful. Mr Newark is not, yet he has a basic honesty."

"Well, don't think too highly of him. When we were in the space corps, Brash, Newark, Johnson, Skinner, and Graham hatched a plan to kill Jenna."

Allessa stared at him, shocked. "Kill her...?"

"She was the Admiral's daughter. Her father kept shunting her from sector to sector because she didn't do too well in any of the areas. When she worked in the landing bay, she nearly got us killed." He glanced at her. "She didn't open the doors in time. Brash decided she needed to be... taken out."

"Taken out?"

"Killed."

Flint had never seen the Sentier's eyes widen before.

"But they seem so... close?" she said, stunned.

"Well, a lot's happened since then."

She looked down, processing that revelation.

Drawing her gaze back to him, she tilted her head, studying him curiously. "You knew about this, yet you did nothing?"

"I was barely there," he replied, regretfully.

Her curious eyes remained fixed on him. Reaching out, she touched his arm, feeling his life in her hand. Her eyes widened. Flint glared at her, pulling his arm away. She carried on staring at him.

"That was not something I wanted to share," he said in a hard voice.

"I am sorry. It is a habit I have. I need to learn to ask." Allessa knew to leave it there.

They fell silent, Flint tense, Allessa absorbing what she had learned.

"So, Jenna was incompetent?" she asked at last. "But she seems so... clever, inventive?"

"She didn't know who she was then. She had no confidence."

"Does she know they tried to kill her?"

"She found out later."

"And she has forgiven them?"

"She's changed. They've all changed."

"But they could have been murderers..."

"At the time, I think they rationalised it as acting for the greater good."

"How can you rationalise murder?" she asked.

31

Flint did not reply.

She bowed her head. "I cannot believe that of Lucas."

"He's changed a lot since then."

"Maybe... but what kind of man would kill an innocent girl because she was incompetent?"

"I wouldn't be telling you this if it wasn't over between you. That's not something you really want to know."

"No..."

"Does it change how you feel about him?"

"Are you trying to make me feel better about losing him?"

"Maybe."

"I suppose it has coloured my perception of him, yes. Maybe it has helped a little." She smiled at him, sadly. "I think I need some time alone."

"I understand."

Allessa climbed to the upper deck and lay in one of the bunks. She couldn't believe the Lucas she knew would contemplate murder. It disturbed her greatly. Maybe Flint *was* helping her. Perhaps now, she could push Lucas from her mind and be the Head Sentier she was appointed to be.

She closed her eyes. Sentier didn't need much sleep but she wanted sleep now.

"Allessa, it's Jenna. Can you hear me?"

"Jenna?"

"Finally. We're in trouble."

"Trouble?"

Disappeared

Jenna hadn't told Allessa the reason they'd left Draztis. It needed to be shared face to face. She, Brash, and Graham headed to the crater but thirty miles began to feel like sixty. They traipsed through the sticky, oppressive heat for days, following the course of a river, the water an unusual shade of turquoise. The dark grass shone with a strange iridescence. When they took a break, the spiky blades required careful negotiation. Despite the heat, Jenna and Brash's spirits had lifted. They would be reunited with Flint and Allessa soon. Graham was more sombre. Daria was a world away. He missed Newark too, missed the good times the three of them had shared.

The temperature dropped at night but Brash managed to get a fire going.

Jenna looked around the dark landscape, wondering if any aliens lived in these parts.

"We didn't bring weapons," Graham said as if reading her mind.

"We don't need them," Brash told him. "We have Jenna."

"Oh, yeah."

"Seems what's left of this crew hasn't been thinking straight lately."

Graham nodded, realising love, or desperation, had turned them into mushy-minded idiots.

A sudden wind blew around them, tugging at their hair. It whined like a plaintive ghost.

"That's weird?" Jenna said.

"What the hell is that?" Graham asked.

"Must be some local weather phenomenon," Brash offered. "We know nothing about this planet."

The pressure became intense, the whining acute, the wind ruthless.

Graham raised his voice against it. "I say we move on."

Leaving the snuffed-out fire, they moved off, pushing against the pressure. Breaking free of it at last, they turned. The whining stopped.

"This planet is starting to spook me," Graham said, looking around.

"It's just weather," Brash told him. "I've come across weirder stuff, believe me."

"Oh yeah?"

"Trees that ambush you?"

"What...?"

"On Juyra. That was one messed-up place."

33

"Yeah," Jenna remarked. "Reglons don't travel through the countryside. They hop from city to city."

As they walked on, Graham rubbed his forehead and glanced at her. "I never asked you but... when you and Daria were slaves, did either of you get...?"

Jenna raised her eyebrows to him. "Raped?"

He nodded. Brash tensed, waiting for her answer. He hadn't braved the question, either. It had been a cop-out, he knew.

She shook her head. "No, we wheedled our way out of that."

Graham breathed out. "How?"

"I created ghosts, did some ghost-busting in exchange for our freedom."

"You created ghosts...?"

"Well, I created bumps in the night. I was getting some of my power back. Course, when the former Head Sentier showed up with his energy-sensing tentacles, I had to manufacture a real ghost."

"You made a ghost...?"

"I compressed energy." Jenna smiled. "Amazing what you can do under pressure."

"And you couldn't do that before?"

"No. That was a new one."

"Thank you for keeping Daria safe," he said, looking at her intently. "I couldn't bear it if..."

She touched his arm. "We ended up having fun, causing a little havoc."

Brash smiled and shook his head. "There's no keeping you down, is there?" he said, fondly. Taking a breath, he looked around. "I suppose we should find somewhere to sleep."

They slept in a thicket of trees. Jenna took first watch, the twisted branches above laden with enormous leaves. Ahead, the hills blended into the dark, star-filled sky. The prospect of seeing Flint again made her smile, yet nerves dampened her excitement. How would Flint react? She'd hurt him, she knew that.

Brash took last watch. Leaning against an alien tree, he stared at the sun rising over the hills. He stood abruptly when a swarm of black dots flew their way. The dots became enormous iridescent-green bats. As they teemed around him, he reached for a non-existent weapon but the creatures hung on the branches, more interested in getting their heads down. Brash settled again, turning his attention to what he would say to Allessa.

Graham opened his eyes to enormous bats hanging over him. Letting out an involuntary shriek, he shot to his feet, waking Jenna. Brash cursed himself for not seeing that coming. The critters didn't take too kindly to having their

34

kip disturbed. The bats attacked, chasing them for a good five minutes before the three of them threw themselves in the river, ducking beneath the water and holding their breath as long as possible.

When their heads emerged, the swarm had gone.

"Sorry," Jenna said, turning to them. "I could have thought of something more inventive than chucking ourselves in the river."

As it turned out, being wet provided some relief from the heat of the day. They pushed through it, climbing a rise and staring out over flat, lush land. Ahead, in the distance, the enormous sides of the crater rose out of the ground as if making a statement. Graham stared, beguiled. "It's beautiful..."

"It's huge," Brash said. "They're not going to miss that."

"Come on." Jenna made her way down.

It took hours to reach the crater. As they neared, the sides loomed up in towering walls. Streams ran down its steep, tree-dotted slopes. Jenna gazed at a waterfall tumbling into a narrow river below, the light creating a rainbow effect. Water roared in their ears as they approached it.

"I'm having a swim," Jenna announced, stripping down to her underwear.

Brash and Graham stripped down too, and jumped in after her.

Rolling onto her back, Jenna stretched out her arms, the cool water caressing her skin. She stared up at the turquoise sky. Turning her head, she watched Lucas and Graham bask in the spray of the waterfall. Lucas looked so carefree, his chest bronzed, his handsome face smiling. She couldn't believe how their relationship had changed. She still cared about him but the spark had gone. There was deep sadness in that.

"Hey," Graham called over. "If you contacted Cornelius from Venulas, can't you contact him now?"

Jenna stared at him. What the hell had happened to her brain? Of course, she could contact Cornelius.

Graham's attention got diverted. She followed his gaze. A dot in the distance got larger until a Bortten craft came into view. The three of them hurried out of the water, throwing on their clothes as the craft landed on the other side of the river. Jenna's heart raced.

Flint and Allessa stepped out of the craft, walking forward like a mirage in the hazy warm air. Jenna gazed at Flint, taking in his ice-blonde hair, his lean, strong body. His eyes fixed on her and she melted inside. Brash stared at the Sentier, yet her eyes did not connect with his.

"Hey, you're on the wrong side," Graham called out.

Flint smiled. "Then swim over. I'm not wasting fuel."

They smiled back. Brash and Graham dove straight in, and swam over, fully clothed. Jenna stood there momentarily, still appreciating Flint's form, her heart bursting inside. She thought she would never see him again, and now, here he was in all his glory. Her attention shifted as the strange weather phenomenon started up. And this time, it was ruthless. She dropped to the ground, bracing herself against the pressure.

Brash and Graham struggled to get out of the choppy water. They turned to see Jenna's hair tugged all over the place.

"Move!" Brash shouted but she couldn't move.

Flint dove into the river, battling to get to her.

The air whined like a craft nose-diving to earth. A whip-like crack belted their eardrums. Blinding light flashed.

Flint climbed out of the river, staring around in horror. "Jenna!"

Brash, Graham, and Allessa came up behind him, dripping wet. "Where the hell is she...?" Brash asked, looking around, bewildered.

"The energy feels different here," Allessa said, extending her tentacles. "Some intense vibration."

"What was it?" Flint asked, raking a hand through his hair. "How do we get her back?"

"I do not know..."

"Can you contact Cornelius?" Graham asked the Sentier.

"This is no time to think of getting back to Marios Prime," Brash shot.

"I'm thinking of getting Cornelius to come here," Graham shot back. "He might be able to help."

"Yes, good idea." Brash looked to Allessa.

"I will try," she said.

"How can she have disappeared...?" Flint asked, looking around, helpless.

Fair Game

Disorientated, Jenna caught hints of a white background, and shady, indistinct figures. The figures got clearer. Around fifty of them. Different species, a couple almost ghostly. She stood in a large round room, the figures standing in a circle around her.

"We finally managed to get a handle on you," a voice said, and she whipped her head to look for the speaker.

An eight-foot being stepped forward. It had large blue eyes, long indigo hair, and pale blue skin with a ridged structure over the cheek-bone. The eyes never left her. "It took us several attempts," he said, studying her curiously, his lips unmoving, "as you may have noticed."

She glanced around at the others. One looked reptilian. One would have had the face of an angel were it not for its yellow slit eyes. One wore a long, hooded cape, its face in shadow.

"W... Where I am?" Jenna asked. "Who are you? What do you want with me?"

The blue being carried on studying her. "You are on a planet called Gatsoi in the Andromeda Galaxy."

"What...?"

"We have dragged you through a portal. Sorry about the disturbances you experienced earlier. Our newest member is responsible for that." He glanced behind him to a slimy, overgrown slug with arms and legs. "He needs more practice but he must start somewhere."

"So, *who* are you?" Jenna asked again.

"My name is Aktimar. We, here, are a council. We come from many parts of the universe. Indeed, two of our number are from a different dimension."

"What...?"

"You could say this is a centre of excellence for those with the power."

"You can create portals and travel to other dimensions...?"

He nodded, his eyes remaining fixed on her.

"How can you travel to another dimension...?"

His blue lips curved. "Now that is giving the game away. Suffice to say, there is much you have not yet explored."

"Okay... So, what am I doing here?"

"We have been watching you for some time."

"Watching me? How?"

"By tapping into the field."

37

"The Erithians could do that..." Jenna remembered. "They could create portals too. Do you know them?"

The being smiled, amused. He shook his head. "No, some do not approve of inter-dimensional hopping. We do not frequent those dimensions."

Jenna stared at him, puzzled. *Those dimensions?* "So, you're a council of beings with the power. Do... you want me to join you or something?"

He shook his head slowly. "You killed the Thunder God, a being with a strong command of the power. What you did was more impressive, though."

They'd watched her kill SLOB? "So, I'm here because you're curious?"

His lips curved, wickedly. "No. You will provide us with fair game."

"Fair game...?"

"We intend to hunt and kill you."

"What...?" she spluttered.

"You see, for beings like us, there is little left to challenge us. You will be given four earthly months to prepare yourself. You might want to find out what you do not know. After that, we will begin our game. If you are still alive after one earthly year, we will release you."

"Are you insane...?" she whispered, looking around at them.

"When the game begins, we will come for you one at a time. A white feather will give you notice each attack is imminent. There will be no more than four a month. We will return you now. Four months, Jenna Trot. Bastira," he said, turning to the slimy freak, "get it right this time."

"Wait-"

"Four months, Jenna Trot." The voice tailed off.

Shattered Dreams

A wind got up. Whining began. The crew pushed back to escape the epicentre. A loud crack tore the air apart, and they turned to see a blinding circle of light. Jenna fell to the ground.

The light vanished. Jenna looked up. The crew stared at her.

"Jenna?" Flint asked, rushing to her side, crouching before her.

Her gaze honed in on him. "They're going to hunt me like game."

"What...? Who is?"

"About fifty of them. Beings from all over, two of them from a different dimension. They said I have four months to prepare." Pressing her hands to her head, she stared at the ground. This wasn't happening. This was *so* not happening.

"D'you think whatever's happened has scrambled her mind?" Graham asked.

"I'm not scrambled," she shot. "I need to... I don't know what I need to do," she threw out, raising her arms.

Flint took hold of her arms, his blue eyes staring into hers. "Whatever's going on, Jenna, we'll help you."

"You can't help," she said feebly. "They have the power, and they know a hell of a lot more than I do." She looked at the ground. "I need Cornelius to bring the SMHD, and I need to get to the old woman on Cyntros. You all have to leave me. We're no match for them."

"I'm not leaving you," Flint said.

"Neither am I," Brash seconded.

"Or me," Graham said.

"Or me," Allessa added.

Jenna looked at them, tears lacing her eyes. "You *have* to."

"I've contacted Cornelius," Allessa told her. "He's coming."

Jenna nodded. This had started off such a good day, and now it had turned into a nightmare.

"Why do these beings want to hunt you, Jenna?" Flint asked gently, masking his fear.

"Because they think I might be 'fair game'. They've been watching me."

"How?"

"They're psychic or something."

Flint turned to Brash and they shared a heavy look. Jenna glanced at Flint. She'd just found him and now she had to let him go. She could no longer tell him how she felt.

"With the SMHD," Graham said, "Cornelius will be here in no time." And so would Johnson, though he kept that excitement off his face.

Biting his lip, Flint looked at Jenna. She had so much courage, so much spirit, but he had never seen her look so lost. He turned to Brash again, wondering why the man wasn't coming over to comfort her.

"Cornelius has a few things to attend to first," Allessa told them.

"Like what?" Graham asked.

"Takeza is pregnant." The crew stared at the Sentier. "He is enlisting her friends to stay with her in his absence."

The news of the pregnancy would have been startling under different circumstances.

Flint brushed a hand through his hair. "Right, well, all we can do is wait for him."

"I vote we wait in the craft," Graham said. He didn't trust this patch of ground.

Flint helped Jenna up. They waded and swam across the river. Flint climbed out, extending his arm back for Jenna. She took it, and he lifted her out, their bodies connecting in excruciating bliss. As they walked to the craft, she looked at him forlornly. His wet clothes clung to his perfectly-proportioned body, his wet hair teasing the bottom of his neck. She wanted to touch it but she had to be strong. Flint had let go of her for her greater good, and now she had to do the same for him.

Flint glanced at her, giving her a reassuring smile. His gaze drifted to Brash, viewing the man with a puzzled frown.

As they approached the craft, Brash caught hold of Allessa's arm. "Could I have a word with you, please?"

She tilted her head but allowed him to lead her away. Brash looked up at the turquoise sky, his throat tightening, not sure how best to say this. He turned to her. "I'm sorry for how I treated you," he began quietly. "The thing is-"

"We are past explanations, Lucas."

"But I-"

"Lucas, you have no need to worry about me. You are no longer what I want. I am here for Jenna now."

"You don't want me anymore...?" he asked, staring at her. "But I thought you-"

40

"I lost my equilibrium for a while. I forgot myself. Even if you begged me to take you back, I would say, no."

"You would...?"

She nodded. "Let us leave the past in the past and move on."

Allessa turned away, determined to get over this man. The cold truth was, murderer or no murderer, seeing him again had unsettled her.

Brash watched her go, swallowing the hard lump in his throat. Wandering to the craft, he let her words sink in.

He entered the flight-deck to find Jenna alone, sitting with her head in her hands. He sat beside her. "How are you feeling?" he asked.

"I can't believe this is happening... How could beings who know so much behave this way...? It's plain evil."

"Maybe they're... bored. You know how thrill seekers look for new kicks?"

"I do, actually," she said, rubbing her forehead. "But I never hunted anyone down and killed them."

"Look, perhaps you're more than a match for them. Perhaps they can't do everything you can."

"They've been watching me," she said with a shudder. "They know what I can do. They've given me four months to get better. They want a worthier challenge."

"Christ..."

"Not helping, Lucas."

"Sorry. Cornelius will be here soon. He'll know what to do."

"Will he?"

Brash rubbed a hand over his mouth, knowing Jenna had overtaken Cornelius in her abilities.

She glanced at him. "You've told Allessa then?"

"I didn't get to tell her." She looked at him, confused. "She pre-empted me, made it clear she wouldn't take me back if I begged her."

"I thought she was crazy about you?"

"Not anymore," he said, swallowing. "I've well and truly fucked it up."

"I'm sorry."

"Have you told Flint?"

"No. And I'm not going to. I can't start a relationship with him if it's likely I'm going to die. Besides, love makes people stupid. I don't want him putting himself in danger for me."

"Jenna, we're all going to put ourselves in danger to protect you. That's a given."

"That's nice to know but I don't want you to."

41

Flint walked in with towels, pleased to see Brash finally talking to Jenna, the pain in his chest secondary to her well-being. Graham came in behind him with a few water bottles. Allessa did not re-appear.

As night descended, Graham hung around outside, waiting for Daria to arrive. At last, a dark shadow moved across the sky.

"They're here," he called out.

The rest of the crew joined him, watching as the large craft came in to land, their hair blown around in the draft. Graham waited with baited breath as the gangway lowered.

Cornelius walked out alone, visibly relieved to see Jenna. He came straight over and hugged her.

Pulling back, he looked at her. "What happened, Jenna?"

"Are the others not here?" Graham asked, disappointed.

Cornelius turned, surprised to see Graham. "No. They are currently working in another city on Kaledia, except Fraza. He is travelling the wilderness."

"She's not come...?" Graham asked, staring at the man.

"Fraza's traveling the wilderness...?" Brash asked.

Fixing his priorities, Cornelius's gaze returned to Jenna. "Tell me what happened."

She told him everything. Cornelius rubbed a hand over his mouth, considering it thoughtfully.

"I'll take you all back to Marios Prime," she said. "Then I'll head for Cyntros."

"No," Brash asserted. "You're not going alone. And besides, you can't even fly this craft."

"It can't be too difficult. Cornelius mastered it. So will I."

"Jenna," Cornelius said, "we are not going to abandon you."

"But Takeza is pregnant," she insisted. "And Graham needs to find Johnson and... and you'll all get killed if you come with me."

"We're not leaving you," Cornelius repeated.

Jenna glanced at Graham.

"You're stuck with us, Trot," Graham said, his courageous smile hiding how gutted he felt.

"Well," she said, relenting, "I've got four months. You can stay with me until then. After that, you need to leave."

No-one replied.

"Come on," Cornelius said. "We need to get moving."

Cornelius led them aboard, heart-broken to be leaving Takeza at this time. Alessa, still heart-broken, determined to move past Lucas. Jenna, still dazed, determined to show no interest in Flint.

"She's not here," Graham murmured to Brash.

Brash placed a hand on his shoulder. "Welcome to the house of shattered dreams."

Horrible Dilemma

Cyntros was in the Spearos galaxy, a great distance from the Milky Way. It would take two weeks to get there. The ship would make a number of leaps, stopping for a while to recharge. This journey, at least, would be more comfortable. Their ship was luxurious, and huge compared to the Bortten craft. It had a bar, gym, and lounge on the lower level. The officers' quarters, located on that level too, had been commandeered by the crew. The spacious flight-deck on the upper level was well kitted out. The Hellgathens had carpeted it in a deep purple pile, and had placed black leather seating around the perimeter. The weapons systems on that deck were top of the range. Newark had spent most of his time in there at first.

Walking through the passageways, the crew made for flight deck. Cornelius led Jenna into the conference room, situated next to it. They sat in black, high-backed leather chairs.

He looked at her, intently. "So, you think this old woman on Cyntros can help you?"

"Everything I can do is because of her. She taught me to change my perspective when using the power. She said, in terms of the power, there is no 'from and to', just the power and intent. It took me a while to master it. Instead of drawing the power up through me, I sort of take myself out of the equation." She frowned. "Why didn't the Erithians teach us this?"

He rubbed his chin, thoughtfully. "Maybe they told us what we needed to know at the time."

"Why? It could have helped me."

"Could it? In order to take the third step in a flight of stairs, you need to be at the second step."

"What...?"

"You may not have been ready for it, Jenna. The Erithians have a broader view of the picture. Maybe they see things we do not."

"Can they see what's happening now?"

"I don't know."

"Is there any way for you to contact them?"

"I'm afraid not..."

"Cornelius, I'm no match for them!"

"How do you know? Because they said so? You trust the word of murderers?"

"They can open portals and travel to other dimensions. They're like fucking gods. Only mean, nasty, scary ones."

"You're allowing yourself to be intimidated, Jenna."

"Damn right, I am."

"Well, stop. You must not allow fear to get in the way. A certain amount of fear might push you on, but too much shuts you down."

"Sorry, I'll adjust my fear-o-meter," she threw out, sarcastically. "Damned Erithians. They could have taught me this shit."

"As I said, you wouldn't have been ready for it. Sometimes, something in you has to shift before you can move on."

She studied him. "How do you always appear so calm in a crisis?"

"Because you need me to be. Now," he said, placing his hands on his knees, "whilst we've got time to spare, why don't I teach you the mind trick I mastered."

Cornelius was alive today because of that mind-trick. At first, the crew thought their mentor's head had been taken from his shoulders, but the headless body belonged to a Sentier he'd been fighting. The twisted, egotistical, former Head Sentier who'd ordered their execution was dead now too. Allessa had been appointed the new Head.

"As I said before, Jenna, projecting images is harder than projecting thoughts. You have to make the image vivid and precise. So, empty your mind and conjure an appealing image. Make it as detailed as possible."

Jenna closed her eyes and pictured Flint's face... the perfect bone structure, the full lips, those intense blue eyes...

*

Leaving Flint at the helm, Brash and Graham wandered to the bar, and sat down with a bottle.

"I blew it," Brash said, knocking his drink back.

"So did I," Graham said, knocking his drink back too. His throat burned. Hellgathen concoctions were potent. The blue ones couldn't be knocked back in one go.

"Thing is, it was always Jenna before. She was the first woman I loved. That colours everything..."

"Daria was *my* first love."

"When Allessa came along, it knocked me sideways."

"Yasnay was sweet. I was a complete bastard, dumping her the way I did. She deserved better."

"I mean, Allessa was a very... sensual creature. The things she did to me on that plantation..." Brash lost track of his thoughts for a moment.

"Yasnay will get over me. I'm not that remarkable."

"I lost my mind, my ability to think."

"She'll find someone who will treat her right."

"When she drove away, I was crushed."

"Daria said she still loved me even when she broke up with me."

"Then it dawned on me she'd been using me. That's when the guilt kicked in. You know, because of Jenna. And I realised sex wasn't everything."

"Trot said it was because of her mother."

"But then I discovered she'd left because she *did* have feelings for me. 'Course, seeing Jenna again made me very conflicted."

"Her mother never got her presents. I always forgot her birthday. What a bastard..."

"I thought it was Jenna I wanted but it wasn't."

"She could be over me by the time I get to see her..."

"But now, Allessa doesn't want me anymore. She's had time to think." Brash stared at the table.

"Daria might realise she doesn't want me, after all." Graham stared at the table. "But... we've always come back together when we've broken up before..."

"Perhaps she can't forgive me for not choosing her."

"But this has been a long break, with someone else involved."

"I let the tentacles sway me. What a shallow bastard..."

"I always got this feeling we were meant to be together. Like... destiny. Maybe it *will* work out in the end."

"So, it's over now."

Graham looked up. "Maybe it's not over. Maybe it's destiny."

Brash looked up, eyeing him oddly. "No, it's over."

Graham stared at him. Did he say that word out loud? What the fuck was wrong him?

Brash retired to his quarters to stew alone.

*

Brash walked onto the flight-deck the next morning to find Flint and Allessa sitting before a patchwork of lights. Allessa stood and walked out, giving him a brief nod as she passed. Brash watched her leave.

"I think it's hard for her to be around you at the moment," Flint said. Brash turned to him and nodded. "So, is Graham the reason you left Draztis? I thought you were staying on there for a while?"

Brash opened his mouth then shut it again. He nodded, wishing Jenna would tell the man the truth. "So, how are we doing?" Brash asked, trying a change of subject.

"Building up for the next leap." Flint's eyes had him under scrutiny. "I'm sorry, Brash," he said, and Brash frowned, confused. "You get the woman of your dreams and now all this..."

God, the man was a good sport. Flint was a continual surprise. Brash nodded, uncomfortably.

"How is Jenna?" Flint asked.

Brash had no idea. "Still shaken."

Flint nodded, concerned.

*

Jenna sat in Cornelius's quarters, continuing her training.

"Now," Cornelius said, "bring up an image, clear and precise, and transfer it to me."

Jenna transferred the image.

"Flint again?" he asked.

She shrugged. "He has a distinct face."

"I see. Well, good job. Now, that's the first stage. I've got a mental image. The second stage is to flood the recipient's mind so it by-passes their sense of sight. You did something similar on Juyra, if you remember? The Governor, who spoke the wrath of God at the citizens? The words flooded him in such a way he felt compelled to utter them. Total sensory overload. And that is what you have to do with your image now. It has to be so strong and powerful it replaces the real image."

"How do I make it so powerful?"

"Belief, focus, and, of course, the power."

"The power?"

"I told you once the power is an all-purpose entity. You use the power to flood the mind, sort of giving the image an injection shot."

"But how do I hold the image for any length of time?"

"By keeping your focus. It's like opening a door. Once you've opened it, you need to hold it open, hold your focus. Try it."

Jenna tried. "Anything yet?" she asked.

"I'm afraid not. You're still sitting in front of me."

Two hours passed. Cornelius continued to wait.

"I can't do it," she threw out.

"Jenna, it took me years to master this."

"Then why am I even bothering?"

"Because, for some reason, which, if I were a different type of personality, would infuriate me immensely, you seem to master things quickly. So, stop whining like a child, and keep practising."

"I can't help but whine. I've got less than four months."

"Fear and panic must not allow you to lose your focus. They are superfluous and will not serve you in any way."

"It's alright for you to say. You're not the one being hunted."

"If I had allowed myself to panic when the Sentier attacked me, my head would not now be sitting on my shoulders." He let out a breath. "I know you are young and maybe I'm expecting a lot, but so much more has been asked of you, Jenna. And you have risen to it." He assessed her. "Why don't you make it into a game? You like games, don't you? Pick one of the crew, and see if you can deceive them."

The idea appealed to Jenna. She could enjoy this. "OK, I'll try."

As Jenna walked out, Cornelius felt, perhaps, he hadn't quite thought that through. He shrugged. Oh, well, needs must.

Jenna tried for days but without success. On hearing Graham and Brash sparring in the gym, she focused on Flint's image, blasting the image with the power as she stepped inside.

"Hi, Trot," Graham called out.

Crap.

More days passed and success wasn't forthcoming. Taking a break, she went for a drink, stopping at the bar entrance. Flint and Allessa sat in there, their backs to her, talking intently with their heads too close together for comfort.

Jenna's heart raced. When Flint got up and walked out, she scurried away, hiding in the games room.

What the hell was that all about...? One way or another, she had to find out.

Conjuring Flint's well-worn image, she brought up the power, feeling a huge injection shot, enough to send the image to Mars and back. She kept her focus as she entered the bar.

Allessa turned, looking surprised. As yet, Jenna wasn't sure who the Sentier saw but she continued to flood her with the image of Flint.

"Have you reconsidered?" Allessa asked.

Jenna sat opposite the Sentier, staring at her, the fact of being Flint overtaken by the fact he had something to reconsider.

Allessa tilted her head. "I know you think sleeping together to get over her will not work, but perhaps it could in time. I find humans appealing, and you are particularly attractive. We Sentier enjoy sex. We are skilled in the art of giving pleasure. If nothing else, I assure you, you would have a good time. They have moved on. We need to move on too." Allessa tilted her head the other way. "You are thinking about it, aren't you?"

What the fuck...? Jenna's fists clenched with a burning need to punch the Sentier. Should she tell Flint the truth? She was caught in a horrible dilemma.

Changing Faces

Rushing out of the bar, Jenna charged to her quarters, slamming the pad to close the door, kicking the crap out of a chair.

"The slut!" she yelled.

Anger spent, she sat on the bed to think this through. She could tell Flint how she felt but in four-months-time she might die, and that would hurt him. Worse still, he might get himself killed trying to protect her. She could talk to Allessa but Allessa would be someone else who knew the truth. Would she tell Flint? She could let the bitch have him but she couldn't stand the thought of that. So, she had to think of something else.

*

Jenna found Cornelius in the gym, working through his katas.

"Cornelius, I did it," she told him.

Cornelius turned around. "You did it *already*...?"

"Yes. So, how do I project a voice?"

Cornelius walked toward her slowly, still processing the fact she'd done it. He had hoped for weeks, perhaps, but days...?

"Is it possible to project voices?" Jenna asked.

He nodded, mutely, still staring at her.

"Are you alright, Cornelius? You look... odd."

He shook his head. "I'm fine. It's just... you are constantly surprising me, Jenna."

Jenna appreciated the sentiment but she didn't have time for compliments. She needed to nip Allessa's scheming in the bud. "So, voices?"

Cornelius gestured for her to sit down, staring at her all the while.

"Voices," he said. "Well... once you have the image transfer firmly in place, the recipient already believes you to be the person you are projecting. That's half the battle but the other half is to project a sound at the same time. This is hard, and the memory of the voice in your head might not be exact. As I said, though, if the recipient is of the firm belief you are, in fact, that person, any slight variations might be ignored. So, first, pick a voice, hear it, the tone, cadence, intonation. When you have it, see if you can flood my mind with it.

51

Once you manage this, we'll see if you can flood me with the image and the sound at the same time."

"Could you demonstrate?" she asked. "To show me it's doable."

Cornelius smiled. "Very well. Get ready to be freaked out, Jenna."

Jenna raised her eyebrows. Within moments, she stared at her twin speaking in *her* voice.

"Holy crap," Jenna exclaimed.

The other Jenna Trot grinned at her. "Freaky, isn't it?"

"OK, you can turn it off now."

Cornelius shut it off. "It took me many years to master that. I imagine it will take you... a matter of days."

Jenna bit her lip. "I'm sorry," she said. "I don't know why it's coming much quicker for me. I know it's not fair."

He touched her arm. "It's alright. I've lived cocooned with the Erithians all my life. You have had so much thrown at you and have had to adapt quickly."

Chewing her lip, she nodded. "Needs must, I suppose." And that was definitely the case now, as far as Jenna was concerned. Still, she felt sorry for the man. "Maybe I can do all this crazy stuff but you're a damn sight calmer and wiser than me."

"That's just age. Shall we start then?"

"Yep," she said, eager to press on.

When Jenna wasn't practising, she tried to keep tabs on Flint and Allessa, watching any conversations they might have. It wasn't easy because of the size of the ship. She'd also studied the flight-deck rota.

*

Flint assumed Brash and Jenna were together all the time. Brash, however, was usually in the bar with Graham. The crew had previously installed a kitchen down there. It killed two birds. Brash watched Graham stuff a sandwich into his face.

"What d'you think our chances are of coming out of this alive?" Graham asked around a mouthful of food.

Brash rubbed his forehead. "I don't know... Our chances of coming out alive were slim when we went to kill SLOB and we made it, so..."

"Yeah, but it sounds like these beings are in a different league to SLOB."

Biting his lip, he nodded. "Well, what are our assets? We've got Jenna and Cornelius, and Allessa can manipulate energy too. You saw what the Sentier were capable of on Juyra. The rest of us have got weapons and we can use them."

"Weapons are useless against these beings and you know it."

Brash nodded, biting his lip harder.

"Trot asked me not to tell Flint how she feels about him," Graham mentioned.

"Yeah, I was told the same."

Graham shook his head. "She thinks it will make a difference. Flint's going to die for her whether she tells him or not. The guy's crazy about her."

"You think he's still crazy about her?"

"He watches her every time she walks past."

"He does?"

"Yeah. Err... you're definitely over her, aren't you?"

"Yeah. Sure."

"Well, if you ask me, she should tell him."

"I suppose she wants him to leave in four months-time. I guess he won't do that if he thinks there's a chance."

Graham smiled. "She's still got a streak of naivety in her, even now."

"I'm not sure she has. Knowing Jenna, she'll find a way to make him leave. Or maybe she'll do a disappearing act."

"Yeah, she always was inventive."

Brash stood. "I'm going to... the little boys' room."

As Brash walked out, Graham stared after him. *Little boys' room?*

Outside the bar, Jenna punched her fist in the air. *Yes! I did it!*

Calming her excitement, she went off to find Flint.

When Brash actually did come into the bar, Graham looked up at him. "You were a long time in the little boys' room?"

Brash looked at him, oddly. "Are you drunk, Graham?"

"Not yet but I'm heading that way."

Jenna approached Flint on the flight-deck. She purposefully tilted her head. "I think you are up here far more than anyone else," she remarked.

"I like it here, like looking out at it all."

"I take it we are between leaps?"

He nodded. "One last leap and we'll be there."

She sat down. "Listen, I have been thinking. It was wrong of me to suggest what I did. In fact, to a human, I might appear... slutty." Flint glanced at her, and she smiled pleasantly. "Please, forget my proposition, and if I ever, in a moment of weakness, mention it again, please ignore me. Sex is not a way to mend a broken heart."

Flint assessed her. "You've changed your tune, Allessa?"

53

"Well, I have been thinking. Maybe you will, at some point in the future, find somebody else but it won't be with a slu-" She cleared her throat. "With a Sentier who is using you for sex."

Flint's eyes widened. "Using me for sex? That isn't how you put it before."

"Well, like I said, I have been thinking."

"You seem... different today, Allessa?"

Jenna purposefully tilted her head, keeping her focus in place. "I think I am tired. I will retire for a while."

As Jenna walked out, Flint's eyes followed her.

She bumped into Cornelius in the corridor.

"Hello, Allessa," Cornelius said.

Nodding graciously, she greeted him. "Cornelius."

Jenna dropped the facade and brought a finger to her lips. "It's working," she whispered, smiling at him.

Cornelius stared at her, shocked. "I can see that..." His brow creased. "I hope you're not getting up to mischief, Jenna."

"Those days are over, Cornelius. I'm a totally responsible, well-adjusted Jenna Trot now."

"Good. Keep it that way."

"What's next?" she asked, excitedly.

"What's next?"

"Is there anything else you can teach me?"

Cornelius shook his head, regretfully. "I'm afraid I've taught you as much as I can. We'll be arriving at Cyntros soon. Let's hope the old woman is there. By the way, does she have a name?"

"Tynia."

The real Allessa walked along the corridor, heading for the flight-deck. Jenna moved forward to intercept her. "Do you want to come to the games room for a while? I need to take my mind off things."

The Sentier bowed her head. "Of course."

Jenna turned to Cornelius. "Why don't you come too?"

"Very well," he said.

Hellgathen games were difficult to get the hang of. A round pool table had four balls and a disk. They couldn't figure out what to do with it. In fact, they couldn't work out what to do with anything.

"Maybe this was a bad idea," Jenna said.

Allessa smiled. "I think I will go and talk to Flint for a while."

"Why?" Jenna shot.

Cornelius appraised her. The Sentier turned to her, tilting her head. "He is... interesting."

"Cornelius is interesting," Jenna said, faking a smile. "Graham's interesting, if you give him a chance. Am I not interesting? Or, are we not interesting enough for *you?*"

Allessa's grey eyes fixed on her. She attempted to touch Jenna's arm but Jenna moved back.

"You should ask before you do that," Jenna said in a hard voice.

"I am sorry. It is a habit. If you want to spend more time with me, Jenna, you only have to ask. I assumed you would be busy with Cornelius and Lucas."

"Well, you assumed wrong."

"Then what would you like to do?"

Send you back to Lixia.

A moment of intense pressure made them stumble.

"I think we are approaching Cyntros," Jenna said, relieved.

As they walked out, Cornelius caught Jenna's arm. "What was that all about?" he asked. "Do you have a problem with Allessa?"

"No," she said, keeping a firm check on her thoughts. "It's just, sometimes, she seems... aloof, snobbish."

"It's how the Sentier appear. I think she's a very nice woman. Perhaps you are being prejudiced."

Jenna nodded, not allowing herself to think that, perhaps, Allessa was being a two-faced slut.

They joined the others on the flight-deck, staring out at the amber planet of Cyntros. They were back in the Spearos galaxy. Jenna briefly wondered where Serza and Hendraz were. She missed their friends and former allies, wished she had time to pay Hellgathen a visit.

"Well," Brash said, "let's hope the old crone's still alive."

Jenna looked at him. Tynia was over two hundred years old. What if she had died? What would she do then?

Panic seized her. She'd pinned all her hopes on Tynia. What if that hope was in vain?

Living Free

Newark, Johnson, and Skinner had been put up in a luxury hotel. The hotel was used by the oil company and many of the employees stayed there. Unfortunately, the mad bitch was there too but she settled for giving Johnson scathing looks.

"She's a bunny-boiler, that one," Newark remarked over the high dining room table. The table had to accommodate large Kaledian bellies. "Her eyes are like fucking lasers."

Johnson nodded. "If she comes near me again, she'll be a dead bunny-boiler."

The god-like form of Emilio walked in. Johnson's eyes followed him. The Spaniard looked over at her and smiled as he went to sit with friends.

"Have you screwed him yet?" Newark asked, stuffing down his breakfast.

Skinner knew the answer to that. He'd seen the Spaniard enter her room late last night but he didn't voice it. Johnson had been touchy since she'd broken up with Graham.

"Concentrate on your own non-existent love-life, Newark," Johnson said, her eyes straying to the Spaniard.

Newark's mood dropped. He'd never had a love-life. Yeah, plenty of one-night stands, tons of them, in fact, but a relationship was something he'd never done. It didn't used to bother him but over the course of the past few months, it had begun to niggle. He turned to Skinner and his spirits lifted. He was sure Skinner hadn't had a relationship, either. Of course, for much of his life, Skinner had been a creepy, cowardly worm, who made women want to barf. Cornelius had altered that with his *die a thousand deaths* programme. Skinner had changed before their eyes, developing a backbone for the first time in his life, together with a god-complex and an air of arrogance. He was over that now, though.

They'd been here nearly three weeks and, as yet, they'd done nothing but lounge about the hotel or wander around Kelparz, the hold-up due to the company doing checks on them. It was taking a long time because they'd provided false names. If they gave their real names, they could land up back on Osiris.

"We're going to get slung out, you know," Newark said, watching the interchange of glances between Emilio and Johnson.

Johnson shrugged. "They're paying us in the meantime."

"What if they want the money back?"

57

"They can sing for it. Anyway, seems to me, they need us more than we need them. They had trouble again last night. Petrol bombs."

"How d'you know that?"

She hesitated. "Overheard a guy talking."

"And what did the security forces do?"

"Fired weapons into the dark wilderness, hitting dust, most likely. They're not getting to the bottom of it, that's for sure."

"Who've they hired?"

"Revlans."

"Revlans? They're as thick as... as... Sure, they look big and scary but they haven't got a brain cell between them."

Johnson laughed. They stared at her; hadn't seen her laugh in ages. "D'you know what one of them did? He tried to make a petrol bomb of his own, and the damn thing blew up in his hand. He's a real mess."

Newark and Skinner joined in the laughter.

"If the company doesn't employ us," Johnson said, wiping her eyes, "they're as stupid as those fucking Revlans."

"So, do we have a plan to deal with the trouble-makers?" Skinner asked.

"Hey, you're the brain box. That's your department."

Skinner's gaze became distance and thoughtful. "We want to be out of the compound when they attack. We need to catch one of them and get information. It would have to be a stealthy snatch."

"We'll need some kind of night goggles," Johnson reasoned.

"Where would we get something like that?" Newark asked.

"We put in a requisition form," Johnson said, shrugging. "Up to the company to sort it out."

Newark nodded. "So, what we doing today then?"

"Don't know about you but I've got plans."

"What plans?"

"Emilio is showing me the sights."

"So, you *are* fucking him."

"Jealous?" she asked, smiling as she rose from the table.

Skinner watched her go. "The man's certainly improving her mood."

"Whatever he's packing is improving her mood."

Skinner sighed. "We need to get back in the game."

*

Johnson and Emilio wore shades as they climbed a scrubby grass hill outside Kelparz. When they got to the top, Johnson turned, staring down at the sprawling city, sheltered by the hills on three sides. Kelparz looked a lot like Jakensk, if marginally smaller. Yacts flew around it like insects, the place a warren of streets, alleyways, and activity.

She turned. Low-lying hills, covered in that same scrubby grass, stretched on into the distance.

"Jakensk is in that direction," Emilio said, pointing over the hills, "and over there," he said, turning her by the waist, "is where our rig is located."

Miles of flat land stretched off to the horizon but she couldn't see any rig.

"It's out in the wasteland," he said. "An hour's ride."

"How long are you going to be on this planet?"

"I'm not sure yet... Could be a long time." His eyes ran over her. "The sundress is very appealing, by the way. You weren't wearing it at breakfast."

She shrugged. "Thought it might be cooler."

He smiled, his dark eyes honing in on hers. "Who are you, really? The checks are coming up blank. Either you don't exist or you have given a false name."

Johnson chewed her lip. She turned away, staring out into the distance. The Spaniard caught a strange kind of pain in those unusual grey eyes. "I don't know who I am..." she said, quietly.

"What are you saying...?"

"I don't know who I was, what I liked, before my mother told me what to be. And... that would have been alright if..."

"If what...?"

"If she had loved me."

The Spaniard didn't know what to say. He barely knew Daria, if Daria was her real name, yet she shared some deep, dark secret.

She turned to him. "I had to say that to someone, and I know I don't mean anything to you and we'll part company eventually." She shrugged. "So, you seemed like the ideal person."

Emilio stared at her.

"My first name *is* Daria. I can't give you my surname. But me and my friends are the best chance you have of ridding yourselves of these trouble-makers."

He scratched his neck. "But it isn't up to me."

She smiled, wryly. "Yes, it is. Emilio De Marco, CEO of Ubro Oil. I riffled through your papers that first night when you were in the shower. You're very young to be in the position you are, and for some reason *you* are travelling incognito. But you get to call the shots, so it *is* your call."

A smile possessed his face. "You're devious."

"Care to share?"

"I am young, I suppose. Twenty-nine. I like to have fun, whilst keeping an eye on the operation. It wouldn't be seemly for someone in my position so, as you say, I travel incognito. Only a few know who I am. Unorthodox, I'll admit, but there you have it. So, are you criminals?"

"No."

"Then you've got the job. Give me a list of your requirements."

She nodded, turning back to the landscape.

"And you're wrong," he said, quietly. "You do mean something."

*

Miles and miles of wasteland passed Fraza by. Nobody lived out here and few, if any, had ventured this far. The sun dazzled, the heat brutal, but the yact was equipped with a weather shield and air conditioning.

The nights would turn cold. Fraza wrapped himself in a couple of blankets, looking up at the stars, thinking of all the places he had been, places he never imagined he'd go. Jenna was out there, with Brash, having an extended holiday. They might be lying on a beach right now, not a care in the world. He missed her terribly. And he missed who he was when he was with her.

Cornelius was right. Somehow, he had to find that Fraza now. He wasn't exactly sure how coming out here would help, and the aching loneliness crushed his heart. Yet... he had been alone for many years before he met the crew. He had never fitted in, didn't have friends. His parents mollycoddled him when they were alive, but they didn't know him, never asked his opinion, never trusted him to do anything, never let him be himself.

Thoughts like that gave him renewed determination, and he'd push on through the night.

As the heat of a new day rose around him, so too did the featureless wasteland. Hours passed, and features *did* appear - scrubby patches of grass, the patches merging as the land became hillier. Wasteland had become wilderness. The air became cooler the further in he went. Clouds appeared overhead, until wind blew the grass, the movement a sharp contrast to the mind-numbing stillness of the past weeks.

Another day brought trees and different vegetation, even tiny bits of colour. He followed the course of a river that wound like a snake through forest. Spotting a clear patch by the bank, he came in to land.

Lifting a panel from the floor, he installed a new fuel rod. He had a stash of rods but he'd kept his speed steady to conserve fuel. Grabbing a few empty bottles, he walked to the river to fill them up. The green water in Kaledia was odd to many species. Some refused to drink it; others took convincing. Once he'd filled the bottles, he sat, staring at the water gliding by, contemplating his loneliness.

He whipped his head up. Standing before the trees on the opposite bank were a couple of naked Kaledians. Fraza stared at them, careful not to drop his gaze.

"Have you been looking for us?" the man called.

Fraza frowned. "Looking for you?"

"For our nudist colony."

"Nudist colony?"

"We'll swim over."

The male and female dove into the water. As they stepped out, Fraza averted his gaze.

"We're hard to find," the man said. "Many get lost."

"I didn't think anyone lived so far out," Fraza said, keeping his eyes up, scratching his ears.

"We live a naturalist existence out here," the woman said, "free from the trappings of modern life."

"How many of you are there?"

"About three hundred. Come, we'll show you around. Err... you'll have to take your clothes off, though."

Fraza stared at her. "Take my clothes off...?"

"That's the idea. We'll show you around, get you some food, and, if you'd like to stay, we'll sort you out with a bed."

The idea of decent food and a bed appealed to him. But taking off his clothes? His parents wouldn't approve of him taking off his clothes in front of strangers. That gave him the push he needed. He undressed, trying to cover himself with his hands, which wasn't easy as he desperately needed to scratch his ears.

"Come on," the man said, diving into the river.

Fraza swam across after them, the water cold on his skin. Walking through the trees, they entered a clearing with wooden huts and naked Kaledians all over the place. Fraza wrapped his arms around himself. Above him, walkways stretched from tree to tree, wooden treehouses interspersing

61

them. Naked children ran around playing as adults attended to chores. A few older white-haired Kaledians dotted the place. He had not expected to find such a bizarre sight on Kaledia.

"Come," the woman said, "we'll introduce you to everyone."

Being introduced without his clothes on made his skin crawl, but nobody looked where they shouldn't, even if Fraza, inadvertently, did. The nudists welcomed him with gusto, the settlement extending through to another large clearing. After being introduced to everyone, he was shown to a hut, sat down, and left in the capable hands of an attractive young woman, called Jabreen. Jabreen didn't seem self-conscious as she leaned over him to retrieve a wooden bowl, her belly inches from his face. Things happened down below. *Oh no, oh no, oh no.* Fraza scratched his ear incessantly with one hand whilst covering himself with the other.

"Do you have itchy ears?" the woman asked. Fraza nodded. "I can rub ointment into them, if you like."

"No," Fraza replied in a high-pitched voice.

"We don't get many visitors," she said. "I think people have forgotten we're out here." She assessed him. "How old are you? Twenty-seven, twenty-eight?"

"Twenty-eight," Fraza replied, his ears becoming sore.

"I'm good at guessing ages. I'm twenty-four."

Fraza needed to put his mind on other things. "So, do you not miss the city?" he asked.

"Sometimes, but I wouldn't want to live there again. You can't wander around naked in Jakensk, can you?"

Fraza shook his head, vigorously.

She handed him a bowl of food, which he took. When she handed him a wooden mug, Fraza stared at it.

"Take it," she urged.

Reluctantly, he took it, revealing his elevated manhood.

Jabreen stared. Lifting her eyes to his, she saw the horror written there. She fetched him a wooden tray. "There, that should make things easier," she said with a breath-taking smile.

As darkness fell, Fraza sat around an enormous campfire where Kaledians sang songs. A few danced with gay abandon, raising their arms in the air. For a moment, he had a flashback to the wild men village on Juyra but he calmed himself. There were no spears and no enormous cooking pot here. As he looked around, he realised these people were... happy.

Fraza slept there that night. He decided to stay.

Tynia

Stepping off the craft, they looked around. For Jenna, Brash, and Graham, the land was just as wild, the purple hills within walking distance, the amber sky giving that same muted feel. Jenna looked toward the copse of trees. Tynia's wooden shack was in there. Beyond it, sand dunes and the sea.

Flint looked at Jenna for direction.

"This way," she said.

They walked through the trees and approached the hut. Jenna knocked on the door. No answer and no sounds inside.

"She's not here," Jenna said, concerned. "D'you think she's dead?"

"Calm down, Jenna," Brash told her. "She could be anywhere."

Flint opened the door and wandered in. "She's not dead," he said, lifting a recent unwashed bowl. He glanced around the cluttered-looking hut, his eyes brushing over a cooking pot hanging above burnt embers, a few tatty chairs, cupboards, a frayed rug covering half of the wooden floor, and a door into a bedroom at the back.

Allessa sat down, feeling faint. The rest of them experienced light-headedness.

"We need that leaf," Graham said, searching around the place.

"Leaf?" Flint asked.

"Bata leaf," Brash replied. "The air on this planet is too thin for most species. The leaf gets oxygen into the bloodstream."

"Found some." Graham dragged a tattered sack from under a chair. He took a handful of leaves before passing the sack around.

Allessa ate some and started laughing. The crew stared at the peculiar sight. They didn't think Sentier *did* laugh.

"This happened to Fraza," Graham said, rooting through cupboards. "Some kind of side-effect. Let's hope that green concoction's knocking about."

Jenna hid a smile. The Sentier looked ridiculous, laughing like a hyena. It didn't look attractive *at all*. When Flint crouched before her, Jenna's smile dropped.

"Are you OK, Allessa?" he asked.

The Sentier couldn't answer for laughing.

"It's just a side-effect," Jenna said. "She'll be fine."

Graham found the bottle and spoon-fed the stuff to Allessa.

"There's always one," a voice said from the doorway.

Jenna whipped her head around. The blue-skinned, hunched-back old woman looked just the same, right down to her loose-fitting trousers and piercing blue eyes. Her voice was communicated telepathically.

"I was worried you were dead," Jenna blurted, relieved.

"Well, I would have been but it seems I'm hanging on, and now I know why." Tynia came over with a generous smile and took Jenna's hands. "You did it, didn't you? I was certain you'd fail."

"Err... thanks?"

"When you left here, you hadn't got a clue what you were doing but somehow you mastered it. You took out the Thunder God," she said, proudly. Tynia rubbed her nose with a wrinkly blue finger. "I had thought you would pay me a visit before you left the galaxy."

"Oh... Sorry..."

The old woman's eyes roamed the room. "So, we have some new faces this time."

Cornelius stepped forward. "A pleasure to meet you," he said, graciously, at which Tynia gave a bashful smile. "My name is Cornelius."

"And I'm Vincent Flint," Flint said, smiling with an acknowledging nod.

Allessa moved to stand but Tynia touched her shoulder. "Stay there for a time, dear."

"My name is Allessa," the Sentier told her.

"What pretty silver skin you have. Most unusual... Well, I must say, you seem politer than the last lot." She rubbed her hands together. "I think I'll make a stew."

"Tynia, I'm here because I need your help," Jenna said. "I'm in trouble."

"I didn't think this was a social call," the old woman said, smiling steadily. Jenna stared at her. "You can tell me everything after tea."

As Tynia busied herself, the crew stood around, aimlessly. The cabin felt cramped. Cornelius found himself a chair and sat down.

"I think I'll take a walk," Flint said, moving to the door.

"I'll join you," Allessa said, moving to get up.

Jenna placed a hand on her shoulder. "You need to stay seated for a while, remember?" she said, sweetly.

"I feel fine now," the Sentier said, looking up at her.

"OK, I'll come out with you."

Watching them leave, Brash hung there awkwardly then decided to take a walk too. After a moment, Graham joined him.

"Was it something I said?" Tynia asked as she collected ingredients.

"They must have a fear of confined spaces," Cornelius remarked, amused.

"That, or intimacy issues."

64

Cornelius's smile broadened. "You have a lovely place here," he commented, looking around.

"Thank you. Jenna mentioned you last time she was here."

"She did?"

"She sounded fond of you. I had an inkling she was coming back."

"Oh?"

"I sense you are worried about her."

"I am." He turned his whole body to her. "She believes you can help."

"I will do my best. Though, at the moment, she seems to have other things on her mind."

"Other things?"

The old woman shook her head. "Love triangles are tricky."

"Love triangles?"

"Is the woman with the dark hair having a relationship with the man with the blonde hair?"

Cornelius shook his head. "I don't think so."

"Um... Jenna seems jealous."

"She does?" he asked, puzzled. "Jenna is with Mr Brash."

"Well, maybe I'm seeing things that aren't there," the woman said with a sweet smile.

Cornelius sat back, rubbing a hand over his mouth. He'd left Jenna with Mr Brash on Draztis, thought they were happy. Had things changed or was the old woman desperate to find some drama?

*

Jenna walked beside Allessa, irritated beyond words. If Allessa read her thoughts, she'd receive a whole lot of vitriol. Jenna knew, however, that Sentier had a code of honour. They only read when you spoke. Still, those hands were a little too touchy-feely. One touch and the Sentier could see inside you. Jenna kept her distance.

"The purple hills are enchanting," Allessa remarked. "The sky gives the place a strange, dreamy feel..."

"Yeah."

Allessa turned to her. "You seem quiet. Are you worried, Jenna? We will all help you in any way we can."

Jenna nodded, not bothering to make eye contact with her. How would she keep Allessa and Flint apart? Much of her time would be tied up with Tynia.

"There is no bitterness," Allessa said, honestly, and Jenna looked at her. "People can't help being drawn to each other. And maybe this is for the best. Before I met Lucas, my life was... uncomplicated. I could devote my energies to my service. I do not do relationships, Jenna. Sex, I enjoy, of course, but relationships unsettle me. Perhaps you coming together with Lucas was a blessing in disguise."

"So, you just want sex now, do you?" *Slut!*

"It is simpler."

Jenna turned away, thinking even harder of a plan.

Still looking at Jenna, Allessa tilted her head. "My life has changed so much since I met you. You opened my eyes. You opened all our eyes to Olixder. The Sentier had lost their way. My one desire now is to help you."

Jenna turned to her, swallowing hard, until she reminded herself of the Sentier's other desire. To screw Flint. Somehow, she had to keep them apart.

*

The green stew tasted much better than it looked. After tea, Tynia led Jenna into the bedroom.

"Now, dear, tell me what trouble you are in."

Jenna explained her situation and the woman listened with rapt attention. When she finished, Jenna waited for her response.

"Oh dear, oh dear," Tynia said, shaking her head.

Not the response Jenna wanted. "It's hopeless then?"

"Sorry? Oh, no, I was thinking about my stew. I forgot to put bren in. It gives it the distinctive flavour."

"What...?"

"I didn't have any myself because-"

"Forget the stew! What about the trouble I'm in!"

"No need to be rude, dear. I don't get visitors often. I want them to enjoy my stew."

Jenna stared at her. "You were so much more focused last time. You even drugged the resistance to give us peace and quiet."

"Yes, dear, that's right," the woman said, smiling. "Though, the universe was in peril at the time, and, much as I like you, you are just one person."

"Good to know."

"Don't be upset, dear. I will help you as much as I can."

"*Can* you help me, though? These beings can open portals to other dimensions. What else will they be capable of?"

"You know, if you travel to a higher dimension, you have to raise your vibration."

"How d'you know that?"

"Because I've done it." The wrinkly old woman smiled in reminiscence. "I keep in touch with a lovely little squigloid on a world called... well, I never get the pronunciation right."

Jenna gaped at her. "A being from another dimension...?"

"Yes, dear. Of course, it's disconcerting because their time runs at a different rate to ours. If you spend a day over there, a month passes here. I missed hiffelfust."

"Hiffelfust?"

"They have wonderful celebrations here around harvest-time. Debauchery gone mad it is."

Jenna gawked at her. "But... you're an old lady, and you seem to keep away from others?"

"Oh, I was young then. No male would look at me twice now," she said, sadly. "Did I tell you I was over two-hundred-years-old?" Jenna nodded. "I've out-lived all my family and friends, and now there's just me and the sea."

A sudden stab of pity hit Jenna's heart. She knew nothing about Tynia. It hadn't occurred to her how lonely the woman might be.

Sadness turned to curiosity. "So, how old were you when you first travelled to that dimension?"

"Forty-four."

"And is that young here?"

"Oh yes, dear."

"And when did you realise you had the power?"

"As a child, strange things happened around me, but I didn't know they came from me. Then I figured it out, but I was in my twenties when I learned to control it. I sort of had to. I travelled off on my own, and was drawn to a man who lived in the hills. Didn't I say those with the power are drawn to each other?" Jenna nodded. "Well, I was so glad I found him. I'd felt alone, being different, you see. But soon it became an adventure, scary at first, yet rich and varied, full of experiences most could only dream of." A gleam came in her eyes. "And maybe some mischief too."

Jenna smiled.

She listened to the old woman all night, forgetting about a council of scumbags out to kill her, forgetting about Flint and Allessa, just listening to this woman whose story needed to be heard. Tynia's love-life had been eye-opening. The old woman transformed before her eyes.

At the end of the evening, Tynia smiled at her, fondly "That's better, isn't it, dear?"

"What is?" Jenna asked.

"You've come back to yourself."

"Come back to myself?"

"To the confident, self-assured woman you'd become."

Jenna eyed her, oddly. "Last time I was here, I was anything but confident and self-assured."

A twinkle came in the old woman's eyes. "I've been keeping an eye on you."

"How?"

"Well, tomorrow, I'm going to show you."

Tuning In

Jenna returned to the craft to find everyone, apart from Allessa, in the bar. Relieved to see Flint there, she took in his amazing form as she walked over.

"Can she help you?" Cornelius asked, appraising her.

"She's going to start tomorrow."

"Do you think I could sit in?"

"I don't see why not."

"It's strange to be back here," Brash said, throwing down his drink.

"Yeah," Graham agreed. "Feels like we've come full circle."

Flint studied Brash and Jenna. Their body language seemed odd, considering they were in love. Brash didn't look at Jenna once, and Jenna sat beside Graham. He considered they might be trying to spare his feelings but they barely seemed aware of each other. Jenna caught him watching her and he looked away quickly. There was something he couldn't put his finger on.

"I wonder what Daria's doing now," Graham said, distantly.

"I could have taken you back there," Jenna said, quietly.

"I'm not a rat deserting the sinking ship." He looked at her. "Not that the ship is sinking or anything."

"It's OK," Jenna said, sombrely. "Right now, it feels pretty far down in the water."

Flint glanced at Brash. Brash refilled his drink, being anything but supportive. Flint leant across the table. "I'm sure this woman can help you, Jenna," he said, gently.

Jenna gazed into Flint's absorbing blue eyes. *Damn that council and their blasted hunt. They've screwed up everything.*

Flint had an overpowering urge to kiss her. He drew back. "I'll go and find Allessa," he said, standing. "See if she's alright now."

Flustered, Jenna blurted, "I think she went to the gym."

All eyes fixed on her. "Gym?" Graham asked, surprised.

Jenna shrugged. "Sentiers must exercise too."

As Flint left, Jenna got up. "I'm going to... bed."

Cornelius watched her go.

*

Flint looked around the empty gym.

"Flint?" Allessa asked.

He turned to the doorway and smiled. "I wouldn't have expected to see you in here?"

The Sentier tilted her head as she came forward. "I have put on a bit of weight around my stomach," she told him.

"Well, it doesn't show."

"Yes, it's like a spare tyre."

He frowned. "I came to see if you felt better now."

"Better? I did not feel ill. Just couldn't stop laughing."

"Yes." He let out a breath. "In truth, I wanted to get away from Jenna."

"Get away from Jenna?"

"It's hard being around her. I thought I wouldn't see her for months, if I went back to Marios Prime at all, and now I'm stuck on a ship with her and Brash."

"I understand."

He scratched his neck. "I wondered, if maybe... I don't know... if your idea might work."

The Sentier stared at him. "What idea?"

"Sleeping together? I know you said you'd changed your mind but... perhaps..."

"I have changed my mind," she said, emphatically. "I was all over the place when I suggested that. I wasn't thinking straight. How can you contemplate sleeping with me if you have feelings for Jenna?"

He stared at her, surprised. "*You* suggested it to me."

"Well, I shouldn't have. Please don't come near me again."

Flint stared after her as she walked out. He stood there, confused. Allessa didn't seem herself. Indeed, she sounded... jealous. Could the Sentier possibly have feelings for him? Had he done anything to encourage it? He usually had a good handle on things but he had to say, he couldn't figure things out at all.

Jenna wiped tears away as she walked to Allessa's quarters. She knocked on the door and it slid open, the Sentier's face brightening on seeing Flint.

"Could I have a word?" Flint asked, off-hand.

"Of course."

Flint marched in and turned to her. "Allessa, I've come to ask you to stay away from me. I need space to get over Jenna, and I don't want any temptation thrown in my way. It's too... complicated. So, I'm asking you to keep your distance."

"I see... For how long?"

"Until I say differently."

She gazed at him, oddly. "Very well... If that is what you want..."

"It is," Flint said, walking out.

Tears streamed down Jenna's face as she strode down the corridor to her quarters.

Cornelius watched her go with a thoughtful expression.

*

A warm, pleasant breeze brushed over Jenna, Cornelius, and Tynia as they walked along the beach, waves lapping at their side.

Jenna stared at the sand with a heavy heart. She'd managed to keep Flint and Allessa apart for now, but he had wanted to sleep with the Sentier. Was he starting to like her?

"This is a nice spot," Tynia said, sitting herself down.

The two of them followed suit.

"Such a lovely day, isn't it?" Tynia remarked.

They nodded, Cornelius pleasantly, Jenna absently.

"Well, I suppose we should begin." The old woman turned to Jenna. "I once said to you, Jenna, in terms of the power, there is no time and space. Well, let's go deeper now. There is a field of energy that runs through everything-"

"Cornelius told me this," Jenna mentioned.

Tynia looked at Cornelius. "Please forgive me if I overlap."

Cornelius smiled, graciously. "Just pretend we're absolute beginners," he said.

Tynia smiled back, bashfully. "Very well. Now, the field is..."

"Alive, all-encompassing," Jenna remembered.

"Yes. That. Anything and everything, including us, is contained in it. Anything can be found and viewed. It is all available at any moment in any place. So, for example, an event occurring across vast stretches of space can be felt or seen by us here and now because the field is one entity. Our common-sense laws of time and space do not apply at this deeper level. Every part of the field contains the whole."

"*Okay,*" Jenna said, soaking this in.

"We simply have to tune in and focus. I always find it helps to visualise yourself becoming one with the field. You are, of course, but you are not normally aware of it. So, it's about learning to connect and plug in."

71

"How do I do that?"

"You're asking too many questions, Jenna. You need to let go of the mind. The mind separates us from the field, erects its own barriers. Don't get me wrong, questions are useful in their place, but sometimes we need to let go of them. Now, to begin, I thought it might be helpful if I plug in, and you and Cornelius can read my mind, see what I see. Seeing is believing and believing drives you on."

"That's a wonderful idea," Cornelius said, and Tynia blushed.

"OK, I'm going to focus on this council of hunters. Feed the image into my mind, Jenna."

Jenna brought up her memories of that place and those beings, focusing on the being with the blue eyes. Tynia winced. "Yes, they seem a very unwholesome bunch. OK, here goes. They'll probably see me, of course."

"Wait. What? See you?" Jenna asked, alarmed. "Do we want them to?"

"They can see what they want. They've given you a certain amount of time, and that time is yours, no matter what they see." She frowned. "Don't allow them to intimidate you, Jenna."

Jenna scratched her temple. Easier said than done.

Tynia fell silent as she connected to the field. Jenna and Cornelius plugged in to her mind.

"Are you with me?" Tynia asked, and they nodded. "OK, here goes."

Stars and planets flashed past, Tynia racing through the universe without a spacecraft, faster than any spacecraft, a gazillion times faster. They travelled a black void, then more stars flew by. A green planet came into view, and like a satellite zooming down, they descended through cloud, over ocean, until platforms with buildings rose out of the water. They zoomed in further to a white room, and a blue-eyed being staring back at them.

Jenna jolted back. Cornelius's eyes shot open. Tynia turned to them. "I think I was being a little dramatic," she said with a sheepish smile. "I could have plugged straight into him but I thought you might enjoy the ride."

"That was him," Jenna said, staring at the woman, transfixed. "He's in the Andromeda galaxy, and we saw across all that distance...?"

"That's just time and space, dear. Don't let it get in the way. Now, see if you can do it without me. Pick someone else, if you like."

Jenna thought about Newark, Skinner, and Johnson. How were they getting on? She decided to focus on Johnson. Cornelius picked Takeza. This time, they lay back on the sand, and closed their eyes.

"Now, remember," Tynia said, "you are part of the field. In a metaphysical sense, you are travelling to another part of yourself."

Jenna opened her eyes at that, closing them again.

72

"Become one with the field," Tynia said, softly, "and focus on who you want to see."

They lay there for a time but nothing happened. At last, the pair opened their eyes, and sat up.

Tynia smiled at them. "It's just words, isn't it?" she said.

"Pardon?" Jenna asked.

"In an intellectual sense, you except the field, and I've even given you a demonstration. But, on a deeper level, neither of you accepts *you* are the field."

Cornelius rubbed a hand over his mouth. All this time and the woman had got to the crux of the matter.

"Lie down again," Tynia instructed. "I want you to stay there and focus on your being. Empty your minds and see if you can feel energy pulsing through you."

"Energy?" Jenna asked.

"Your energy."

"My energy?"

"Just that."

They lay back down.

Tynia waited patiently, gazing out at the sea. She thought about Hiffelfust and tortured herself with glorious memories from times gone by.

"I can't feel anything," Jenna said.

"You have only been at it for five minutes, Jenna." She determined not to get cross with the girl this time. "You need patience. If we have to sit out here for hours, hours it will be."

The first hour passed.

"I have it," Cornelius said. "I can feel it."

Tynia's heart warmed. It was so good for older people to discover new things. "Stay with it."

She looked at Jenna, knowing the girl was trying too hard.

"I can't do it," Jenna said, frustrated.

"You are not doing anything. You're a passive observer, nothing more."

Tynia knew the girl had achieved so much, done so much, changed so much. Yet, coming up against this council had set her back. What seemed like the impossible did tend to do that, but even the impossible must not hold you back.

At long last, Jenna gasped. "I feel it. It's like... pulsing, buzzing... alive..."

"You are energy," Tynia said, "vibrating at a certain rate. Energy is all around you. Everything is energy. Everything is connected. Do you see now you are part of the field?" Jenna nodded. Cornelius nodded. "So, shall we try to plug in to a certain object of interest?"

They closed their eyes, and Tynia sat patiently, remembering her first love.

Jenna plugged in to Johnson. There was no trip through space this time. She found herself in a hotel room, staring at Johnson screwing a dark-haired, insanely attractive man on the bed. It was raw, passionate sex. A silk slip lay carelessly discarded on the floor. Was that Johnson's...?

The trip was over quickly and she'd seen more than enough.

When she opened her eyes, Tynia asked, "What did you see?"

"I saw Johnson, my friend..." Jenna murmured, stunned, "across all that distance..." No way was she mentioning this to Graham.

"I saw Takeza," Cornelius said, happily. "She seemed fine."

"Takeza?" Tynia asked.

"My girlfriend."

Tynia's face fell.

When they returned to the shack, Tynia told them she would make a stew. She got her hands on the bren straight away. Cornelius said he'd round everyone up.

As Tynia gathered more ingredients, she glanced at Jenna. "You are with Mr Brash, are you, Jenna?" Jenna averted her gaze and nodded. A moment of silence followed. "But you like the other one."

Jenna whipped her head to the woman. "Why d'you say that?"

"I've lived a long time. I pick up on the nuances."

Jenna looked at her for a long moment then let out a sigh. "It's a big mess. Lucas- Mr Brash and I aren't together. He likes Allessa and I like Flint." Jenna explained the whole situation. "So, you can't say anything, OK?"

The old woman studied her. "What you're doing is noble but if you want to spare his feelings, you'd let him start a relationship with the Sentier and get over you."

Jenna stared at her. "I'm not *that* noble."

"No, you want to keep him on hold in case you make it through this."

"That's unfair," Jenna shot.

"Keep him alive and keep him on hold."

"OK, maybe I do. Once I'm dead, I won't care who he screws."

"Your language has become colourful, Jenna."

Jenna scowled. "So, you think I should let her have him?"

"God no. I think you should tell him."

Graham and Cornelius entered the shack.

"You saw Daria?" Graham asked.

"Err... yes," Jenna replied, glancing at Cornelius.

"What was she doing?"

"Err... sleeping."

"I loved watching her sleep."

Jenna busied herself looking in the cupboards for bowls. The crew drifted in and Tynia told them to sit down. Flint, Brash, and Graham sat on the floor as there weren't enough seats for all of them. Tynia scooped out the stew and Jenna handed the bowls around.

It was an uncomfortable gathering, everyone quiet, Graham wondering if Johnson missed him, Brash wondering if he could win Allessa back, and Flint wondering if the Sentier did like him. He stole odd fleeting glances at her. Jenna noticed and felt sick.

Cornelius studied them all, realising he'd been missing things lately. He needed to tune back in.

Punching the Pixie

Emilio showed them around the compound and they stared at the huge rig.

"We're opening other sites soon," the Spaniard told them. "Come on, I'll show you where you're based."

He took them to a porta cabin set against the perimeter wall. Situated near the gate, it belonged to a cluster of porta cabins. They stared up at the wall that appeared more like a rampart. A few Revlans on top kept look-out.

"It's like a castle," Newark remarked.

Emilio followed his gaze. "Yes, we had to fortify the place. These gangs are costing us money."

The Spaniard led them into the porta cabin. A couple of beefy Revlans loafed about in there, their rubbery faces sizing them up. Newark looked around, disappointed at how basic it was. His eyes brushed over a couple of desks, a few chairs, the comfy ones taken by the loafers, and a few cupboards. At least, they had a coffee machine.

"You requested night googles," Emilio said, walking to a cupboard and bringing out three pairs. He moved to another cupboard. "And the weapons are in here if you need them."

"Cool," Newark said.

"So, you're going out there tonight?" Emilio asked, turning to Johnson.

"Yep. You said you'd had no trouble for the past two nights?"

"That's right."

"Well, we'll be going out until they show up."

"Be careful," he said, looking deep into her eyes.

Skinner looked at the Revlans. "Do they speak English?"

Emilio glanced at them. "Pigeon-style English. They've been told to defer to you, so make use of them in any way you want." His eyes returned to Johnson. "The shuttles leave at certain times but I've given instruction that you may use them when you need." His eyes lingered on her. "I'll leave you to it then."

As he walked out, the two Revlans stood, trying to look intimidating. "We not tak ords from anyon," one of them said in a hard, if funny-sounding, voice.

Johnson, Newark, and Skinner glanced at one another then steamed forward to kick the crap out of them. The aliens might have been big but the lumbering creatures were no match for the crazy manoeuvres this team pulled off.

Johnson kicked one in the groin to finish him and make a point. "You do what the fuck we say," she told him. "Or next time, I won't be kicking your goods, I'll be ripping them out."

The Revlan's eyes widened.

"Fucking pond scum," she said, turning away from them and looking around the cabin. Walking over to the coffee machine, she switched it on, looking back at the Revlan. "Go find me some sugar. *Now.*"

Keeping hold of his groin, the injured Revlan stumbled to his feet, and hobbled out. The other creature kept his eyes on the floor. "Dere den of us, algether," he mumbled. "And dat just dayshit."

Newark laughed.

Johnson scowled. "So, we'll kick the crap out of ten of you, if we have to. And the nightshit too."

Newark sat on a chair and stretched his arms back. "What are we going to do with these bastards?" he asked, glancing at the Revlan. "If you ask me, they're useless."

"We'll find something," Johnson said, searching for mugs.

"We could use a couple as a decoy," Skinner suggested.

"How d'you mean?"

"To draw the main bulk of the gang away while we knab one."

Johnson nodded, thoughtfully.

"Me not daco," the Revlan protested.

"Hey, you work for us now," Newark said.

Skinner assessed the Revlan. "They're probably too cowardly to be decoys. They'd run off before the gangs arrive."

"Is that right?" Newark asked the creature. "Are you Revlans cowardly worms?"

"Me not dowad."

"Yeah, you and your mates are scared-shit pussies, aren't you?"

"Revlans bave!"

Johnson pulled guns out of the cupboard and tossed a couple to Newark and Skinner. Moments later, the hobbling guy re-entered with a whole gang of angry Revlans.

"You pay for dis!" one of them shouted, steaming forward.

Johnson shot him in the leg and he dropped. The others backed up, their hands in the air.

"A bit over the top," Newark remarked.

"They need to learn discipline," Johnson said, pointing the gun at the others. She gave them a hard look. "We've been put in charge, so you either follow our orders or your sacked. Not that we need you anyway. Bunch of cowards."

"We not dowads," a few asserted.

"No? We need decoys to catch a gang member, and this sniffling worm," she said, pointing at the sore, aching Revlan behind her, "says he can't do it."

"Too *scary* for him," Newark added in a boo-hoo voice.

"We be dacos," one asserted. "Revlan not dared anython!"

"I'll believe that when I see it," Johnson remarked, glancing at Newark. "OK," she said, "we'll give you a chance. We need a couple to head out with us tonight."

Every Revlan volunteered. Apart from the one with blood oozing from his leg. That guy had passed out.

"OK, you two," she said, pointing at a couple of them. She glanced at the Revlan she'd kicked in the groin. "Where's my sugar?"

As he left again, the Revlans edged further in and sat.

"Right, Skinner," Johnson said, "go over the plan."

"Which direction did this gang come from last time?" Skinner asked the group.

"Sowt," one answered.

"Do they always come from the south?"

"Des."

"Which way's south?"

The Revlan pointed.

"Right, well, the only cover we've got is night. No features, as such, to hide behind. When they show up, you two," he said, pointing at the volunteers, "run in front of the gang and lead them west. The three of us will grab a straggler."

"Dey kill us," one of the two protested.

"We'll position a jeep to the west. We'll take it out there shortly. You make off in that. Meanwhile, we take our hostage into the compound and get information on who's behind this."

"So, are we all set then?" Johnson asked.

"Yes, cep, we don wok nightshit. Nightshit wok nightshit."

"Fucks sake. OK, how about this? You two work at night and you'll get overtime rate."

"What dat?"

"It means you get paid double."

79

*

Skinner, Johnson, and Newark hung around under cover of night. The two decoys appeared nervous, one wringing his hands, the other trembling. The roar of vehicles came their way. The five of them ducked, blending into the darkness.

The vehicles stopped. A large group of beings jumped out, unloading arsenal. Within minutes, they lobbed objects at the compound. Explosions lit the night.

"They're upping their game," Skinner said, watching the walls of the compound take severe blows. "They're using make-shift bombs."

"OK, it's time to draw them away," Johnson said, looking at the two Revlans.

The Revlans appeared frozen.

"You're up," Johnson said. "Move it."

"Told you they were a bunch of pussies," Newark remarked, disgusted.

Fuelled by the insult, the Revlans stood and charged forward, running in front of the terrorist protestors then quickly running away. The protestors took the bait, storming after them. Newark, Skinner, and Johnson sprang into action.

The terrorists yelled and jeered as they chased their prey. Johnson hoped to God they didn't catch them. A straggler soon became apparent. Making ground, Newark nabbed him, clamping a hand over his mouth as he brought him down. The riotous chase carried on in front as they dragged their victim back to base.

Personnel put fires out when they arrived back. Revlans were on high alert, for what good it did. The crew took their hostage to the porta cabin. Chucking him in a chair, Newark ripped the ski mask off his head.

The eyes gaping back at them belonged to a her, not a him. A human her. The girl had messy black hair and a pixie-looking face.

"You're human," Johnson said, shocked. "Are you all human?"

The girl shook her head, her hands trembling.

"So, what's going on here? Who's behind this?"

"I'm saying nothing," the girl said. "You won't hurt me. There's due process."

"Process this," Johnson said, stepping forward and punching her in the face.

Knocked back, the girl lost focus. As her senses returned, she held her cheek, staring at Johnson in shock.

"You tell us what you know," Johnson said, "or the face gets it again."

"Dahlia Solares," the girl blurted. "But she's just protecting the planet. They're hurting it with those drills. Planets have feelings too."

The three of them stared at her then burst out laughing.

"It's not funny," she asserted. "Just because you can't see the truth of it. This drilling needs to stop and we're not stopping until it does."

"OK," Johnson said, collecting herself, "you take us to this Dahlia Solares, so she can explain it all to us."

"I can't do that. She's our spiritual leader. You'll have her arrested."

Johnson clenched her fist. The girl stared at it then caved.

Skinner felt compelled to offer the girl a hand up. This had never happened to him before and even Newark registered it.

They exited the porta cabin, relieved to see the two Revlans climb out of their jeep.

"Good work," Johnson called over. The Revlans looked pleased, if jaded.

Finding a Kaledian shuttle pilot, they instructed him to take them to the city.

It was an hour's flight over dark wasteland, the girl viewing them with contempt. Skinner viewed her curiously, her pixie-like features intriguing. He found them appealing.

"*Are* you human?" Newark asked, considering she *was* actually a pixie.

"Of course, I'm human." The girl turned her head away from him.

The crew fell silent, Johnson remembering the heavenly experience she'd had last night. The Spaniard knew what he was doing. Newark wondered why he hadn't been getting any lately. Was he off his game? Skinner studied the girl with interest. Did she really buy all that crap about hurting the planet?

The lights of the city came into view. Touching down in an area reserved for Ubro oil, they disembarked. Leaving the deserted air base, the girl led them through a labyrinth of streets and alleys.

"How far?" Johnson asked, impatiently.

"She's on the outskirts of the city," the girl mumbled.

Darkness turned to the grey light of dawn. Skinner kept glancing at the girl. Her lithe body was... sort of perfect. The way it moved hypnotised him...

He snapped to attention when that body made a break for it.

They chased her down alleyways, knocking various low-lives out of their way. Skinner took the lead, knowing if Johnson caught her, the girl's face would need surgery.

81

Careering around another corner, he tackled her to the ground. She struggled against him but he held her firm. Twisting in his grasp, she spat in his face. Standing, he grabbed her up, manoeuvring her out of the way as Johnson's fist came in.

Johnson stared at him in askance.

"If you knock her out, we'll never get there," Skinner insisted.

Considering this, Johnson unfurled her fist. "Don't let her get away again."

Skinner kept a firm hold of the girl, intensely aware of her heat, her scent...

The girl took them to an old stone building. The sun, rising over the hills, highlighted the flaking paint on the double door entrance.

"This is it?" Johnson asked.

"This is our temple," the girl told her.

"Temple?" Newark asked. "Looks like some grotty, derelict building."

"What are you going to do?" the girl shot.

"We're going to have a little chat," Johnson told her.

"You'll be interrupting their dawn worship."

"Then we'll stand at the back and watch."

The crew pushed open the wooden doors. A long dim corridor stretched ahead of them, another set of double doors at the end.

"Is that where they're worshipping?" Johnson asked.

The girl nodded.

Walking down the corridor, they opened the doors to find a bizarre, if not grotesque, sight. Men and women of all species screwed on rugs in an open-air courtyard.

"Holy fuck..." Newark murmured, watching a blue Stilgen and a pot-bellied Kaledian doing it.

"I thought they were worshipping...?" Johnson mumbled, staring on in horror.

"They are," the girl replied. "They are worshipping life, nature, our bodies, sex..."

"Christ," Skinner said. It was inter-species connection on a grossed-out scale.

The crew backed up, closing the door behind them.

"I think I'm going to puke," Newark said, covering his mouth. "This is fucked-up."

Skinner glanced at the girl. He couldn't be sure, but he thought he caught an amused gleam in her eyes.

As the daily worshippers departed, the crew's eyes followed them. Hesitantly, they re-entered the courtyard. The girl led them over to Dahlia

Solares, the woman of a species unknown to them. She had a long, thin body, shocking white skin, and bulging brown eyes. She fastened a robe but Newark had no desire to see what lay beneath. She reminded him of a long stick insect.

"I'm sorry," the girl said to the woman. "They work for the oil company. They forced me to bring them here."

The stick insect stroked the girl's cheek. "I understand. All are welcome," she said, her voice sultry.

"You speak English?" Johnson asked.

The stick insect's huge brown eyes fixed on her. "I speak many languages. We are a race of missionaries. Spreading our message is important."

Spreading diseases too, Johnson thought, eyeing her with revulsion. "You have been inciting trouble and causing damage to property."

"I don't believe I have."

"You have been inciting your followers, telling them the oil company is hurting the planet."

"I might express a view but I cannot be responsible for the actions of others. I do not condone violence."

Johnson turned to Skinner. "She's going to wriggle out of this, isn't she?"

Skinner was thoughtful. "What race are you?" he asked the woman.

"Orpadian."

Skinner motioned for them to leave. Once outside, he turned to Newark and Johnson. "Let's see if there's been any Orpadian bids for drilling here."

Johnson frowned. "You think this Dahlia Solares might not just be a sex-craved fruit-loop, but part of a bigger opposition?"

"It's a possibility."

"So, either she's a freaky witch or she's a calculated freak."

"You don't believe she's genuine, do you?" the girl said behind them.

The crew turned to her.

"No," Skinner said, his eyes lingering on her. "You're welcome to tag along while we find out." Skinner had no idea why he'd said that.

"Maybe I will," she asserted, "to prove to you you're wrong."

Newark's mind still processed what he'd seen. "That Dahlia woman was doing it with a Kaledian..." he murmured.

"Why shouldn't she do it with a Kaledian?" the girl asked.

"Duh." His eyes narrowed. "Have you done it with a Kaledian?" He stared at her, horrified. Skinner waited for her answer.

"I do not attend dawn worship."

"You think it's sick too, don't you?" Johnson said.

"No, I... I have many boundaries to overcome."

"You keep hold of those boundaries, sister," she said, walking on ahead.

The three of them followed, making their way to the hotel.

Skinner kept glancing at the girl, intrigued by her pixie-like features. Who knew he had a type?

"What's your name?" he asked her.

"Sophia."

"Your face looks sore," he said, staring at a large bruise.

"That's because it got punched. Are you in the habit of punching girls?"

"I don't punch girls," Skinner insisted.

"She did," Sophia accused, pointing.

"*Technically* she's a girl too."

"She's not a girl," Sophia said, sourly. "She's more a man than most men I know."

Johnson overheard and the words stung. She'd bought lots of new clothes recently. Emilio had complimented her on them. But none of it made her feel... feminine. Did she seem feminine to him? She thought, tonight, she'd do something different with her hair.

Pulling out a slim communicator, she woke Emilio.

Newark fell silent. They'd seen many things on their travels but that about topped the lot.

*

Emilio sat in the lounge, listening to their report with interest. "There *was* an Orpadian bid," he said.

"Dahlia Solares is genuine," Sophia insisted.

Emilio turned to her. "What is she doing here?"

"Skinner brought her," Newark told him.

"She wants the truth," Skinner remarked, shrugging.

"Or she wants to report back," Emilio said. "Take her somewhere else, Skinner."

Skinner got up and motioned for the girl to follow him. He led her to the far side of the lounge.

"We'll run checks on this Dahlia Solares," Emilio said, "and the company will start to investigate possible Orpadian involvement. If this theory is correct, it could be the beginning of our trouble."

"How will you investigate?" Johnson asked.

"We'll buy intelligence services."

84

"And if Orpadians *are* involved?"

"Then the Kaledian government will need to get involved too." Emilio rubbed his forehead.

Johnson touched his arm. "Maybe it doesn't go that far. Maybe this woman really *is* a fruitcake."

He glanced at her hand, appreciating her concern. "In the mean-time, I'll inform the security forces. They can round up Dahlia Solares followers."

"They'll have gone to ground by now," Newark said. "But if we want more information, we could always punch the pixie again."

Emilio looked at Newark, puzzled. "Punch the pixie?"

"Johnson whacked the girl. Squealed like a pig, she did."

"It was a tap," Johnson insisted, wishing Newark would shut the fuck up.

"It probably wasn't the best idea, steaming into that shagging pad," Newark realised. "Fuckers will be keeping away from there now."

Johnson cringed. Who made her leader anyway? She'd never been captain before. This just wasn't her thing.

Emilio turned to her. "You punched the pixie?" he asked, an amused gleam in his eyes. "What *am* I going to do with you?" His low, seductive voice was flavoured with Spain. It drew a smile from her.

Across the room, Skinner attempted to initiate a conversation. "How old are you?"

Sophia's dark exotic eyes fixed on him. "Twenty-one."

"So, how did you end up on Kaledia?"

"I'd rather not say."

"Right." He glanced around the empty bar. "So, how did you end up with Dahlia Solares?"

"I'd been struggling to survive and she gave me refuge."

"I see."

"I handed out leaflets for her and did menial jobs but I got food and shelter. She was kind to me."

"Can you speak Kaledian?"

"Yes. I was always good with languages."

The angry bruise on her face made him feel something new. Guilt. It mingled with the insane attraction, taking him into deep unchartered waters. Apart from temporarily falling in love with Trot, he'd only used women for sex. What he felt now had an added component and he wasn't sure what to do with it.

The girl looked over at Johnson and Emilio. Skinner couldn't take his eyes off her. She glanced at him. "You want to sleep with me, don't you?" she said, bluntly.

"Err... yes."

Her look turned hard. "Then you shouldn't have punched me."

Glancing over at the others again, she got up and left the hotel. Skinner stared at the door for some time before realising he shouldn't have let her go.

Newark walked over. "Emilio says we can help ourselves to a drink."

Skinner looked around. "Where've they gone?"

"Where d'you think?"

*

Emilio took Johnson to his room. "What am I going to do with you?" he asked mischievously, closing the door behind him.

"I don't know," Johnson replied with equal mischief. "What *are* you going to do?"

"You've been a very bad girl, lashing out with those fists. D'you want me to show you what I do to bad girls?"

His words started a fire. "Show me," she breathed.

"Lie on the bed."

She did as he asked, the room left in darkness. He stood by the door for a few moments, pulling his t-shirt over his head, placing it on a set of drawers. Her anticipation mounted as his dark form moved forward. He lowered to the bed, his weight pressing down on her. She breathed in his exotic fragrance. He stretched her arms back, sliding his hands along them, his touch electrifying. Already, she was losing herself but her eyes widened as he quickly and deftly tied her hands to the bed posts.

"What are you doing?" she asked, panicking.

"Trust me," he whispered in her ear.

She writhed to break free. "Get these fucking things off me!"

She kicked out in helpless fury as he unfastened her jeans, pushed up her t-shirt.

"Get off me," she raged, yanking on the restraints.

He kissed her stomach, her body bucking beneath him.

"Get off me!"

He came up and leaned over her, staring into her eyes. "You'd really like this," he said, his teeth nipping her lip. She bit his lip hard but he smiled. "Do you want me to stop?"

"Yes!"

Sighing regretfully, he untied her. Pushing him aside, she got up and stormed out of the room. Lying on her own bed, she tossed and turned, wanting something she shouldn't want. Finally, she shot to her feet and strode to Emilio's room.

When he opened the door, she glared at him.

He smiled, a god-damned sexy smile. "Do you want something?"

"You fucking know I do."

Johnson succumbed to the unthinkable. She let a man take full control. He took control with his hands, his tongue, and when he entered her, she discovered that in bondage she found a new kind of freedom. Her arms strained against the ties. She dropped into excruciating bliss. If this was what happened when she punched the pixie, she'd gladly do it again.

Questionable Motives

"Now," Tynia said, "you asked about travelling to other dimensions, Jenna. But I must warn you, some dimensions are not, shall we say, higher. There are sick, twisted dimensions you do not want to stumble into by mistake." She shuddered. "I've seen things that, to this day, I cannot bring myself to speak of." Tynia fell silent and Jenna stared at her.

The woman collected herself. "However, if you stay on known pathways, it can be a rich and rewarding experience."

"You think I might be able to do this?" Jenna asked.

"Well, I suppose we will find out." Tynia glanced at Cornelius to find him staring over the sea. "Are you alright, Cornelius?" she asked. "You seem distant."

"I was wondering how Takeza is?"

"You saw her yesterday," she snapped. Biting her lip, Tynia looked down, fiddling with her skirt. "This material's itchy," she flustered. Jenna hadn't seen her wear a skirt before. She usually wore loose fitting trousers.

Tynia drew in a resolute breath. "Now, where was I? Oh, yes. In order to travel to another dimension, you have to open a portal. That's a subject for later. However, if you travel to another dimension, depending on where you travel to, you either raise your vibration or lower it."

"The Erithians lowered their vibration to come here," Jenna said. "Did they not teach you how to do this, Cornelius?"

Cornelius pulled his gaze away from the sea. "No. Why would they?"

"Err... It might have come in handy? Didn't you ask?"

"I suppose I felt it was out of my power. They are from a higher dimension, after all." He glanced at Tynia, assessing her for a moment. "You really are a remarkable woman, aren't you?"

She blushed, fiddling with her skirt again.

Jenna watched those fidgety blue hands. "So, how do you raise your vibration?"

"Well, for one," Tynia said, "you have to get limiting thoughts out of your head. Then, you plug in to your own vibration, and focus on raising it, as if you are tuning a musical instrument. Should we give it a go? Why don't you lie down? Try to connect with your energy again."

Tynia glanced at Cornelius. He had slipped back into his own world. "Cornelius," she said. "You need to focus. Put all other concerns aside. You need to forget about them. Keep your focus on me."

He turned to her with a gracious smile. "I'm sorry. You have my undivided attention."

Tynia went weak at the knees.

They spent the rest of the day out there on the beach but neither Jenna nor Cornelius made much progress. Cornelius was distracted, and Jenna had limiting thoughts. Despite all she'd done, raising her vibration seemed a step too far.

*

Brash spent the day trying to win Allessa over. Needing to regain her trust, he suggested they could still be friends. He even persuaded her to take a walk with him. They climbed the hills to find them laden with bata plants.

"This is where she gets the stuff," Brash remarked with a smile, absorbing the Sentier's long dark hair as it stirred in the breeze.

Allessa nodded, turning to look over the sea. She had been foolish, agreeing to come out here with him. She tried to avoid looking at his handsome face. She still wanted him, despite what Flint had told her, despite him being with someone else. Somehow, she had to find a way past this man. She couldn't be his friend.

"Lucas, I do not think we can be friends," she said, steadfastly looking at the sea.

"Why not? I really am sorry for how I treated you. Or is it...? Do you still have feelings for me?" His tone was hopeful.

She turned, fixing him with those captivating grey eyes. "I cannot be friends with a man who plots murder."

His brow creased. "What...?"

"Flint told me about your plot to kill Jenna. Maybe she can overlook it, but that is not the sort of person I take for a friend."

Brash stared at her, shame crawling up his spine. Allessa turned and walked off down the hill, Brash still staring at the spot where she'd stood.

The Sentier's eyes rimmed with tears. She could think of only one thing to take them away. Flint.

*

Flint and Graham took a walk too.

"I didn't know much about her mother," Graham said. "She never spoke about her. I knew she didn't have a father but she didn't say much about her past."

"What were *your* parents like?" Flint asked. Aside from knowing nothing about Graham's past, the man had talked about Johnson non-stop.

"Average. I was an only child. My dad had this fun side. That's why I'm called Graham Graham." Graham scratched his neck. "Bastard. Apart from the name, they were OK. I was happy enough." He turned to Flint. "Trot said you gave Daria therapy?"

Flint glanced at him. "We... had a talk."

"So, what did she tell you?"

"I don't think I should repeat it."

"Oh, come on, Flint. We could die soon. You can give me something."

Flint chewed his lip, considering whether to share anything of what he knew.

"The thing is," Graham said, "I might have been a tad... insensitive at times. I don't see things like you do, Flint. You seem to know what's going on. I'm starting to feel like... Newark."

Flint smiled. He missed Newark. He took in Graham's desperate face and sighed. "OK. Anytime she cried or showed signs of weakness, she got locked in a dark cupboard. Anytime she giggled *like a girl,* she got locked in a dark cupboard. Basically, she spent a lot of time in that cupboard. The only way to get out of the cupboard was to toughen up. If she wasn't locked in there, she got sense knocked into her, and all the time her mother told her she did it for her own good. There's more but..." Flint shrugged. "You get the picture."

Graham stared at him. "God... She never told me any of that..." He lowered to the ground.

Flint joined him and they sat in silence for a time.

"No wonder she's hard as nails..." Graham whispered.

Flint scratched his cheek. "She had no choice but to be."

Graham glanced at him. "You know, they'd be times, if she was happy about something, her smile was... different. Sort of... sweet." He shook his head. "Although, if I told her that, she'd knock me out."

"Maybe there are things about her even she doesn't know," Flint reflected, sadly. "Things often go unnoticed until they scream for attention."

"Flint!"

The two of them turned, their eyes widening on seeing Brash charge over. He looked like the scary captain he used to be.

"What the hell did you tell her!" Brash yelled.

Graham and Flint stood, Graham jumping back as Brash's fists came flying in. Flint pulled off insane manoeuvres, Graham marvelling at his skill, even now. He moved like an acrobat, avoiding Brash's punches with ease, his own punches landing with deadly precision. A lethal round kick to the head had Brash staggering back. A follow-up punch laid him out flat. Flint spun him onto his front, twisting his arms up his back.

"What's going on, Brash?" Flint asked in a hard voice.

"You told Allessa," he spat. "You bastard!"

"Told her what?"

"About us trying to kill Jenna." Flint stared down at him. "Why did you fucking do that!"

"I'm sorry, Brash. I didn't think you'd ever see her again. I thought it would help her move on."

"Do *you* want her? Is that it? Thought you'd stick the knife in? Make me look like a complete shit. You're a scheming worm!"

Flint had thought they were past this. "Look, you and Allessa were over. I was thinking of her. I didn't think-"

"It doesn't matter if we were over! You're always going to laud that over me, aren't you?"

Flint stared at Brash, wondering if he was right. *Was* he bitter Brash had got Jenna? He hadn't been getting a handle on anything lately.

"Look, I'm going to release you now," he said. "Let it go. I said I'm sorry and I mean it."

Flint released him, and Brash sat back, wiping his bloodied lip, glaring at Flint with hatred.

Flint looked at him briefly then turned and walked away, wondering about his own motives.

"You were never going to win that one," Graham remarked.

"I've lost any chance of getting her back now," Brash spat, angrily.

"Yeah," Graham reflected, "he's well and truly screwed things up for you."

*

The crew, tired of eating Tynia's stew, ate in the craft that night. Flint and Brash kept to their quarters. The rest of them ate in the bar. Graham told them about the fight earlier.

"They were fighting over me?" Allessa asked.

"They were fighting over what Flint had said," Jenna shot.

92

"Yes, of course. That is what I meant."

"They were going at it," Graham remarked. "Brash was out of his mind, and I wasn't sure Flint was going to stop."

Cornelius, being able to mind-read, had known about the initial plot to kill Jenna. Consequently, he was not surprised. He was surprised with the Sentier, though. From where he sat, he would say the woman liked both men. He wondered if she realised this. He looked at Jenna, wondering if she'd crack and confess her feelings for Flint. She held firm. The girl truly was remarkable. Mentally, he shook his head. This crew were masters at creating farce. He supposed it gave them something to focus on to relieve the boredom. As long as it didn't interfere with Jenna's training, he'd let them work it out themselves.

When Allessa left, Jenna huffed. "Fighting over her. She has a big opinion of herself."

Tynia came in, flustered, struggling to catch her breath. Cornelius rose and placed a hand on her arm, his touch soothing.

"I've been searching everywhere for you," Tynia managed between breaths. "Then I went searching for the exit again but I couldn't find it. Has anyone got a paper bag?"

"That's right," Jenna said. "You're claustrophobic, aren't you? Come on, let's get you out of here."

Jenna escorted Tynia off the craft, Cornelius following behind them. Once she hit fresh air, Tynia placed her hands on her knees and drew in large gulps.

"Oh, that's better," the old woman said, straightening. She looked at them. "You have enough bata leaf, do you?" she asked.

Jenna nodded.

"Good. Now, I don't want you to panic, but something strange has arrived on the shore."

A little Push

"What the hell's that?" Jenna asked, staring at a mutilated carcass. The green, four-legged beast had its head cut off.

"I think it's intended either as a cruel joke," Tynia said, "or it's meant to intimidate you."

"What...?"

"As this counsel of beings want you to improve," Tynia considered, "it's probably a sick, twisted joke."

"*They've* sent this...?"

"Don't panic, dear. Don't give them the reaction they want. They're just having a bit of fun. Watching now, no doubt. Don't rise to it."

"Don't rise to it...?" Shock turned to fury. She screamed at the sky. "When I find you, I'm going to mutilate *you!* You hear me, you sick bastards!"

"Jenna, they are messing with you."

"Messing with me? Mess with this," she yelled, sticking up fingers in repeated rude gestures.

"Jenna," Cornelius said, "they won't know what that means. Calm down. Don't give them any reaction."

"Well said," Tynia remarked, smiling at him.

Jenna continued to rant at the sky.

"Um... I suppose she's getting it out of her system," Tynia considered.

Cornelius nodded in agreement. "And anger *is* a step up from fear."

"Yes. Maybe they're trying to see where she is with everything."

Jenna whipped her head to the woman. "Where I am? Well, I could send them a note, rip out a page of my diary, maybe call them in for an interim fucking meeting!"

"There's no need for sarcasm, dear."

Jenna was pumping. She didn't think she'd ever been as furious in her life. She wouldn't rest until every one of those twisted fucks was erased from existence.

"You think you're coming for *me?*" she yelled at the sky. "I'm coming for *you!* Every single one of you!"

"Lovely sentiment, dear. Let's hope we acquire the goods to back it up."

Jenna turned to Tynia, her face hard. "I've got the intention. You give me the goods."

Aktimar smiled. Scratching his ridged cheekbone, he turned to Helmus. "You were right about her. We've given her the little push she needs."

Helmus smiled back, his face in hooded shadow.

"Send another one," Aktimar said to Bastira.

"Do you think that's necessary?" Bastira asked. The slimy freak sweated slime. He wasn't sure he could do it twice in a row.

"No, it is not necessary. But it is *so* entertaining."

Reconnecting

"You're putting too much pressure on yourself, dear," Tynia said. "Determination will work against you. In a sense, you have to let go."

"But I want to do this," Jenna said, frustrated.

Cornelius sat up and touched Jenna's arm. "Jenna, what have I said to you about patience?"

"But I don't have much *time*."

"Letting go in the direst of circumstances is a strength you have to acquire now. You can't force your will on this."

Jenna lifted her head and stared at him. Time was running out but the more she pushed, the harder it became. She let out a hopeless breath, her head falling back on the sand. "Can someone get rid of those carcasses," she threw out. They'd been there for days. She'd wanted them kept there to spur her on. Now, they taunted her.

"I'll sort it out," Cornelius said, getting to his feet.

Tynia watched him walk off, studying the calm grace of his movement. Jenna felt the sting of tears in her eyes. She swiped them away, the constant crash of waves mirroring her mood.

"He's a lovely man, isn't he?" Tynia remarked.

"Who?"

"Cornelius."

"Yeah."

Jenna closed her eyes, wishing none of this was happening, wishing Flint knew how she felt about him, wishing he lay beside her now.

On hearing voices, she sat up. Cornelius walked along the beach with Flint and Graham, who carried a stretcher from the ship. Jenna took in Flint's glorious form... his perfectly proportioned frame, his loose, run-your-fingers-through-it hair. He looked over at her and smiled. The sexiest smile in the universe. She smiled back, staring at him as they loaded the carcasses onto the stretcher, and carted them away.

Tynia's attention diverted to Jenna. "Your Mr Flint is dreamy, isn't he?" she remarked.

Jenna nodded.

"If I were you, I wouldn't let anyone get their tentacles into him."

Jenna bit her lip hard. Had she done enough to keep Flint and Allessa apart? Did it matter anyway? Did Flint have feelings for the Sentier now? She wished she could be a fly on the wall.

"Come on, dear, let's press on. Just keep out of your own way. Try to reconnect with your energy again."

Jenna lay back down, the maudlin thoughts quashing her fighting spirit. She stayed there until, eventually, she felt her energy.

"I've found it," she said.

At last, Tynia thought. "Excellent. Now, you are vibrating at a certain rate. Think of it as a note on a scale. So, we want to reach for a higher note. To do this, we use the power and intent. The higher note is all there is. Try it."

Jenna used the power and her intent. The higher note was all there was... She kept her focus there, space and time dissolving around her.

"You're doing it, Jenna," Tynia said. Jenna's eyes shot open. "Well, you've lost it again but you had it. It will take practice to keep it there but you're on the first step."

Jenna noticed Cornelius standing beside them. "I did it," she said to him.

"Yes," Cornelius replied, looking like he'd seen a ghost.

"Are you alright?"

He smiled. "Fine." He glanced at Tynia.

"Are you going to join us again, Cornelius?" Tynia asked.

He nodded.

*

Flint and Graham buried the carcasses. Cornelius felt it best if indigenous aliens did not find non-indigenous alien corpses.

"Has Brash spoken to you today?" Graham asked.

Flint shook his head. He felt guilty about Brash. The man had changed a lot since that plot to kill Jenna. He wasn't the man he'd been back then. And Flint realised, deep down, he *was* bitter. In truth, he didn't think Brash deserved Jenna. The man had completely forgotten about her on Juyra after he'd met the Sentier.

He caught sight of Allessa, wandering down from the hills. She cut a lonely figure. He had respected her wishes and kept away, but he wondered what was going on with her. He couldn't get a handle on her at all. *Did* she have feelings for him?

Graham followed the direction of his gaze, thinking everything had got messed up since that portal appeared. He wasn't sure who liked who anymore. He'd kept his promise to Trot, but Flint was slipping through her fingers. Panic seized him. Was Daria slipping through *his* fingers? Daria believed him to be with Yasnay. He wished he could let her know he wasn't. A sudden thought occurred to him. Trot had seen Daria. Could she communicate with her?

After they'd buried the bodies, Graham wandered around, biding his time until Jenna finished training. Finally, he walked to the beach to wait there.

Jenna sat alone on the sand and he moved over to her. "You alright?" he asked.

She turned to him. "Yeah. Having some down time. Tynia's gone off to make a stew."

He smiled. "You didn't try to stop her?"

She smiled back. "No. She never has guests. We should let her get on with it."

He sat beside her. "Listen, I was wondering... D'you think you could do that crazy trip thing again, and talk to Daria for me?"

She looked at him. "I can't communicate with her. I'm like a ghost. She can't see me. It's like... remote viewing."

"Oh," he said, disappointed.

"I'm sorry, Graham."

"I want her to know I'm not with Yasnay anymore."

She nodded, chewing her lip. "I wish I could help."

"D'you think you could do that viewing thing anyway, so I could see what she's up to?"

"Err..."

"Please, Jenna."

"Jenna? You must be desperate."

He smiled, impishly.

"OK, if it means that much, I'll try."

Jenna lay back and closed her eyes, Graham watching her intently. She plugged into Johnson and found herself in that same room, staring at Johnson tied to the bed. The dark-haired man had full control, and Johnson gave it him. A flimsy dress lay on the floor.

Jenna's eyes shot open. She sat up, unable to look at Graham.

"What did you see?" Graham asked.

"Err... she was... shopping."

"*Shopping...?* Really?"

Jenna nodded, dazed, thinking it best to prepare him gently for any changes he might find when he eventually met up with Johnson. She looked at him. "You ever seen her in a dress, Graham?"

Graham's eyes widened.

"Yeah, she was buying a dress."

"A *dress...?*"

*

Flint bumped into Allessa outside Tynia's hut. They looked at each other, uncomfortably.

The Sentier stepped forward. "I need to speak to you," she said, her grey eyes intent. "I know you wanted me to keep apart from you but I... I need you, Flint."

He stared at her, confused. "You wanted me to stay away from you, remember?"

The Sentier tilted her head. "No. My sentiments have not changed since we spoke in the bar."

"Allessa, what's going on here? You can't keep changing your mind."

"I have not changed my mind. I want you," she said, moving closer and touching his arm. "Let us be a comfort to each other."

The door burst open. "Oh good, I've made stew. Anyone fancy a nibble?" Tynia asked, her blue eyes fixed on the Sentier.

One Date

The nights brought bliss, the mornings torment. Johnson was becoming addicted to something she should not be addicted to. After the first two times, she'd left Emilio's room straight away then had steamed back to kick the crap out of him. But the Spaniard could handle himself, and they had ended up back in bed together. Now, she was learning restraint, learning to ride it through, yet two sides of her warred with each other. One fragile, emerging side was becoming liberated for the first time, but the old familiar side raged against this male domination.

Emilio always gave her time to cool off. He had an instinctive feel for this woman, knew how to handle her, how much pressure to apply, when to back off. He was helping her discover herself. He'd watched, fascinated, as she'd experimented with different hair styles, different styles of clothing... It didn't matter to him what she wore. He liked her in jeans and t-shirt as much as dresses. He'd been spending most of his free time with her and it wasn't like him.

Tonight, they dined together in the hotel, one of the few places that served half-decent human food. Emilio's gaze fixed on those unusual grey eyes.

Those eyes looked down at her plate. "So, do you use that bondage shit on all your girlfriends?"

"I only have one girlfriend, and that is you."

"I mean, have you used it on other girlfriends?"

"Yes. Does that bother you?"

She shook her head. "No, why should it?"

"Then why do you ask?"

"Just curious."

He reached across the table and took her hand. "I've never done it with anyone I had feelings for."

Johnson stared at him. She pulled her hand away. "Don't feed me bullshit."

"You don't trust me much, do you?"

"Look. I'm having a good time. So are you. You don't need to pretend it's anything more. Save yourself the effort."

He smiled to hide a troubled frown. "I'm not bullshitting."

She took a sip of her drink, glancing away. "So, did you find out if there *is* Orpadian involvement?"

Emilio shook his head. "Nothing's turning up. They've rounded up all Dahlia Solares's followers." The Spaniard smiled. "After their first incursion into the dawn worship, some of the security officers had to take the afternoon off."

Johnson smiled. "You're bullshitting me again."

He held up his hands. "Straight up."

Johnson shook her head. "That was one fucked-up place."

"Well, the trouble's stopped, so I guess we have the culprits."

She nodded.

"And just so you know," Emilio said, "I'd like to keep you on."

"You still need us?"

His dark eyes fixed her. "I still need *you.*"

She sipped her drink, glancing away again. The man had a disarming effect on her. She needed to redress the balance. "Well, there's something I need," she said.

"What's that?"

"I need to tie *you* up."

A slow smile spread on Emilio's face. "I thought you'd never ask."

Newark watched Johnson from across the room. "What the hell's he done to her?"

Skinner looked around. "I don't think it's all him. You said she had a meltdown on Draztis, didn't you? After Flint's therapy? Something about her mother?"

"Yeah, the same time you had your meltdown. You both went fucking nuts."

"Maybe there's more to it than a Spaniard that's good in bed."

"Like what?"

Skinner shrugged. "You'd have to ask Flint."

"That guy knows tons of shit. I wonder what he's doing... Hope he comes back."

"You're missing Flint?"

"Hey, the guy rescued me from a village of demented wild men and a boiling pot. He was a one-man fucking army."

"Thought he'd end up with Jenna," Skinner remarked, confused.

"Me too. Weeks we stayed on that plantation because Brash was screwing the Sentier. Weeks. And then he blows the poor cow off."

"I think it was the tentacles."

"Yeah, they were fucking gross."

"Tentacles that extend from the fingers... It's..."

"Fucking gross."

"She's watching them again," Skinner observed.

"Who? The bunny-boiler? Does she never give up? The woman's desperate."

"She's not the only one. I haven't been laid since I got here."

Newark sighed. "Neither have I. Everyone in this place is paired up."

Skinner smiled. "At this rate, we'll be hooking up with Kaledians."

"Hey, that's not funny." Newark watched Johnson and the Spaniard get up. "D'you think he's going to dump her?"

"Who? The Spaniard?" Newark nodded. "Probably."

"Poor cow..."

Skinner, Newark, and the bunny-boiler watched as Johnson and Emilio left the room.

"Lucky bitch is going to get laid," Newark said. "D'you think they'll sack us now the trouble's over?"

"I think they'll keep us on for a while longer," Skinner said, looking to the door.

The question soon became irrelevant because the next evening, the troubles began again. Revlans were in disarray. Johnson yelled at them to keep their shit together as bombs pounded the perimeter wall. A few got over. Down below, in the compound, staff scrambled to put out flames. The crew fired into wasteland, discharging round after round. Johnson threw out flares to light up the terrorists, and the crew managed to hit a couple, but for the most part, they operated blind.

"We need powerful spotlights!" Johnson yelled. "Why has no-one thought of that!"

"Dat your dob," one Revlan said.

"Fuck off."

"Where your night 'ogles?" a second Revlan said.

"Newark, go get the night goggles," Johnson shouted.

"'umans dupid."

"Say that again and I'll knock you out."

It was a long, gruelling night. In the morning, staff began a clean-up job.

"Fuckers have totalled our porta cabin," Newark complained.

A few porta cabins had been burned to the ground.

"Dahlia Solares was a red herring," Skinner said, thoughtfully.

"So, who's behind this?" Johnson asked, wiping her brow with the back of her wrist. She pulled shades out of her pocket and put them on. The sunlight dazzled already.

Emilio arrived on a shuttle. Johnson soaked in his manly form as he stepped out. He came over to her straight away. "Are you OK?" he asked, taking hold of her arms, looking her over.

"Yeah. Fine," she replied. "We need spotlights. Powerful ones. And more night goggles. Enough for everyone."

Emilio nodded. Rubbing his forehead, he looked around at the damage. "Who the hell's doing this?

Skinner spent the next few days trying to find out. He wandered around Kelparz in the hopes of finding clues... any strange gatherings, any unusual activity. He roamed streets and alleyways, looking in windows, watching beings as they walked by. Kelparz was a big place. Johnson and Newark told him he was wasting his time but they were out of options. They couldn't knab another terrorist. They'd be prepared for that.

Night closed in on another day. The green twilight glow faded into darkness. As Skinner rounded a corner, he stopped dead in his tracks. Further down the alley, the pixie entered a doorway. His heart sped at the sight of her. Walking over, he carefully pushed on a rickety door. Steps led down a gloomy stairwell. He took the steps, the walls to either side, rough and flaking.

At the bottom, he entered a squalid cellar dwelling that hadn't been renovated in years. Light and voices spilled from a doorway down a narrow corridor to his right. Carefully, he moved to the door, peeking into a large room. At least fifty beings sat around on old chairs, tables, the floor... A hotchpotch of species - Kaledians, Guthrins, Stilgens, even a couple of Revlans. Skinner surmised they served as the local low-life.

His eyes fixed on Sophia, handing out money. A human man did the same. Cash in hand, the assembly checked their dosh as Sophia addressed them in the Kaledian tongue. Skinner stared at her in awe. *She* was behind this? He gazed at her, transfixed. She was fabulous.

As the meeting came to a close, Skinner left the building, watching from a doorway further down the alley. The assembly dispersed. Sophia stepped out with the other human, and Skinner followed at a discreet distance. When the two parted company, Skinner darted forward, grabbing Sophia from behind. She struggled desperately but he held her firm.

"Remember me?" he said in her ear. She stiffened. "I'm going to loosen my grip. If you run, I'll catch you."

He loosened his grip and she turned to face him.

Skinner absorbed the appealing features. "You're behind this?" he asked with a hint of reverence.

"Behind what?" she said, guardedly.

"Who are you working for? A rival human company? Which company?"

"I don't know what you're talking about."

"What were you doing down there? Why were you handing out money?"

"I... I..."

"If you give me the information I need, and go on a date with me, I'll not turn you in."

She stared at him, wide-eyed. "Go on a date with you...?"

"It's prison time or a date."

Sophia bit her lip. "If I go on a date with you, you'll let me go?"

"I won't turn you in. You can go when the matter is resolved."

"Where will you keep me?"

"At the hotel."

"I'm not sleeping with you."

"I'm not asking you too. I just want one date."

A flurry of thoughts flashed through her head. Jail time wasn't what she had planned for her future. One date? How hard could that be?"

Pairing Up

"How did you end up in this line of work?" Skinner asked, marvelling at those dark, exotic eyes.

"I speak Kaledian," she answered without looking at him.

For their impromptu date, he had taken her to a quiet bar off the beaten track, somewhere with no crowds she could slip through. Apart from the serving Stilgen, only two other customers sat in the drab room. Sophia looked around, disappointed.

"So, you volunteered for this job?" he asked, intrigued. She glanced at him but was not forthcoming. "You promised information, remember?"

"I was offered a hefty pay rise and a promotion."

"That's it?"

"Isn't that enough?"

He assessed her. "Not for you."

She frowned. "You don't know anything about me."

"I know. I want that to change."

"Why?"

"I don't know."

She looked at him, oddly. "You're a strange person."

He looked down. His parents often called him strange. His siblings too, when they weren't ridiculing him.

He raised his head to find the large eyes studying him.

"Have you ever *had* a date before?" she asked.

He looked deep into her eyes as if baring his soul. "I've been with many women but I've never had a date."

Sophia felt a surge of pity for the man, sensed a kind of emptiness in him. It engaged her interest. "You do realise I have no job now and no means of support?"

"Give me all the information you have and I'll get you a job."

"How?"

"I'm a good friend of the boss's girlfriend. Translators are always in demand."

She chewed her lip. "How big is your hotel room?"

"Big enough. I'll let you take the bed."

"Or," she said, studying him, "we could always share."

Skinner stared at her.

"He's not the boss," Johnson said.

"Yes, he is. One favour. That's all I ask. Look, we've cracked the case. She's called another meeting to round them up, and he now knows who's behind it. So, one favour's not much to ask."

"You've gone soft, Skinner. She should be banged up like the rest of them."

Skinner gave her a hard look. She'd never seen that look before. "No-one must know she's involved," he insisted.

"Where is she?"

"In my room."

"What is she, your girlfriend or something?"

"Maybe."

Johnson's eyes widened. "Since when do you do girlfriends?

"Since now. So?"

She shook her head in disbelief. Skinner had got himself a bird...? "Alright, I'll see what I can do."

*

Skinner and his new girlfriend spent a lot of time in his room. Skinner wasn't too clued in on the dating side of things, but he had become adept in the bedroom department. Sophia was pleasantly surprised. Between their insatiable love-making, Sophia instructed Skinner on the finer points of relationships.

"Loosen up a bit," she said. "I'm not an alien species. Don't look so stiff around me."

He nodded, his eyes tracing the contours of her face.

"I liked that you asked me how I was. That's good. Two people in a relationship need to be thoughtful to each other."

He nodded.

"Oh, and after sex, you're supposed to lie there for a while."

"I wanted to but I didn't know what to say."

"You don't need to talk after sex. You can if you want but it's not mandatory."

He nodded. In the past, after sex, he'd always sodded off. He'd never experienced any awkwardness before.

Sophia found his awkwardness charming. He was someone who needed to be mentored. A lost soul needing guidance. And with her influence, the man started to grow. Indeed, he experienced happiness for the first time in his life.

Newark wasn't quite so happy. In fact, he was miserable. In what universe did Skinner get a girlfriend before *him*? It made him feel like a failure. It also made him feel lonely. Lonely and desperate. Desperate people did desperate things, sought out other desperate people. One evening, he found himself chatting up the bunny-boiler. As other men avoided her, she was a sure thing. So, Newark, for the first time ever, found himself landed with a girlfriend. A clingy, needy, possessive one.

Waking Up

"Holy fuck," Jenna exclaimed.

"Jenna, I haven't said anything before," Tynia said, "but your language is becoming quite offensive."

Jenna stared at the woman. Cornelius stared at Jenna, who, a moment ago, had appeared as flimsy as a ghost. Jenna gazed at her outstretched arm, solid and visible now. She opened her mouth but nothing came out.

"Yes, it's startling at first, isn't it?" Tynia said. "You'll get used to it."

"I *disappeared...*"

"No. Not quite. You have to raise your vibration much higher for that. And that's a feat, believe me."

"Why did I disappear...?"

"You didn't disappear, dear. On this plane, when your vibration is that high, you become less solid. In a higher dimension, you *would* appear solid."

Tynia turned to Cornelius. "Keep practising, Cornelius," she encouraged. "It's all to do with how you use the power. You'll get there." She gave a him bolstering smile but Cornelius just stared at her.

"Now, Jenna," she said, glancing back at him, briefly, "you kept it there for some time before you saw yourself and... freaked out. So, we need to practice keeping that state in place."

"I disappeared..." Jenna repeated.

"No, you didn't, dear."

"Wow..."

"Um... We're not going to achieve much more at the moment. Let's take a break. Give this time to sink in."

"No, I want to become invisible," Jenna said. "I can go higher."

Tynia appraised her. "Well, if you're sure, you could try. But don't get your hopes up. Becoming invisible can take months of practice."

Jenna closed her eyes to resume.

Tynia motioned for Cornelius to get up. He did, and she drew him away.

"We'll let her try," she said. "She won't get there, of course." The old woman assessed Cornelius. "It must be a strange feeling, having the student surpass the master?"

"I'm hardly a master. But it's a good feeling, knowing I gave her a start."

"Yes. That's a good way to look at it."

"The girl continues to surprise me," Cornelius said, shaking his head. "I caught a glimpse of it before but this time, she sat in that state for ten minutes."

"Yes, I noticed you had taken a break." He glanced at her and she smiled, sweetly. "Why don't we start working on changing your perspective when using the power. From the level of the power, there is no time and space. We have to get into that mindset."

"Yes," Cornelius replied, nodding thoughtfully. "I believe I do."

Tynia led him to the shoreline and instructed him as she had instructed Jenna all that time ago. She told him to raise the water, and he did what Jenna initially did. He produced a column by pushing the water up. Tynia produced a towering wall. Next to her wall, his column appeared feeble.

"Now," Tynia said, "I'm not drawing the power up through me. I'm using the entirety of the whole universe..."

*

Graham sought out Trot. He wanted to see Johnson again. He knew Trot was training but they must take a break sometime. As he walked up the dunes, he gazed at a towering wall of water. "Fuck me..." This stuff never failed to amaze him.

The wall sunk into the sea. He dragged his gaze to Cornelius and Tynia then searched around for Trot but he couldn't see her anywhere.

Moving away, he looked in Tynia's hut to find it empty. Wandering through the trees, he emerged, looking around the wild landscape, spotting Flint and Allessa climbing the hills.

"You alright, Graham?" Brash asked from behind.

He whipped his head to the man. "Yeah. I'm looking for Jenna." He manoeuvred himself around so Brash had his back to the hills.

"Have you seen Allessa?" Brash asked. Graham shook his head. "She's avoiding me." Brash raked a hand through his hair. "I've given her a few days space but I need to talk to her now, explain I was different then. People change, don't they?"

Graham nodded, vigorously. He wasn't good at giving advice and, in this situation, he had nothing, so he deflected. "Perhaps we should concentrate on what we're going to face soon. We could all get killed."

Brash nodded. "You're right. But I need to sort this out."

"I'm not sure how we can help her," Graham said, heavily, waking up to the gravity of the situation.

"Who? Allessa?"

"No. Trot." Graham stared at the man, annoyed. His ex-girlfriend faced all manner of unknowns. Did that mean nothing to him? Flint rambled over the hills with the Sentier; Brash rambled on about her. He felt sorry for Trot. She'd saved the universe and shit still got dumped on her. "Jenna should be our primary focus," he shot, stomping off.

As he headed to the craft, Graham realised he was taking a stance. A pretty good stance. Jenna had sacrificed a relationship with Flint for the man's own good. He respected her and, in doing so, found a new respect for himself.

*

Cornelius turned around. "Holy..."

Jenna came back into form. "Did I manage it?" she asked.

"Yes..." Tynia uttered, staring at her, transfixed. "You went all the way..." The woman felt renewed pity for Cornelius. How the heck must *he* feel?

"So, are we ready to start opening portals?" Jenna asked.

"I... suppose so..."

Jenna recognised the look on the old woman's face. Cornelius had that same look on the ship. Wondrous inadequacy. She never thought she'd see Tynia carry it. "You must be a remarkable teacher, Tynia," Jenna said, smiling.

Tynia smiled back, bashfully. "Well, I... I suppose so." She pulled herself together. "Portals. Right."

"I think you are leaving me behind," Cornelius said.

Tynia turned and touched his arm. "Why don't you sit out and watch for a while." Looking at her hand on his arm, she reluctantly removed it.

"Now," she said, turning to Jenna, "to open portals, we use the power and intent again. It's better to focus on an exact location, otherwise you could end up anywhere. And it does help to have a map. I can give you mine, if you like?"

"You made a map?"

"Yes. Well, I copied it from rather nice Philian I met on a planet called... I forget the name of the place. The most unusual landscape. Stunning. But I'm going off on a tangent. Now, opening portals requires an added ingredient."

113

"What's that?"

"You have to raise your level of consciousness."

"*What...?*"

"Well, you are breaking through space-time, dear. Granted, it might be an illusion, in a manner of speaking, but from this level of being, it's a tough nut to crack."

"I have no idea what you're taking about..." Jenna said, staring at her.

"I know. I think we might need to drug you, so you get the gist of things."

"*Drug me...?*"

"We have to expand your boundaries, dear. This is how I started. It gives you a view of the underlying reality. It's this we need to tap into."

"But I can't be drugged," she insisted. "Last time I took a drug, I forgot who I was. It took me ages to find myself again."

"I see. Well, don't worry. It's not *that* type of drug. You'll lose yourself for a time, of course, but you'll know who you are when you come back."

"Err... Maybe I don't need to do this. Opening portals? Is it *that* necessary?"

"Well, you need to be able to move quickly. They can. It's up to you, but you need everything at your disposal."

Jenna rubbed her forehead. She glanced at Cornelius. "You gave Lucas a drug like that, didn't you, Cornelius? But he can't raise his consciousness."

"No," Cornelius reflected. Mr Brash's consciousness often slipped beneath the radar.

"I'll take the trip with you," Tynia said. "Help you process the experience you're having for future reference."

"What...? How...?"

"Let me worry about that."

"When...?"

"Tonight, at my home. You'll be there, won't you, Cornelius?"

"Wouldn't miss it."

*

Jenna rubbed her sweaty palms on her jeans as she sat on the floor of Tynia's shack. Candles lit the room. The woman had put a bundle of blankets down. Cornelius sat on a chair. Tynia prepared the concoction.

"How can I open a portal alone?" Jenna asked. "It took tons of Erithians to do it on Marios Prime?"

114

"Who are these Erithians?" Tynia asked.

Cornelius explained about the beings he grew up with, how they'd come from another dimension to help them.

"It only took one of them to open the portal," Cornelius confessed, and Jenna looked at him, confused. "You were all nervous," he said. "The Erithians wanted you to have faith in the procedure."

Jenna's brow creased. "It wouldn't have made a difference to me."

"Not to you, but the others... well, they didn't accept the... extraordinary as easily as you did. Plus, the whole place wanted to come and see you off."

"So, it was Llamia that opened the portal?"

"Yes."

Jenna chewed her lip in thought. "This council would have to raise their level of consciousness to open a portal." She looked at Tynia. "That doesn't fit. If they can do that, why are they murderers?"

Tynia looked at her. "All they need is a moment in that state."

"Yes, but even so..."

"Some use intricate breathing techniques to elevate their state but its temporary. They're still existing at the level of personhood." Jenna's brow creased. How could Tynia put this? Oh, well, no point in being bashful. "An orgasm is a blissful, liberating experience, but it's short and sweet, and when it wears off, you're the same as you were before." Tynia glanced at Cornelius. "Do forgive the analogy, Cornelius, but I'm trying to convey my meaning."

He stared at her then shook his head. "No, that's quite alright. It's a... good analogy."

She smiled, bashfully, looking back at Jenna. "Well, many people reach that state temporarily, don't they? But they don't live in a continual... orgasm." She smiled. "They'd never get anything done." She turned back to the potion, stirring vigorously, her thoughts taking her to places that would make Cornelius blush.

"Right," Tynia said, coming over, "drink it in one, dear."

Jenna peered into the mug. The purple liquid smelt weird. She wasn't sure about this.

"Come on, dear. Don't think about it. Leap in."

Jenna glanced at Cornelius. He gave her an encouraging nod, so she downed the whole drink. "God, that tastes vile," she said, wiping her mouth with the back of her hand. "Aren't you having one?" she asked Tynia.

"I don't need it, dear."

Jenna felt peculiar. The room spun. She fell back on the blankets, staring up at the undulating ceiling. "Tynia," she said, afraid. "What's happening?"

"Keep with it, dear."

Jenna experienced a strange whooshing sensation and got sucked out of her body. *Holy crap!* She stared down at herself. Tynia lay on the blankets with her eyes shut. The whooshing happened again and she stared down on the roof of the hut. She floated in thin air, smelt the trees and grass in a way she never had before... rich, alive... A thought occurred to her. *Am I dead...?*

"No, you're not dead, dear."

"Tynia, where are you? I can't see you?"

"Don't worry about that. Now, things are going to get a little... weird."

"What...? I want to go back! I don't like this!"

"I'm afraid you can't get off until the ride's over. Are you ready?"

"No...!"

*

Cornelius waited patiently. He knew they wouldn't be back for hours, so his thoughts turned to Takeza, allowing the sadness he kept at bay to well up in him. He wished he could be there with her and their unborn baby but he couldn't leave Jenna to face this alone. He reminded himself Takeza had friends to support her.

Graham barged in. "Is Trot here?" He stared down at Tynia and Trot lying out of it on the blankets. "What's going on?"

"They have taken a drug."

"What...? After what happened last time? We'll get the Admiral's daughter back and no way can she-"

"It's not that kind of drug. It is to help her with her training."

"Really?"

"Really. Did you want something, Mr Graham?"

Graham looked at Trot. "I wanted a word with Jenna. It'll have to wait."

He left the hut, wondering if it *could* wait. Flint and Allessa were walking on the beach. They'd been spending a lot of time together. Brash hadn't clocked them yet. At the moment, he was in the bar getting trashed. If Trot didn't come clean, she'd lose Flint for good, and Brash might get the shit kicked out of him. In the past, stuff like this didn't bother him too much but it wasn't the best time for the crew to fall apart. They needed to be on their game for whatever came at them. Jenna's plan to protect Flint could put them all in danger. Graham felt *he* had to take the responsible role but he didn't want it.

116

"It's beautiful, isn't it?" Flint said, staring up at the stars. The hazy atmosphere gave the twinkling stars a faint hint of blue, red, and yellow.

"Yes," Allessa agreed, looking at his handsome face.

Flint caught her watching him. "I need to come to this in my own time," he said, honestly.

"I understand... I enjoy being with you. The rest can wait."

He nodded, staring over the dark, churning sea. He chewed his lip. "Do you think Jenna is coping?"

The Sentier tilted her head. "She seems to cope remarkably well."

"She's had a lot thrown at her, though..."

"Yes." She tilted her head the other way. "It does not get easier seeing the two of them together, does it?" The Sentier's eyes probed his.

"No." Flint's brow creased. "But I haven't seen them together much."

"Jenna is busy, I suppose."

He nodded.

"Lucas wants to be friends with me," she said, "but I cannot be friends. Too much has passed between us. I am sorry you got into a fight with him. I used what you told me to put a barrier between us."

"I wish you hadn't," he said, glancing away.

"I am sorry. It was a spur of the moment decision." She studied his pursed lips. "I am sorry," she repeated.

Nodding, he drew in a breath. "Well, seems he still cares about what you think. That's better than being dismissed."

"I'm not sure it is..."

He turned to her. "Allessa, I have to ask. Do you have feelings for me?"

The Sentier stared at him. She'd been struggling to answer that herself. "I... enjoy your company. I find you attractive. But I do not intend to enter into another relationship."

"You didn't answer my question."

"I think it is better left unanswered."

*

Dawn filtered through the window. Jenna and Tynia stirred. Cornelius watched Jenna sit up and gaze wondrously around her. She turned to him with wide, incredulous eyes. "It's all one... It's all beautiful... I can see it... It's like waking up..." She rose to her feet and wandered around, studying everything with a fascinated interest. A small pot absorbed her attention.

Tynia sat up, glancing at her. "I remember my first time," she said, smiling in reminiscence.

Cornelius nodded, smiling too.

"It's dawn," Jenna announced in rapture. She rushed out to gaze at the sunrise.

"So, you achieved what you wanted?" Cornelius asked the woman.

"I think so."

"What did you do?"

"You know how you lose yourself completely in that blissful state?" Cornelius nodded. "I didn't, and I didn't allow her to, either."

"I don't understand?"

"I pulled Jenna back so she, the individual, was as close as possible. Flipped her in and out of the picture, as it were. This should have a profound effect on her, should make it easier for her to get into that higher state again."

He stared at Tynia in awe. "How do you pull *yourself* back?"

"I have done this many times, Cornelius. I had help initially too."

His eyes lingered on her. "So, in effect, you experienced oneness and separation at the same time?"

"No, that is not possible, but if you undulate between the two states, it's pretty close."

He shook his head. "You really are remarkable."

She blushed. "Should we go and look at the sunrise too?" she suggested, feeling rather buoyant.

"Good idea."

They walked to the beach and stared at the sun rising over the waves.

Jenna gazed at it, entranced. "It's sublime..." she murmured, tears trailing down her cheeks.

"Pity she has to come down," Cornelius said, quietly.

Tynia nodded, sadly. "Every silver lining..."

"Indeed." He glanced at the woman. "You seem unaffected, Tynia?"

She turned to him. "Two hundred years, Cornelius. I've had lots of practice."

He smiled. "And you don't look a day over eighty."

She blushed.

Thoughtful

Graham and Flint sat on the flight deck, talking about Johnson. Graham had the urge to spill the beans, tell Flint how Jenna felt about him. But Trot would be furious, and the girl had become one of the best fighters he'd seen. Newark put that down to his mentoring skills. His missed Newark, missed having a laugh with his mate.

"So," Graham mused, nonchalantly, "you're spending a lot of time with Allessa?"

Flint looked at him. "Well, there are only four of us. Brash hasn't forgiven me, and you seem to spend... Actually, how do you pass the time?"

"I've been in my quarters." He sniffed. "Working on some stuff."

"Stuff?" Flint asked, intrigued.

"Designs. Architectural designs. It's... a dream of mine."

"And you've never pursued it?"

"I was shit at exams but maybe one day..." He shrugged.

Flint appraised him. He didn't know the man had dreams. "I suppose a lot's been getting in the way this past couple of years, hasn't it?"

"Yeah."

Allessa walked in. She smiled at Graham, her smile becoming warmer as she looked at Flint. Graham clocked the way her eyes lingered on him.

Graham stood. "Why don't we take a walk," he suggested. He decided to spend the day with them. It was the least he could do for Trot.

*

Brash had a hangover. He left the craft to get some fresh air, knowing getting drunk wasn't the answer. But she kept refusing to talk to him. As he entered the copse of trees, he stopped and stared at Jenna. She knelt on the floor, gazing at a cluster of wildflowers.

"Jenna? What are you doing?"

She looked up at him, her eyes lighting. "I love you, Lucas..." She jumped up and wrapped her arms around him.

"Jenna, I..." *She loved him...?* "Jenna, you'll always be important to me but I'm not in that place anymore."

119

Her arms released him and she ran out of the trees. He turned to see her running up to Flint, throwing her arms around him.

"I love you..." she said and Flint's heart soared. Allessa's heart took a nosedive. Graham breathed out, relieved. Finally.

Jenna turned to Graham. "I love you, Graham..." Squeezing the life out of him, she turned, throwing her arms around Allessa. "I love you, Allessa..."

Ah, Graham thought. "She's taken a drug."

"What?" Brash asked, joining them.

"The old woman gave her a drug."

Brash's hackles rose. "A drug?"

"It's got something to do with her training." Graham shrugged. "That's what Cornelius said."

"He knows what the last drug did to her!"

"He said she'd be fine."

Brash did an about turn and stormed off to find Cornelius.

Jenna gazed at the hills. Flint stood in front of her. "Jenna, do you know who you are?"

Her eyes settled on his. "You have incredible eyes..." she effused. "The clearest, most beautiful eyes... Pools of blue light..."

"So do you," he said with a fond smile.

He turned to the others. "We're not going to get much out of her at the moment but she shouldn't be left alone." He stared after Brash, who seemed more interested in having an argument. "I'll keep with her today," he said.

"Look at that!" Jenna exclaimed and their heads turned.

She ran off, chasing a blue-winged insect. Allessa watched Flint follow after her.

Flint tagged Jenna for hours. She was in her own wondrous world, a world he couldn't see, yet it held a deep, hypnotic fascination for her.

"Look at the sky..." she said, craning her head. "It's incredible..."

He caught up to her, the words spilling out of him. "*You're* incredible."

She brought her head down. "You're incredible," she murmured, gazing at his face as if it held mysteries untold. Flint wanted to kiss her. He used all his willpower to restrain himself. Jenna stepped forward and wrapped her arms around his neck, kissing his cheek. "Everything's incredible..." she declared, looking around.

He swallowed hard, watching her skip away.

Damn you, Brash. Damn you for taking her, and for not appreciating her when you have her!

He laid her in bed that night, and in the morning, his annoyance turned to concern. She didn't emerge from her quarters, and the crew found her sitting

120

on the bed with her arms wrapped around her middle, staring at one point on the floor.

"She's coming down," Brash said, sadly.

Flint turned to him. "What...?"

"She's going to be in a bad way for a day or two."

"This happened to you, didn't it?" Graham said, looking at Brash.

"Jenna?" Allessa asked, crouching before her.

"You won't get anything out of her," Cornelius said from the doorway.

Brash spun around. "Happy now?" he shot. "Look at the state of her!"

"As I told you yesterday, Mr Brash, this is necessary. In case you've forgotten, Jenna has a council of powerful beings out to kill her."

"And *this* is going to help?" he accused, pointing at Jenna.

"If I remember correctly, Mr Brash, the experience had a beneficial effect on you. For a time."

"What's *that* supposed to mean?"

Cornelius looked him squarely in the eyes. "It means, it appears to me, Mr Brash, you are losing yourself again."

Brash moved toward Cornelius but Flint held him back.

"Get your fucking hands off me," Brash yelled, shoving Flint away.

Graham placed a hand on Brash's shoulder. "Come on, Brash. Let's get out of here."

Brash glared at Flint and Cornelius as Graham led him away.

When they got outside the craft, Graham turned to him. "Listen, Brash, we need to talk. Cornelius is right."

"What...?"

"You're letting your obsession with this woman alter who you are. You're better than this."

"This is about Jenna!"

"Is it? You've barely thought of Jenna since you've been here. You're angry, I get that but-"

"Damn right, I'm angry. That snake has-"

"It's done now. There's nothing you can do about that. And, as for Allessa, the more you push, the more you'll drive her away. For the time being, you have to leave her alone."

Brash stared at him, oddly. "Since when do *you* give advice?"

"Since I'm stuck here with you lot. I've sacrificed being with Daria to be here. There are other, more important things to focus on. We need to support Jenna. She's under a lot of pressure."

121

"I didn't take you for the thoughtful type," he said, eyeing Graham oddly. "And you've done nothing but harp on about Johnson the whole time we've been here."

"I know. I'll try to stop that. So, are we going to put Jenna first?"

"Yes. After I speak to Allessa."

Graham shook his head. "Cornelius is right. That drug was wasted on you. You're the same selfish captain you used to be."

"When I was captain, this crew loved me," he insisted.

"Yeah, well, we've changed since then."

Graham walked away, Brash staring after him. Graham had never spoken to him that way before.

A Day Out

Jenna had come back to herself. She sat in the copse, gazing at the flowers, forlornly, a painful ache in her chest, a deep sense of loss in her soul.

Tynia approached her. She sat on the grass beside her, leaning back against a tree. "So, I expect you're feeling... disconcerted."

"It's gone..."

"Yes, you've landed back inside your brain."

Jenna looked at her, confused.

"The brain filters reality. You're back to two-dimensional black and white. But don't worry, dear. You get to keep what many don't. When beings undergo such a blissful experience, they dissolve completely. As did you. But because I kept flipping you in and out of the picture, so to speak, Jenna Trot was as close to that picture as any get. That leaves a firm imprint, and I believe you can experience that state again without the drug. A lot of this works beneath the surface, of course, but so many things do."

Jenna looked at her, strangely. "Who are you really, Tynia?

Tynia smiled, enigmatically. "Who are any of us?"

"I don't think you are who you seem."

"Yes, well, you'll forget about that soon enough. So, why don't you try it now? Close your eyes, empty yourself, cast Jenna Trot aside. Let the memory of that state suffuse you. Let it come to *you*. Give it a go."

"Will I feel awful afterwards?"

"No, you're just taking a glimpse. A glimpse is all we need to open a portal."

Jenna's gaze lingered on the woman. She closed her eyes. She would do anything to return to that blissful state.

"Don't try to make it happen," Tynia said. "Empty yourself. Let it come to you."

Tynia waited patiently, wondering if Cornelius was up yet. Pity he had a pregnant girlfriend. It definitely put the brake on things. She would have liked one more dalliance before she was through. She was too old for Cornelius, she knew, but he had a quality of spirit that was so damned appealing. Oh well, pregnant girlfriend aside, it was late in the game to switch forms now.

A look of rapture possessed Jenna's face. Tynia agreed with the girl's assessment. She *was* a good teacher.

123

Flint walked past. He stopped, staring at Jenna, thinking she looked even more radiant today.

Tynia smiled at him. "Good morning, Mr Flint." She *did* like this man. He was so polite.

"Morning," he replied with a nod and a smile.

Jenna opened her eyes. She and Flint shared a long look. Smiling awkwardly, Flint continued on.

"I like him," Tynia said, watching him go.

"I like him too..."

"Well, how do you feel?"

"Amazing."

"It's a tonic, isn't it? A pick-me-up. Now, are you ready for a day out?"

"A day out...?"

"Come on, we'll collect Cornelius and my map."

*

They found Cornelius on the beach. Tynia did like an early riser.

He turned to them. "I love the sea air," he said. "Makes one feel alive."

"Yes," Tynia agreed, watching the breeze tease his white hair. "I've got something wonderful planned for today. Jenna is going to take us on a lovely trip."

"I am?" Jenna asked.

"Hopefully."

Tynia studied the map. "Right, this is your destination." She pointed at the paper. "It's a small planet, called Gadestria, and there's a wonderful little place called, Kesian. It has a quaint taverna by a lake." Jenna eyed her, oddly. "This is part of your intention. The other part is to open up space-time. To do this, you must raise your consciousness, rising above space-time itself. So, if you could get into that higher state. Once you have it, you use the power and your intent. Remember, Kesian. It's lovely."

"I can *really* open up space-time?"

"At a higher level of consciousness, space-time is malleable. Your intention and the power bring Kesian to you. But you need to intend the portal too. No point having a nice house, if you haven't got a door to get into it."

"No point at all," Jenna said, shaking her head slowly.

"Come on, dear. You've come so far. Don't start with limiting thoughts now."

Jenna straightened. "You're right. Why let a chunk of space-time stand in my way?" She started to laugh. Creasing up, she laughed harder.

Tynia and Cornelius shared a glance.

"Are you OK, Jenna?" Cornelius asked.

Jenna tried to compose herself. "Yes." Taking a deep, collecting breath, she straightened. "I'm fine. I can do this."

*

Flint watched them from the sand dunes. A stirring breeze blew over him. It ruffled Jenna's blonde hair. His eyes travelled over her. She was the most perfect woman he had ever seen. Every cell in his body craved her. She had no idea how beautiful she was, and not just on the outside. He wanted to discover everything there was to discover about her but he would never get the chance. She had chosen Brash, not him.

Jenna's hair got tugged around as the air became charged. A pressure built. A whining grew. Cornelius, Tynia, and Jenna struggled to remain standing. A loud crack ripped the air apart, and a blinding circle of light appeared.

Flint stumbled back in shock, watching Tynia, Jenna, and Cornelius walk into the light.

The light disappeared, taking them with it.

Flint stood there, unmoving.

Remembering Friends

"Well, that was a lovely little excursion," Tynia said happily as they returned to the beach.

"Kesian... Yes," Cornelius said. "The crystal blue lake was stunning, the taverna was, indeed, quaint, and the odd-looking inhabitants couldn't have been more welcoming. I'd like to take Takeza there."

Tynia's face fell.

"I'm going for a walk," Jenna said, quietly.

"Are you alright?" Cornelius asked.

"I'm fine."

He watched her wander off down the beach. "It's a lot to assimilate, isn't it?" he said, thoughtfully.

"Yes," Tynia agreed. "Her whole concept of herself and the universe has been blown wide open. And she's still so young..."

"The years bring a perspective she does not yet have. Certain things get easier with age."

"You would think." Cornelius turned to her and she smiled, sweetly. "Well, it's been a long day," she said. "I'm going to retire."

"Good night, Tynia." He watched her for a moment then turned to look at Jenna. Concerned, he wondered what might help.

Jenna wrapped her arms around her middle, anxiety spreading through her like poison. She should have felt ecstatic but she felt... lost.

She sat at the edge of the dunes, staring out. Darkness closed in, turning the sea to a black roiling mass. Burying her head in her knees, she didn't move from that spot as the waves crashed relentlessly on the shore.

"Jenna?"

She looked up to find Flint. The sight of him made her want to cry but she couldn't.

He sat beside her. "What's wrong, Jenna?" he gently asked.

"I... I don't know..."

"You do. You just need to get hold of it."

She stared deep into his eyes. "I don't know who I am anymore... I can do all this insane *stuff*... I mean, I've already done a lot of insane things but there's more of it, and I can do it. I'm falling down a rabbit hole that never ends. It's... scary, lonely."

"I saw the portal. Cornelius told me you made it."

"Yes, I did."

His eyes held concern. "You need time to process everything that's happening to you. Even good things, or amazing things, can be scary because we have to adjust who we are to accommodate them. Letting go of notions of ourselves can be... difficult."

"You'd think I'd have managed it by now."

"Yes, but you've just broken through space-time. You know, that could give some people a god complex." He smiled, trying to brighten her mood but she chewed her lip, nodding morosely. "You are one of the bravest people I've ever met, Jenna, but you can't steam ahead. You have to think of yourself in all this. If a child became an adult overnight, how the hell would they cope?"

She nodded, thoughtfully.

He rubbed his chin. "Maybe I'm speaking out of turn here, but I don't think Brash has been as supportive as he could be. You need to take time out and spend it with him. Perhaps I could have a word with him on your behalf."

"*No.*" She glanced at him. "I'll talk to him."

He nodded. "Do it soon." Throwing caution to the wind, he took her hand. "Jenna, it might not sound like much when you're feeling this way, but we're all here for you. You're not alone. Maybe I can't understand everything you're going through but I want to. I'd share it with you if I could."

She battled to fight back tears, wanting to let her feelings out, needing him so much. She was going to do it. She was going to tell him.

"We're with you in this," he said. "Each one of us would fight to the death for you."

She choked the words back.

"Go and find Brash," he said. "If you don't talk to him, I will."

She smiled briefly. Rising to her feet, she walked away, tears streaming down her cheeks.

*

Jenna found Brash alone in the bar.

"Hi," she said.

He looked up, surprised to see her. "Jenna. I've been meaning to see how you're getting on."

"Fine," she said with a brief smile. She sat opposite him. "How are *you* getting on?"

He smiled, humourlessly. "Allessa hates me because I tried to kill you."

"Yes, I heard about that." She chewed her lip, taking in his sombre state. "Do you want to spend some time with me tomorrow? I need a day off."

He looked at her. "That would be good." He shook his head. "I haven't been thinking of how everything's affecting you. Graham was right. I am a selfish arsehole."

"He said that?"

"Not in so many words."

She smiled at him, gently, knowing whatever they were to each other now, she held a deep affection for this man.

"I'll see you tomorrow then," she said, getting up.

"Wait. Don't you want to stay for a drink?"

She cocked her head. "A drink would be good."

*

Brash and Jenna enjoyed each other's company, forgot about Flint and Allessa, started the process of becoming friends.

"I opened a portal yesterday," she said as they rambled over the hills.

Brash stopped and looked at her. "What did you say?"

She turned. "I opened a portal."

"You opened a *portal*...?"

"Yeah. Never thought I'd be saying *that*."

He stared at her, his mouth falling open.

"I'm freaked-out myself," she said to him. "I don't need *you* to freak out."

He shook his head. "You are one remarkable lady."

"Well, I'm not a lady, and as for remarkable? Maybe I *can* do all manner of strange stuff. That's just... stuff."

"Pretty cool stuff?"

"You would think."

He assessed her. "Aren't you pleased?"

"Yes, but... The universe keeps on getting less... solid, real... And it's like I have a power I've done nothing to earn. Maybe I can do all this stuff, but I suppose I was born this way."

"It isn't just what you can do, it's your spirit, your courage, your determination. You manage to get there, rise above yourself. That's something I haven't been able to do."

His words made her feel better. She smiled. "Maybe you have a few weak spots. You know, things that need working on?"

He smiled at her. "I'm glad we came out together."

"So am I."

They sat on the side of the hill and looked out at the sea. The amber sky gave a muted, almost mystical flavour.

"I'm sorry I haven't been there for you," he said. "Not much of a friend, huh?"

"Well, we're new to this, I suppose."

"Yeah... I wonder how Johnson, Newark, and Skinner are getting on."

Johnson had been weighing on her mind. "I need to tell someone this."

"OK. What is it?"

"Johnson's got another bloke. I think... I think it might be serious." She told him what she'd seen.

He looked at her, shocked. "Tied up...?"

She nodded.

"A dress...?"

She nodded again.

"Graham's going to be gutted."

"Maybe it's not *that* serious," Jenna amended. "But... she seems different."

"I don't know what's more shocking," Brash said, shaking his head, "you opening a portal or Johnson wearing a dress?"

They looked at each other and laughed, both of them needing the release.

As their laughter faded, Brash's dark brown eyes turned serious. "I really did love you, you know?"

"I know. Sometimes people move on. It can't be helped, Lucas."

*

"What the fuck's he doing?" Johnson asked, staring at Newark from across the lounge.

Emilio glanced around. "Landing himself in a whole heap of trouble."

The bunny-boiler was pleased with her new trophy. At first, she'd lauded it over Emilio in the vain hope the Spaniard would be jealous. Now, her attention was absorbed in Newark.

Johnson couldn't take it anymore. She got up and moved across to the bar. "Newark, a word, please?"

The bunny boiler glared at her. Newark turned. "Yeah, what's up?"

Johnson drew him away. "What the fuck are you doing?"

"Trying to get a beer."

"What are you doing with *her?* You've been with her every night."

"Oh, yeah. She's my new bird."

Johnson gawked at him. "Are you fucking nuts? I thought you were just screwing her?"

Newark leaned closer. "She's fucking ace in the sack. Desperate to please."

"She's your girlfriend?"

"Hey, you and Skinner have one."

"Yeah, but you're jumping in the deep end with her. She's unhinged." Johnson realised she had been neglecting her mates. Newark should never have been left alone. "Right, well," she said, "you, me, and Skinner are going out tonight."

"Out? Where?"

"For a piss up, like we used to."

"Oh. OK."

"Good."

Glaring at the bunny-boiler, she went back to join Emilio.

"Everything OK?" he asked.

"I need to get him away from that nut job."

Newark came over. "Sorry, can't go out tonight."

"Why not?" Johnson asked.

"She says she'll dump me if I go anywhere near you."

"What!" Johnson got up to knock the nut-job's lights out but Emilio held her back.

"Hey, sorry," Newark said, holding up his hands. "She's the best lay I've ever had." Newark shrugged helplessly and walked off.

"Let him make his own mistakes," Emilio said.

So, they left him to it and Newark basked in new-found adoration. The woman worshipped him. He felt like a god. It was intoxicating. But an odd thing started to happen. The woman began to exert a strange hold on him. He agreed with her a lot, did things she suggested all the time. He found himself attempting to please her and would do anything to avoid the tears or anger. Sometimes, he got both at once. The old Newark would have told him to get a grip but this wasn't the old Newark. This was Newark in relationship, and relationship was unexplored territory for him. This behaviour continued even as the frequency of sex declined. He was a lost soul but he didn't even know it.

Johnson called Newark out on his lap dog behaviour, telling him the bunny boiler was a controlling witch, but Newark defended his bunny-boiler, and he and Johnson ended up in a fight.

Even Skinner worried. "Never thought I'd see Newark brought to heel."

"It's the first relationship he's had," Johnson said, concerned.

"Still..."

"He was one of ten kids. Probably didn't get much attention as a child. It must be frying his brain now."

"Pity he got trawled up in her net," Sophia lamented. "He needs someone to mentor him.

"That's a good idea," Johnson agreed. "We need to hook him up with another bird."

"Who?" Skinner asked.

"We could pay a hooker."

They found a human willing to prostitute herself for money. But Newark even turned his nose up at that. Things were bad. Johnson didn't know how to save her buddy. She wished Graham was here. He'd know how to snap him out of this.

"Maybe he'll reach his breaking point eventually," Sophia said.

Johnson wasn't so sure. She'd been careless. Newark shouldn't have been left to his own devices. She'd been too wrapped up in Emilio. The guy *was* seriously hot, talented in bed, great company... but she needed to remember her mates. She thought of the others. How were Trot and Brash getting on? What had become of Flint? Was Fraza still alive?

*

Fraza had been taking part in the nude games, throwing himself into them without a care for what might be flopping around. He, too, had had a relationship for the first time. Jabreen was a skilled and sensitive lover. Unfortunately, he discovered she loved other men too.

"We experience free love here, Fraza," she told him. "Didn't you know that?"

Fraza scratched his ears violently. "Nobody told me," he spat.

"You should try it."

Fraza didn't want to try it. He'd had his fill of sexual adventures. He'd experienced all that on Venulas. The Jaleans had opened him to a whole new world. Here, he thought he'd experienced something else. But it had been a lie.

He lay awake all night, knowing his time in this place was over. He couldn't watch his girlfriend screwing other men. He had to let go and move on.

He stole out of the place before dawn. As he climbed into his yact, fully clothed, he remembered his friends. He hadn't thought much about them these past weeks. He wondered if he'd ever see them again. He realised something profound. Though he loved Jenna dearly, his attachment to her had been broken.

Parting Ways

Flint watched them from down below. They looked like a couple again. Part of him was pleased for Jenna, another part incredibly sad. Since they'd arrived on this planet, everything had been confusing. But it wasn't now. Now it was clear. He had to move on.

He walked back to the craft, sought out Allessa, and spent the day with her. They wandered in a different direction, exploring areas they hadn't trod before.

Graham held up in his quarters, working on his designs. He stared at the papers, a dawning realisation settling on him. He would never be an architect. He was going to die. Why was he even doing this?

Chucking the stupid papers away, he stood and walked outside, wandering around aimlessly.

Tynia approached him. "When everyone comes back, will you tell them I'm making a stew."

That was all he fucking needed.

*

"What's this added ingredient?" Cornelius asked.

"Linnel," Tynia said, looking around for some response. "Thought I'd experiment. Do you like it?" Her gaze travelled the group.

The crew nodded but not even the linnel could relieve the monotony of three stews a week.

Jenna noticed Flint and Allessa share a smile. What the hell...? They shared smiles now? A sick feeling took hold of her. She struggled to swallow each mouthful.

After tea, the crew headed back to the craft, Flint and Allessa walking up ahead. Jenna's eyes followed them. Weren't they supposed to be keeping apart? Her plan had failed.

She walked faster to catch up but Tynia called her back.

"Jenna," the woman said, "I wanted to ask if you had a nice day today?"

"Yes," she answered, distractedly.

"It's so important to take time out." Jenna nodded impatiently. "OK, well, I'll see you tomorrow."

Nodding, Jenna hurried off. She caught up to Graham and Brash, watching Flint and Allessa enter the craft. Brash watched them too.

"You coming for a drink?" Graham asked her.

"I'm tired," she lied. She had a very bad feeling.

Walking up the gangway, she split from Brash and Graham, her head spinning. Where would they be? She checked the flight-deck, the lounge, then peeked her head around the door of the bar, avoiding being seen by Graham and Brash. She even looked in the gym. At last, she arrived at Flint's quarters.

Trembling, she hung outside. Taking a deep breath, she focused, raising her vibration as high as she could, looking at her invisible arm. Coming back into form, she took another deep breath, knocked on the door, then quickly raised her vibration again. The door did not open.

Moving to the Sentier's quarters, she did the same thing. This time, the door slid open, and her heart stopped. Flint sat on the bed. Jenna slipped into the dimly-lit room, disappearing into the shadows.

"There's no-one there," Allessa said, gazing down the corridor.

Confused, the Sentier hit the pad to close the door, and moved back to the bed. "It is good to make a decision, isn't it?" she said, taking his hand.

He nodded and Jenna stared on, horrified, as his other hand brushed through the Sentier's long dark hair. When his hand came around her neck and he kissed her, Jenna shot into corporeal form. She couldn't move, couldn't look away, her eyes glued to the nightmare unfolding before her. The kiss became heated. They fumbled to undress, coming together naked on the bed, skin on skin, the Sentier's hands and tentacles going everywhere. Jenna stared at Flint's hands moving over silver flesh, the Sentier responding to his touch.

Her heart split down the middle. The naked pair were so absorbed, they didn't notice her slip through the room. Hitting the pad quickly, she ran out.

Flint sat up. "What was that?"

Allessa sat up. "The door is open?" She frowned. "There must be a fault."

She went to close the door. Returning to the bed, she moved to get back to where they were.

Flint rubbed his brow. "Listen, I don't think I can do this, Allessa."

"But we were so... engaged."

"I know but..."

"Please, I can get you back in the mood."

*

136

Charging into her quarters, Jenna ran to the bathroom and threw up. After heaving Tynia's stew, she fell on the bed and sobbed. How could she have hoped to keep them apart with that horny slut on board! She'd wanted to protect Flint. She hadn't wanted him screwing the Sentier. Her future looked bleak. She'd probably die but even if she survived, she had lost the man she loved. The tears wouldn't stop. The image of them together burned on her retinas, was seared onto her heart. Tanned flesh on silvery flesh. And the way he kissed her? Jenna had only one kiss with Flint. One broken kiss. And that trollop was taking the lot! There was no coming back from this. Somehow, it made her care less about dying.

It was sooner than expected, but it was now time to part ways.

Time to Unplug

"Gone...?" Graham asked, pulling on his pants. "She *can't* have gone."

"Read the letter." Brash shoved it at him. "It was stuck to my door. Says she has to do this on her own. We won't find her because she's opened a fucking portal."

"She can do that...?" Graham asked, staring at him.

Brash raked a hand through his hair. "Yes. Maybe Tynia can get her back. Come on."

Graham grabbed a t-shirt as they charged out of his quarters.

"What's going on?" Flint asked, watching them race by.

"Jenna's gone," Graham called behind him.

"Gone...?"

Allessa and Cornelius emerged from their quarters. "Did he say, Jenna's gone?" Cornelius asked.

Without answering, Flint charged after Graham and Brash. Tearing through the trees, the three of them burst into Tynia's shack.

"Jenna's gone," Brash shouted.

The woman looked around at him. "Gone...?"

"Read the letter." He snatched it from Graham and handed it to her.

"I can't read this, Mr Brash."

Flint took the letter and read it out loud:

"Sorry to skip out on you all but I have to do this on my own. Thank you for standing by me and for being willing to risk your lives. I can't let you do that. I love you guys and I totally forgive you for trying to kill me. We're past that, right? Tell the others I love them too. Fraza, if you ever read this, you're incredible. Never stop believing that. Cornelius, you are incredible too. Tynia, you're amazing. Graham, I hope you get Johnson back. Johnson, you were my first female friend too. Newark, never stop being you. Skinner, bye. Lucas, we shared a lot together. You'll always have a place in my heart. Vincent – I never called you

139

Vincent, did I? Wherever you go, Vincent, I wish you a world of happiness.

Time to move on, guys.

Jenna x

"Can you get her back?" Brash asked.

The woman rubbed her forehead. "No. It would be like looking for a grain of sand on a beach."

"There must be something we can do?" Flint pressed, raking a hand through his hair.

Cornelius and Allessa entered the hut.

"Jenna's gone?" Cornelius asked, worried.

Brash handed him the letter.

"Wait a minute," Graham said, "you can do that remote viewing thing."

"I could," Tynia said, "but I wouldn't be able to discern where she was. And remote viewing is a one-way process."

"Can't you do that mind-linking shit?" He turned to Allessa. "*You* can link with her."

Tynia sighed. The guy was on top form. "We could but, seeing as she's skipped out, do you think she will answer?"

"You have to try," Flint insisted.

Tynia appraised him, her heart squeezing. She recognised pain when she saw it. "I will try, Mr Flint," she said, graciously.

She sat and closed her eyes, humming a tune in her head to pass the time, conjuring a pretty scenic landscape.

At last, she opened her eyes. "Nothing. I am sorry."

"Did you see anything?" Graham asked.

"Hills and a river," she said. "How many hills and rivers are there in the universe?"

Flint lowered into a chair.

"She was always planning to leave, wasn't she?" Graham said, sombrely.

Flint raised his head to Brash. "She said nothing to *you*? Gave no hint of this?"

Letting out a sigh, Brash glanced at him. "She wasn't *with* me."

"What?"

"She was crazy about *you*." Flint's brow furrowed. "She didn't want to rekindle your relationship when she thought she was going to die. She wanted to spare your feelings and your life."

"*What...?*"

140

"The reason we got stranded on that planet was because we had made a terrible mistake. There's nothing between Jenna and me anymore. We were trying to get to you and Allessa, praying you'd forgive us."

Flint and Allessa stared at Brash. Flint's gaze transferred to the floor, soaking it all in.

"There must be something we can do?" Brash said, turning back to Tynia.

"All we can do is pray," the old woman said.

Cornelius sat down, heavily. "Why now?" he quietly asked. "Her time isn't through."

"Why indeed?" Tynia reiterated, her gaze moving to Flint.

Flint lurched to his feet. Flinging the door wide, he walked out. He strode over the dunes to the beach, a pressure building inside him. Wind tugged at his hair and clothes. Waves crashed against the shore.

"Damn you, Jenna Trot!" he screamed at the sky.

*

The crew waited in the vain hope Jenna would return. At last, they convened in the meeting room of the ship.

"What should we do then?" Graham asked Cornelius.

"There is nothing we *can* do." Cornelius rubbed his forehead. "I need to leave. I need to be with Takeza."

"I'm staying here," Flint said.

"Me too," Brash seconded.

Flint looked at Cornelius. "Try to contact her again," he pressed.

"I have tried. Repeatedly. She isn't responding."

"So, that's it then," Graham said, staring at the table. "We'll never know if she lives or dies."

Cornelius wiped a tear from under his eye. "We have to pray she'll come through this, come back to us."

"I need to return to Lixia," Allessa said, soberly. She realised she had lost her balance. Had she focused more on Jenna, she might have foreseen this. She needed to go home.

"Won't you stay with us?" Brash asked, a pleading note in his voice.

"I am the Head Sentier, Lucas. I can't stay away forever."

Brash wondered if it was time to let her go. If she couldn't be friends with him, how could they be lovers? Maybe he had to accept it was over.

Flint looked at Cornelius. "Can anyone train in the power?"

141

The question took Cornelius by surprise. "Anyone?"

"Is this power available to everyone?"

Cornelius scratched his temple. "On paper, the power should be available to everyone but...."

"What makes Jenna different?"

"The power comes through freely in her."

"Why?"

"I don't know..."

Flint got up. Leaving the craft, he strode to Tynia's hut and asked her the same question.

Tynia studied him. "Some are born musical geniuses. They have a gift. Others become brilliant by sheer practice. It is possible for others to command the power but you have so little time, Mr Flint." She assessed him. "What do you hope to achieve? You will never find her."

"I need to do something," he shouted, banging his fists into a cupboard.

"Sit down, Mr Flint," she said, gently.

Dropping into a chair, he put his head in his hands.

"It's a good job you have a head start then, isn't it?" Tynia told him.

He looked up at her.

The woman sat opposite him. "How do you think you survived your childhood, Mr Flint?"

He stared at her, strangely. "What do you know of my childhood?"

"More than I'd like to," she answered, moisture welling in her eyes. "You shut down for many years, didn't you? Do you remember how you got out of that place?"

He glared at her. "Has Cornelius been talking to you?"

She shook her head. "I see too much, Mr Flint. I see what a remarkable young man you are. You have managed to rise above the horror. But some memories, understandably, have been buried." She leaned forward and took both his hands, lifting her eyes to his. "Now do you remember how you got out?"

He stared into her intense blue eyes, seeing his past through them. He was eleven. He'd been in that place so long he couldn't remember not being there. A dark, airless void. The beatings had become more vicious. The monster used a knife too. He carried one now; was going to cut him, maybe even kill him. Something snapped inside, something powerful. It wasn't terror. He'd had too much of that. It was a cry for freedom, at any cost, and if that meant death, he'd gladly take it. His chains broke, the roof caved in, crashing down around them. Through the dusty, choking blackness, he clawed his way to freedom.

"That was you, Mr Flint," she said, gently.

"That was me...?"

"The power surging through you." She looked at him with compassion. "You closed down, didn't you? Couldn't live with it all, but it haunted you like a malignant shadow, a shadow covering more than you realise. It is time to unplug, Mr Flint."

A Tricky Subject

Takeza threw her arms around Cornelius. "You're back!"

Brash and Graham stared at her enormous belly.

Drawing his attention away from it, Brash looked around Daka's old gaff. The empty place needed filling out. He clocked two Kaledian women sitting in a lounge over to the right but he was in no mood to socialise. He drew in a jaded breath. They had taken Allessa home before coming here. She had hugged him, which made the parting more painful.

Graham, by contrast, was energised. He planned to travel to Kelparz as soon as possible to find Johnson.

Brash glanced at him. He needed to have that chat now.

Takeza untangled herself from Cornelius and greeted the two of them. "Where is Jenna?" she asked.

"I'm afraid she left us," Cornelius said, heavily. "She didn't want us risking our lives."

Takeza let out a relieved sigh. She liked Jenna but her child needed its father. As she steered Cornelius over to her friends, Brash asked, "D'you have any beer, Cornelius?"

Cornelius pointed the way.

"We need to talk," Brash said to Graham.

Walking over to the kitchen, Brash retrieved a keg of beer, and poured two glasses, handing one to Graham before taking a large swig.

"What's up?" Graham asked.

Brash rubbed his forehead. It was a tricky subject to broach. "Listen, Graham, I've got something to tell you. I think Johnson might have... someone else."

Graham's glass stopped half-way to his mouth. "What...?"

"Jenna wasn't completely honest about what she saw."

"What did she see?"

Brash told him the lot. Colour drained from Graham's face. His gaze transferred to the floor, taking it all in. Appearing dazed, he threw back his drink. Brash watched him pour a second drink and throw that back too.

As a third glass emptied, Graham sunk into denial. "She's a woman with needs," he said, nodding thoughtfully. "She's experimenting. It's probably not serious. Hell, I was with Yasnay for ages and look at me now. Johnson and I are meant to be together."

Brash nodded, thinking the poor bastard was going to get his heart ripped out.

*

It kept getting better and better. No man had ever made her feel this way. He was an incredible lover. She was pushing boundaries she didn't know existed.

Flopping back spent, she stared at the ceiling.

Emilio came over her, looking down with those incredible dark eyes and that intoxicating smile. "I have a surprise for you."

She smiled back. "I think we've tried everything, Emilio. You can't have any surprises left."

"Not that kind of surprise."

"Oh?"

"I'm taking you away for a couple of days."

"Away? *Is* there an away on Marios Prime?"

"Wait and see."

"I've never *been* taken away before," she said, thoughtfully.

"Another first then. You'd better pack. We're leaving in a few hours."

"I'll pack. In a while," she said with a meaningful look.

The Spaniard's lips curved. He leant down to kiss her and the marathon of pleasure began all over.

When he finally left, she took her time bathing and packing, reliving each glorious detail of their incredible morning of passion. She sauntered to the window, looking over Kelparz, taking it all in. Scruffy alleys became quaint, charming pathways. The weird freaks that occupied the city were now a cosmopolitan celebration of difference. The city breathed with life.

They boarded the shuttle early evening. "So, where are you taking me?" she asked. "Where's the pilot, by the way?"

"I'm piloting."

"Cool."

She sat in the cock-pit with him, looking out as they took to the air. She felt... feminine. Emilio made her feel feminine. She wore a low-cut, light grey dress, which matched her eyes. A part deep inside revelled in the fact she was rebelling against her mother. As a child, she was the only girl dressed in jeans at parties. That wasn't the problem. The problem was, she never got a choice.

They left Kelparz behind, flying over the hills.

146

"Are we going to Jakensk?" she asked.

"No."

They flew for over an hour until she spotted a green lake sitting in a relatively deep valley. Newly constructed buildings surrounded the lake. They reminded her of the buildings on Draztis, white and kind of classy-looking. Taller ones rose high in the air. Hotels?

"What's this place called?" she asked.

"San Paulo."

"Sounds Spanish"

"It is. It's a new holiday construction."

She turned to him. "Yours?"

"Our company is expanding. There are no holiday resorts here. We're capturing the market."

"Cool."

The craft came in to land on a round concourse behind the resort. They disembarked and Emilio took her hand, leading her into the town. Johnson looked around the clean, expensive-looking place. Not a scrap of litter in sight. Of course, the scrubby hills and green lake weren't ideal, but on Marios Prime it was quite something. Well-dressed Kaledians milled around, a few staring over the lake. Restaurants lined the street, the noise and chatter drifting over to her.

"So, this is where rich Kaledians hang out?" Johnson asked.

"They do now. Come on, I have my own place."

Emilio's place was a whole top floor of an expensive hotel. The lift opened straight onto it. Ahead, a wall of glass looked over the lake. Johnson walked onto the terrace to take in the view. The lake looked like a large murky pond but here, it was class.

She turned to a table laid out with food. Human food.

"Hungry?" Emilio asked.

"God, you must be rich," she said to him.

He smiled. "I am. I'm with the best-looking woman in the place."

She crossed her arms. "I'm probably the only human woman here."

"Not true, but I'll amend. The best-looking woman I've ever met."

Her cheeks heated. She turned away. She wasn't used to compliments and she still didn't trust they were genuine. What the hell did it matter? The food looked good and the sex was great.

They had a romantic dinner and an incredible night of passion. No bondage, but wild sex, interspersed with slow sensuous moments. Emilio had a tender side. Johnson found she did too. She brushed his face in a way she never had before. The eyes staring back at her contained so much depth. It was hard not to look away. When she did, he touched her chin, bringing her gaze back to him. With Emilio, she felt like someone else.

In the morning, he suggested they take a swim in the lake.

"I'm not going in there," she objected. "I might catch something."

He laughed. "It's perfectly safe. It's the same water you drink. Come on, don't be chicken."

"OK but if anything swims past me, I'll kill the crap out of it."

Smiling, he wrapped his arms around her waist. "You have such a way with words."

He saw that look come in her eyes, a softening, a sweetness she kept at bay much of the time. He knew it was hard for her to show vulnerability. He only got glimpses but those glimpses were becoming more frequent.

They walked out, hand in hand, and Johnson braved the lake. They messed around in the water. She dove on his shoulders, trying to shove his head under. Emilio retaliated. It was so freeing not to have to worry about hurting him. She'd injured Graham a few times when they'd been jerking around. Graham wasn't soft but few men were strong enough for her.

As they calmed down, she looked at him. "You can handle yourself, can't you? How come?"

"My father taught me to fight from an early age. Various types of martial arts. He wasn't raising a sissy."

Johnson stared at him. "Did you get locked in a cupboard too?"

Emilio stared back at her, shocked.

Realising what she'd said, she glanced away. "So, you're expanding?"

"Yeah," he replied, his eyes remaining on her.

"You're a driven man."

"I am when I want something."

"And what if you can't get it?"

"I never give up."

She turned to find him looking at her. "What the hell are you doing with me, Emilio? I'm a foul-mouthed, coarse woman, who a CEO should not be consorting with."

Smiling, he wrapped his arms around her waist. "You're my foul-mouthed woman, and I'll consort with who I like."

She assessed him. "Just so you know, I'm never going to be CEO girlfriend material.

"Just so you know, I don't want you to be. Marry me."

Johnson blinked. "What...?"

"I'd planned to ask you tonight but I can't help myself."

She stepped away from him. "Are you shitting me?"

148

"Not the response I was hoping for."

"Have you gone nuts?" Johnson waded out of the water, threw on her sundress, and walked off.

Emilio caught her arm. "It's too soon, I know. I'm sorry. I misjudged the situation."

She stopped and stared at him, raking her hands through her wet hair. "Look, marriage is... a tricky subject for me."

"I love you, Daria. Do you love me?"

"What the hell's love got to do with marriage?" His brow creased. She let out a breath. "Listen, if you feel the same way in a year, ask me then."

"I'll hold you to that."

She stared at him. What an idealistic fool. "I'll see you back at the hotel. I need some time to myself."

Johnson walked off, Emilio staring after her.

She felt awkward with him after that but she tried not to let it show. Emilio gave her space, knowing he'd freaked her out.

They returned to Kelparz the following night but over the next few days, Johnson felt hemmed in. She tried to fight against it but old patterns resurfaced.

Meanwhile, new patterns became the problem for Newark. He constantly had to reassure his woman. He couldn't talk to anyone without her beady eyes on him, and he often felt he wasn't quite good enough. He strived to be better.

Skinner and Sophia watched Newark with a studious interest.

"How long before he cracks, do you think?" Skinner asked.

"Well," Sophia said, moving her head to the side, "I don't know him that well. Sometimes, these situations can go on for years but she *is* an extreme case."

"What is he getting out of it?"

"It's his first girlfriend, you say, so I suppose he's getting a valuable lesson." Skinner smiled at her. She smiled back. "What do you think?"

"I think he's under the mistaken illusion he's getting something, without realising he actually isn't. He just has to figure that out."

"I'm glad we hooked up," she said, leaning her elbow on the table, smiling at him with her chin resting on her hand. "You're not what you first seemed."

"How do you mean?"

"Well, at first, I thought you were... creepy."

Skinner's face dropped. "Creepy?"

"It's probably because you're not good around women." She touched his hand. "But you see things, don't you?"

149

Her praise touched him deeply. "I'm still trying to figure *you* out. Why were you down here, rustling up trouble?"

"The truth?" He nodded. "I wanted adventure."

He smiled at her. "You should have met me a year ago. You'd be up to your neck in adventure."

Sophia cocked her head, intrigued. Skinner told her the crew's story. She listened, rapt, and when he'd finished, she stared at him in awe. "Why didn't you mention all that before...?"

He shrugged. It hadn't occurred to him to mention it.

"D'you want to go to bed?" she asked, still staring at him.

Johnson plonked herself beside them. "Newark still in chains?" she asked, glancing across the lounge.

Skinner and Sophia shared a disappointed glance. "Yes," Skinner replied. Johnson seemed restless and he wondered why she wasn't in bed with the Spaniard.

"Where's Emilio?" Sophia asked.

Johnson sniffed. "Told him I was spending time with my mates."

"Great," Sophia said with a strained smile. Johnson had grown on her, but Skinner had just transformed into a superhero and she wanted to bang his brains out.

"It's depressing as hell seeing Newark like that," Johnson lamented.

"Let's hope she doesn't ask him to marry her," Skinner remarked.

Johnson whipped her head to him.

*

At breakfast the following morning, Johnson appeared restless again, Skinner and Sophia surprised when she came to sit with them. Across the room, Emilio kept glancing at her.

"Not sitting with Emilio?" Sophia asked.

"What am I, joined at the hip? No way am I ending up like Newark."

"Emilio's not a bunny-boiler. He seems very... together. Confident, self-assured."

"He asked me to marry him," she whispered over the table. She needed to get that out.

"Wow... That's great."

"No, it isn't. He'll either get sick of me and throw me away like trash, or I'll end up chained to the kitchen sink. No bloke treats me like that. I'm my own fucking person."

"It doesn't have to be that way."

"Trust me. Never let a man take control." She quickly glanced between the two of them. "That doesn't apply to Skinner, of course. He's different. You'll dump him first."

Skinner's face fell. Inside, he knew the truth of it.

"I've no intention of dumping him," Sophia said, taking Skinner's hand. Johnson didn't hear her. She stared at the doorway.

The two of them followed the direction of her gaze. Johnson didn't know what to feel. Life had got a whole lot trickier.

Meetings and Partings

Graham stood frozen in the doorway, gazing at Johnson. Her hair had been curled but she was the same woman he loved. He moved over to her slowly as if drawn by a magnet.

Brash strode forward, slapping Skinner on the back, touching Johnson's arm. "You two are a welcome sight."

Skinner and Johnson stared at him in shock.

Graham gave Skinner an acknowledging nod before looking at Johnson. "How are you?" he asked, taking in every detail of her face.

"What are you doing here...?" she said in a whisper.

He sat beside her, glancing at the others uncomfortably. "I made a mistake, Daria," he said, softly. "By the time I realised, you'd already gone."

Weeks ago, those words would have been light in the darkness. Now, she didn't know what to feel, what to say. Graham searched her face, looking for a positive sign. She'd gone pale.

Brash, realising Graham wasn't getting a response, explained the events of the last few weeks. Skinner, Johnson, and Sophia listened, absorbed.

"She can open portals...?" Skinner uttered.

"Where is she now?" Johnson asked.

Brash shook his head. "We have no idea and no way of finding her."

"She shouldn't be dealing with this shit on her own. We're a team."

"Try telling Jenna that."

"So, where's Flint?"

"I think he's gone nuts. He's with the old woman on Cyntros, trying to turn himself into a Jedi master."

"What...?"

"We left him to it. Said we'd pick him up in a few weeks. So, are you coming with us?"

Johnson rubbed her forehead. Trot was her mate. She couldn't abandon her but this was a difficult decision.

"Where's Newark?" Graham asked.

Johnson and Skinner shared a glance.

"He's a bunny-boiler's bitch," Sophia blurted, carried away by all she'd heard.

Brash and Graham looked at her. "And you are?" Brash asked.

"Jeremy's girlfriend."

Graham and Brash's eyes widened. They slowly transferred to Skinner.

"Yeah," Johnson said. "You think that's shocking, you should see Newark."

A man appeared at Johnson's side. Graham looked up. Whoever he was, he was shockingly handsome, virile, and exotic-looking.

"Aren't you going to introduce me to your friends, Daria?" the man said.

"This is Emilio," Johnson mumbled. "He works for Ubro oil."

The Spaniard smiled. "I'm also Daria's boyfriend," he added, extending his hand.

Graham nearly choked on his fluids. His fears were confirmed in the worst possible way. Johnson clenched her fists.

Brash shook the man's hand. "I expect you've heard of us. We're Johnson's crew."

Emilio's brow creased. He hadn't heard of them; had no idea she *had* a crew. "I see. Well, good to meet you. Excuse me, I have a lot to do." He smiled briefly before walking away. Johnson watched him go.

Graham slumped in his chair. "So, you've got a boyfriend?" he accused.

Johnson glared at him. "What was I supposed to do, Graham? Stay celibate my whole fucking life."

She got up and stormed off. One man had just asked her to marry him, the other had driven her away by wanting to marry her. Couldn't they keep their fucking proposals to themselves? Head in pieces, she charged up to her room.

Brash turned to Skinner, glancing briefly at his girlfriend. "Well, Skinner, we brought Cornelius back but we're not giving up on Jenna. You in?"

"If Sophia can come too."

The girl beamed at him.

"We haven't got room for dead weight," Brash said and Sophia's face fell.

"She might look fragile but she can be underhanded, deceitful, organisational, and... insightful. Qualities that could prove useful."

"How can those qualities prove useful?"

"I don't know yet but it's coming to me. Plus, I can teach her to fight and fire a gun."

Sophia gazed at him in adoration.

Brash assessed her. She was certainly eager. "Fine. We need to collect Newark."

The man appeared, as if on command, walking into the room with a blonde. Brash shouted his name. Newark's face lit up. Graham lurched to his feet, grabbed Newark's arm, and slapped him on the back. "I've missed you, you fucking bastard!"

Brash slapped Newark on the back too. Newark smiled at them both, yet he seemed subdued. "What are you doing here?" he asked, gazing at them.

"It's a long story," Brash said.

The woman at his side coughed loudly.

"Oh, yeah," Newark said, "this is Claire. My girlfriend."

Claire looked them over as if checking for design flaws. She smiled briefly, taking Newark's arm and leading him away.

"What the fuck...?" Graham asked. "Newark, we've got a lot to tell you."

Newark looked around. "Yeah, bud, I'll speak to you later. We don't want to miss breakfast."

"You won't speak later," the woman shot, glaring at Newark. "It's our day off. We're going shopping, remember?"

"Oh, yeah. Sorry bud," Newark said. "Maybe tonight."

As they walked off, Graham stared after them, confounded. "The bitch has sucked Newark out of Newark."

Graham and Brash had a mission to save Newark. Sophia's underhanded deceitfulness came in handy. So, too, did her organisational skills. She breezed around, telling everyone she'd got engaged, and insisting all the women come out for a hen night. The bunny-boiler seemed reluctant but Sophia wouldn't have her being left out.

So, that night, while the bunny-boiler was away, Brash, Graham, and Skinner had a chat with Newark.

"You have to break this off, bud," Graham said. "She's no good for you. You're losing yourself, man. Kick her into touch."

"But she's the only girlfriend I'll ever get."

"Who told you that?"

"She did. I'm stupid and coarse."

"That's bullshit. The woman's unhinged. Snap out of it, Newark."

"She's the only woman who's ever loved me."

"That's not love."

"It isn't?"

"Love is letting people be themselves."

"The woman's got serious issues," Skinner contributed. He shook his head. "Classic narcissistic symptoms of manipulation and control."

Graham nodded. "Yes, she's controlling you, man. You can't be yourself with her. You can with us. And we need you, bud."

"You need me?"

"Trot's in danger."

"Trot's in danger...?"

Brash explained. Newark listened, spellbound, but he still wasn't taking the bait.

"Trot does love you," Graham said. "In a non-sexual way. She saved your neck twice, remember? Even though we tried to kill her. We'd all die for you, man. This crew is your family."

Newark looked at him. Something registered. Something clicked. "Family...?"

"That's us."

A dormant pressure surged up. Pent-up fury found release. Newark exploded out of himself. "The bitch said I was a shit lay. I'm a fucking god in the sack!"

"Welcome back, man."

Brash slapped Newark on the back. "Yeah. Welcome back."

*

Johnson sat in her room, torn in two, darkness closing around her. After hours of struggle, she made up her mind. She couldn't abandon Trot. She should say goodbye to Emilio but she couldn't bring herself to. He might beg her to stay, and that would be awful. She would hate to see the confident, self-assured man brought so low. She told herself he would be better off without her. He was a top-exec. She was a... well, she wasn't sure what she was, but one day he would inhabit his CEO role and she wouldn't fit in. He'd probably want kids too, and that wasn't her bag. All in all, she was doing him a favour. She wiped tears from under her eyes. The guy had turned her soft. She needed to leave.

Standing abruptly, she packed a bag, leaving all her dresses behind.

She found the crew drinking in the lounge. Hanging back in the doorway, she glanced around, checking Emilio wasn't there. Sophia appeared at her side.

"Where's the bunny boiler? Johnson asked.

"Legless in a bar." Sophia walked into the room.

Nodding approvingly, Johnson followed her in.

"Newark's back," Skinner told them.

"Thank fucking God," Johnson said. "Let's go."

"What's the rush?" Brash asked.

"Trot's in danger."

Graham's heart soared. The boyfriend was toast.

Emilio stood in the shadows, watching them leave the hotel. He could have gone to her room and talked to her, asked her to stay, but then it wouldn't have been her decision. He shouldn't have asked her to marry him. He lost her the moment he did. He realised he was wrong about himself. He didn't always get what he wanted. He'd had a powerful lesson in letting go, and one that would leave a hole in his heart.

Back in the Game

Time was running out. What would happen when it did? They said they'd come for her one at a time, so she assumed they'd send their weakest first. But how strong were *they*?

Jenna shook her head. She'd slipped into fear, and she wasn't giving them that. She brought to mind those carcasses on the beach.

"There. Now, eat."

She looked up at the yellow-skinned ogre. Venulian hospitality was overwhelming. The yellow eyes brimmed with expectation, and Jenna had no idea how she would cram a fourth course in. She took a spoonful with an appreciative smile, breathing out, relieved, when the woman left the room. Looking around, she opened a cupboard door, found a fancy dish, and deposited the fourth course in there. She would dispose of it later.

She was staying with Serza's friends. Though Serza wasn't with her this time, his friends had welcomed her enthusiastically, bowing their heads and pressing their hands together before grabbing her in crushing hugs. She had only met them once? Though, after taking out SLOB, she and the crew had become heroes here. In fact, she could have got free room and board at a hotel but she didn't want to draw attention to herself.

Unlike last time, she could communicate with the couple using thought transference, and she found them to be chatty, the woman relentlessly so. The older woman, unfortunately, had died. She got a full run-down of the burial ceremony.

She planned to leave this place when her time was up but, for now, she needed somewhere to anchor.

Putting her empty bowl on the oversized table, she left the room, wandering through the tunnel-shaped corridors, feeling like a hobbit in an over-ground burrow. She had long since discovered Venulians had an aversion to angles.

Venturing out, she walked over the grass, staring up at the ringed planet. Their sun was setting and the planet had a pink glow. The last time she'd stood here, she was in love with Lucas. She could never have imagined that would change. She supposed she had changed.

She wondered what the rest of the crew were doing now. Was Fraza alright? Was Flint in love? Pain stabbed her heart. A wave of nausea rose up. She pushed it down. It didn't matter now. The odds of her surviving this were slim. Her one objective was to take out as many of them as she could. On the off chance they were viewing her, she stuck her fingers up to the sky. "That means 'fuck off!'" she shouted.

"Hello, Jenna Trot." She turned around to find Gati. The Venulian man smiled, bowed his head, and pressed his hands together. "Mita said you have eaten. I am sorry to be late this evening."

"Don't mention it. And call me Jenna. Trot's a surname."

The last word seemed lost on him. "If you tell the Council you are here, Jenna Trot, they will throw a ball in your honour. They would do anything for you."

"I don't what any fuss. I just want a bit of... quiet time on your beautiful moon."

"I understand." He smiled and turned but turned back again, looking concerned. "There is no further threat here, is there?"

She shook her head. "No," she assured him. "I'm not here in... an official capacity." What was she? Bloody superwoman?

Gati pressed his hands together and bowed his head before walking to the farmstead.

Jenna turned back to the planet. Taking a deep breath, she summoned determination. Time to get practising. What else could she discover about this power? If it was a game they wanted, she determined to give them the best game she could.

*

"Excellent, Mr Flint," Tynia said. "See, you're a natural."

Flint let go and the pot smashed on the floor.

"Well, don't wreck the place," Tynia complained.

"Sorry, I didn't know how to bring it down gently."

"Power and intent. You don't just switch it off, you intend it down gradually."

"Yes, it's all a little... alien."

"It is, isn't it? It's a different way of looking at things. Not your average, run of the mill, common sense. But I must say, Mr Flint, for a complete beginner, you're doing remarkably well."

Flint sat down, deflated. "I'm not going to be ready in time, am I?"

"Did you really think you could be?"

He didn't answer.

160

She looked at him with compassion. "You have to accept this will take time. You can't possibly be ready when they start coming for her. The best we can hope for is that you can, at some point, help her."

"If I can find her," he said, despondently. He rubbed his forehead. "She could be dead by then."

"You know," she said, taking the seat opposite him, "this is all to do with removing the barriers inside yourself. Your command of the power is there. It was there as a boy, and we're unplugging it now. You always were that musical genius. But your mind needs... a little expansion. I could help you with that."

He looked at her. "How?"

"Take the drug Jenna took."

"That will help?"

"It will loosen the constraints of the mind. I'll be with you, as I was for Jenna."

He considered it then nodded. "OK, I'll do it."

"Excellent. I'll make us a snack first," she said, getting up. "You shouldn't travel on an empty stomach."

Flint leaned back, raking a hand through his hair. Over the past two years, he had done everything he had set his mind to. This required something else.

"So, you screwed the Sentier," Tynia remarked.

Flint whipped his head to her. "What...?"

"Jenna told me. I think you should know." She *so* wanted them to get together. They were made for each other.

He stared at her in shock. "Jenna...?"

"She saw you, Mr Flint."

His heart stopped. "Saw me...?"

"She can raise her vibration. At the highest rates, you appear invisible."

Amazed horror washed over his face. He remembered the door opening by itself. He put a hand to his mouth, his insides shrivelling.

"Allessa reminds me of a siren," Tynia mused. "Drawing men to their peril."

"I didn't sleep with her," he threw out. "I nearly did but I didn't."

Tynia smiled, pleased. "I knew she wouldn't get her tentacles into you. Just because it's offered, doesn't mean you have to take it. Now, Mr Brash is a different kettle of fish. He would have snapped it up." She leaned toward him. "I always liked you best," she whispered, conspiratorially.

Flint gazed at her, punch-struck. "Is that why she left...?"

"She always planned to leave, Mr Flint. This gave her a shove."

He fell silent, his head in pieces. "Wait a minute, you knew she was leaving?" She nodded meekly. "And you let her *go*?"

"She was quite determined."

"But you looked shocked when we told you she'd gone?"

"Yes. Mr Brash was highly charged. That man seems to have lost his equanimity. I wasn't going to be his emotional punch bag. I'm an old woman, for God's sake."

"You could lay him out flat and you know it," Flint said, annoyed. "You should have stopped her."

"It was her time to go, Mr Flint."

He looked at her, oddly, then leaned forward with his hands in his hair. "She saw me..." he muttered, distraught.

"Pretty steamy by all accounts."

"Not helping, Tynia."

"Jenna might have felt... inadequate."

"I was thinking of Jenna the whole time!"

"Ah. Well, if you do see her again, you might want to mention that. Sex matters, even when it doesn't."

He got up and paced around. Finally, he walked out.

Tynia hummed a tune. She *did* like that man. And the power flowed in him freely. She just had to get his mind out of the way. The mind was the toughest nut to crack, far tougher than space-time. She stared down at herself making a stew. Maybe she would try a different dish tomorrow. Yes, Mr Flint deserved a treat. He was a knight in shining armour, doing all this for the woman he loved. She thought about Cornelius. She missed him. She shook her head. She had lived far too long for romantic notions. The game of life was compelling, kept dragging you back in. But her service here was nearly done. A greater bliss awaited her.

*

Graham existed in a blissful state. He had snatched Daria from the clutches of the Spaniard. Now, all he needed to do was reconnect with her, remind her what they were to each other. And he had plenty of time to do that because this wasn't going to be a short mission. None of them would give up on Trot. It felt like old times again, having Daria and Newark back. Hell, he'd even missed Skinner. Sophia was decent enough company too. Things were looking up.

162

He sat in the bar with Newark, who was having a blow-out.

"You know," Newark said, "we should pay Hellgathen a visit. Stock the bar up. Nothing blows your head off like this shit."

"Good idea." Graham looked at his buddy. "Listen man, if you ever become a bunny-boiler's bitch again, I'll knock your fucking lights out."

Newark choked up. It was enough to make him tear. He was back where he belonged. He sniffed. "Yeah, lost my fucking head for a while." He sat up straight. "So, a council of evil scumbags, eh? I'm ready for a bit of action."

"Might not be so easy."

"When has that ever stopped us? We mutilate the fuckers or we die trying." Newark turned to him and grinned. "I'm back in the game."

Time Will Tell

A light whip. And she had created it. Jenna whirled it round, marvelling at the dazzling display. She cracked it on a thick branch. The branch fell as if cut by a laser beam. Excitement pumped through her veins.

Five minutes later, the whole tree lay in ruins. This was *fun*.

She realised her imagination had to catch up with what she could do. She employed it diligently. The hours flew by. She was a kid in an adventure playground. Trees got battered by light arrows, light sabres... She even played around with lightening balls again, only this time making them bigger.

She raised her vibration but discovered she couldn't affect the physical world in that state. So, she could hide and move, but not fight. *Could* she hide, though? Could they detect her? She had no idea what they were capable of.

As she experimented and practised, she devised strategies, trying to consider all angles, all possibilities. She had to be sneaky. And maybe it was time for her to start watching *them*.

*

Aktimar stared over the green ocean. "How's she doing?" he asked Tastari.

"Having a blast, by the looks of things."

Aktimar glanced at the lizard. Looking back at the ocean, he smiled. "And she is progressing?"

"In leaps and bounds."

He smiled again. "Her time is nearly through."

"Bastira will die."

"Then he should have improved."

"How long do you think she will last?"

"Not long enough... I doubt we'll get a turn."

A hard voice came in his head. *"You'll get your turn."*

A smile possessed Aktimar's face and he turned his head. He saw her, sitting on grass, staring him boldly in the eye.

"Think you're invincible, Aktimar?" she said. "Don't get too comfortable with that thought. I've got nothing to lose anymore." His brow creased. "You cost me something precious. I have every intention of meeting up with you."

165

"What did I cost you?" he asked, curiously.

"What do you care? I'm fully engaged in your game now and I intend to win."

He gave a little laugh. "Bold words. I hope you can back them up."

"There are many ways to play a game." Her lips twisted in a humourless smile.

Her image vanished.

Aktimar turned to Tastari. "She is intriguing, is she not?"

"Or desperate."

"Um... Time will tell."

It begins

Fraza travelled to the furthest reaches, yet, he wasn't concerned about getting back. Jabreen had affected him deeply. Old cares melted under the loss of his first romantic relationship.

Strange plants passed by beneath him. Humidity hung over lush forest. He would be the first to explore this territory, but his sense of accomplishment was dampened by the feeling he was skimming the surface. When he spotted a clearing, he came in to land.

Wiping his brow, he got off the yact. Moisture dripped from leaves. The chirrup of insects rang from the grass. Many creatures probably lurked in that dense undergrowth but he didn't care. Grabbing the axe he had taken from the colony, he set about constructing a fortified camp. He had seen enough of the planet. He would stay here for a time, do a different kind of exploring. He would begin to explore his gift. How far could he travel with that?

*

"So, how should I play it?" Graham asked Brash as they sat on the flight-deck.

"Well, don't go steaming straight in. You've been away for a long time and there's been another bloke in the mix. You need to become friends again, then hopefully things will go from there."

Graham nodded, thoughtfully. He went off to become friends with Daria.

Newark walked onto the flight-deck. "Preparing for the next leap?"

"Yep," Brash said.

Newark coughed, uncomfortably. "Listen, I lost my mind back there. Don't know what the fuck happened to me."

"Don't worry about it. I've lost my own head over women recently."

Newark sat down. "So, you shafted Allessa, realised you'd made a mistake, and now she doesn't want you back?"

"That's a pretty good summation."

"And you don't want Trot anymore?"

Brash shook his head. "Jenna and I are just friends now."

Newark sniffed. He'd been proved right. "So, Flint's gone nuts?"

167

"Thinks he can learn to do what Jenna can."

Newark shook his head. "Never thought *he'd* lose it. He'd become my fucking hero."

Brash looked at him. *He* had once been Newark's hero. "Well, even he has limits," he said sourly.

"Yeah."

"D'you know, he told Allessa we planned to kill Jenna?"

Newark frowned. "Why would he do that?"

"The man's a snake."

"I thought you liked him now?"

"Yeah, well, a leopard and all that…"

Newark's brow creased, a thought occurring to him. "D'you think he wanted to screw the Sentier himself?"

"Makes you wonder." Brash took a big collecting sniff. "Anyway, she's gone now, thanks to him. We need to focus on helping Jenna."

"I miss Trot," Newark said, reflectively. "Hope she's alright. What's the plan then?"

"Well, seeing as we've no idea where she is, I'm not sure…"

Newark racked his brains but nothing presented itself.

*

Graham found Johnson in the bar, staring at her drink.

"You OK," he asked, studying her.

"Yep."

Nervously, he sat down. "Quite a turnaround, isn't it, finding ourselves here?" She nodded. "We're still friends, though, right?"

"Why wouldn't we be?"

"I was… hard on you in Draztis."

"I got over it."

That was not what Graham wanted to hear. She was uncommunicative and he had no idea what it meant. Give her time, he told himself, but impatience by-passed his thought process. "Do you still have feelings for me, Daria?" he blurted.

She stared at him, shocked, shock turning to anger. "You set up camp with your Saffria girlfriend, tell us you're going to stay there, and as far as I'm concerned, I'm never going to see you again. Then you barge into my life because you've changed your mind, and expect me to pick up where we left off? You are one selfish, insensitive bastard." She glared at him harshly then stormed off.

Graham sat, winded. Selfish, insensitive bastard...? She'd never said *that* before.

Things did not improve the next day. Johnson had no desire to speak to him. Newark found him in the bar, looking miserable.

"What's up?" Newark asked.

"Daria. She called me a selfish, insensitive bastard."

"Oh."

"I don't know what to do."

Newark decided to cheer him up. "Don't worry about it, bud. She was madly in love with the Spaniard. They were in the sack together all the time. And he changed her. It's not you. She just needs to get him out of her system."

"She was in love with him...?" Graham asked, looking at Newark, shell-shocked.

"Maybe not so much love as... hot steamy sex. She'll be coming down off that. He would have dumped her anyway."

"Hot, steamy sex...?"

"Hey, he was way out of her league. She must have known that."

Skinner and Sophia walked in.

"Everything alright?" Skinner asked, taking in Graham's despondent face.

"Johnson thinks he's an insensitive bastard," Newark told them.

Graham looked at Skinner. "*Was* it serious with the Spaniard?"

"Well, she left him, didn't she?" Skinner replied, though she was so obviously nuts about him.

Graham nodded. That was a good sign.

"Don't worry, bud," Newark said, patting his back. "Johnson knows her limits."

Skinner wasn't sure, but he thought Newark had actually got thicker. Had the bunny-boiler addled his brain?

Shaking the thought off, he moved to the bar, realising he was the only member of the crew with a girlfriend. He might have felt sorry for Graham if he wasn't so stoked. For the first time in his life, he was on top.

*

169

Johnson hung in her quarters, feeling weird. She didn't know what to do with herself. She should be her old self now she was back with the crew, but she didn't feel comfortable in her own skin. She'd opened a door she couldn't close, and felt stuck in no-man's land.

Getting up, she went to the gym to kick the crap out of a punch bag.

Exhausted, she sat on the floor, staring into nowhere.

*

Jenna sat on the grass outside the farmstead, staring ahead, remote viewing. Three platforms rose out of the ocean on long, strong legs. Connected by walkways, two held a conglomeration of buildings. The third served as a landing platform. The buildings soared into the air, mainly metal and glass, though she spotted a round stone structure. A mix of species milled through narrow pathways. The complex was too small to be a city or a town. Was this some kind of meeting place?

Zooming in, she watched a variety of beings enter a towering building. Zooming in further, she stared around an enormous chamber. Beings filed into tiered seats. It reminded her of a lecture theatre. She kept her mind empty to avoid detection.

When the assembly had seated, a blue being at the front stood, his eyes roaming the chamber. He was the same species as Aktimar but she knew it wasn't him. She had a feel for that man now.

The blue being spoke without moving his lips. "Welcome," he said. "We hope you enjoy your stay with us. But let me remind you, we only retain the best. If you *are* accepted, it will be a great honour for you. Few are chosen to join us. Many come and go, passing briefly through our halls, even those with the highest of expectations."

A green-skinned grinch with white hair lifted his hand. The blue nodded for him to speak. "Do any make it onto the Council?"

"Only in exceptional cases."

Jenna pulled away, staring at the whole complex again. It was some kind of... university? A university for those with the power? Did those beings down there know the Council was a bunch of sick, twisted murderers?

She spotted Aktimar striding over the walkway to the landing platform. He got into a silver craft and took off. Keeping back, she tagged him.

The craft flew over water. Miles of it. Jagged mountains cut the skyline in the distance. Flat land came into view, stretching from the shore to the

170

mountains. Flying over a golden beach, the craft came down before a red-roofed, white-walled villa. A blue woman and two blue children ran out to greet Aktimar. Jenna stared as they threw their arms around him. What the hell...? Aktimar had a family...?

She broke the link and came back, staring ahead. *He had a family.* She sat there, thinking. Her time wasn't quite up but, for her, the game was starting. The Venulians owed her a favour, and she was about to cash it in. Aktimar would *so* regret messing with her.

She stood. "It begins."

Sticking Points

"That's excellent, Mr Flint."

Flint stared at the collapsing column of water.

"You know," Tynia said, "I think you're the best student I've ever had. You don't complain, don't get distracted, you just get on with it." The woman beamed. "I can't tell you how many moping whingers I've had over the years. Sometimes, it was all I could do to stop myself cracking them over the head." Flint raised his eyebrows. "It's so refreshing to meet you."

"Was Jenna a moping whinger?" he asked with smiling eyes.

"The first time, yes. But she's grown a lot."

"Yes..." He took a deep breath. "So, I need a wall?"

"Yes. There's no difference between the wall and the column. The only difference is in your mind."

Flint nodded. He was grasping this now, grasping it in an intuitive way. He turned to the sea and focused again.

When the wall appeared, Tynia stared at it, beguiled. She attempted to jump up and down. "We're whizzing ahead," she said, excitedly. "We'll put off tea and carry on. I think we're on a roll."

Her face dropped. Flint followed the direction of her gaze. A craft entered the atmosphere.

Tynia took a deep collecting breath. "Well, we'll leave them to create their own little dramas. We'll press on."

"You're not going to make a stew?" he asked with an amused smile.

"D'you know, Mr Flint, I think it's about time someone cooked for *me*. I'm an old woman, for God's sake."

"I don't know *who* you are, exactly," he said, leaning closer, "but you're not just an old woman."

She batted a hand at him and blushed.

He smiled at her, fondly, seeing her as the mother figure he never had.

"Now, come on," she said, shaking her head, playfully, "let's carry on. Act as if they're not here."

*

173

"Look at that," Sophia said, staring out and pointing as they came in to land. "It looks like a tidal wave."

Skinner looked over her shoulder. "No, it's the old woman."

She turned, gazing at him. "So, everything you said was true...?"

"You didn't believe me?"

"Well, I did but... I didn't..."

"Wonder if she's got tea on," Newark said, hopeful. "I'm starving."

"You won't be after weeks of eating the stuff," Brash said over his shoulder as he brought the craft down.

Johnson looked out too, Graham acutely aware of her presence. Two weeks had passed and still nothing. How much time did she need?

They landed on the far side of the copse. Disembarking, they walked to the shore, staring at the wall of water.

"How does she do it...?" Sophia murmured.

"Power and intent," Skinner replied. "But they're just words, aren't they?"

She stared at him, puzzled.

"We're back," Brash called out.

"Any chance of some stew," Newark called after him.

The wall collapsed. The old woman turned with a scary look. Avoiding her, Newark walked over to Flint, grabbed his arm, and slapped him on the back. Brash frowned.

"Hey, man," Newark said. "Heard you've gone nuts?"

Flint glanced at Brash. "Good to see you too, Newark."

"Any word on where Jenna is?" Brash asked Tynia.

"No, Mr Brash," she replied.

"Shouldn't we be trying to find her, instead of fucking about with Flint?"

An invisible force knocked him on his arse. He sat up, staring at the woman, thrown.

"You do not direct that language at me," Tynia said in a hard voice. "You're half the man you were the first time you came here."

Fuck me, Newark thought, he wasn't messing with *her*. Jeez.

Brash pulled himself up and stomped off. He couldn't argue. Who swears at an old woman?

Tynia turned to Johnson. "Nice to see you again, dear," she said, studying her.

Johnson smiled briefly and nodded. She did the same to Flint. Flint studied her too.

"I'm Sophia," the girl said, stepping forward with an outstretched hand.

Tynia took it. "A pleasure to meet you, dear."

"I'm Jeremy's girlfriend."

174

"Jeremy?"

"Skinner."

"Ah." Tynia turned to him. "You have a girlfriend, Mr Skinner. How lovely. Well, if you'll excuse us, we're a little tied up here."

Newark's face fell. They weren't getting any stew?

As the crew walked off, Flint's eyes followed Skinner. "Miracles do happen," he said, amused.

"They do indeed," Tynia agreed. "Let's make a few more."

*

"What's he been saying to her?" Brash asked Graham as they entered Tynia's hut.

"How d'you mean?"

"Did you see what she did to me...? He'll have been whispering in her ear."

Graham thought bitterness was driving Brash crazy.

Newark rooted through the cupboards. "Nothing worth eating in this place. May as well go back to the craft."

Skinner retrieved the sack of bata leaf and handed some to Sophia. "We need this to breathe here," he told her, passing the sack to Brash.

Johnson glanced around the hut, remembering the last time she'd been here. She'd spent most of that time screwing Graham in the trees.

"I'm going back to the craft," Brash said, striding out.

As the door closed, Graham turned to the others. "I think he's losing it."

"What? Why?" Newark asked.

"He's lost Allessa and he blames Flint."

Skinner expanded. "He lost Jenna to Flint. Now he's lost Allessa because of Flint, and the crew has come to respect Flint more than him. It's an alpha male thing. Only, he isn't the alpha male anymore."

Newark considered this, thoughtfully. "Well, perhaps it's not that bad. I mean, Flint's gone nuts, Brash doesn't like Trot anymore, and Allessa did have gross fucking tentacles."

Skinner thought, as valid as those points might be, this was Newark but not quite. Newark had grown somewhat these past two years. Had his first relationship set him back? Did having your balls chopped off make you lose brain cells? Interesting...

Graham shook his head. "Well, the man needs a chill pill." He glanced at Johnson, wondering when she'd snap out of it. She was distant and weird. He

175

wished she'd wake up and come back to him. They were going to get together sooner or later.

Feeling frustrated, he left too. Skinner, seeing the problem, ventured out after him. Graham paced around, raking a hand through his hair. He looked at Skinner. "She's punishing me, isn't she?"

"No, I don't think so," Skinner replied, calmly.

"No?"

Glancing back at the hut, Skinner led Graham away. "You didn't see how she was on Draztis. She had a meltdown. I didn't see much of it myself but I heard about it. Johnson's gone through a lot of changes. You might need to accept that you'll never have what you had before."

Graham scowled. "What d'you know? You've had a girlfriend for what? Five minutes?" He viewed Skinner oddly. "And since when do *you* give advice?"

Skinner realised this *was* a first for him. He didn't give advice, he made observations.

"Deep down, Daria loves me," Graham asserted. "I know she does."

Glaring at Skinner, he marched off.

Tynia and Flint entered the hut an hour later, Tynia relieved to find the place empty. She flopped in a chair and Flint crouched before her. "Are you alright, Tynia?"

"Yes, dear. Just a little tired from all the excitement. I haven't been so excited in years. You're coming along so well, Mr Flint."

He smiled. "I'll make you something to eat."

"I don't mind cooking for *you*. You're so appreciative."

"You shouldn't have to cook all the time."

He rooted in cupboards, stopping momentarily. "Do you ever get lonely here, Tynia?" he asked, turning to her.

"Not enough to worry about. I can't do with too much commotion. I don't think I could live around others now."

He nodded. "I need time to myself too."

Tynia smiled. "Some need it, others are afraid of it..."

He pulled out the bren but stopped, bowing his head. "They'll come for her soon, won't they?"

"You can't think about that," she said, softly. "You have to focus on what's at hand. Jenna's inventive and determined. I'm sure she's got a few tricks up her sleeve."

He rubbed his forehead. "I want to protect her but I can't..."

"It's a helpless feeling, isn't it?"

"Yes..."

She assessed him, sadly, seeing the helpless boy who no-one protected. She swallowed the hard lump in her throat. "Maybe you need to trust that she can protect herself."

"But the odds are against her."

"They were against you but you came through. Perhaps, you need to have faith."

He turned to her. "It's not always easy to have faith."

She gave him a fond smile. "We all have our sticking points."

Fully Committed

Aktimar stared around in shock. The place was a mess. Furniture upturned, graffiti on the walls? He shouted his wife's name, called out for his children. No-one answered. He charged upstairs to find no sign of them. Running outside, he scanned the surrounding land, his mind racing, his heart hammering in his chest.

Before long, the whole Council was involved in the search. And they had boots on the ground, looking for unusual tracks. They remote viewed the entire planet but nothing turned up.

"It's like they've disappeared," Helmus said, his hooded face looking back at the house.

"Who would do this?" Tastari asked. "They were untouchable. Nobody would take what's yours. Everyone knows that."

Aktimar raked his long fingers through his indigo hair. "Who *would* do this...?"

"*I would,*" a hard voice said.

He whipped his head, looking for her. Spiky mountains cut the skyline, the land blinding white. Fine-tuning his perception, he saw her.

"Invisibility is great, isn't it?" she mused. "Didn't think you were going to see me at first. How do you manage it?"

"Where are they?" he barked, his blood pumping.

"Where indeed? Are they being looked after? Are they being harmed? Abused? Sold into slavery? Are things happening to them you don't even want to imagine?"

"You wouldn't hurt them," he spat. "It's not in your nature."

"What do you know of my nature? Your evil game cost me something precious. Well, losing things can turn sane people crazy. And I'm hopping fucking mad. You have a debt to pay and this is no longer a game. This is war. There are many casualties of war. You're going to kill me, right? Well, maybe I'll kill a piece of you first. Your game has already started."

"You're going to *die*, Jenna Trot."

"Tell me something I don't know. But here's some information for *you*. If I die, strict instructions have been given to terminate your family. In the meantime, how *are* they being treated? Is your wife being... entertained in your absence? Are they even being fed? You shouldn't have messed with me, Aktimar."

"I'll find them."

She gave him a twisted smile then broke the link.

Aktimar stared at the place she'd been.

"It starts in two days," Helmus said. "Do we postpone it?"

"She hasn't got it in her to kill them."

The air became charged. Wind got up. Whining turned to a violent crack as a portal appeared, and a headless carcass dropped to the ground. Aktimar gaped at it.

Helmus hid a smile. He was starting to like this girl. Aktimar had set the date himself. Helmus wondered what the man would do. If he postponed the game, his respect for Aktimar would diminish.

"I'm going to locate my family," Aktimar said, storming off.

*

Jenna looked around the bleak Hellgathen landscape... frozen, empty moorland, broken by spiky mountains, topped with a grey sky.

She stared at the blood on the ground. She'd pilfered the creature from a slaughter house, brought it out here, and stabbed the carcass repeatedly, before lasering its head off. If the old Jenna Trot, the Admiral's daughter, could have witnessed that, she would have been appalled.

She turned and walked away, fully committed now.

Alone

Fraza hung suspended in the air, staring down at the forest. He had levitated himself further than he ever had before, and now he was going to attempt flight. Even Jenna hadn't done this.

Initially, he would have directed the power to push him along. But that was the old way of thinking. There was only the power and his intention. Flight was all there was.

Soon he was flying, watching the forest glide by beneath him. His heart soared, like a bird, free and unlimited. But limiting thoughts impinged and he plummeted at an alarming rate.

Focusing as he fell, he intended an energy cushion to soften the impact. Careering through the trees, he found the cushion in place and landed relatively intact.

He sat up, rubbing his sore arm. This was good. He hadn't panicked. He had managed to correct it. His mind was still a problem but its power was diminishing. This was very good.

What was not so good was the snarling beast edging toward him through the trees. Yellow stripes marked its grey fur. Long razor-sharp teeth dripped saliva. Fraza stood straight, refusing to be intimidated. As the beast charged, Fraza thrust out a hand and knocked it back several feet. He needed to kill it and he thought of an inventive way - he'd been finding lots of inventive ways to use the power. Closing his eyes, he intended a light whip. As the beast came at him again, he struck out, cutting the creature in two.

He stared at the animal for several moments. Grabbing up the two halves, he carried them through the forest, eyeing the trees. He was proud of himself. He was getting his better-self back and he was doing it on his own.

When he got to camp, he threw the mutilated carcass down, made a fire, and cooked it.

The twilight glow emerged as he sat at the side of his yact to eat alone. He didn't feel lonely. He had himself.

*

Allessa tried to inhabit her Head Sentier role. She stayed on in Lixia for a time, reacquainting herself with other Sentier. She had always loved her home planet, with its stunning lilac sky and towering grey mountains. Yet, she felt empty.

In a bid to shake off the emptiness, she travelled the region, as Sentier often did, introducing herself as Head Sentier to the planet leaders. They always showed her courtesy and respect. The Sentier were healers, they worked with energies. They helped. Their role was that of service but, as the weeks passed, she found service wasn't fulfilling her anymore. When she visited Juyra, memories of Lucas haunted her. She wasn't thinking of the Lucas who had plotted to kill Jenna, or the Lucas who had dumped her without a word. She thought of their times together on the plantation. No-one had ever made her feel that way, and no-one ever would again. She had changed, and she didn't know how to change back.

She pushed the memories down. She had made her decision. Lucas was galaxies away from her. Even if she could shrug off her responsibilities, he was too far away to reach. She never used to feel alone. Now, loneliness pressed around her heart.

Round One

Jenna paced around the icy wilderness, a woollen blanket covering her shoulders. She had acquired materials, and had constructed a makeshift tent. She'd also pilfered food and warm clothing. Packets of Hellgathen food lay discarded on the ground.

She'd hung around for days, knowing her four months were up but not knowing exactly when they'd come. She kept calm, focusing her energies. Fear was her greatest enemy, and she had enough enemies to deal with. Losing Flint had made it easier, made her less afraid to die. She intended to throw herself into this with everything she had.

She stopped pacing when the air became charged. She turned. Pressure built. An unnatural wind blew her hair around. Nature whined in protest until the air ripped apart, and a blinding circle of light appeared.

As the light vanished, a white feather floated to the ground.

Taking a breath, Jenna threw off the blanket, and braced herself. Minutes later, another portal opened, and a slimy slug dropped onto the hard earth. It stared up at her, confused.

The slug transferred a thought. "Have you seen a young girl around here?"

Jenna pointed with her chin behind him.

Looking at her oddly, Bastira followed the direction of her gaze, scanning the barren land. His eyes flared wide as a raft of burning arrows struck his chest, sticking him like a pin-cushion. Ink blue blood oozed from his fat body. He fell to his knees, staring up at his prey, the old woman now gone.

Jenna moved closer. "I expected so much more," she said, summoning her light whip. Spinning around, she took his head from his shoulders.

"One down," she said, walking away.

*

Aktimar could not locate his family. He hadn't slept at all. He couldn't tune in to them and he wasn't sure why. He was a master at this. What blocked him?

Jenna could have told him what it was. It was breathtakingly simple. Fear. Cornelius often told her how fear blocked. And what greater fear than fear for your family? She would play to his fears whenever she could.

Of course, his family was safe, detained at her pleasure with the Venulian Council, who would be spoiling them rotten, no doubt. Jenna had travelled to the Council, unnoticed, using Cornelius's mind trick. Being swamped by over-enthusiastic ogres was not what she needed.

She'd walked through the broad, curving streets, remembering her previous time in this city. Stone buildings turned to round glass structures in the centre. Entering the lobby of the tallest building, she approached the Venulian at the desk, dropping the disguise. The man stared at her in awe. Jumping to his feet, he pressed his hands together and bowed his head, before ushering her to a back room, and into a lift. He spoke into a headpiece as he accompanied her to top. When the doors opened, he bowed with a flourish, keeping his eyes to the ground.

Jenna's gaze lingered on him as she exited. That was new.

The round, glass-walled room, far too spacious for the small seating area in the centre, gave a stunning view of the city. She turned when the five members of the Council appeared, the yellow-skinned ogres overjoyed to see her. Bowing their heads, they pressed their hands together.

She didn't need to use thought transference. They handed her a translator headpiece, which she put on.

"You have English in here now?" she asked.

"Yes," the Head replied. "Whilst we repaired your craft, Fraza programmed English in. We wanted your language to commemorate you. Indeed, many Venulians have attempted to learn it."

"Wow..." What a colossal waste of time.

"Sit down, Jenna Trot," the Head said. She sat, dwarfed by Venulian furniture. "Will you have fish or Yola?" he asked.

Jenna knew better than to argue. Indeed, in preparation for this meeting, she had deposited most of her breakfast in the cupboard. She made a mental note to clear it out later.

After she'd eaten, she explained the situation.

"You intend to kidnap them?" one of the members asked, astounded.

"I understand if you don't want to do this, and if he comes for them, you must hand them over."

"How will this help you, Jenna Trot?"

"It is a card to play, and I need every card I can get hold of."

"We usually do not act without a sign," one of them said, thoughtfully.

"Yes, I remember. And I know this is a lot to ask."

The Council members went away to discuss the request between themselves. This would be risky for them. She felt sure they'd say no.

They came back. "You helped us, Jenna Trot," the Head said. "We will help you."

"Really?"

"You risked your life for us. You showed great courage. We will help you."

"No sign?"

"Of course, there is a sign. It is you. You are the sign to repay the debt."

After depositing Aktimar's family with the Council, she left Venulas, opening a portal to Hellgathen. The capital, Akmenuth, was cold, drab, and as dreary as its inhabitants. She struggled to acclimatise.

Wandering through the streets now, her eyes ran over the decrepit buildings. This was SLOB's home planet but he, like that slug out on the frozen moors, was dead. The down-trodden citizens had their heads down, barely registering her. Hendraz and Serza, though Hellgathen, were nothing like them. Had they returned here? She'd love to see them again but she couldn't put them in danger.

She found the run-down bar she and the crew had visited the first time she was here. Walking in, she could communicate with the barmaid this time, though the woman stared at her lips oddly. Jenna took her drink and sat in a quiet corner, wondering if she passed for a Hellgathen here. She had blonde hair, like all Hellgathens did. As long as she didn't take her clothes off. Johnson had seen Serza naked once. Only once. Everything was around the back. Jenna smiled. She missed Johnson.

Taking a long drink, her mind turned to serious matters. When would they send the next one? She had a year of this. What was going through Aktimar's head right now?

*

Aktimar sat in one of the secluded, black-out booths. The students used the booths when learning to remote view. It blocked out all sensory input.

He looked up when the door opened.

"Bastira is dead," Helmus informed him.

"That's no surprise." The game was losing its appeal for Aktimar. He had anticipated it greatly but he hadn't even watched the first round. He wanted nothing more than to rip the bitch's heart out but the others wanted their turn. The Council would lose all respect for him if he didn't play the game properly.

"Have you not found them yet?" Helmus asked.

185

"No. But I will."

"Do you think they could have been harmed?" Helmus asked, tactfully. The dead were impossible to find.

"No. She's bluffing. She's desperate."

Helmus thought Aktimar didn't seem too sure. From what he'd seen so far, the girl didn't look desperate. She'd been entertaining. How *had* she managed to distract Bastira?

"The next one is Tirius," Helmus remarked. "Are we continuing?" Helmus studied Aktimar, wondering what his response would be.

Aktimar's blue eyes fixed him. "Of course, we're continuing."

Helmus bowed his head, graciously, then turned to leave. Already, he anticipated the next round. Bastira's death had been quick but nobody expected much from him. Tirius was a step up. Tall and willowy, with huge black eyes, the Ventrian was deceptively weak-looking but those bony arms took some snapping. Bastira was a novice compared to this man.

Needing Sleep

Jenna's eyes drooped. She sat up straight. She'd barely slept this week. How could she possibly do this on her own? She needed someone to keep watch for those blasted feathers.

Climbing out of the tent, she moved around to wake herself up. Her breath misted in front of her. Cold seeped into her bones. How long could she wait this out? It was hopeless. She had no choice. As much as she didn't want to, she was going to look for Hendraz.

Walking off, she stilled as the air became charged. Wind blew her hair. She turned, quelling the rising fear. The whining turned to a loud crack, and the blinding light appeared. It vanished to reveal a second feather. Taking off her jacket, she threw it into the tent, bracing herself.

The moments stretched. She wouldn't use her mind trick this time. She assumed they were watching, and she didn't want them to get wise to it. This would only get harder, so she needed to save it.

A second crack. A blinding flash. The portal opened, depositing a tall, willowy figure with pale yellow skin, a bald head, and enormous black eyes. Jenna let loose with her light arrows, the being batting them away effortlessly, throwing balls of lightning her way. She deflected them, returning fire with even bigger balls. Yet, they seemed to be at stalemate. She tried to block his power, as she had done once before with SLOB, but this being's power and intent were as strong as hers. Changing tactic, she conjured a sword of light, her eyes challenging him to a duel. The being smiled and took the bait, summoning a sword of his own.

Light crashed on light against a backdrop of bleak wilderness. He was physically stronger than her and he knew it. He would win the sword fight. But this was a distraction. Summoning a whip in her other hand, she lashed it through his neck, lasering his head from his shoulders.

"Two down," she said, staring at the body. She looked at the sky. "Are you all so fucking stupid!"

In a galaxy far away, Helmus smiled. He couldn't wait for round three.

*

Jenna trudged through the streets of Akmenuth. She couldn't do this alone. She didn't know if Hendraz and Serza had returned to this planet, but before Hendraz became part of the resistance, he was in government here. She looked around for the least grotty building. She couldn't find one, so she asked an unfriendly local to point the way.

Following his directions, she came across a plain, grey stone building. In other places, it might have been considered derelict. Here, it was grand. Climbing up the few steps, she walked inside. A guard loitered by a desk, talking to the man behind it. That man scowled at her.

She walked forward, not bothering with pleasantries. "Is there a man called Hendraz here?"

The Hellgathen behind the desk stared at her mouth, unable to figure out the discrepancy. "What do you want with him?"

Relief flooded her. "He's here?" After all this time, she would see Hendraz again.

"He is a First Minister," the man said, haughtily, "which means you only get to see him by appointment. There are cards over there," he said, pointing. "Fill one out."

"He's my friend," Jenna insisted. "Tell him, Jenna Trot is here to see him."

The man shook his head as if she was stupid. "You need an appointment card. Now, be off with you."

Jenna moved forward and hauled the man over the desk by his collar. The guard made a grab for her but she side-kicked him in the guts and he dropped. "You get him or I'll shove that card right up-"

"Jenna...?"

She turned. Hendraz stood there, staring at her in disbelief. Blonde, with a scar on his face, the tall, muscular Hellgathen was a welcome sight. She took in his dark, tailed suit, the clothes too formal for his wild, rebellious nature.

She dropped the shocked Hellgathen and moved over to Hendraz. "I've missed you," she said, smiling broadly.

Smiling back, he grabbed her in a fierce embrace. "It's good to see you. What are you doing here? Wait. How are you speaking to me...?" He pulled back, appraising her. "You speak Hellgathen now?"

"No. It's a long story."

His eyes lingered on her. "Come with me."

Saying a few strong words to the man at the desk, Hendraz led Jenna up a creaky staircase, the two men in the lobby staring after them. The narrow, gloomy corridors depressed the hell out of her. Hendraz's dark, dismal office didn't suit him at all.

"Sit," he invited.

He sat opposite her, taking her in.

"Is *everyone* unfriendly here?" she complained.

"I'm not," he said, smiling at her. "But then I've travelled. It's a miserable planet, to be sure. I've realised that more since I've returned." Placing his hands behind his head, he stretched back. "So, tell me everything. What are you doing here? How can you speak to me? Are the others here?"

"No," she said, shaking her head.

She told him everything that had happened to the crew since she had last seen him. He listened, rapt, his eyes widening at various points. When she finished, he stared at her.

"I didn't intend to contact you," she insisted, "but I do need sleep."

"I can see that," he said, chewing his lip and nodding. Sitting forward, he rubbed a hand over his chin. "So, you are part of a game to these beings?"

"Yes. Part of a bloody game."

After all this girl had gone through, it seemed unjust to Hendraz. He wished *he* had the power. He wanted to fight beside her.

"I'm glad you sought me out," he said. "I will help you."

"Are you sure? I know you have a life here."

He gave a short laugh. "If you can call it a life? This planet is a gods-forsaken hell hole. I came back to try and change things but Hellgathens are set in their ways. They are comfortable being miserable. I can't get new ideas passed. Nobody can see future benefits. I'm on the brink of quitting." He looked at her, seriously. "In truth, I don't feel I belong here anymore."

"Coming with me could be dangerous, though," she warned.

He smiled at her. "When has that ever bothered me? I'll get hold of Serza."

"He's here?"

"Yes, and as miserable as I am."

"So, what happened to your crew?"

"They disbanded. No point in having a resistance if there's no-one to resist." His gaze became distant. "Good times," he reflected.

Standing, he hit a few buttons on an antiquated machine. "Serza, could you come over? I've got a surprise for you."

"Have you turned gay, Hendraz?" the man asked.

Hendraz laughed. "Just come."

Serza arrived, staring at Jenna in shock.

Jenna smiled at the young, fresh-faced Hellgathen. "I hear you're bored, Serza," she said. "Need more adventure?"

"You're talking to me," he said, freaked out.

"She's transferring thoughts," Hendraz told him.

Serza's mouth dropped open.

After Jenna explained the situation, Hendraz clapped his hands and rubbed them. "I'll get my ship ready. It'll be like old times."

Enjoying the Show

Hendraz and Serza marvelled at Jenna as she hammered the tables in an alien gambling house.

"I never knew she could do *this*," Serza said.

"Neither did I..." A smile possessed Hendraz's face. "She's ruthless, isn't she?"

"She's amazing..."

Dragging his gaze away from her, Serza looked around. The indigenous people were attractive - pale skin with a bluish sheen and white hair. Other species not so. He stared at a large being with rust-coloured skin and huge pot-holes on his forehead. Tearing his gaze away, he looked up at a crystal-studded ceiling. This was one rich city, a far cry from Akmenuth. Serza hadn't needed any persuasion to come with them. He'd been dying on Hellgathen. He missed being part of the resistance, and had kept in touch with Hendraz since they had disbanded. Hendraz, knowing how unhappy he was, suggested he find a woman but Hellgathen women were miserable and bad tempered. The two relationships he'd ventured into had put him off relationships for life. He looked around at the white-haired beauties, cursing his anatomy. He was coming to believe Hellgathen anatomy might not be the norm. He had once had an embarrassing incident with Johnson. When they had taken their clothes off, he discovered things were back to front. Hendraz told him of similar embarrassing incidents he had endured. Serza wondered if there was a way to work around it. Would there be anyone willing to try?

"Right," Jenna said, "we've got enough for now."

"But you're doing so well," Hendraz said, amused.

"If I carry on, the goons will come out."

"Goons?"

"The muscle. All these places have them. Let's collect and go for a drink."

They left the building, trouble-free, looking around as they walked through busy streets. This city, Jenna had discovered, was called, Iskus, and it had the most unusual architecture. Purple stone structures tapered in then out again to silver-domed roofs. They reminded Jenna of fancy chimneys. Purple stone paved the streets too, and long slender vehicles hovered a foot above ground.

Jenna communicated with one of the residents. "Do you know where we could find a bar?"

The beautiful being didn't understand the concept of bar.

"Alcohol?" Jenna tried.

Again, it was lost on her.

"I don't think they drink here," Jenna remarked, and the Hellgathens' faces dropped. She turned back to the woman. "Hotel?" she asked. The face lit up and the alien gave directions.

"Thank you," Jenna said.

Serza looked around at the woman as they walked away. "I wonder if they have prostitutes here..."

Jenna and Hendraz stopped to look at him. Serza stared at them. Had he spoken that out loud? He explained his predicament.

"Are Hellgathen women that bad?" Jenna asked, staring at him.

"They're... scary."

Hendraz nodded in agreement.

Jenna contemplated that as she walked on.

The hotel comprised a series of purple chimneys with walkways connecting them. The plush lobby, floored in a shimmering mother-of-pearl, with a huge, curving mirror for a wall, produced a disorientating effect.

Having tons of cash, they booked good rooms but their priority was food.

The dining area on the top floor had an excellent view. Beyond the city, fields of ink blue grass stretched on to purple mountains in the distance. Orange clouds floated in a pink sky, the dying sun creating a stunning effect.

"Are you still with Brash?" Hendraz asked as they waited to be served. He'd always had a thing for this girl. Damn shame human anatomy was back to front. He and Brash had come to blows over her once, before Serza filled him in.

"No. It didn't work out."

"I see... So, the crew's on Cyntros with the old crone."

"Yes. Her name's Tynia, by the way."

Serza stared at her. "It's so strange being able to communicate with you. It's a bit..."

"Freaky?"

He nodded. "How is Fraza, by the way. I miss the Kaledian."

"I'm not sure," Jenna replied, concerned. He wasn't in great shape when she left him.

"And Johnson?" he asked.

"Keeping herself busy." Jenna looked at them, seriously. "Listen, I'm grateful you're helping me, but you must *not* put yourselves in danger. No matter what's happening, even if they're killing me, you don't intervene."

Hendraz scratched his neck. "That will be hard."

"You'll die if you try to help me. These beings are stronger than SLOB. There's nothing you can do. Promise me you won't get involved."

"But-"

"Promise me," she said, looking at them intently.

They nodded but they couldn't make that promise.

"Tomorrow," she said, "we'll get provisions and start sleeping outside. I don't want to be here in the city when they come."

"You get the feather as warning?" Hendraz asked.

"Yes. And listen, I just need you to watch out while I sleep. Other than that, you can do whatever you want."

When the waitress appeared, Serza gazed at her. His eyes followed her as she walked away.

The food was not at all odd or repulsive. The white succulent meat looked like chicken, though it tasted like beef, and the star-shaped, green vegetables had a spicy flavour. The rest of the crew would have approved, Jenna thought. A wave of sorrow swept through her. Would she ever see her friends again?

After the meal, she stood. "Come on, let's find out if there are any prostitutes in this city."

"What...?" Hendraz asked, looking up at her.

"You two need to get laid," she said, walking on ahead.

Serza stared after her. "I love that girl..."

*

Warm air brushed their skin, the breeze laced with a citrusy scent. Grass and trees had a deep-blue tint, the sky above, cloudless.

Finding a spot near a river, Jenna looked at the trees, set twenty feet behind.

"Here?" Hendraz asked.

"Yes, we'll set the camp back against the trees. That way, you'll be able to disappear when they come."

They erected two makeshift tents, and unloaded their provisions. Jenna dug out cold snacks - fish in an elastic pastry.

She glanced at Hendraz and Serza as they ate. "So... did it work out for you last night?"

Serza grinned. "Yes," he said with a gleam in his eye.

Jenna smiled. "Not everything's insurmountable then."

193

"There are ways and means," Hendraz said, reflectively. Taking a bite of his snack, he glanced at her. "So, you don't have a boyfriend, Jenna?"

"No," she answered, quietly. What were Flint and Allessa doing right now?

"That surprises me."

"Well, what with saving the universe, eradicating slavery in a whole region of the milky way, and being pursued by evil maniacs, it doesn't leave much room for a relationship."

She was being flippant but Hendraz saw the sad look in her eyes. His lips pressed. She was far too young to have such weight on her shoulders.

"This, what's happening to you, is not fair, Jenna," he said gently. "If anyone deserves this, you don't."

"It's not about fair, though, is it?"

"I'm glad we can help."

"I just need to sleep, remember. Need you to keep watch. Nothing more."

They passed the rest of the afternoon reminiscing, the temperature turning cooler as night approached. Hendraz took first watch, Serza second.

Jenna awoke in the morning to find Serza spearing fish in the river, his blonde hair shining in the early light. It reminded her of Flint, and she swallowed hard.

Throwing the wriggling body in a bag, Serza walked over. "Breakfast?" he asked her.

"What have you got there?"

"I have no idea and it's very ugly. Let's hope it tastes good."

Jenna watched him make a fire. "Didn't know you were the outdoorsy type, Serza?"

"I used to fish with my dad when I was young."

She smiled fondly as he gutted the fish, remembering the many times she'd watched him stagger around the bars on Venulas. Serza could never handle his drink. Yet, drunk or sober, he was always considerate and thoughtful. He'd been the first resistance they'd encountered, though he had once been part of SLOB's fleet.

"How did you end up in SLOB's fleet?" she asked, curiously.

He looked at her. "SLOB had a good sales pitch, and I had a desperate need to travel. When I joined, I had no idea who SLOB was. He sold it as a peace-keeping venture. Thing was, after I'd signed up, I couldn't leave."

She tilted her head. "How old are you, Serza?"

"Thirty-three."

"*What?* You look twenty-three. How old's Hendraz?"

"Forty-five."

"*What...?* He looks thirty."

Hellgathens looked young for their age? That meant SLOB would have been older than he had appeared. As she sat there, contemplating that, Hendraz emerged with messy hair. Venturing out, he stretched, looking at the fish cooking in the pan.

"Knew the smell would wake you up," Serza remarked.

Hendraz's fingers reached in the pan but Serza batted the hand away.

Jenna smiled.

Hendraz's head turned, his gaze intent. Jenna stilled. The air became charged.

"Couldn't they wait until after breakfast," she shot. "They've done this deliberately."

"It's them?" Hendraz asked.

"They're coming. Get in the trees," she said, rising.

"What's happening?" Serza asked.

"They're opening a portal."

The pressure intensified, a wind got up, blowing their hair around.

"Go," Jenna said.

The air cracked, the Hellgathens shielding their eyes against the blinding light. As it vanished, a white feather floated to the ground.

"Get in the trees," Jenna said, urgently.

The Hellgathens moved back as the air became charged again. Jenna walked out, ready to engage whatever came through.

The second portal opened. Aktimar's double jumped to the ground. The imposing, eight-foot being studied her, hard confidence oozing from his eyes. She intended a shield around her, waiting for its move. She couldn't shield and fight at the same time but she wanted to see what it would go with.

The being conjured a light sabre and came at her, trying to tear through her shield. Jumping back, she dropped the shield and summoned her own light sabre. They crashed together, the Hellgathens watching the dazzling display. They'd never seen anything like it.

The alien was stronger than her and he knew it, his eyes taunting her as she struggled to keep up. She couldn't use the whip again. He would be ready for that. But the sabre fight was still a distraction. She had another trick to play.

She was about to play it, when the creature's eyes widened, and he dropped down dead. She stared at him, her gaze transferring to Serza, and the laser gun in his hand. Staring at it for several moments, she doubled up in a fit of laughter.

Serza walked over. "I thought you'd be cross," he remarked, a smile breaking on his face.

She looked at him, wiping her eyes. "That was priceless. Arrogant fucker didn't see that coming."

Hendraz watched her, amused. "See, we can help you."

She pulled herself together, attempting a more serious expression. "No," she said, injecting authority into her voice. "You must never do that again. Next time, they will see it coming. These are the easy ones. It will get harder. When they come again, you mustn't be anywhere near me. But... this time... thanks."

Serza slapped her on the back. "How the hell did you *do* that? A light sabre?"

"I've been experimenting."

As they walked back to camp, a voice came in her head. *"You are breaking all the rules, Jenna trot, but I have never laughed so hard."*

She whipped her head to the left. A hooded figure stood in that white room, his face in shadow.

"What's your name?" she silently asked.

"Helmus."

"Glad you enjoyed the show, Helmus. Bye the way, has Aktimar located his family yet? Bet he's been a pain in the arse to live with, hasn't he? Good job he doesn't know what you've been plotting behind his back. He might be an evil scumbag but, really, you and that lizard should show more loyalty. Shouldn't evil scumbags stick together? Well, don't worry, your secret's safe with me. For now."

Helmus's image disappeared.

"What are you staring at?" Hendraz asked, studying her.

*

"What does she mean?" Aktimar accused.

"Nothing," Helmus said. "She is trying to create division."

Aktimar glanced at Tastari. "Why would she mention you?"

The lizard shrugged.

"You need to get some sleep, Aktimar," Helmus said, carefully. "Would you like *me* to try to locate your family?"

Scowling, Aktimar shook his head. He shouldn't need Helmus's help. He was the leader of this council. If Helmus helped, how would it reflect on him? "I'll find them," he said, striding off.

Helmus had never seen the man so thrown off course. His opinion of Aktimar was declining. His opinion of the girl, however, was increasing. She was inventive, calm under pressure, and could think on her feet. But she was no match for this council. As yet, she had only come up against interns. There were fifteen full members of the council. If she *did* get through the interns, she had no idea what would come at her. Her little tricks would seem like child's play then. Still, for now, he was enjoying the show.

A Touch of Indigestion

Weeks turned to months, the crew going stir crazy, Graham increasingly frustrated with Johnson. Yeah, she would talk to him but he wasn't getting anywhere. She gave him no signs, no indications to advance things. He wanted to shake sense into her. Newark, bored and restless, persuaded him to take a short trip to Canker, and it became a weekly event. When Graham told Newark about the shape-shifting prostitute Brash had slept with in Canker, Newark laughed his head off.

"So that was why Trot dumped him in Venulas," Newark said.

"Don't mention it to Brash. Mood he's in, he'll rip your head off."

Brash kept complaining they needed to do something but he didn't know what. Jenna could be dead, for all they knew. The thought pained him greatly, and it made him furious with Flint for having a meltdown when they needed to be a strong team. He couldn't stomach the man anymore. On the upside, at least the crew could see what a fallible human being he was. Why on earth would the old woman encourage his delusions? He hadn't spoken much to her, either, since she'd knocked him on his arse.

Johnson spent much of the time wandering around, lost. Graham and Newark kept asking her to come to Canker with them but she couldn't summon any enthusiasm. Skinner told her she was depressed.

"I'm not fucking depressed," she barked at him. "I don't get depressed. Depressed is for sissies." She glared at him, slugging back her drink.

"Did your mother say that?"

"What are you, my fucking therapist?"

"You don't seem yourself," Sophia ventured.

"You've been around for what? Five minutes? And you know me, do you?"

Sophia shrugged. "I'm trying to help."

Brash walked in and got himself a drink. Knocking it back, he poured another one then came over and dumped himself down. A pressure built inside him. "We need to do something," he spat.

"Well, why *don't* we do something?" Sophia asked. "Nobody's keeping us here."

Brash looked at her. They *could* go looking for Jenna. Sure, they didn't know where to go but going somewhere was better than going nowhere. "You're right. We need to try to find Jenna," he decided. "Where's Newark and Graham?"

"Canker," Skinner replied.

199

"Christ."

Skinner and Sophia shared a glance and a smile.

"We'll have to wait till they... *reappear*," Skinner said, looking at Sophia.

"Maybe they'll *change* their minds and come back sooner," Sophia said.

"I'm sure they'll *rematerialize* at some point."

Brash stared at them, oddly. "What's wrong with you two?"

"Newark has told them about the shape-shifting prostitute you slept with," Johnson remarked, matter-of-factly. Brash turned to her. "He told me too."

The pressure built to breaking point. Brash shot up and stormed out.

"Why did you tell him that...?" Skinner asked, staring at Johnson.

"I'm depressed, remember?" she said with a shrug. "I say all kinds of shit."

"Whatever your problem is," Sophia snapped, "there's no need to take it out on us."

"I'll tell you what my problem is," Johnson said, eyeballing the girl. "You two, all coy and sickly sweet, sharing your little joke together. It's enough to turn anyone's stomach."

"This isn't about us, is it?" Sophia asserted. "It's about you, running out on the man you love."

"I don't love anyone."

"Yeah. Right. You threw him away, without even saying goodbye."

"D'you want laying out," Johnson growled, standing in a menacing way.

Skinner stood too. "You touch her, you go through me."

"Bring it on."

The bar room became littered as Johnson and Skinner fought it out. Sophia marvelled at them. She wanted to learn to fight like that. They'd been putting it off in favour of sex but now...

Johnson got the better of Skinner. Sophia's mind raced. Retrieving a heavy bottle from behind the bar, she stood on the counter and smashed it over Johnson's head. As Johnson dropped, Skinner gazed up at Sophia in adoration.

She jumped down and they kissed passionately.

*

As soon as Graham and Newark returned, Brash assembled the crew in the meeting room.

"What happened to you two...?" Graham asked, looking between Johnson and Skinner, who sported black eyes.

200

"We had a disagreement," Johnson said.

"About?"

"About nothing."

"Tensions are running high," Brash said. "We need to get moving, go search for Jenna."

Newark looked at him, puzzled. "It would be like looking for a... for a... drop of piss in a cesspit."

"Nice analogy," Graham remarked, staring at the man.

"Mind you, I wouldn't mind heading to Venulas," Newark said. "We're heroes there, aren't we?"

"Venulas..." Brash reiterated. "Maybe she went there. It was familiar territory, after all."

It *was* familiar territory, Graham realised. He and Johnson had good times there. She needed to be reminded of them.

Skinner wasn't fussed as long as he was with Sophia. Sophia couldn't wait for a change of scenery.

"Are we all agreed then?" Brash asked.

The crew nodded.

"I'll go get Flint," Newark said.

"Forget Flint," Brash spat with hatred. "The man's off his trolley. He's dead weight!" The crew stared at him. Brash raked a hand through his hair. "In his current state, Flint's better off here," he amended, more calmly.

The crew went to ask Flint anyway. At the very least, they wanted to say goodbye. Tynia told them he was on the beach but when they got there, they couldn't see him anywhere. Walking back, they searched the area but couldn't find him.

"Come on," Brash said, "we can't hang around all day for him."

"Who made you Captain?" Newark said. Hanging around on that plantation weeks longer than necessary had forced a profound shift in Newark.

Brash stared at him, realising how far things had come. He had once been like a god to Newark. He looked at Newark sternly. "The Space Corps made me captain. I was captain before Flint, and led you on the mission to kill SLOB. Or have you forgotten that?"

The crew shared a moment of silent reminiscence. They had all changed since then but old bonds remained strong.

"Are we ready?" Brash asked with authority. The crew nodded. "And one more thing," he said, looking at Skinner and Johnson. "No more fighting."

Graham looked at them too.

Boarding the craft, they took off.

As the craft ascended, Sophia spotted Flint on the beach. "He's there," she said, pointing.

*

Flint watched the craft leave the atmosphere. Tynia appeared at his side.

"They've left?" Flint asked.

"Mr Brash had a bee in his bonnet. They didn't come to say goodbye?"

"No."

"Well, don't feel too bad. They've been here for weeks and none of them have noticed what you are capable of. Self-involved doesn't begin to explain it."

"They've been wrapped up in other things," Flint said, thoughtfully. "Graham with Johnson, Johnson with..." He wasn't sure where Johnson was. "Skinner with his girlfriend, and Brash with..."

"Himself?"

He glanced at her and smiled.

She shook her head. "You've been busy training and you know all that. They've got nothing to do and they haven't noticed you. I do hate selfish people. I tell you, I've had terrible indigestion since they arrived."

"Well, they are here for Jenna, not me."

"If you ask me, she doesn't need a bunch of bored, restless idiots running all over the place. They'll never find her."

"Sometimes, doing something is better than doing nothing."

"In this case, it amounts to the same thing." She took a breath. "Now, come and get some tea, Mr Flint. You've been out here all day. You must be chilled to the bone."

Flint turned to her and smiled. "You're looking after me, aren't you, Tynia?" Tynia thought it was about time someone did. "And, by the way," he said, "call me, Vincent."

"Vincent. Yes. Such a lovely name."

They walked away from the shoreline.

"So, how long this time?" she asked.

"Ten minutes. That's all I can manage."

"That's absolutely astounding, Mr Flint. I mean, Vincent," she amended, smiling. "You've been at this such a short time."

"I want to make a portal."

"You're not quite ready for that. Remember to follow the process."

"Do you think she's still alive?"

Tynia stopped in her tracks, turning pale.

"Are you OK, Tynia?" he asked. The woman stared ahead. "Tynia?"

Placing a hand on her chest, she let out a breath and looked at him. "I'm fine now. A touch of indigestion."

Creating Division

"I'm OK," Jenna insisted. "Just caught the tip of it."

Hendraz ripped the material from her shoulder. The skin was badly burned. "We'll have to get something for that."

"Give me a minute. I'll do it myself."

Looking at her, he nodded. The Hellgathens had witnessed this before. Fraza had revived Jenna after being mortally wounded by SLOB. They'd witnessed a miracle before their eyes.

Hendraz turned as the portal appeared to take the body away. For some reason, they always left it a few minutes. The grey, willowy alien hung suspended then disappeared as the light vanished. He'd struck her moments before she made the death blow. Hendraz and Serza had watched, amazed, as a laser sword, completely unconnected to Jenna, came down from the sky, slicing through the grey's oblong head.

"How did you do that?" Hendraz asked. "Your light sword came from the *sky...*?"

"Power and intent. It doesn't have to come from me."

Serza frowned. "If you can do that, why haven't you done it before?"

"I didn't need to do it before. Like I said, these are the easier ones. I just do what I need to do to kill them. I don't want this council seeing what I'm capable of. They'll be prepared."

"Don't they see you practising?"

"Maybe, but a lot of stuff I practise in my head."

Hendraz scratched his temple. "What *can't* you do...?"

"Stick with me. You might find out." She sat on the ground, working her magic on the burnt skin.

"How many has it been now?" Serza asked, staring at her shoulder as the skin began to heal. Being with Jenna was like being on a magical mystery ride.

"Twelve." She looked up at them. "Why don't you go into the city. They won't come again. No more than four a month, remember?"

"Are you coming with us?"

She shook her head. "No. You go and have fun."

"You sure?"

"Sure."

Hendraz touched her arm. "We'll see you later."

Jenna watched them walk off through the twilight, their shapes becoming silhouettes. The attackers were getting stronger. She had the feeling this council was just playing with her at the moment. There would come a time when she would struggle, and Serza and Hendraz would get involved. She'd have to leave them before that time came. She bowed her head. Everyone she loved, she had to leave...

*

Helmus watched her curiously. He always watched her after a battle but she was different this time. No spirited jubilation, no fingers in the air. He hoped the girl wasn't losing her spirit. That *would* be disappointing. She raised her head, staring at the river, her eyes far and distant.

"Hello, Helmus," she said. He whipped his head, seeing the same scene from a different perspective. "You and your bunch of murderers will never break my spirit. You've taken everything. I'm not giving you that. Maybe your Head is losing *his* spirit, though. Has he figured out what you're plotting?"

Helmus turned to see Aktimar viewing him with suspicion. The man had barely slept these past weeks. He was a shadow of his former self. Should he even *be* Head anymore?

Aktimar lurched to his feet, and threw out an arm, slamming Helmus into the wall. "Thoughts like that will be your undoing, Helmus," Aktimar growled at him. He stalked forward, standing over him. "What is she talking about?" he barked.

"She is trying to create division. Can't you see that?"

"I see what was in your mind!"

"Forgive me," Helmus said. "It was an erroneous thought. I don't even know where it came from."

Aktimar's blue eyes bore into him. "You are no match for me and you know it. I suggest you get your thoughts in order."

In the background, Jenna's laughter taunted them. It cut off abruptly.

"She's making a mockery of us," Aktimar spat, angrily. "Do not engage with her again. Is that clear?"

Helmus bowed his head.

Aktimar strode out to try, yet again, to locate his family. He knew now that fear worked against him. He determined to overcome it.

Back to Cyntros

Johnson stared at the ringed planet as they approached the moon of Venulas. "It's beautiful…"

Graham glanced at her, oddly. "Looks as impressive as last time we came, doesn't it?"

Docking above Venulas proved to be a problem as none of them spoke the language.

"We haven't thought this through," Newark complained to Brash. Nuts or not, least Flint was an ace with languages.

Johnson pressed the coms button. "Jenna Trot," she said.

The Venulian voice became effusive. They heard flustered voices in the background. A docking station was being cleared, the craft approaching it veering off course. An English voice came through the coms. "You are cleared to land. Docking station three, please."

"It's good to be back," Newark said.

From that point on, they received help every step of the way. As they disembarked, they were handed translator headpieces. They put them on to find English had been programmed in.

"They have English in here?" Newark asked, astounded.

"Yeah," Johnson remembered. "Fraza was fucking about with the things for ages, wasn't he?"

"That was what he was doing?"

A Venulian led them to a shuttle. Indeed, he took them to the front of the queue. The shuttle was larger than an average shuttle, each seat twice the size to accommodate ogre arses. As ogres passed their seats, they pressed their hands together and bowed their heads to them. The crew nodded intermittently. As the shuttle departed for the moon, ogres talked amongst themselves. Were these the humans that had defeated SLOB?

Descending through a cloudless atmosphere, the crew stared over rolling green land. The tall glass buildings of the capital, Venulas, shone in the daylight. Graham gazed at the architecture. The city was a mixture of glass and stone, the outlying districts made of stone roundhouses. The Venulians liked curves, compromising only for the sake of space.

Landing on a busy concourse, they disembarked to find a Venulian with a headpiece waiting for them. He pressed his hands together and bowed his head, before looking at them in awe. "Welcome back," he said. "We have arranged a craft to take you to the best hotel."

"I've missed these fuckers," Newark said as the ogre led them away. Smiling, he looked around, hoping to spot some Jaleans. Not only were Jaleans attractive - as close to humans as you could find in these parts - they were promiscuous and adventurous. Newark had slept with tons of them.

Climbing into a small circular craft, they flew to the grounds of an expensive hotel. Graham couldn't believe his luck. It was the same hotel as last time. Entering the building, he looked around the familiar oblong-shaped lounge, his eyes settling on the round bar at the centre. Surely, this would jog Daria's memory. The glass wall at the back afforded a clear view of the garden. The glass at the front gave a view of the street. Graham glanced at Johnson, wondering if she felt nostalgic yet.

They sat down, Venulian furniture dwarfing them.

"What is it with the aversion to angles?" Newark asked Skinner, looking around for Jaleans and finding none.

"I'm not sure," Skinner replied, "but it's coming to me."

The staff couldn't do enough for them. Food and drink were on tap. After a while, the staff hanging around constantly, irritated the hell out of them. Newark had forgotten how creepy Venulian hospitality was.

The staff were not their only problem. As news of their return spread, Venulians descended from all over the city. The lounge became packed with plump yellow bodies, all bowing their heads, pressing their hands together, and staring at them like they were gods.

Sophia looked around, amazed. "You're heroes..." she murmured.

Skinner beamed inside. For the first time, he actually felt like a hero. Newark lamented the fact Venulians were God-damned ugly. He could have ridden the back of this.

"I'll have a word with management," Brash said, pushing through the crowd, ogres talking to him incessantly.

Newark turned to Skinner. "Come on, let's fuck off and get laid."

Skinner pointed out the flaws with that plan. "Firstly, I have a girlfriend. Secondly, there will be no Jaleans this time. They'll be back on their own planet now. So, unless you want to try your luck with a Venulian..."

"Downer." Newark's mood dropped.

The Venulian manager sported a shiny new headpiece. He smiled graciously as he replied to Brash's request. "Asking them all to leave would be the height of bad manners."

Brash raked a hand through his hair, plastering a smile on his face. "I understand, but my crew are very tired. Keeping the universe safe is a demanding job."

The yellow eyes widened. "Oh. Of course. I'll see to it," he said, bowing his head and pressing his hands together.

"Wait. You haven't, by any chance, seen Jenna Trot around here, have you?"

"No," the manager said with regret and disappointment. "Although... there has been a tumour she's been here."

Brash's brow creased. "Oh, you mean a rumour."

The manager's brow creased. "The tumour is that she has visited the Council."

It was a ray of hope.

The manager took forever clearing the place, the guy explaining to each individual. Brash frowned. Didn't he have a megaphone or something?

As the ogres left, Brash sat with his crew. "Right, there's a rumour Jenna's been here."

"A rumour?" Newark asked.

"Yes. It's not much, I know, but it's something. The rumour is, she visited the Council."

"If that was the case," Skinner said, thoughtfully, "the whole place would have seen her."

"Yes," Brash said, rubbing his chin, "but it's all we've got. We need to head over there."

Johnson turned to look at the crush of Venulians loitering outside. "We're going to get flattened."

Brash glanced around. "Christ-sakes." He looked out of the back window to see the craft gone. Blowing out a breath, he stood. "Come on, let's get this over with."

Throwing backs their drinks, they left the hotel, braving the over-enthusiastic mob. Cheers, shouts, and clapping echoed around them. Brash kept a smile on his face, checking his murderous impulses.

Newark kept getting shoved. "I swear, I'm gonna knock one of these fuckers out," he spat under his breath, bowing his head intermittently.

Skinner kept tight hold of Sophia. The girl gazed around, star-struck.

Johnson got separated. Graham searched for her through the sea of beaming yellow faces. Spotting her at last, he reached back and pulled her through. In that brief moment, he found her staring at him in a way she never had before. A distant, yet alluring way. He took it as a positive sign. He kept hold of her hand until she pulled it free.

Nerves frayed, they arrived at the tall, round, glass building. Inside, glass lifts surrounded the lobby, the occupants staring down at them in wonder. The man from the desk got up to greet them, bowing his head and pressing his hands together before ushering them to a room at the back. There, he indicated for them to get in the lift.

"Well, that was nuts," Newark said, smiling and bowing his head at the Venulian man, who escorted them up.

"Completely over the top," Brash remarked.

Sophia stared at them all.

Emerging into the spacious, bare room, Sophia would have rushed to take in the view but she didn't get chance. The Council awaited them, stationed at the seating area in the middle. Wearing their red robes, the five Venulians stood in greeting. The crew put their headpieces on.

"It is an honour to receive you back here," the Head of the Council said.

"The honour is ours," Brash replied.

Again, Venulian furniture drowned them. Again, they had to be fed, and it was unfortunate they'd eaten at the hotel. The Head told them a Yola had been sacrificed - a rare treat, as Venulians mostly ate fish. The meals were brought straight away.

"You expected us?" Brash asked.

"Yes. We were informed when you left the hotel."

Creepy fuckers, Newark thought.

The crew forced down every mouthful, which seemed sinful as the animal had been sacrificed especially. And hastily. At least, communication was easier. Brash steered himself through the pleasantries then, finally, he asked, "Have you seen Jenna Trot?"

"Yes. She visited us..." The Head conferred with another. "A little over three of your months ago."

"Has she gone?"

"Yes."

Brash bowed his head.

"She told us of her current predicament," the Venulian said. "Indeed, she enlisted our help."

Brash looked at him. "Your help?"

"Yes. Come, I'll show you." The Head stood. "Please, follow me."

Descending in the lift, the Head led them through a door and back into the building. They knew the place well. A long, tunnel-like corridor stretched ahead of them. The large council chamber lay behind a door on the left, the right wall lined with windows.

"So, why the glass and the aversion to angles?" Newark asked Skinner.

Skinner thought about it. "My theory? Glass is see-through. Honest, nothing hidden. The curves relate to a similar principle. No sticking points, no dark corners. Everything above board."

"No shit? D'you think they know that?"

"No."

The corridor curved into another corridor. The Head led them to a round, guarded door, opening it to reveal a plush room where three blue beings tucked into a Venulian banquet - a woman, over seven feet tall, and two four-foot boys. They stopped eating and looked at the newcomers.

"Who are *they*?" Brash asked.

"Aktimar's family."

"Who?"

"Apparently, he is the leader of this council that has decided to kill Jenna Trot."

Brash's eyes widened. "His *family*? How did they *get* here?"

"Jenna Trot brought them."

"What...?"

"She asked us to... look after them for the time being."

"She brought them here? Why?" The how had dawned on him.

"She said it was a card to play. This council sounds ruthless. She is playing every card she can."

"What good can this do, though?" Graham asked, confused.

"An insurance policy, maybe," Newark offered with a shrug. All heads turned to him. Sometimes, the man astounded them.

Brash rubbed his forehead. Jenna hadn't been sitting around, waiting. She had been proactive. But he couldn't grasp how this would help her. Aktimar would be furious. That couldn't be good for either Jenna or the Venulians.

"Them being here is putting you at risk," Brash said.

"She told us not to fight if he comes for them," the Head told him.

"But you've been harbouring them. Why would you do that?"

"We owe you all a debt."

Brash stared at him. This debt could cost them dearly. Jenna obviously thought this card worth playing but it wasn't like her to risk others.

"And you have no idea where she is?" Brash asked.

"I'm afraid not."

"Right." Brash straightened. "OK. We'll take them."

"What?" the crew asked in unison.

"I'm not sure what Jenna's thinking is, exactly, but they will find them eventually. Maybe Tynia can hide them more effectively. We'll take them back to Cyntros."

"But we just got here," Newark said, gutted.

"We don't have to stay on Cyntros," Brash told him. "Just drop them off."

"Oh. OK."

Brash looked at the Head. "Let's hope, for your sakes, this Aktimar guy doesn't yet know they're here."

"Oh," the Head said, "I nearly forgot. Jenna Trot was explicit about this. She told me to tell Aktimar that she will be checking in on us. If anyone here is harmed, she will kill herself."

"What...?" Newark asked. "Is she insane? She's doing their job for them."

"No," Skinner said, thoughtfully. "She is their sport. They want to challenge themselves, and if the game is over too soon, so is their challenge. There is more than this Aktimar involved. This council wants their game. It has started and it sounds like they are committed."

"We don't know that for sure," Brash said.

"No, but Jenna does."

"D'you think she'd really kill herself...?" Graham asked.

"She's probably reasoned she's going to die anyway," Skinner said, sadly.

A sharp pang of loss stabbed Johnson's heart. She missed her friend, didn't know how to help her. "Let's take the blues," she said, decisively. "Make the bastard suffer."

"Back to Cyntros then," Brash said.

Hands Are Tied

Tynia and Flint looked at the aliens. The sea breeze blew through their indigo hair. The large blue woman had an arrogant tilt to her jaw, and her eyes stared at them boldly.

"So, is there a way to make them less visible?" Brash asked.

Tynia couldn't deny Brash's logic in bringing them here, even if it was damned inconvenient at the moment. She didn't usually get this involved. That wasn't her role. Yet, she had to admire Jenna's bravado and courage. She liked the girl. She liked Vincent. She thought she'd make an exception for them. She would shield the three aliens from detection but the problem was keeping them contained.

"You will have to build them a hut and place a guard on them," she informed Brash.

"No. We're leaving again," he told her.

"You brought them here, you need to guard them. If you want to help Jenna, this is the best way. Running around all over the place won't help her at all."

"I don't know," Newark remarked, glibly, "we might find more aliens she's stashed away." God, he missed Trot. She was so much fun.

"What about Flint?" Brash asked, curtly. "Couldn't he guard them?"

"Mr Flint is busy," Tynia stated.

"Busy?" Brash turned to look at Flint for the first time in weeks. "Snap out of it, Flint. Stop fuc-" He glanced at Tynia. "Stop deluding yourself and be of some use to us. You've turned into goddam Fraza!"

Newark spared a moment to wonder if his buddy had made it. He shook his head. The poor bastard would be dead by now. Sorrow welled up in him.

Flint's eyes found Brash. "Me snap out of it?" he asked, calmly. "Perhaps *you* need to snap out of it. You're becoming the egotistical captain you once were."

Brash's temper flared. "Do you remember how *you* were, Flint? You were barely there. A fucking ghost!"

"If you want the captain role back, I suggest you start earning it. The best thing you can do for Jenna right now is to guard the aliens. So, fucking guard them."

The aliens watched the exchange, not knowing what was going on. The crew watched the exchange, thinking Brash was going to get laid out again.

Flint didn't sound too nuts to them. Tynia wondered why they always had to include swear words.

Brash's muscles clenched. Fury burned in his eyes. He wanted nothing more than to punch Flint, but he knew where that would end up. His hands were tied. His crew couldn't see him take a battering. Using tremendous willpower, he allowed the fury to subside. He turned to Tynia. "Seems we'll have to guard them after all then. We'll guard them on the ship."

"No, Mr Brash," she said. "They will need their own home for the duration."

"What are they?" Newark asked. "Guests?"

"That is exactly what they are," Tynia said. "Their father might be a ruthless, twisted murderer but there is no need to take it out on the children."

"If you ask me, they'll turn out the same," Newark muttered.

"Well, let's give them the benefit of the doubt, should we? Why don't you all get started while I have a little chat with them. Oh, and a couple of you will have to go to Canker. You'll need glass for a window."

Glaring at Tynia and Flint, Brash strode off, the rest of the crew following, morosely. Apart from Sophia, who was pumping.

"We're going to build a hut?" she asked, excitedly. "I've never done that before."

Skinner smiled at her. "Neither have we."

Flint's attention turned to the three blue beings. The woman, far taller than a human, had big blue eyes and a ridged structure over her cheek bones.

Tynia smiled at them, pleasantly, using thought transference to communicate. "Now, my... friends over there are going to build you a hut for the duration of your stay. Unfortunately, you will need to be guarded but please enjoy the area, and try to make yourselves at home here."

The young women raised her chin. "He will find us," she said, defiantly, "and you will all suffer."

"Would you like us to suffer, dear?"

She looked at her, oddly. "Of course, I would like you to suffer. You will pay for this outrage!"

"Do you know why you are here, dear?"

She shrugged. "Aktimar has many enemies."

"That does not surprise me. What kind of man do you think your husband is?"

The young woman stood straighter. "He is strong, formidable. He is the Head of the Pramordis Council. He is stronger than you could imagine, old woman. He is respected, revered, honourable."

"Well, that depends on your definition of honourable, doesn't it? If it means hunting down an innocent girl for fun, then I'm sure you're right."

She viewed Tynia with suspicion. "What sick game are you playing here?"

"No game, dear. That's your husband's department. From all accounts, he sounds like a ruthless, unpleasant... whatever your species are called."

"I'll kill you for that slur," the woman hissed, lunging forward. She got flung back, landing on the sand with a painful thud. She stared up, shocked, her children rushing to her side.

"Now, dear, let's not have any more unpleasantness. I understand you are in the dark, but really, I'm an old woman, for God's sake."

Tynia turned to Flint. "Poor dears, they don't have a clue."

Flint looked at the three beings. "Which suggests this council has deviated from its cultural norm."

"Yes."

Flint felt sorry for the woman and her children. But he felt sorrier for Jenna, and if keeping them here could help her, that's how it would be.

Tynia sighed. "I suppose we'll have to entertain them until they build that hut."

Newark glanced back to see the blue alien on the sand. He laughed. "Looks like the old woman's put *her* on her arse too."

The crew looked around.

"Come on," Brash said, irritably. "Let's build that damned hut."

"How?" Newark asked.

"We start by chopping wood," Graham said with a spark of enthusiasm. "I'll draw a design."

As it was morning on Cyntros, they had hours of daylight ahead of them. Graham sprang into action, issuing commands, the crew kept busy as the day progressed.

"Ow!" Newark shrieked. "I nearly chopped my bloody toe off!"

Johnson and Graham burst out laughing.

"It's not funny, you bastards!"

"Newark, take a break," Brash said. "Go and see to your foot."

Newark glared at Brash. Didn't need his permission. As far as Newark was concerned, Flint was still the Cap, even if he had gone slightly nuts. The man had saved his bacon on Juyra, putting his life on the line for them, whilst Brash had kept him on that plantation for weeks. Weeks!

As Newark walked off, Graham glanced at Johnson. She wiped her eyes. It lifted him to see her laugh.

Skinner and Sophia returned, carrying bundles of twining materials.

"Are these OK?" Sophia asked, dumping her bundle down.

215

Graham picked up a reedy leaf and inspected it, testing its elasticity and strength. "Yeah, they'll do."

As Graham looked over his drawing, Johnson viewed him, fondly. He was starting to live his dream. Maybe one day he'd build his own town. Her look took on a reflective quality. Graham raised his head, catching the look, taking it as a positive sign.

Tynia walked past. Finally, she thought, something constructive to keep them occupied. They had chopped down a few trees, making a tiny clearing in the wood.

Moving on, she searched out a quiet spot to work on shielding the aliens. Deflection was a tricky business. She had to create a blind spot in the field. This was usually impossible, but she would be working from a very high level of consciousness. She shook her head. This Aktimar had nothing on her.

*

Aktimar stared at the ugly yellow creature. "So, where are they?" he demanded, his blue eyes boring into the thing.

The Venulian Head stared at the unmoving mouth. The rest of the Council lay sprawled on the floor behind him. The blue being had not reacted well to the news his family wasn't there.

"They would not tell me," the Head insisted.

Aktimar's look turned hard. "Then you will die."

The Head quickly repeated Jenna's message, praying this would have the desired effect. "Jenna Trot said she would kill herself if you kill us."

Fury and sleepless nights blazed in Aktimar's eyes but reason pierced the anger. If Jenna Trot killed herself, his council would not be happy. The way things were at present, Helmus could well take charge. Jenna Trot might be bluffing, but could he take the chance?

Aktimar settled for raising his fist but before he struck, the Venulian quickly added, "Harmed. She said harmed."

"Damn it!" Aktimar punched his fist into one of the plush seats. The seating area took a severe battering until the raging blue's anger was spent. The Venulian Council stared at the destroyed remains. The alien had anger issues. Aktimar heard their thoughts. But they were wrong. He was one of the calmest beings alive. Jenna Trot had struck at the heart of him. The bitch knew what she was doing. He desperately wanted to end her, but his hands were tied.

216

Going All Out

Six months had passed since Jenna's disappearance. The crew had a rota, taking shifts to guard Aktimar's family. When Skinner and Sophia were off duty, he took her to the gym to teach her to fight. She was enthusiastic but not particularly strong, and he had to be gentle with her. She was fast, though, and this would be her strength.

Brash spent his time going on long walks. He worried about Jenna, wondered if she was coping, prayed she was still alive. Between times, he thought of Allessa. The Sentier haunted his dreams but he began to believe he wasn't good enough for her. He knew he had been slipping back to his former self... the same old patterns, and even if he could see this, he felt powerless to stop it. His resentment toward Flint festered, took on a life of its own.

Newark would tag along with him sometimes, like a dog he couldn't shake. Today, Newark wanted to... talk.

"She always had a problem with me," Newark said, scratching his head, "but I never knew what it was. You know, like she was taking offense at stuff all the time."

"Yeah, see, that was her problem, not yours."

Newark nodded then shook his head. "Can't believe I got sucked into that."

"You traded yourself for the illusion of love because that's what you got little of as a child."

Newark stared at him. "Is that what it was?"

Brash shrugged. "I don't know but it makes good sense."

Newark thought about that.

Brash looked at him. "According to Skinner, you knew the women was unbalanced. So, why did you get involved?"

"She was the only one available."

"Yeah, see, you have to be more picky."

Newark nodded. "So, I didn't get enough love as a child?"

"You were one of ten kids, weren't you? Stands to reason."

Newark nodded, thoughtfully. Then he frowned "D'you think you can sue your parents?"

Brash glanced at him. "Not for that."

"Bitch said I was stupid."

"Your mother said *that*?"

"No. Claire."

Brash stopped and looked at him. Newark had never been the brightest button but he had to admit, since they'd met up again, Newark's intelligence quotient had taken a dip. "Did your parents ever call you stupid, Newark?"

Newark scratched his messy head. "Sometimes. Can you sue for that?"

"No."

Newark reminded Brash of a stray, neglected puppy. Maybe he should invest time in him. "Well, seeing as you lied on your application form, and are not, in fact, technically proficient, how about we spend time teaching you to live up to that form."

Newark's eyes brightened. "Cool."

So, Brash helped Newark, starting with the basics of how a spaceship flew. He used child-like drawings to begin with, and many times Brash wanted to rip his hair out. He enlisted Skinner's help, and Skinner wanted to rip Newark's hair out. Skinner had taught Graham, but where Graham's brain had been a sponge, Newark's was a thick steel wall.

Brash tried to get Graham to join the effort but he point-blank refused. Graham's energies were focused elsewhere. They had been focused on Daria, but he'd got mixed messages from her. Sometimes, he'd find her staring at him with an odd, reflective look. Other times, she'd talk to him as if there had never been anything between them. He couldn't gauge her at all. He'd tried to be thoughtful and sensitive, giving her time, but it was frustrating as hell, so he channelled his frustration into a second architectural project. He wanted to make a grander home for Tynia, and his endeavour occupied much of his time.

Johnson wandered around on her own, aimless and distant, wondering when she would start to feel better. Was Skinner right? Was she depressed? She ambled to the beach now, looking for Flint but he was busy with Tynia. She turned and walked away.

Brash came across her outside Tynia's hut. "Are you alright, Johnson?"

She straightened and sniffed. "Yeah. Just bored."

"Johnson," he said, tentatively, "you haven't been yourself since you came back. Are you sure you're OK?"

"Hanging around here's making me restless," she said, avoiding eye contact.

He assessed her. "Yes, but... you've not been yourself since Draztis, have you?"

She stared at him. He wanted her to open up? She needed Flint, not Brash.

"I'm fine," she said, dismissively. "Just bored as fuck. How's Newark getting on? Anything going in?"

"It's slow going."

Smiling briefly, she walked away. Brash watched her go, wondering what he could do to improve the crew's morale. An idea came to him.

He assembled the crew outside the ship, dragging the blues along too, as they couldn't be left unattended.

"Right," he said, enthusiastically. "I'm going to resume the team-building activities."

The crew didn't look too excited.

"This will be good for us," he insisted. "You enjoyed it first time around, didn't you?"

Still no response.

"Alright," he said, "I'll cook for the rest of the week."

"Done," Newark said, snatching his hand off.

Leading them over flat land, he marked out starting and ending points, and the crew began a relay race. Graham, Skinner, and Sophia formed one team; Brash, Newark, and Johnson formed another. The blue children wanted to join in, much to their mother's annoyance. They put one on each team, and Newark thought the blues were nippy little bastards. Within no time, the crew's spirits lifted. It reminded them of old times, brought a renewed sense of camaraderie.

The team building became a daily event. Brash exercised his brain to think of different activities.

Flint and Tynia watched them from a distance. "Finally," Tynia said. "He's going all out to think of others, not just himself."

Flint nodded. "I'm not sure he really wants to be captain anymore, though."

"Maybe not. But it's what he needs right now." She looked at him, cocking her head. "Did *you* want to be captain, Vincent?"

"Not really. It was a means to an end."

"Seems you were very good at it."

He gave her a wry smile. "Who knew?" His look turned serious. "All I want now is to see Jenna again."

"Well, maybe we should take a look. I'll teach you to tune in to her. Find out where she is."

His gaze narrowed. "You said you couldn't discern where she was?"

She smiled, sheepishly. "I lied."

*

Hendraz and Serza watched, fascinated, as Jenna slammed down from the sky, reigning thunderbolts. She was like a superhero or a goddess. A fast one. The lithe, turquoise-skinned alien with a cone-shaped skull, was fast too, quickly dodging the onslaught. Jenna flew at him and performed a total body shot. The alien got blasted back as if hit by an explosion. Disorientated, he took arrow after arrow until he scrambled to get away. Jenna went in for the kill. Flooding the creature's brain with her intention to move down, the alien ascended, and she came up beneath him, her light sword striking through a poorly protected scrotum. The alien's eyes widened before he plummeted through the air. Jenna flew down after him, lashing out with her light whip, splitting him in two.

The Hellgathens stared at the body as it fell in two halves on the ground.

Jenna came in to land.

Hendraz and Serza stared at her. "You can fly...?" Hendraz said, stunned.

"Power and intent," Jenna remarked, looking around at the body.

"That was incredible..." Serza murmured.

"You can fly..." Hendraz said again.

She scowled at him. "How many times do I have to tell you to keep out of sight. And you," she said, glaring at Serza. "What did I say about firing that gun?"

"I thought you were in trouble."

"It doesn't matter. You never intervene. He blocked your fire easily, and if I hadn't got in his line, you would be dead now. You shouldn't even *be* watching," she threw out. "Keep to the trees. Do *not* draw attention to yourselves."

"Did anyone tell you, you're very sexy when you're angry?" Hendraz teased.

"I'm serious! They're getting stronger. You can't help me."

Pressure grew. The air cracked, and blinding light appeared. The two halves of the body lifted, vanishing with the portal.

"How many has that been?" Hendraz asked.

"Twenty-three."

"So, one more left this month."

She nodded. For some reason, she thought of Flint and the bottom fell out of her heart. She frowned. She was out here facing all this shit and he was probably in bed with Allessa. Life fucking sucked.

She dumped herself on the ground.

Hendraz sat beside her and touched her arm. "You'll get through this."

She turned to him. "No, Hendraz, I won't."

"You expect to die?" he asked, sombrely.

"They're getting stronger. I intend to rid the universe of as many of them as I can, but... yes, at some point, I expect to die."

He looked at her, sadly. "You are the bravest woman I have ever met."

Serza sat on her other side. "I'm glad you brought me along. I would rather die beside a hero than live with no purpose."

She smiled at him. "Thank you. But if you get hurt, Serza, I'll throttle you."

They turned, confused. The air became charged again. Pressure built.

"They're opening another portal...?" Hendraz asked, frowning.

Jenna stood. "I think they're sending twenty-four."

"They can't do that, can they?" Serza objected.

"They can do what they like."

The pressure intensified. They braced themselves against it. The portal opened, and a white feather floated to the ground.

"Disappear," Jenna urged. "Now."

The Hellgathens moved back. The next portal brought a nine-foot being with a scaly face and razor-sharp teeth. Its piercing green eyes observed her like she was an insect.

A carpet of fire swept toward her. She leapt into the air, the creature leaping up too, fire raining in on her from all angles. She shielded, desperate to buy herself time, and though the shield blocked her from the flames, scorching heat engulfed her.

It didn't stop. He was relentless. And she was tired, wasn't prepared for a second attack. She could do nothing with her shield up, couldn't even see the alien through the wall of flames. Taking a chance, she dropped, ditching her shield. A force slammed into her, sending her spinning through the air. When the motion slowed, so did time. She watched Serza's gun fall from his hand as a light javelin impaled him, his limp body collapsing on the ground.

"No!" she screamed. Fuelled with adrenaline, she flew at the alien, desperate to finish him, desperate to get to Serza. She went all out, raining a host of wrath - light arrows, lightening balls, light javelins, anything that came into her head. He blocked and deflected, and time was running out.

Hendraz grabbed Serza's gun and aimed. The alien repelled the fire, but in that moment of distraction, Jenna summoned her power and intent. Black thunderclouds spewed out lightning, targeting the alien. Blocking the lightening and the laser fire, the alien didn't notice Jenna's light whip until it struck from behind, sent his head flying from his shoulders.

As the alien dropped, Jenna flew down. Hendraz tried to revive Serza.

"Move over, Hendraz," she said, kneeling beside him.

Remaining calm, she laid her hands over Serza and focused, letting the power pour through her and into him, imagining it healing every cell. She carried on until she felt it spill back into her. She could do no more.

They waited, watching intently. This had worked for Newark. It would work for Serza. But Serza's eyes did not open. His lungs did not draw breath. She tried again, unable to accept it was too late.

Hendraz, at last, laid a hand on her arm. "He's gone," he said in a broken whisper. "He isn't coming back, Jenna."

Jenna stared at Serza, a sob tearing from her throat.

The Trip of his Life

Tears blurred her vision. "Take Serza home, Hendraz," she whispered at last, pulling her head up.

"I'm not leaving you," he insisted.

"No, I'm leaving you."

"But you need my help."

"My mind's made up. I'm sorry I dragged you into this. I shouldn't have done that."

"Jenna, I can't let you do this alone."

She turned to him, smiling, sadly, tears trailing down her cheeks. "You have no choice." She wrapped her arms around him and hugged him tight. Letting go, she got to her feet, looking down at Serza's lifeless body. "Tell his family..." She had no words.

"I'll tell them he died fighting evil, which he did."

She collected the map, smiling at Hendraz one last time, before walking away.

"He wouldn't have regretted coming," Hendraz called after her, and she turned. "He said he'd had the trip of his life."

She smiled at him, fondly. "Goodbye, Hendraz."

Hendraz watched her become a distant figure. A portal opened, swallowing her.

He looked down at his friend, allowing the tears to come.

*

Flint sat back, staring ahead with moist eyes. "Who were the men?"

"Hellgathens," Tynia replied. "Part of the resistance. They were here with the crew last time."

"She seemed very close to them."

"Yes."

"She said they're getting stronger."

"Yes."

"She struggled with that last one."

"Yes."

"I need to be able to tune into her myself."

"Yes."

"I can open a portal now, so once I learn this, I can go."

"Yes."

He looked at her. "You saved this for last so I wouldn't go too soon, didn't you?"

"Yes. I'm going to miss you, Vincent."

*

Fraza had managed it. He had flown all the way to Jakensk, taking a few stops here and there.

When Cornelius opened the door, he nearly fell over. "Fraza? You're back?"

"And in one piece," Fraza said with a smile.

Cornelius noticed the difference in him immediately. His OCD wasn't apparent and the smile... well, he was smiling.

"Come in, come in," Cornelius insisted, calling Takeza over. Fraza stared at her gigantic belly. It was a miracle she was on her feet.

"Is the baby due soon?" Fraza asked her.

"No-one can tell us."

Takeza hugged Fraza before going off to prepare him food.

"Well, come along," Cornelius said, guiding him to the sitting area. "Tell me everything."

Fraza sat on a couch, and told Cornelius of his adventures.

"A nudist colony?" Cornelius asked. "Did you take your clothes off?"

"It was a requirement."

Cornelius listened with interest to his life there, hearing latent anger when he spoke of Jabreen. Cornelius was even more interested to learn of Fraza's further travels. Not only had he subsisted on his own, but he had explored his gift.

"This is excellent, Fraza," the man said with delight. "You have fought back and come through."

Fraza looked around. "Where are the crew?"

"I'm afraid there is much to tell here too."

Cornelius described events and Fraza stared at him, alarmed. "We need to help her," Fraza insisted.

"I don't have the SMHD and I cannot leave Takeza now," Cornelius said, regretfully. "But maybe..."

Cornelius had been practising what Tynia taught him. He'd briefly produced a portal, even if it was fleeting and insubstantial. What harm could it do to instruct Fraza? Cornelius would prepare the drug. If he hadn't already, Fraza was going to have the trip of his life.

The End of the Kiss

Graham and Johnson sat outside the aliens' hut, Johnson currently on duty. The blue woman was in a mood today and showed no inclination to come out.

"Newark thinks she's pre-menstrual," Graham remarked, turning to Johnson with a smile.

Johnson smiled back. "Newark puts everything down to that. It's probably the biggest word he knows so he likes using it."

Graham thought Daria seemed mellower than she used to be.

"If you ask me," she said, staring ahead, thoughtfully, "she's miffed her hubby's not found her yet."

"I bet *he* is too." Graham thought this might be a good time to 'talk'. He tensed. "Listen, Daria, we've never talked about your... mother, have we?" Johnson turned to look at him. "It was... because of her you didn't want to marry me, isn't it?"

She sniffed. "In an indirect way, I suppose."

"If I'd understood that at the time, I wouldn't have gone off with Yasnay."

"I didn't understand it myself."

Graham trod carefully. He and Daria hadn't talked too deeply about stuff before, and he didn't want to make a mess of it. "I wish I *had* understood."

She nodded, looking away.

This was it. He was going to ask if they could start over. Before he got the chance, Newark appeared. "You won't *believe* the shit I've just seen."

Johnson raised her chin to him. "What have you seen?"

"This portal thing appeared on the beach, and Flint walked through it. Fucking walked through it."

"What...?" Graham asked, confused.

Johnson looked at Graham. "You said Trot went through a portal, didn't you?"

"Yeah... but what's Flint doing walking through one?" He stood up. "Newark, stay here. Guard the blues."

"Fuck off, it's not my shift," Newark said, insulted.

Graham turned to Johnson. "I won't be long."

Johnson's eyes followed him as he walked off with Newark.

Tynia came up from the beach, wiping a tear from under her eye.

"Where have you sent Flint?" Graham asked.

"I haven't sent him anywhere," the old woman replied. "He left himself."

"Well, how will he get back?"

"He will open a portal, I assume."

Graham and Newark stared at her. "He can do that...?" Graham asked, incredulous.

"He has been doing a lot of things these past months. He is an incredibly gifted young man with a firm command of the power. Whether you have chosen to notice that or not is your own business."

"Fuck me..." Newark mouthed.

"Flint *can* do anything..." Graham realised.

The rest of the crew were equally astounded when they found out. Brash appeared shell shocked.

*

He stepped out from behind a wall of rock. The view looked the same, but now he smelled the salty ocean. A wave crashed against the rocks, sent a cold spray onto his face. She stood further down the shoreline but she hadn't noticed him yet. She stared out over the ocean, as if the ocean could lead her home. He swallowed. She cut a lonely figure and his heart went out to her.

Taking a breath, he moved along the shore.

Her head turned.

Jenna couldn't comprehend what she saw. Was it a mirage? Flint...? That couldn't be Flint, *could* it...? His amazing blonde hair stirred in the breeze. His strong, lean body walked with slow, calm, elegance. How could Flint *be* here? A dreadful thought occurred to her. Her attackers could project false images too?

As Flint drew nearer, she brought out her light sabre.

His eyes widened. "Jenna?" he asked, staring at the weapon. "What are you doing?"

"Nice try. Now drop the act."

"The act?"

She kept her guard up, waiting for its first move.

"You think I'm one of them?" he asked, confused.

"Well, unless Flint has suddenly developed the ability to open portals, I'd say it's a safe bet. And where was the fucking feather!"

"Jenna, I *can* open portals. Tynia taught me. I can command the power." He smiled, gently. "Who knew?"

"Drop the act," she said in a hard voice.

228

He frowned, concerned. "Can these beings switch form?"

"Oh, you're good. Nearly as good as me."

His brows raised. "*You* can switch form?"

"Stop stalling and get on with it."

Assessing her, thoughtfully, he moved forward slowly, coming close to the end of her light sabre. "It's really me, Jenna," he said, looking into her eyes.

She took a step back, not sure what to believe.

"Jenna, would that council know we got only one broken kiss on the beach in Hercillen, or the impact that kiss would have? Would they know how I've wanted to repeat that kiss every day? Would they know the kind, caring girl whose heart went out to me when I was most broken, or the girl who infuriated me by disobeying my orders?"

"They might," she said, uncertainly.

"They wouldn't know you when I was broken because you hadn't killed SLOB then. You hadn't even found yourself. But you were kind to me. As lost as I was, I remember that."

"Flint...?"

"It's me, Jenna."

No alien could fake those eyes. His soul shone through them. She dropped the light sabre. "What... What are you doing here...?"

"When you left, I asked Tynia if anyone could train to use the power. She told me I already had it."

"You did...?"

"I didn't know. I'd blocked many things out."

She struggled take this in. Flint was like *her*...?

He looked down briefly. "I need to explain about Allessa."

Reality kicked back in. The image of him and Allessa flooded her mind. A fist wrapped around her heart. She stepped back. "Listen, you need to go. You've been practising for what? Six months? You can't possibly hold your own against-"

"I know why you left Draztis," he said, his blue eyes holding hers. "You made a mistake, didn't you? And then you kept me in the dark about it."

Her eyes narrowed. "Who told you?"

"Does it matter?"

"No, it doesn't, because you need to go."

"Pushing me away again?" His voice took on a hard edge.

She responded in kind. "I didn't have to push too hard, did I? Now leave before you get killed." She turned to walk away.

He grabbed her arm. "I don't want Allessa. It's you I want."

"You have a strange way of showing it," she shot, pulling her arm free. "I saw you!"

"I know you saw me but I didn't go through with it."

"I saw how much you wanted her."

"It's you I want."

"I saw you!"

"I was thinking of you the whole time! Your body, your skin, your hands on me. I couldn't help it. I was with you."

She stared at him.

"It was you," he repeated, softly.

"Me...?"

"Do you think it's been easy for me, watching you with Brash? I needed to take my mind off you." He bit his lip. "Turns out I couldn't."

"Me...?"

"You took the decision away from me, Jenna. You don't get to decide if I live or die. I do."

The vehemence in his voice shocked her. So, too, the pained look in his eyes. She wasn't sure what it meant but it touched her deep inside.

Moving closer, she reached out, brushing a hand over his cheek. "I'm sorry. I was trying to protect you."

The trace of a smile ghosted his face. "You always were impossible."

He reached for her and kissed her, as he had wanted to do for so long. Jenna finally experienced the end of the kiss. Her whole body sunk into it. Her heart kicked back to life.

Flying Together

Jenna's hands clawed the grass as he entered her again. It was a night of passion, never spent. And this man knew what he was doing, taking her to places she'd never been before. She rolled on top of him, staring down at his breath-taking face, her eyes locking with his as they moved together again. He reached up and grabbed her into a kiss... a ravenous kiss, full of months of unsatiated hunger. She drew up, her back arching as the pressure intensified, her rapturous face turned to the stars. Blasphemous swear words tore from Flint's throat as he joined in the rapture...

Gradually, she brought her head down and smiled at him. "I think I should call you Vincent now."

He smiled back. "I think you should."

Their smiles dropped. The air became charged.

"No!" Jenna threw out. "Not now!"

She climbed off Vincent and they dressed quickly, the wind blowing their hair, the air whining under the unnatural pressure. A lashing crack struck. Blinding light appeared. As the portal vanished, the light of two moons revealed a single white feather.

"Stay back, Vincent," she said.

"It's always one, right?" he asked.

"Yes, but you're not ready for this." She couldn't spend time protecting him. "Vincent, please, stay back."

Glancing at her, he moved to the trees.

The pressure grew again. Bracing herself against it, she focused, getting into the right mindset. The second portal opened and a blue, like Aktimar, jumped down, landing steadily on his feet. She sensed its power and strength. Fixing her with cold steely eyes, it brought up a light sword. She manifested two swords, one in her hand, one in the sky above. The sword in her hand didn't distract him. He quickly dodged the falling weapon then steamed in, sword raised. Ditching her sword, she took to the air, throwing everything at him... arrows, javelins, lightening balls. He deflected it all with ease before taking to the air and launching a counter-attack, his weapons firing like bullets, a battery assault of them. She shielded, the weapons tearing through her shield, this alien so much stronger than the others.

She shot out of range. He came after her. Swinging around, she flung out her light whip but he caught it around his sword, jerking it away, a massive light whip manifesting in his other hand. His eyes toyed with her; the

231

message clear. Mine's bigger than yours. Whichever way she went, that whip would catch her. She made a last stand, firing out more arsenal, which he deflected, effortlessly. Her heart hammered in her chest. She shot off, the whip arching toward her...

When it didn't strike, she turned. Vincent's light spear skewered the alien from below. As the body fell, Vincent spun mid-air, his spear slicing through the thick blue neck.

Jenna hung there, gazing at Vincent.

He flew over to her. "Are you OK?"

"How did you do that...?"

"Tynia gave me a few tips."

"You were incredible..."

"*You* were incredible."

"No, I wasn't. He was too strong for me."

"Come on." He took her hand and led her down.

Back on solid ground, she stood, staring at him in awe. "You shouldn't be able to do all that..."

"I don't like the word, shouldn't," he said with a smile. "Besides, I took him by surprise." He turned, scanning the surrounding countryside. "Do you know when the next one will come?" He turned back to find her still gazing at him. "The next one, Jenna?"

"It's been twenty-eight now. They said no more than four a month. That means we get a week off, I suppose." She frowned. "If you ask me, they sent that last one deliberately early." She shuddered to think of what they'd seen.

"Deliberately? Are they always watching you?"

"I don't know how often they watch."

Vincent thought about this. "OK, well, you need a bed and some rest. Are there any towns or cities around here?"

"I don't know. I've just got here."

"OK, come on."

As they walked over the moon-drenched land, Jenna glanced at him. "I think taking the head was unnecessary," she remarked, her eyes shining with humour. "Were you showing off?"

He smiled. "Just practising."

"Ah."

His smile deepened. He turned to her with soft eyes. "I've missed you."

Her heart melted. "I've missed you too."

His look turned sad. "I'm sorry about your friend."

"My friend?"

"The Hellgathen. Tynia was teaching me to remote view."

"You can do that too...?"

"Yes. I... saw how upset you were."

Chewing her lip, she nodded. "I shouldn't have contacted them. I needed sleep."

"You needed help. You shouldn't have left us, Jenna."

"It's getting harder," she whispered. "If you hadn't been here tonight..."

He assessed her. "You're tired, aren't you?"

"It's relentless." Tears came in her eyes. "I want to make them pay for Serza but I don't think I can."

He took her in his arms and kissed her forehead. "You've got me now."

"I know but... I don't know how long we're going to last..."

"Then we have to be inventive." Pulling back, he smiled, gently. "You were always good at that, weren't you?"

She managed a strained, lifeless smile.

He pressed her to him, and she rested her head on his chest. All this time, she'd tried to keep him away from this. Now, she was grateful he was here. She couldn't believe how far he had come in such a short time. Was she dreaming?

"We need to find somewhere for you to sleep," he said, taking her hand.

As they walked on, he glanced at her. "You can switch form?"

She shook her head. "It's a mind trick. Cornelius taught me."

"Could you show me?"

She glanced at him. "OK. Prepare to be freaked out."

As he stared at his double, he stumbled back. When she spoke with his voice, he backed up further.

She quickly dropped the act. "It's just a mind trick," she insisted. "I don't change. I use the power to flood your mind. Cornelius did it when he was fighting the Sentier. Remember?" Vincent nodded, mutely. "Are you... OK?" she asked, studying him.

Collecting himself, he nodded. "Could you teach me that?"

"Yes. You'll probably pick it up in... a day," she said with a wave of her hand. Now she knew how Cornelius felt. But she wasn't complaining. Vincent was a gift from the gods.

They slept in a hollow of a hill that night, Jenna resting her head on his chest, savouring the feel of him. He didn't want the Sentier. He wanted her. She smiled.

As the sun rose on a new day, they pressed on. Jenna looked at him. "Why are we walking?"

Vincent shook his head. "I have no idea"

233

They took to the air like giant birds, flying over the verdant landscape. It reminded Jenna of a lucid dream she'd once had. She couldn't have imagined doing this for real. The boundaries of reality had shifted considerably, the miraculous had become the commonplace.

For Vincent, this was newer, though his progress had been swift. When he first took to the air, he felt his soul expand. He and Tynia had flown over the purple hills one morning as the crew slept in their beds. Touching down, they stared over the sea.

Tynia turned to him. "Do you know why you are picking this up so quickly, Vincent?"

"I had wondered."

"Well, let's just say, you are an old soul."

"An old soul?"

"You have commanded the power over other lives."

Vincent's eyebrows rose. "How would you know that?"

She smiled, sweetly. Without answering, she took to the air, leaving him staring after her.

Vincent watched Jenna now, flying low, skimming her fingers over the surface of a river. Smiling, he dove after her, skimming the water too, reaching out to take her hand.

Jenna smiled at him. Vincent was like her. They were flying together in every sense.

Tall sandy buildings appeared in the distance.

Landing, they walked, hand in hand, staring at the city before them.

"Do you think they're tall, slim, and beautiful, like the Erithians?" Jenna asked.

"Why do you say that?"

"This place reminds me of there." A wave of nostalgia swept over her.

He smiled. "Well, we're about to find out."

Entering the city, they strolled through broad pedestrianised streets, edged with willowy trees. The tall buildings dwarfed the short, portly inhabitants, who had light grey skin and goblin faces.

"Not like the Erithians then," Jenna said, and Vincent smiled.

The goblins peered up at them as they passed by. Jenna and Vincent had visited so many places, they'd become accustomed to being stared at. Vincent listened to the language, picking out words. He'd always had a knack for languages – like codes he could crack.

"They seem to aspire to the tall and slim," he remarked, looking up at the buildings.

Jenna glanced at them too. "They're far too big for them. I hope they have a casino here. I need that bed."

She stopped to ask a resident. The creature, predictably, gazed at her lips.

The goblin nodded, even showed them the way. He took them to a sprawling building, which looked out of place amongst the rest.

"There?" Jenna asked.

The alien nodded, holding out his small grey hand.

Staring at it, Jenna took the hand and shook it.

The creature gave her a cross look before marching off.

Vincent laughed. "I think he wanted paying."

"Paying? Well, that's one enchanting custom I won't be buying into. Come on, let's fleece the creeps."

He smiled, appreciating her form as she walked up to the building.

She turned. "You coming?" she asked, tilting her head.

"Yeah. Just checking you out."

Jenna stared at him. That was new.

Entering the building through tall metal doors, they looked around. This wasn't like any casino they'd seen before. A series of circus rings filled the space. Goblins placed bets on other goblins doing all manner of things... wrestling, boxing, groin kicking?

"Right, well," Vincent said, scratching his cheek, "we'll have to try and get money another way."

Jenna shook her head. "No, this will be fine."

He turned to her, a smile playing on his lips. "Didn't Cornelius tell you off for doing this?"

"Yes, but he's not here and they're kicking the crap out of each other anyway." She gave him a wry smile. "Surely, Cornelius wouldn't begrudge me a bed."

"Cornelius might, but I won't."

"Vincent, you're a rebel."

He leaned into her with a sexy smile. "I've got a good teacher."

The smile captivated her. Dragging her gaze away, she looked around, spotting a booth, where two goblins handed out chips for cash. "You distract the cashiers. I'll... borrow."

The goblins in the booth gawked at the strange creatures as they approached. Vincent had picked up a few words but he hadn't had time to make sense of them yet. Still, he only needed to distract them.

"Ka Stilgos per ontro?" he asked the gawking aliens. "Ontro. Per ontro?"

"Ka Slilgos?" the creature replied. "Per rushi? Per rushi?"

Jenna levitated a few chips from a pile on the counter. Depositing them in her pocket, she glanced at Vincent.

"Stilgos per ontro," Vincent said again as he and Jenna walked away.

The cashiers' eyes followed them. "What did he mean, free lunch on me?"

"I don't know but he was very insistent."

"What did you say?" Jenna asked.

"I've no idea. So, who's going first?"

"You're going to join me?" she asked, surprised.

"Why not?"

"OK, watch and learn."

Jenna placed a bet and when the fight started, her goblin lost control of his limbs, for which he should have been extremely grateful because he annihilated his opponent. The other guy staggered senseless until her man finished him with a brutal kick to the head.

"You're ruthless, Jenna Trot," Vincent said in a seductive voice that had her staring, brainlessly. He planted a kiss on her forehead before turning to place a bet.

When the next fight began, Jenna gaped at Vincent's guy. It was like being with Fraza. How had Vincent got so good at this? And in such a short space of time? As the opponent fell, Vincent turned to her and winked. She nearly dropped. Where had *this* guy come from? She didn't know Vincent's deep dark secret, but she knew this was the man he was born to be.

They collected their cash, leaving behind four very confused goblins. Two stared at their limbs with suspicion. Two waited for a free lunch that never came.

Outside, Jenna asked a passer-by to direct them to the best hotel, though, for best, it didn't look too grand. The foyer had plain white walls and floor, the blinding monotony punctuated by stark metal chairs. Jenna asked for the most expensive room but the room was as minimalistic as the foyer, the bed disappointingly short. Vincent walked out onto a narrow balcony, looking over the sun-drenched city, the goblins tiny below.

Jenna joined him. "This planet is called Soskia, by the way," she remarked. He glanced at her. "I have Tynia's map," she said, holding it up.

Vincent reached into his back pocket and held up a folded paper. "I have Tynia's map too."

She frowned. "I thought there was only one."

He smiled. "Apparently not." He looked into the room. "Can you tell if they are viewing us at the moment?"

"If I still my mind, I can sense it."

"Then could you do that?"

"OK." She went to sit on the bed and quietened her mind, remaining there for a time. "I can't sense them," she said, opening her eyes. "What are you thinking?" she asked, looking at him suggestively.

"I'm thinking, I need to learn that mind-trick. Fast. And we need a plan."

"Oh."

"You say they are getting stronger, yet we have five months left. We can't fight them this way alone."

"No..."

He came over, crouching before her. "Why did you stop with Aktimar? You found his weakness but what about the others?"

"Aktimar? How d'you know about him?"

"Because his family is on Cyntros. The crew found them on Venulas and brought them back." Her brow creased. "The crew were looking for you. Tynia is shielding the family now."

"Really? Right. Well, Aktimar had a family. I'm not sure about the others. Many of them aren't even from that planet. I couldn't discern what their weaknesses would be."

"You're slipping, Jenna. Everyone's got a weakness."

She half-smiled, half frowned. "I've had a lot to contend with."

"I know. We need to spend time watching them without them knowing. When you view them, can you make yourself undetectable?"

"If I don't want to be seen, I keep my distance, keep my mind clear, and hope for the best." She shrugged. "That's as much as I know. Are we doing that now?"

"Yes." He moved in with a seductive smile. "After other things."

"What other things?" she asked, toying with him.

"What do you think?"

He came over her and gently pushed her back on the bed. She dragged his t-shirt over his head, gazing at his firm, bronzed chest.

She sat up, suddenly, staring at a scar on his stomach, noticing other scars... faded white lines all over him. Her eyes moved to his.

"Can you ignore them?" he said, his eyes pleading with her.

She swallowed hard, pushing down the pain in her chest. She reached up to kiss him, to make him forget whatever had caused those scars.

Before long, their naked bodies pressed together, her skin waking beneath his expert fingers.

"What if they're watching now?" she asked, breathlessly.

"Then they'll get a good show because I'm not stopping for anyone."

Soon, she forgot about voyeuristic aliens. She became lost in the moment, her body immersed in pleasure. There might be aliens out to kill her, but for the moment, life was sweet.

Two problems

Flint's amazing new abilities knocked Brash's confidence to such a degree, he stopped the team-building activities. And all other pursuits he'd initiated. He'd turned a corner to smash into a brick wall. Or rather, a great stone slab had fallen on him, crushing his spirit. The crew witnessed the strange shift in him, before he locked himself away in his room. Johnson thought he had depression. As they didn't know what to do, they left him to ride it out.

Today, the crew hung in the gym with the blues. Johnson thought the kids could use some exercise, and she showed them around the equipment. The blue woman watched from the side lines.

Skinner sparred with Sophia. To Johnson, the girl looked like an over-excited pixie. She thought Skinner was pampering her. If he wanted her to learn fast, he should drop her a few times.

Graham suggested he and Johnson have a turn. Shrugging, she walked out onto the mat. Newark plonked himself beside the blue. The woman glanced at him, shuffling down a few inches.

"Johnson always beats him," Newark remarked to the alien but she couldn't understand a word he said. "I'll give it three rounds. Want to place a bet?" Newark glanced at her uncomprehending face. "You could learn to speak the language, you know? Even those brats of yours have picked up a few words."

The blue woman followed the direction of Newark's gaze, watching her children use the equipment. The youngest child ran to a high climbing frame and started up it. As he reached the top, the older child called his name and the younger one lost his footing. His mother shot to her feet, crying out as her child fell. The dark-haired girl moved in fast to catch him. He landed on top of her, nearly crushing her. The girl emerged intact. The blue woman stared at the girl, who checked her child over. Her gaze transferred to the brown-haired man, who ruffled her child's hair. Newark stared at the brown-haired man too. Skinner was being touchy-feely?

The woman lowered herself back onto the bench.

"That was a close shave," Newark remarked. She turned to look at him. "Least you're not an overprotective mother, rushing over to pamper him. My mum left us to it too. Although, she would have cracked me over the head for being an idiot."

"Crack, head," the woman repeated.

Newark's eyes widened. "Crack head, yes." His excited brain buzzed into gear. He pointed at himself and said, "Newark."

The woman looked at his hand then pointed at herself and said, "Damensa."

"You're called, Damensa. Right." He pointed at himself again, and at the others too. "Human."

The woman, cottoning on, pointed at herself and said, "Calibstra."

"I'm fucking communicating with her!" Newark called out.

Johnson dropped Graham on the floor. Legs astride him, she stared down with a *you'll never beat me* look.

Graham's eyes turned misty. Feeling awkward, Johnson climbed off. "What was that, Newark?" she asked.

"Her name's *Damensa*. She's a *Calibstra.*"

"No shit," Johnson said, coming over. "Johnson," Johnson said, pointing at herself.

"Damensa," the woman said in like fashion.

"I think I'll try to teach her English," Newark decided.

"Good luck with that." Johnson pointed at Newark. "Knobhead."

"Knobhead," the alien repeated.

"Stop confusing her," Newark complained.

Johnson shrugged. "Where's the confusion?" Newark frowned. "Hey, you know I love you."

Johnson stared at him, realising what she'd said. Newark stared back at her. She scratched her ear. "Err... I'm going out for a walk."

Graham followed after her. "D'you want to come and see the new house I'm working on?"

She glanced at him. "Sure."

Leaving the craft, they entered the trees, passing Damensa's place, and continuing on until they entered another small clearing. The house was a hut but still impressive. He'd even made a long veranda at the front.

"Christ, you have been busy," Johnson said, impressed.

As they stepped inside, she breathed in the smell of wood, spotting an attic section above with a ladder leading up to it. "Will she be able to get up there?"

"She's already been up. Here, let me show you it." He stretched out his hand for her.

She stared at the hand then looked at him. "I think I can manage," she said, quietly.

Graham climbed the ladder, and she followed.

"She could get a bed up here," Graham said, "free space downstairs."

Johnson looked around. "This is quite something. You're really good at this."

Graham beamed with pride. "Well, I haven't got much to work with but... it's OK."

"You should definitely do this."

He had already planned their house. It would sit beside a lake, and he saw three children running around. The only problem with this plan at present was Johnson. "Listen, Daria," he began awkwardly. "I want to talk to you about... us."

"Us?" she asked, staring at him. "There isn't an us."

"But we've been getting on so well."

"We have, so why wreck it?"

He scratched his temple. "You know what we were to each other. I know you better than anyone. You're just scared because of what happened."

She continued to stare at him. How could he know her when she didn't even know herself? She had changed and she didn't think she could change back. Didn't know if she wanted to. She wondered if Graham had ever known her. He never did take the time to find out.

He shifted his weight, uncomfortably. "I've seen the way you've looked at me these past weeks." Her brow furrowed. "That dreamy, faraway expression?"

"I've never looked at you like that."

"You're in denial, Daria. You can't lie to me."

"Don't tell me what I am!"

"And you've become mellower. I think, maybe, I can handle you better now."

"What...?"

"Well, what I mean is, I didn't understand what made you the way you were, but-"

"The way I was?"

"Don't get me wrong, I loved you and all, but you were quite... forceful. I'm saying this all wrong. What I mean to say is-" Graham stopped. He'd got lost. He wasn't sure *what* he was trying to say.

"So, you loved me but I was a pain in the arse?"

"No, I don't mean that."

"Some people might love me for being a pain in the arse."

"No, I..."

"Perhaps you should have asked me why I was a pain in the arse because, let's face it, you weren't the most sensitive man, were you? And how many times did you forget my fucking birthday!"

241

"I know. I never got that right," Graham blundered. "I thought it didn't bother you."

"Well, it fucking did!"

"My point is, I can be more thoughtful. I'll try to understand you more. I'll try to make you happy."

"Seems like an awful lot of trying," she impressed on him. "Perhaps you should find a lower maintenance woman."

"But I want you."

"Maybe you only think you want me. Truth is, it shouldn't be so much hard work."

"You *have* to work at relationships. I figured that out."

"When?"

"When you were away."

Christ, he really did want her back. "Listen, I don't even know who the fuck *I* am. I don't want a relationship."

"But what about those looks?"

"What looks?"

"Hello," Tynia called from below.

Graham and Johnson peered over the railing.

"I thought I could hear voices," the old woman said. "My, this place is taking shape. We've got a little village in the trees now, haven't we?"

"D'you want something, Tynia?" Graham asked with forced patience.

"No, not particularly. With Mr Flint gone, I'm feeling at a loose end."

Great fucking timing. An idea came to him. "You could always talk to Brash. He's... depressed."

"Angry depressed or sad depressed?"

"Weird depressed. He's shut himself off in his room."

"Ah, now see, I can't board your spacecraft. If you could get him out of there, I'd be happy to talk to him."

Damn. "OK," he called. He turned to Johnson. "Look, we'll talk later."

"There's nothing to talk about."

"Yes, there is. I flew across a fucking galaxy for you."

"I didn't ask you to."

"I dumped Yasnay for you."

"Well, if you'd figured relationships out, you'd know you shouldn't have dumped her for me. Either you want to be with her or you don't."

"Stop being so clever!"

"Stop being a brat!"

Down below, Tynia slinked away.

"It's the Spaniard, isn't it?" he accused.

242

"I left the Spaniard. Like I said, I don't want any bloke. I want to find out who *I* am. And now Flint's pissed off, that isn't going to be easy."

"Let *me* help you. I know you better than Flint."

"You're not fucking listening!"

Johnson moved to the ladder and got out of there fast.

Graham stared after her. How could he have screwed that up so badly?

He spent the rest of the afternoon, wandering around, dejectedly. He found Newark in the bar later, and confided in him.

Newark became pensive. "You know, if you love someone, you should let them go."

"Who told you that?"

"Some bollocks Sophia said. Thing is, though, if you carry on like this, you'll end up like the bunny-boiler. And *she* was fucking nuts."

Graham studied Newark. That was wisdom. Newark had learned something. "So, you're completely over her now?"

"Yeah. Brash helped me make sense of it. It was my parents' fault."

"Right," Graham said, his gaze lingering on him. "Have you seen Brash today?"

"No."

Graham knew they had to deal with Brash. "Tynia said if we can get him off the ship, she'll talk to him."

"How? He won't come out of his room."

"He must come out sometimes or he'd starve."

"Maybe he has starved. Maybe he's dead." Newark's eyes widened.

Graham stared at him. "He wouldn't kill himself. Would he?"

Jumping up, they rushed through the corridors to Brash's quarters.

"Brash, are you alright in there?" Graham shouted through the door.

"Let's get Skinner to open it," Newark suggested.

"We're going to get Skinner to open the door," Graham called.

An eerily detached voice called back. "Leave me alone."

Graham and Newark looked at each other.

"We need to get him to Tynia," Graham said.

"How?

"We'll have to lie to him."

"He's going to be pissed."

"Pissed has got to be better than this."

"Yeah." Newark shook his head. "He was just starting to remind me of the Cap again," he said, sadly.

"This is all to do with how he feels about Flint."

"Yeah. The man's a fucking god."

243

"Shush. Don't let Brash hear you say that."

Newark frowned. "Aren't you supposed to be guarding the blues tonight?"

"Shit. We'll have to sort Brash out tomorrow."

Graham rushed off. He got to the hut to find Skinner and Sophia hanging around outside.

"You're late," Sophia said.

"I know. I'm sorry."

As they walked off, hand in hand, Graham sat back against the wall, realising he had two problems to deal with. Brash and Daria. If you love someone let them go, Newark, of all people, had said. He could do that, he supposed, because, after all, Daria would come back to him eventually.

Down to the Council

Aktimar stood in the empty council room. He walked out onto the rear balcony, and stared over the ocean. He had a headache. He'd been having a lot of them lately. His mood had not been good, either. Finally, he'd caved. The whole council had searched for his family. No-one could locate them.

"Aktimar," Rogran said.

He turned. The stocky Dalgagan rubbed his rust-coloured, uneven forehead. "I have disturbing news," he said, looking up at him, uncomfortably.

"Go on."

"Ingamar and Carsuis have been found dead."

Aktimar's eyes widened. "Dead...? How?"

"Talimoe and Carsuis were having a relationship." Aktimar gaped at him. "Talimoe thought Ingamar was muscling in on his boyfriend."

"But Ingamar and Carsuis are completely different species...?"

"Apparently, Drutesh saw them... kissing and stuff."

Aktimar tried to take that in. "And he had to tell Talimoe?"

"Drutesh was close to Talimoe. In a friendship kind of way. Anyway, after Talimoe had finished with Ingamar, he went to finish Carsuis. Drutesh saw it all."

"And he didn't stop it?"

"Talimoe can be quite... scary when he loses it."

"Where is Talimoe now?"

"He's left. I think he's gone back to his home planet."

"Talimoe was always highly strung," Aktimar spat with contempt. He should have thrown him out long ago. His grip on things had been slipping.

"So, what shall we do with the bodies?" Rogran asked.

"Throw them in the ocean."

"No... err... ceremony?"

"What are we? Their family?" Pain gripped Aktimar's chest but he didn't let it show. "If they can't conduct themselves as befits interns of this council, they don't get accorded due respect."

"Err... Ingamar and Carsuis never got to refute the accusations, though," Rogran pointed out.

"And now they never will."

"I'll see to that then. Oh, and just to mention, we are now three down for the next round."

"We'll send Drutesh out."

"Drutesh is... disturbed at the moment. I don't think he realised how highly strung Talimoe was. Ingamar and Carsuis are not pretty sights."

Aktimar stared at him. "OK, we'll send Coppia out."

"Coppia was Ingamar's best friend. He's destroyed. He has no will to fight."

"Jathan?" Aktimar asked, gauging the Dalgagan.

"Jathan was Carsuis's friend. He's in shock too. Unfortunately, he saw the body."

"What did Talimoe *do* to them?"

"They're virtually unrecognisable."

God, Aktimar thought, what kind of interns had they taken on? Three pussies, one psycho, and two God only knows what. That meant just one intern remained. Anamar. A Calibstra like himself. And Calibstra didn't get thrown off course easily.

Tastari walked toward them through the council room. "I've got some disturbing news, Aktimar," he called out, seriously. "Anamar has killed himself."

Aktimar gazed at Tastari in disbelief. "Killed himself...?"

"He was found at his home. Poisoned himself. The poison was in his drink."

None of this made sense. "Could *she* be behind this?" Aktimar asked.

Rogran looked at him. "How could she do all this?"

"I don't know," Aktimar said, clenching his fists. "Why would Anamar kill himself?"

"He had lost his parents recently," Tastari informed him. "He said the house was big without them."

"He lived with his parents...?"

"He was devoted to them."

"What idiots and numbskulls have we taken on!"

Helmus walked up. "Quite a morning, by all accounts," he remarked.

"You've heard?"

"I've seen Drutesh. The man's shook up. I think he's wishing he had kept his mouth shut." Helmus hid a smile. "And now Anamar?"

"How do you know about Anamar?"

"Tastari told me."

"He told you before me?" Aktimar growled, his gaze narrowing.

"He passed me on the way here."

"Last I knew, I was Head of this Council," Aktimar shot, his gaze descending on Tastari. "Matters are reported to me first!"

The lizard kept his head down.

Aktimar's hard gaze transferred to Helmus. "Seems these interns you have taken on are not up to standard," he levelled at him. "In future, I vet the interns personally."

"They all had a firm command of the power," Helmus assured him.

"What good is that if they haven't got a firm command of themselves!"

Helmus couldn't fail to see the irony. Aktimar was losing his cool. He gave him a moment. "So, will the game continue?" he asked, studying him.

"Of course," Aktimar snapped.

"We are down to the Council then."

"Farogen is the fifteenth member," Rogran pointed out. "I'll go and inform him."

Helmus couldn't wait to see the look on her face when she saw Farogen. A hairy Gasidian with two long fangs, he had a rough, uncouth presence. He stunk like a dog and reminded Helmus of a yeti.

For Aktimar, it was bittersweet. He wanted to see her suffer but if she died, would he ever find his family? His hope dwindled. He contemplated something outrageous. Keeping her alive until he got them back.

*

Jenna and Vincent lay on the bed. Coming back to the room, they looked at each other.

"Aktimar is ruffled," Vincent said, pleased.

"I had no idea how many of them that would affect. We potted tons of balls at once. We only had to kill one." Jenna chewed her lip. "Pity about his parents..."

"If we didn't kill him, he would have tried to kill us."

"I know." She shook her head. "I thought they'd have been onto us."

"Seems they don't switch forms, after all."

She rolled onto her side. "You were amazing yesterday. So convincing. Drutesh totally bought it.

"Surprised you kissed me?"

"My mind's not as suggestible as his."

"Ah, and there was me thinking you'd kiss me however I looked."

She smiled. "I didn't look too hot myself."

He smiled back, turning his gaze to the ceiling. "You said Aktimar saw you once when you were invisible?"

"He didn't at first. Why?"

"Just mulling things over... But you can't do anything in that higher state?"

"No. Can't affect anything."

"Um..." He turned onto his side and looked at her. "We have to work together, know what each other's doing. It's our only strength. You heard them, they're down to the council now. It won't be easy."

She nodded then let out a sigh. "We've spent the whole week focused on them," she said, sadly. "And it could be the last week we get."

He touched her cheek, his eyes looking into hers. She was the bravest person he knew. She was everything he ever wanted and more. He wished time would stand still, that a moment could stretch forever, and he could share that moment with her. He leaned in and kissed her, feeling, for the first time in his life, what it meant to be home.

Something Shocking

Newark and Graham glanced at each other as they closed the door of Tynia's hut. They would have closed it from the outside, but they couldn't let the old woman face the onslaught alone.

"Where is she?" Brash asked, looking around.

"Jenna's not here, Mr Brash," Tynia said. "They told you that to get you off your spacecraft."

Graham and Newark braced themselves for impact but impact didn't come. Brash fell into the nearest chair. Even Tynia looked surprised.

"Would you leave us, please?" she said to Graham and Newark.

Closing the door from the other side, they glanced at each other again.

Tynia assessed Brash. "How are you feeling, Mr Brash?"

He dragged his gaze to her. "Pretty fucking pointless," he said in a spiritless voice.

"And why is that, Mr Brash?"

"I'm stuck here, babysitting, while the hero of the hour is off to save the day." He stared at the floor.

"This has been building for a long time, hasn't it?" He shrugged. "You have sunk into depression, Mr Brash. You don't know who you are, or who you want to be. I'd say you are lost. So, should we start at the beginning? Who was the boy? Lucas?"

He lifted his head and looked at her. "Why?"

"Because I'm trying to help you. So, what were you like as a child?"

He shrugged.

She leaned forward. "May I?" she asked, reaching for his hands.

He looked at her oddly but didn't object, staring at the wrinkly blue fingers holding his.

"Ah. Yes," she said. "Intelligent, but prone to follow one's own rules. Your father saw your wasted potential, didn't he? So did your mother. She told you to set an example for your younger siblings, but you ignored her. You were... angry with her." She paused for a few moments. "When she became ill, you finally knuckled down, worked even harder when she died. You buried yourself in ambition because by doing so, it took away the pain of her death. And the... guilt..." She paused again. "You carried on burying yourself until you became a driven man, not even questioning if you were on the right path, not facing your grief, not facing yourself. When you met Jenna, you came off that path, didn't you? You dared to venture off it. But you lost her. And then

249

you lost Allessa. In your mind, to Mr Flint. So, you struggle to get back on that familiar, well-trodden path, but Mr Flint has taken your place, and now there is nowhere for you to be, nowhere to bury yourself. You are in no-man's land, adrift..."

Brash gawped at the old woman. "You got all that from holding my hand...?"

"I am... gifted." She sat back and appraised him. "Sometimes," she said, "the only control we have is to let go. Let go of the need to control, let go of your jealously. Reconnect with the boy you were. Let him express his grief, his guilt. Remove the stopper, Mr Brash." She smiled at him, gently. "What was your mother like, Lucas?"

His mother's image was clear in his mind. "She had raven hair. She was beautiful, kind, but very unhappy..."

*

Graham and Newark came across Skinner and Sophia canoodling in the trees.

"Get a fucking room," Graham snapped.

Newark glanced at him. "It's not his fault you're not getting any."

"You're not getting any, either," Graham shot.

Newark's face fell.

Passing the blues' hut, they saw Johnson through the window.

"She guarding them from inside?" Newark asked. "Why didn't I think of that?"

Inside, Damensa worked on a dress. Tynia had supplied her with material. Johnson couldn't understand most of what Damensa said, though a few words of English broke through.

"Newark been teaching you English?" Johnson asked slowly.

"Newark Knobhead."

Johnson laughed. "Yes. Newark Knobhead."

Damensa looked at her, oddly. "Newark, man. Johnson," she said, pointing at her, "woman."

"Yes. That's good." Johnson pointed at Damensa's dress. "Dress," she said.

"Dress," Damensa repeated. "Johnson, dress?" she asked.

"You want to make me a dress?" Johnson touched the material. She nodded, thoughtfully. "Yes. Johnson, dress."

The alien smiled.

Johnson spent more and more time with Damensa. It was a way of avoiding Graham. Newark thought Johnson was muscling in on his language sessions, but he realised he was bored of them anyway.

Brash spent a lot of time with Tynia and the crew left them to it.

Graham, biding his time with Johnson, threw himself into finishing Tynia's new hut.

Newark, feeling at a loose end, hung around Skinner and Sophia, not realising he was a third wheel. In the end, Skinner reasoned he might as well carry on with Newark's technical training. Sophia thought she'd spend time with Johnson and Damensa.

"Could you get her to make me one of those dresses?" Sophia asked.

"Sure," Johnson said. "Damensa. Dress. Sophia."

The alien nodded.

Sophia turned to the children. "They look bored," she remarked. "We should take them out hiking. Bring a picnic."

Johnson turned to look at the kids. They'd been drawing but now they lay, restless, on the floor. She felt a strange surge of pity for them, cooped up in this tiny hut. "Perhaps we could take them out on those boats too."

"Yes. Then maybe tree climbing."

"And raft building."

"We could fashion an obstacle course for them."

They set about the task of keeping the kids occupied.

Newark's brain was kept occupied too. "Where does this wire go again?"

Skinner explained but Newark got distracted. "Johnson was wearing a dress last night," he remarked. "Saw her quaffing a drink in Damensa's gaff, wearing a dress. What's that about then?"

Skinner thought about it. "I'm not sure. Maybe she's picking up where she left off in Kelparz."

"Thought that was a temporary bout of insanity."

"Is it insane for a woman to want to wear a dress?" Skinner asked, considering this.

Newark considered it too. "I think Graham's given up on her. He's still fucking about with that hut. By the way, has Brash spoken to anyone yet?"

"Not to me. Sophia said he and Tynia have headed off to Canker."

"Why?"

"I don't know but he carried a sack of her coin."

"I bet she's going to buy him a prostitute to cheer him up."

"I doubt it, considering what would be on offer there."

"He might go for a shape-shifter again."

The two of them smiled.

Graham made an appearance. "Anyone fancy a drink?"

"Isn't it your turn on duty?" Skinner asked.

"Fuck's sake."

The last of the light faded as Graham arrived at Damensa's hut. He saw Sophia in there, and wondered if he needed to be here at all.

He knocked on the door. Sophia answered it with a bright smile. "Hi, Graham."

"Are you staying here?" he asked.

"No. Johnson and me are going to the bar."

"Great," he said, disappointed. He spotted Daria in a dress, ruffling one of the kids' hair. *What the...?*

As she came out, she smiled at him, awkwardly, not stopping to talk. His eyes followed her as she walked away with Sophia. Whoever that was, it wasn't Daria.

Taking up position outside the hut, he leaned back, disconcerted.

The door opened, and the blue woman came out. She offered Graham a mug. "Drink," she said, her blue lips smiling.

He stared at the mug suspiciously, so she took a sip first, handing it to him.

Looking at her oddly, he accepted it. "Have you been learning English?" he asked, not expecting much of a reply.

"English. Yes. Newark Knobhead, Johnson, Sophia, teach Damensa. Damensa learn words."

"That's very good," he said, staring at her.

"Drink," she encouraged.

"Thanks."

Bowing her head in answer, she moved back inside.

Graham realised he'd been missing stuff. With Daria most of all. Her behaviour shocked him. But as evening fell on another day, something far more shocking would occur.

Two Enigmas

Skinner, Newark, and Graham heard it but they couldn't make sense of it. Leaving their drinks, they stood, following the direction of the melodic sound. It drew them to the lounge. Walking in, they stopped dead in their tracks. A man played a strange-looking piano. A maestro. *Brash?*

"Are you seeing this too...?" Newark asked, spellbound.

"I'm not sure what I'm seeing..." Graham uttered.

They moved forward, staring at the fingers working the keys. Newark knew fuck all about classical music but he knew this was good. And where the hell had the piano come from...?

They watched Brash, transfixed.

When the last note played, Brash turned to them.

"You can play the fucking piano..." Newark said, staring at him.

"I haven't played for years," Brash said, looking at the instrument. The blue, square piano wasn't up to human standard, but it would do.

"Where did you learn that...?" Graham asked.

"I learned to play when I was young. Had a gift for it but... I messed about too much. My father wouldn't pay for any more lessons, and told me to get a job, make something of myself."

"That was... amazing," Skinner remarked, distantly.

"Where did the piano come from?" Newark asked.

"We had it shipped in from Canker. It's not quite to speck," Brash said, staring at the thing. "The sounds are not exactly the same but... it's good to play again."

"You're a musician," Graham murmured, staring at Brash as if he was an alien.

"If I'd carried on, maybe..."

"Play some more," Newark said.

They sat down, expectantly. Brash turned back to his instrument and gave them a recital. When the performance came to a close, they stood and clapped.

"I bet Flint can't do that," Newark muttered.

Graham hoped to God he couldn't.

*

253

Brash poured himself into the piano over the days to come. It was balm to his soul. All his unexpressed grief flowed into it. Johnson, Sophia, and the blues joined the audience. Graham stared at Johnson's moisture-filled eyes. Was she having a breakdown? He walked outside, feeling thrown. The two problems had become two enigmas.

Staring up at the hazy, star-filled sky, he thought of Trot. Was she still alive? Was Flint still alive? The reason for them being here had got forgotten. Other stuff was playing out, and it was totally beyond him.

His gaze narrowed. A strange shape moved across the sky, coming in their direction. His eyes widened. Had Aktimar found them?

He ran back inside, shouting for the others.

Too Many tears

The crew stood outside on full alert, weapons at the ready. Johnson and Sophia remained inside with the blues.

Tynia stood beside the crew, watching the craft come in to land. As the gangway lowered, the backlight revealed a surprisingly familiar figure.

"Hendraz...?" Graham asked, peering at him.

"It's Hendraz," Newark said, dumbfounded.

The Hellgathen walked toward them, grinning at their shocked expressions. They grinned back, walking out to meet him, clasping hands with their old friend. As Hendraz spoke minimal English, and Fraza wasn't around, he directed his words to Tynia.

"Hello, Tynia, how are you?"

"Very well, thank you," she said with a bashful smile. She liked this man. His men had been loud and crude but this man had... an appealing presence. He was also manly and virile.

"Could you speak for me?" he asked.

"Of course. It would be my pleasure."

Hendraz told the crew he'd been helping Jenna. When he told them of Serza's death, they stared at him, stunned. Serza had been one of them.

Bowing his head, the Hellgathen gave them time to absorb the news.

"I waited until after the funeral to come here," he said, quietly, "but I want to help now in any way I can."

"We don't know how to help," Brash said, sombrely. "We don't know how to find her."

Graham turned to Tynia. His mind had been so full of Daria, he'd missed something obvious. "You sent Flint off so you must know where she is."

"Yes, Mr Graham," Tynia replied, "but they could be moving around. By the time you get there, they might have gone and you'd still be-"

"Then come with us, Tynia."

"I'm sorry but I point blank refuse to get on a spaceship."

"But that's the obvious solution."

"As obvious as it is, it is not going to happen. You are best placed here, guarding Damensa and her family."

"But we have six guns. How can that not help?"

"If you try to spoil their game, they will kill you. Easily."

Tynia turned to Hendraz. "I'm afraid there is nothing you can do for Jenna at the moment. But we would love you to stay," she said, pleasantly.

Hendraz had no intention of returning to Hellgathen. He felt more at home with this group of humans than he ever did on his own planet. "I'd like to stay."

Tynia translated and the crew smiled in welcome.

"Let's get you a drink," Graham said.

Newark wanted one himself. He liked Serza, had shared many drinks with him.

When they walked into the bar, Johnson stood. "Hendraz...?"

The Hellgathen smiled at her. "Johnson," he said, coming over and clasping her hand as he drew her into a half embrace.

"What's he doing here...?"

Brash explained.

"Serza's dead...?" she asked. She lowered herself down, a tidal wave of sadness crushing her heart.

"Here," Newark said, handing Hendraz a Hellgathen concoction. Hendraz slugged the blue drink back in one go. Newark stared at the empty glass. Nodding in admiration, he fetched Hendraz another one.

Communication proved difficult. Hendraz determined to learn the language this time. He glanced at the blue aliens, wondering who and what they were.

The crew brought up fond memories of Serza.

"The bastard could never take his grog," Newark reflected with a sad smile. "I'd often catch him puking up outside..."

"He liked to knock 'em back, though," Graham remembered.

"He was lovely..." Johnson said, distantly. Graham glanced at her.

Damensa didn't know why everyone was glum or why Johnson surreptitiously wiped a tear from under her eye. She placed a hand on Johnson's arm, which made more tears fall. Johnson caught Graham looking at her oddly. She got up and walked out before the tears gushed. She needed help. This wasn't right. Flint might not be here but Tynia was.

Wiping her eyes, she made her way to Tynia's hut, hesitating before knocking on the door.

"Come in," the woman called.

Johnson entered, looking around idly. "You know, if you'd come on the ship, you wouldn't be sitting here alone."

Tynia smiled. "I appreciate your concern, but I can only handle so much company."

Johnson nodded, thoughtfully.

"Why don't you sit down?" Tynia said, studying her. "Tell me what is troubling you."

256

Johnson lowered into a seat, still looking around, anywhere but at Tynia. "How d'you know something's troubling me?"

"Your demeanour, and, of course, your puffy eyes."

Johnson leaned forward, looking at the woman intently. "That's just it. I don't cry."

Tynia sat up. "May I?" She took Johnson's hands. Johnson looked at her oddly but made no protest. Silent for a few moments, the old woman's eyes glazed with moisture.

Tynia sat back, looking at Johnson, sadly. "You were never allowed to cry, were you? Ever." Johnson stared at her. "The part of you that was squashed is fighting to be heard. I'd say it's even rebelling against your mother."

"What do you know of my mother...?"

"A lot more than I did a few moments ago. A part of you is crying out for expression."

"Well, it needs to stop. I don't want to be some soft sissy."

"I understand, but the pendulum needs to sway the other way for a time. This other side of you is demanding expression. It wants its freedom."

"I can't let the crew see me like this."

"Why not? Be your own person, whoever that might be."

"But I *like* being strong and in control."

"Who says you're not? You never got to find out *who* you were. You never got to choose. Give in to your deepest nature, Daria, and see where it takes you. Stop being who your mother wanted you to be."

"And what if I *am* some soft sissy at heart?"

"Being kind, compassionate, caring, is not weakness. Coupled with other qualities, it can lead to wholeness. And making the right decisions from a compassionate place requires far more strength."

Johnson rubbed her forehead.

"You need to take a leap into yourself," Tynia said, "despite what others may think. That is strength."

Johnson looked troubled.

"Cry here, now, if you want to. I'll not judge. Cry for the child you were. Someone should. Tell me one thing your mother denied that child."

Johnson gazed into the woman's kind eyes. "I always wanted a pet," she said, tears welling up. "Something to love, something to keep me company."

"Something to love you?"

"She said the fury fuckers would turn me soft, locked me away for asking."

"You do realise your mother was an unhinged bully, don't you?"

"Yes... I see that now..."

"You need to leave her behind, Daria."

Johnson looked at her. "I know, but it's not that easy."
Tynia nodded. "Then let the exorcism begin."

Changing the Rules

Farogen scanned the empty field. He sensed her. As she materialised in front of him, he smiled, wickedly, his long fangs glistening with saliva. A noise from above made him look up. Jenna's light whip sliced through his neck before he even processed what he saw.

"One down, fourteen left," Jenna said, staring at the ugly, hairy body.

Vincent landed beside her. "Come on, let's go."

*

"They're making fools of us," Rogran threw out. "Making us look like amateurs. Farogen is better than that. And who *is* that man with her?"

Helmus had to agree. They *were* making them look like amateurs. He glanced at Aktimar, wondering what his response would be.

"We wanted challenge," Aktimar said. "She is doing that. We should be thanking her. If Farogen let himself be fooled, he deserved to die."

"Perhaps we should level the field," Helmus suggested. "There are two of them now, so perhaps we should send two of us."

Helmus had no desire to change the rules. This game proved better than expected, but he wanted to ruffle Aktimar's feathers. He knew Aktimar wanted the girl to survive long enough to get to her himself. His priority was his family.

"Losing confidence?" Aktimar levelled at him, calmly. "We set the rules, remember?"

"We set the rules when there was only one player in the game. The game seems to have changed."

Aktimar's cool blue eyes never left him. "You don't believe we are a match for two, Helmus?"

The Head had him at checkmate. "Of course," Helmus said, graciously. "This Council is more than capable. Farogen allowed himself to be fooled. He deserved to die."

*

As the council watched the next disaster, the same question ran through their minds. Zeyros landed and looked around. The muscular, green-skinned Orath had a long black braid trailing down his back, a mark of the warrior people he descended from. Tattoos covered his broad, bare chest. Holding a light sword in each hand, he altered his perception but sensed no-one. He kept his wits about him, his dark eyes scanning the sky, the land behind him, the forest in front. He held his position for over twenty minutes until he wasn't sure what to do. He couldn't return without killing the prey. That would be unthinkable.

He moved around but nothing presented itself. Taking to the air, he scanned the forest, looking for any movement in the trees.

His state of alert gradually dwindled as he reasoned they'd scarpered. He had only one option left. Find out where they'd gone.

Coming in to land, he stretched his muscles and took a few moments. A few moments were all Jenna and Vincent needed to race forward, unseen.

Zeyros sat on the ground, closed his eyes, and focused, tuning in to them.

His eyes shot open. Bodies materialised. A sword swung through his neck.

"Two down, thirteen left," Jenna said, staring at the body.

*

The Council had to endure two more fuck-ups. As their Calibstra hopeful, Asima, jumped out of the portal, he turned to face a deluge of arrows, spears, lightning... He blocked and deflected it, effortlessly, but that man materialised behind him, swinging a light whip through his neck. The Council stared at the head rolling on the ground.

"Three down, twelve to go," the girl said.

The council shook their heads.

Their next hopeful, Draityn, a Dalgagan like Rogran, performed a massive body shot as soon as he landed. On seeing no-one, he altered his perception. Still nothing.

Parched grassland stretched around him. No forest to hide them today. He took to the sky, scanning the land keenly, keeping his wits sharp, altering his perception.

They weren't here.

Coming in to land, he remote-viewed the surrounding area and, at last, he saw them. Sitting by the pool of a hotel? Basking in the sunshine? *What the...?*

He rose into the air, flying until he came upon the holiday complex. Ahead, the sea sparkled. He spotted the pool, and descended, landing in a quiet alleyway. The hum of voices got louder as he walked through a gate and approached the pool. Slender lilac beings with flat faces sat on loungers, drinking and chatting. All of them stared at him but he ignored them, looking around for his prey.

It was oppressively hot. He pulled at his collar, eyeing drinks enviously, his footsteps leading him to the bar. He sat on a stool, his attention on full alert. They wouldn't catch *him* off-guard. An ugly lilac creature, wearing a hooded bathrobe, offered him a drink. He took it, slugging thirstily. A few moments later, he dropped down dead.

*

"They poisoned him...?" Rogran asked.

"They must have bribed someone..." Tastari reasoned.

"So, they waited for him to focus, drew him there, and got someone to poison him...?"

"Pure genius," Helmus remarked, smiling.

"They are making fools of us," Tastari said, shaking his head.

"They weren't even there to engage him," Rogran spat, disgusted.

"Why should they be?" Aktimar asked, annoyed. "This is our game. Not theirs."

Wyshoi, a being from another dimension, stepped forward. Aktimar frowned, irritated. Why did the gelatinous, rotund creature never lower his vibration enough to materialise properly? "If you want surprises," the disgusting blob asserted, "let me handle this."

Aktimar shook his head. "It isn't your turn. We play by the rules. Weakest first."

"But they are not playing by the rules."

"They are the prey. Prey don't follow rules. Prey do whatever they can to survive. If the hunters are not good enough, they become the hunted." He viewed them with disdain. "You thought it would be easier, didn't you? Well, if you want easy, you shouldn't be here. It's our game and we have four rules. The feather. Four a month. One at a time. And weakest first. By all means, be

261

inventive, but you follow the rules set down." He stood. "If this council is intimidated, I suggest you work on getting better."

Helmus appraised Aktimar. He spoke like his former self but it saddened him greatly that his motives had changed. If the girl didn't die before Helmus's turn, she would die at his hand. And when she did, it would be time for a change of leadership. The rules would change when the game was over.

A Moment of Truth

Damensa's English was coming along. Sophia had started a class for the three Calibstra and Hendraz. She threw herself into the endeavour with gusto. They learned against a backdrop of music. Brash constantly played the piano. Skinner persevered with Newark but it was slow-going. After a session, he'd take himself down to the gym, and hammer the hell out of a punch bag. Graham had halted work, worried that Johnson might slip his grip. The *if you love them, let them go* strategy wasn't working for him. He developed a panicked, *if you love them, cling on at any cost* strategy.

He rarely found Johnson, though. Johnson didn't want to be found. She took herself on long walks, avoiding everyone, tearful most of the time.

Today, she sat on the side of a hill, staring out over a calm sea. She had expressed a lot of anger toward her mother since Draztis. Now, her feelings moved to the unloved child. As a small kid, she'd reach up her arms to her mother, wanting to love her as much as she wanted to be loved. The arms were always shoved away.

Sadness filled her heart. Tears flowed again, a whole torrent of them. Would they ever stop?

"Daria?" Graham asked. She whipped her head to him, desperately wiping the tears away. "What's wrong?"

She shrugged, not knowing what to say. How could she explain all this to someone who didn't understand?

"Listen," he said, sitting beside her. "You need to pull yourself together. I don't know what's happening to you but it seems to me, you're having some kind of... meltdown."

"Do you even give a fuck about me, Graham?"

"Of course, I do. That's why I'm saying this."

"How about asking me what's wrong?"

His brow creased. "I just did."

"Did you? Did you take the fucking time to find out?"

His frown deepened. "Is this about your mother again?"

"It's not about my mother. Again. It's about me. D'you know what a shit childhood I had?"

"Yes," he said quietly, and she looked at him, surprised. "Flint told me." He rubbed his forehead. "He said your mother... locked you up a lot."

"In a dark, scary cupboard."

"I know... It must have been awful... The point is, though, you can't let it drag you down. You're not a child anymore."

Johnson stared at him. He *so* didn't know how to help her, *so* didn't understand.

Taking in her disturbed look, he raked a hand through his hair. "I'm trying to help here, Daria."

"Well, don't bother," she said, getting up.

He got up too. "I don't know how to deal with this," he said, indicating her with his hands. "I want things how they were."

"So, it's all about what you want then."

"You know how much you mean to me."

"Do I?"

"Yes. And I know I mean the same to you."

"How do you know?"

"Because we're meant to be together. I've seen the way you've looked at me."

"What?"

"Those looks, like you're remembering stuff, stuff about us."

"I don't know what you're talking about."

"You do."

"I don't!"

"Stop lying to me."

"I'm not lying!"

"You're remembering me!"

"I'm remembering him!" She stared at him, shocked.

He stared at her, shocked. "Him...?"

"Emilio..." she whispered, staring at the ground as it sunk in. It was the truth, and she could no longer deny it.

She dropped to the ground, bringing her arms around her, the feeling of loss choking her. More tears fell. She'd tossed the man she loved aside.

Graham stared at her, horrified. Backing up, he stumbled away.

Feeling Lost

Graham hammered the bar. Newark and Skinner found him half-baked.

"You alright, man?" Newark asked.

"Daria wants the Spaniard," he slurred, tossing back a blue drink.

"Do easy on them. You'll fucking kill yourself."

"Like a care…"

"Did Johnson say that?" Skinner asked, looking at Graham, thoughtfully.

Graham nodded. He rose to his unsteady feet, and staggered behind the bar. Lilting, he crouched to retrieve another bottle of blue.

Sophia came through the door, wrapping her arms around Skinner. "The lessons are going great, if I do say so myself. Hendraz is guarding the blues. Means I get a night off. What's up? You look like you're at a funeral."

"Johnson wants Emilio," Newark said.

"So, what's new?"

Graham appeared with a bottle. He zig-zagged his way over, and fell into his chair.

"Ah." Glancing at Skinner, Sophia sat in front of Graham. "Johnson wants Emilio?" she tentatively asked.

"She was sobbing her heart out for him," he spat, his unfocused gaze fixed on the table.

"You know, sometimes people change, and there's nothing you can do about that. As painful as it is now, it won't always feel this way."

All Graham heard was, *blah, blah, blah.*

Sophia turned to Skinner. "There's nothing we can do," she whispered. "He has to ride it out."

Newark hated seeing his buddy like this. His brain scrambled for something to help. "We could go into Canker, bud, get you one of those shape-shifting prostitutes. We won't tell anyone."

Graham rose to his unsteady feet. "Yes, get me a whore! That'll teach her!"

"Is that wise?" Sophia asked, wrinkling her nose.

"I shouldn't imagine he'll be able to do anything," Skinner replied, "but it'll sure as hell make Newark feel better."

*

Graham didn't manage to do anything. Consequently, he had less to worry about in the morning... after he'd asked Newark what the fuck he was doing in Cankar.

Hungover and sullen all day, Graham's mood didn't improve as the days passed. He wandered and moped, his hopes and dreams shattered.

As shattered as Johnson's heart. She'd woken up to a nightmare. She'd lost the man she loved, and he'd never take her back now.

Brash continued to pour himself into his music. Johnson would sit in the lounge and listen, not caring about the tears trailing down her cheeks.

Hendraz, still astounded Brash could play like that, was equally astounded to see Johnson crying in the corner. He never took her for the sensitive type. This crew had changed, he reflected. Skinner smiled more. And he had a girlfriend. Conversely, Graham didn't smile much and didn't have a girlfriend. What *had* happened between him and Johnson? Only Newark seemed the same.

Hendraz tried hard to learn their language. He wanted to plug in. Tynia filled in a few blanks one night when he came across her taking an evening stroll.

"Mr Brash and Ms Johnson are struggling with... issues," she told him. "Come into my hut, Hendraz. We'll have a nice little chat."

Following her into her meagre dwelling, he looked around. "Isn't there a bigger place, further over in the trees?"

"Yes, but I can't bring myself to move."

Hendraz smiled as he sat in the chair opposite her.

Tynia did like this man. Her eyes lingered on those firm bulging biceps. "So, you're tired of Hellgathen, are you?" she asked.

"Once you've visited other places..." He rubbed his chin. "Well, they kind of put it in the shade."

"I see... So, with the exception of Mr Skinner, Sophia, and Mr Newark, you're feeling as lost as the rest of this crew."

"I suppose so."

She assessed him. "It's hard for you, not having a purpose, isn't it? But don't worry, purposes tend to find people. These humans need time to be a fully functioning crew again but they could use a strong captain."

"I thought Brash was captain."

"He fit into the role quite well for a time, but that wasn't what he was born to do."

Hendraz looked at her, strangely. "What was he born to do?"

"Only he can figure that out." She smiled at him, pleasantly. "How's your English coming along?"

266

"I'm stringing sentences together now."

"Excellent. I believe Damensa's steaming ahead. Sophia's thrilled."

He nodded. "Yes, Sophia is very... enthusiastic. I never thought I'd see Skinner with a girlfriend."

"She's done wonders for him. I do hope she doesn't dump him."

"She seems to like him?"

"Yes... Remarkable really. Tiny little thing. Very flitty."

"You don't like her?"

"Not at all. She's just so... upbeat. Doesn't seem to have a lot of... dimension."

He smiled, glancing around.

Tynia studied him. "You blame yourself for Serza's death, don't you?"

He brought his eyes to her. "I... A little. I shouldn't have taken him with us."

"But he wanted to go."

"Yes, but..."

"You didn't kill him, Hendraz."

"I knew it would be dangerous."

"And so did he."

Chewing his lip, he nodded. "I wish I could help Jenna."

"We need to leave this to Jenna and Mr Flint."

"Mr Flint?"

"Oh, yes, she has a partner in crime now, so to speak. Let me tell you about him. He's wonderful. They're madly in love, you know."

Hendraz frowned. "She never mentioned him."

"No? Well, she might have been trying to forget him at the time."

A knock came at the door.

"Come in," Tynia called.

Sophia poked her head in, smiling briefly at Hendraz. "Damensa wants to know if you'd like a new dress?"

"Err... yes, that would be very kind of her."

Sophia disappeared as fast as she'd come.

"I rarely wear dresses," Tynia remarked. "But it keeps her occupied. Now, Mr Flint. He's dreamy."

*

Sophia returned to Damensa's hut to find Graham outside.

267

"You're not on duty tonight, Graham. It's me."

"Fucks sake," the man muttered, wandering off. He reeled around, coming back at her. "You left them unguarded?" he sniped.

"I was two minutes. And the kids are asleep." Sophia entered the hut before he could take his pissy mood out on her. Arsehole.

Closing the door on Graham, she stared at Damensa, crying at the table. Frowning, Sophia walked over, and lowered into the chair beside her. "What's wrong, Damensa?"

The Calibstra turned her head, fixing her large blue eyes on her. "I not know husband."

"You don't know your husband?"

"Not know man he be. Who Jenna Trot? Why he want kill her?"

"I don't know her myself but he is using her in his game."

"Is she bad person?"

"No. She is a good person." Sophia looked at her, sadly. "He is not the man you think he is, Damensa."

"He..." She couldn't find the word. She tapped her head with her hand.

"Think, brain, remember, forget?"

"He forget Damensa and children."

"You think he has forgotten you? Why?"

"Aktimar find anyone."

"No. That's not it. Tynia is shielding you."

"Shielding?"

Sophia picked up a piece of material and hid behind it. "Material shielding me. See?"

The woman got it. "Why he play game with Jenna Trot?"

"I don't know. You'd have to ask him."

Damensa put her head in her hands, and cried some more. Sophia sat there, silently.

"You should sleep, Damensa," she said at last.

The woman pulled her weary head up. "You stay hut," she said, fetching Sophia a blanket. "Stay, chair," she said, pointing. "Outside, cold."

Sophia sat in the comfortable chair, and put the blanket over her, getting herself cosy.

Damensa went to bed but she didn't sleep. Hours passed and thoughts plagued her. Finally, she got up. Checking Sophia was asleep, she tiptoed through the hut, retrieved a knife, then sneaked outside.

Making her way to Tynia's hut, she opened the door. Soft sounds of snoring came from the bedroom. Moving across the room with stealth, she pushed the door gently, stealing over to the bed. She brought the knife up, hesitating...

A force slammed her against the wall. A fist ploughed into her face. A second punch to the gut took her down, the knife wrested from her hand.

Tynia lit a candle, her eyes fixed on Sophia standing over Damensa.

"I'm nice," Sophia said, "but I'm no pushover, and I never trust anyone unless they give me damn good reason. You crossed a fucking line."

Tynia translated. It was such a heart-felt speech, she didn't want any of it to get missed.

"Damensa sorry," the woman pleaded. "Need see Aktimar."

"By killing Tynia?" Sophia asked in a hard voice.

The Calibstra woman broke down in tears.

Tynia glanced at Sophia. She had the feeling she had misjudged the girl. That so rarely ever happened. Turning her attention to Damensa, she transferred thoughts. "You were going to murder me in my sleep?"

Damensa couldn't look at her. "You are keeping us prisoner. I wanted to see Aktimar, confront him, wanted him to tell me himself, wanted him to refute it."

"Your husband is a murderer. No need for you to become one too. We can no longer trust you. You'll have to be locked up."

Damensa raised her head. "Please don't lock up my children," she pleaded.

"If your children suffer, that is on you." Tynia turned to Sophia. "I'll help you escort her to the ship. One of the others can collect the children. Those poor children..." she said, shaking her head.

"We can still take them out under guard," Sophia said.

"I suppose. Just when you start to trust people." Tynia looked at Damensa, disappointed.

The Calibstra already regretted her actions. Desperation had driven her. Desperation for a man she loved but didn't know. And now, her family's life here would be more uncomfortable, and she had blood on her hands. It didn't matter that she couldn't go through with it. The intention had been there. One thing she did know, though. She hadn't done it for a bloody game!

Feeling Concerned

Jenna and Vincent sat by that same pool. Lilac aliens lazed around, paying them little attention now. As soon as the feather had appeared, they'd flown over here.

"It's like being on holiday," Jenna remarked, taking a sip of her drink. "What's in this stuff? It tastes good."

"No idea."

"How long d'you think they'll fuck around this time?"

"Not sure." He glanced at her and smiled. "You swear a lot more than you used to."

"Does it bother you?"

"No. It's part of your charm."

"I have charm?" she asked, smiling at him.

"You know damn well you do."

"Who's swearing now?

His eyes lit with amusement.

Jenna looked around. "Wish this was a real holiday."

"Well, don't get too settled. After this next one, we should leave. There's only so many times you can pull the same stunt."

"Yeah."

"We've taken out four of the council now but we can't afford to get complacent."

"Who's getting complacent? My attention is on full alert."

"D'you feel anything yet?"

She shook her head. "Oh, hold on. He's coming."

They stood.

*

Vashier walked around the pool, viewing the skinny lilacs with disdain. The lilacs shied away from him, many wondering about their immigration policy. It wasn't just his imposing form. It was the insect quality attached to it. Odd wiry hairs poked out of his grey, bald head. Large slanted eyes sat on either side of a thin protruding face. The proboscis nose put many off their food.

271

Walking past the bar, Vashier viewed the barmaid with suspicion. He couldn't see the humans anywhere but he had his shield up.

Turning, he approached the modern, five-storey hotel, and opened a glass door.

"I'm afraid you can't come in if you are not a guest," a nervous voice told him. Vashier fixed cold black eyes on the man. "T-Though I could make an exception." The lilac stepped aside.

Vashier stalked through white airy corridors, opening various doors, the guests staring at him, horrified

He combed the building thoroughly. The top floor contained kitchens and dining rooms, the staff staring at him as he scoped the place out. To Vashier, the food smelt disgusting. He walked into an empty, sun-drenched dining room, and moved to the window, which covered the entire length of the room.

Two lilac serving staff came in behind him. His attention shifted to them.

"Have you seen any strange aliens in this place?" he asked without moving his lips. He went on to describe them.

One of the lilacs' eyes widened and it nodded. It pointed toward the kitchen.

"Show me."

The lilac led him through the busy kitchen, other lilacs staring, not wanting to halt his progress. His guide took him to a quiet room at the end, and pointed at a closed door.

"They're in there?" he asked

The lilac creature nodded.

Vashier took a moment then opened the door. The lilac shoved him hard, slamming the door shut, and hitting a button. The garbage deposal system in this place was ruthless.

As the lilac ran off, the kitchen staff came to see what the god-awful racket was.

*

The Council sat, stunned. A couple of them felt sick.

"What just happened...?" Rogran asked.

Even Helmus was stumped. They'd just seen Vashier talk to his prey, seen the prey lead him to a door, and watched as the human man pushed Vashier into a... garbage disposal system...?

"Did they hypnotise him...?" Tastari asked, bewildered.

Aktimar frowned, thoughtful and concerned. "It must be a suggestive power," he considered, "which means nothing can be taken for granted." Whatever it was, Aktimar didn't think it would work on the rest of them, and definitely not him, Helmus, or Tastari.

"They are certainly making the game... interesting," Helmus remarked.

"Which is what we wanted," Aktimar said. "We are down to ten. None of us thought she would get this far. Previous games have been... disappointing. So, stop complaining we have a worthy opponent, and start upping your game."

Aktimar got up and walked off, relief vying with concern. She had nine more to go through before him, and it would get harder, despite her tricks. What concerned him most, though, was what she had just done. They had shoved Vashier into a mincing machine. If she was capable of that, would she be capable of killing his family? Why the hell couldn't he find them!

Complete Head Fuck

"Mr Brash," Tynia said, opening her door to find him standing there. "What can I do for you?"

"I'd like to take the craft and go to Lixia."

"Oh?"

"We're achieving nothing here. And there are things I need to say to Allessa."

"I see. Well, it isn't up to me, is it? It's up to your crew. Although, some of them will have to stay behind to guard Damensa and her children."

"Yes... I'm aware of that."

"Why don't you speak to them? In fact, bring them here. I'll make some punch. It's a special recipe I've been developing."

Brash asked the crew to assemble in Tynia's hut. After securing the blues, they made their way over, thinking there might be news of Jenna. Newark wondered if Brash was getting his mojo back.

Johnson and Graham sat poles apart... well, as poles apart as they could in such a confined space. Tynia sat next to Hendraz to translate. She breathed in his scent.

Brash told it straight. "I want to go to Lixia to see Allessa."

"Are you serious?" Graham asked. "You're still obsessing about her? Wake up, Brash. She's not worth it." He shot Johnson a bitter glance.

Johnson caught it. As screwed up as she was, she couldn't let it slide. "Not worth it? It isn't Allessa's fault he chases after her like some salivating dog."

"She's probably been stringing him along."

"He's probably seeing things that aren't there and can't accept it's fucking over."

"Maybe that's because he was fool enough to believe she actually gave a damn about him."

"Maybe she gives more a damn about him than he does about her."

"How can she when she's moping over a fucking Spaniard?"

"Spaniard...?" Brash asked, cottoning on.

"Let's get back to the issue at hand, should we?" Tynia said, redirecting everyone's attention to Brash.

Brash scratched his forehead, thrown. "Right." *Salivating dog...?* "Well, we're doing nothing here, and I would like to see her. I need our ship, and I know some of you will need to stay behind to guard the blues, but I'm asking you to help me out with this."

The crew stared at him. When did he ever ask for help?

"You should go," Johnson told him.

"Yeah, if you want to get your heart broken," Graham threw out.

"I didn't ask you to come find me," Johnson shot. "Didn't ask you to dump your fucking girlfriend."

"Didn't ask me to dump her...? You punched her in the face because you were jealous, remember?"

"Yeah, and you threatened to knock me out, *remember?*"

"Can we focus on matters at hand," Tynia interjected.

"Can I come?" Newark asked. "We've been hanging around here for ages now."

"I'll come too," Graham said. "I could use a change of scenery." He threw Johnson another look.

"Who is Allessa?" Hendraz asked.

"Unrequited love," Graham muttered. "The poor bastard's going back for more."

"D'you want knocking out," Johnson said, standing.

"That's right, use your fists. At least, Yasnay was a girl."

He braced himself for impact but the punch didn't land. She stared at him as if he'd punched *her*. She walked out, Graham staring after her.

"So, we're going to Lixia," Newark announced. "Wait a minute. That place was dull as sin."

*

The rest of the crew watched as their ship took off. Johnson breathed out. Now, she could mope in peace. Skinner breathed out. No more struggling with Newark's brain.

The Calibstra stretched their legs before being transferred to Hendraz's ship. A wave of nostalgia swept over Jonson as she stepped aboard. The dirty dust bucket brought back fond memories.

She and Hendraz escorted the blues to their new quarters. Johnson looked at the miserable children. "We'll take you out tomorrow," she promised.

Closing the door on them, Hendraz studied Johnson. "You, Graham, apart now?"

"Very apart."

"Who is... Spaniard?"

276

Johnson looked at him, her eyes misting over. "Someone I loved and lost." Tears pooled and fell as she walked away.

Hendraz watched her go. She wasn't the scary Johnson he remembered.

Sophia gave Damensa a wide birth now. Johnson took over teaching the Calibstra, and although she didn't completely trust the woman, she knew Damensa cared about her children. She had to give her credit for that.

"Why you so sad?" Damensa asked her.

Johnson glanced at her. "My mother didn't love me, and I let the man of my dreams slip away because I'm a complete screw-up."

Damensa's brow creased. She didn't get all of that but she joined the pity party. "Damensa's man liar. I not know him."

"Yeah, he's a fucking scumbag..."

Johnson looked around the space. Bunks lined the walls. The crew had been quartered here when they'd travelled the Spearos Galaxy, drumming up support for the resistance. She smiled, wistfully, wondering how Trot was getting on. She missed her mate. She should be fighting beside her, not falling apart. She'd become a bottomless pit of sorrow and tears. And the bottomless pit was widening. It encompassed others too. She felt sorry for Damensa, sorry for Graham, sorry for Brash on his desperate and hopeless quest to win Allessa back.

The tears erupted again. Damensa put a hand on her arm but Johnson walked off to find Tynia.

"Look at the fucking state of me," she threw at her.

"You were a compassionate child who was never allowed to feel," the old woman said, gently. "You have a lot of feelings to express."

"But when will it stop?"

"When the reservoir has drained. Stay with it, Daria. You're incredibly brave."

"Brave...? I'm a fucking sissy."

"Ah, now that's your mother talking. She's gone, and now you have to allow your nature full expression. It will settle when it's had its say."

So, Johnson's unexpressed nature continued to have its say. And as the tears abated, it started speaking a different language. It tried its hand at cooking, it swam naked in the sea, it made stuffed toys, particularly a teddy, which it had never been allowed to have, and it was currently decorating a tree for a party. Hendraz stared at her. The short dress she wore showed off toned legs.

Sophia breezed past him, holding glasses.

"What occurring?" Hendraz asked.

"Happening would be a better word," she suggested, smiling at him. "Johnson's having her first birthday party."

Hendraz's brow creased. Tynia walked up behind him, carrying a jug of purple punch.

"It is Johnson's birthday?" he asked the old woman.

"No," Tynia said. "But she's got many to make up for." The woman leaned in. "I've arranged a nice surprise." God, he smelt divine.

Tynia poured the punch. She'd been refining it. This version would certainly get the party started.

Skinner returned with the blue woman and her children. He had rigged up a sound system and he kicked it into gear. Music blasted through the trees. Sophia danced. Johnson studied her moves then joined in. Hendraz stared at Johnson, entranced. Her arms and hips swayed in a mesmerising way. He wouldn't have thought her capable of such movement.

Sophia got the kids to dance, before dragging Skinner up too. Hendraz found himself drawn to Johnson, his feet edging closer. He moved in to dance with her.

Tynia didn't drink. She kept her eye on Damensa. When someone tries to stab you to death in your sleep, it leaves an indelible impression. She'd had an apology but sorry didn't cut it somehow.

After a couple of drinks, Damensa danced too, though the large Calibstra woman waddled in an ungainly fashion.

Tynia's gaze transferred to Skinner. His dancing left much to be desired, though she could discern *some* sense of rhythm. Sophia was certainly dragging a personality out of him.

Half an hour later, Tynia's surprise arrived. A four-piece band from Canker. They played an odd ensemble of instruments, the music uplifting and catchy. Johnson clapped and cheered after the opening number. Tynia smiled. She did want her to enjoy her first party.

They partied through the night, heading back to the craft in the early hours. Skinner locked in the blues then tucked himself up with Sophia.

Johnson and Hendraz carried on drinking in Hendraz's quarters. They laughed and flirted outrageously.

In the morning, Johnson awoke with a mammoth hangover. She turned her head, her eyes widening on seeing Hendraz sleeping beside her. She couldn't remember anything. Did they...? *Could* they...?

She scarpered before he woke up, her head completely fucked.

Twists and Turns

Koldran looked around. The rocky plateau stretched in all directions, the sky an unusual shade of orange. They weren't here. He could sense it. Draityn and Vashier were children compared to him. He stared ahead and focused, tuning in to his prey. Again, they had chosen a populated location - some kind of alien fair. White-skinned stick insects milled around various rides and stalls. Taking an invigorating breath, he moved forward, anticipating his victory.

*

"He's seen us," Jenna said. "He's coming."

"Let's move." Vincent led her away.

Thin white beings turned to look at them as they moved through the crowd. This fair in no way resembled a human fair. Stick insects mud wrestled in soggy green slime. Children threw knives at animals in a pit, their parents applauding when the blades hit home. Other sticks held their breath in a large tank of murky water.

Finding a quiet spot, Jenna and Vincent waited. They had their plan set up. This alien was going through a door too. A door with vicious creatures behind it. The white-skinned aliens were not wholesome at all, despite the family day out atmosphere. Jenna and Vincent had stared into a dark, glass-covered pit to see lights come on, and a hoard of alien animals that looked like hyenas. A door opened and a cute, furry creature got tossed to the ferocious pack. They ripped it to shreds in a blood-lust frenzy. The crowd applauded. Jenna had nearly thrown up her lunch. Then a bright idea occurred to her.

"He's here," she said.

Their new opponent moved through the crowd, turning stick insect heads. His short, golden hair had a feathery cut. Tall, slim, and perfectly-formed, he had the face of an angel... with devilish yellow slit eyes. Those eyes scanned the crowds, the head turning in a slow fluid motion, until the eyes fixed on them.

"Shit, it's not working," Jenna said. "He can see us."

"We'll have to lead him away, engage him."

"But-"

"We have no choice, Jenna. Work together, remember."

The hunter moved fast, pushing through the crowd to get to them. As they took the air, he followed suit, the indigenous population gazing skyward.

Jenna and Vincent flew away from the city, over rocky terrain, the alien coming after them.

"Now," Vincent said.

Jenna turned to face their pursuer, throwing out lightning bolts as Vincent soared high. When the being came in, Vincent dove, firing an array of arsenal. The alien deflected it all with ease, blasting them with an atom bomb body shot that catapulted them off in opposite directions. Vincent took the brunt of it, spinning away, his senses addled. The alien flew at Jenna. She shielded but her shield got stripped away as if he'd sucked it from her. *Holy fuck*. She dodged a huge lightning ball, then another. Retreating, she intended a strong wall but the alien blasted through it, coming in for the kill.

Vincent, back in action, steamed toward the alien's back, throwing light javelins that failed to pierce his shield. In desperation, he lashed out with the power, shunting the alien away from Jenna. The alien swung around with a light sword, and powered toward him. Vincent conjured a sword too. Light crashed on light, the being far outmatching him in strength, speed, and skill. Jenna charged its back, swinging her light whip. It veered wildly off course. She fired arrows, javelins, whatever she could manifest, but nothing got through that shield. This being was in a different league. He could shield, deflect, and fight at the same time. Even with his back turned. They were screwed.

Vincent lived on borrowed time. Jenna scrambled for options, her eyes widening as a thought occurred to her, Cornelius's words echoing in her mind. *Letting go in the direst of circumstances is a strength you have to acquire now.* Remaining calm, she let the whole situation drop away, let herself drop away, as she raised her state of consciousness.

Reaching that golden moment, she intended the portal. Pressure intensified. The alien glanced around, his yellow-slit eyes transferring to her as the air ripped apart, and blinding light appeared. She thrust out both hands, simultaneously knocking Vincent away, and shoving the alien through the portal.

The light disappeared, devouring the weird-eyed freak.

Vincent flew over to her, staring at her in wonder. "That was amazing. Where have you sent him?"

"To that pit. Hopefully, he's a collection of bones by now."

His look of awe turned to soft amusement. "You were getting him in that pit one way or another, weren't you?"

"Why ruin a good plan?"

He grabbed hold of her and kissed her.

As they came down to earth, Jenna looked at him, concerned. "They're getting too strong for us, and I'm running out of ideas."

That proved to be the case when the next hunter, a Calibstra, came through. The female wore her hair tied back. Fast and furious, she kept her wits about her. Jenna tried the portal again but the alien had it covered, shooting away at the first hint of pressure. The blue steamed back in, deflecting their fire, blasting them with an atomic body shot, several megatons more powerful than the last one. They spiralled off, haphazardly, arms and legs flailing wildly. Jenna managed to steady herself, her eyes widening as the alien bore down on her, its swinging sword inches from her neck. Abruptly, the sword swerved off course. As the alien corrected, Jenna lunged up, jamming a light dagger into the startled hunter's ribs. The blue buckled. Jenna moved back, summoning her light whip. Vincent flew in like an avenging angel, swinging his sword through the thick blue neck.

The dead alien fell, thudding on the frozen ground.

"Are you OK?" he asked.

Jenna nodded.

He grabbed her in a fierce embrace. "I thought I'd lost you."

Hearing the pain in his voice, she squeezed him tight. "You saved me. You knocked her sword off course."

He held her at arm's length. "No, Jenna, I didn't..."

*

Aktimar walked in. "Is it over?"

"Pystara is dead," Helmus informed him.

"Dead...?"

"I was sure she had them," Helmus said, thoughtfully.

"They got lucky," Tastari reasoned. "They won't last much longer."

Sengrode rubbed his long grey chin. "If it wasn't for that man, she'd be dead by now."

"Yes," Helmus agreed. "But the portal trick was a touch of genius..."

As much as Aktimar detested the bitch, he had to admire her ingenuity.

Helmus appraised him. "Did you attend to your matter?"

"I did."

Helmus's eyes lingered on him.

Tastari stood. "Well, show's over for today."

Aktimar watched them disperse, knowing the humans wouldn't survive another round. If he hadn't intervened, she'd be dead now. He'd had no choice but to take matters into his hands. She couldn't die before he had his family back.

A dark scheme formulated in his head, a scheme his former self would never have contemplated.

He put it into operation that night, taking out Sengrode and Oblene in their sleep with a powerful stab to the heart. Rogran woke up. The Dalgagan bled out, staring up at Aktimar in shock and horror. Aktimar put a hand over Rogran's mouth and finished him.

This would be a lesson for new interns, Aktimar reflected. How to guard themselves whilst asleep. He wouldn't even try this with Tastari or Helmus. And he couldn't take out the next opponents, Wyshoi and Vishigad, as they were other dimensional beings. They only turned up for meetings and rounds.

Aktimar walked away from the scene of his crimes, his guts twisting. This was a low point for him. But his family came first. His face hardened, his jaw pressed so tight, it hurt. The girl would die a long and painful death for forcing this decision on him.

*

Tastari reported the deaths in the morning.

"What...?" Aktimar said.

"They've brought it onto home turf," the lizard threw out, incensed. "Murdered them in their sleep!"

Aktimar shook his head. "We've been stupid... This should have occurred to us..." He looked up to see Helmus arrive.

"Tastari has informed me of the deaths," Helmus said.

Aktimar's eyes descended on the lizard. "You report to me first!"

Tastari frowned, confused. He and Helmus had discovered the bodies together. They'd walked down the corridor noticing spots of blood on the floor. On finding the bodies, Helmus had told him to report to Aktimar immediately.

282

Aktimar viewed the two of them with suspicion. Then he spied an opportunity. "Perhaps, under the circumstances, we should call off the game, apprehend them. Make them suffer for the deaths last night."

Helmus looked at him, oddly. "Call off the game? You said yourself, prey does what it can to survive. You think we can't handle them?"

Helmus and Tastari's eyes fixed on Aktimar

Aktimar nodded, conceding. "Of course, we can. You are right. Just because the prey is sneaky is no reason to call off the hunt."

Helmus smiled inside. This game had twists and turns. He could never have imagined the Head murdering his own members to protect the prey. Jenna Trot was truly inventive to have led the game in this direction. He hoped he got to meet her.

"Well," Helmus said, his eyes lingering on Aktimar, "we shall have to guard our sleep, shan't we?"

A Complicated Issue

Johnson and Sophia took the blues to the beach. The children ran around as Damensa stared over the sea in a world on her own.

"Johnson," Hendraz called.

Cringing, she turned.

The Hellgathen approached, surveying her with mischief in his eyes. "How be you?"

Biting her lip until it hurt, she led him away. "Listen," she said, scratching her temple, "did you and I?"

He nodded, his blue eyes studying her.

"That's... impossible," she said, staring at him.

"There be ways," he said with a grin. "You want it again, you know where I be."

His eyes lingered on her as he moved away. She stared after him. Was he screwing with her? She wouldn't put it past him. Why couldn't she remember? How much had she drunk?

As the day passed, snippets of memories returned. She tilted her head this way and that until a full and fucked-up picture emerged.

Soon, the fucked-up picture became less fucked-up. In fact, it became compelling. Emilio had opened her up to new things, and this thing with Hendraz was as new as they got. Yet, it was a bitter pill. It reminded her of what she had lost. A deep connection, far more than just sex.

She avoided Hendraz for a time. Going there with him would be too... complicated. But another drunken night brought a repeat performance. Indeed, there were a number of repeat performances.

Skinner and Sophia clocked something happening between them.

"What d'you think that's about?" Sophia asked Skinner.

"I'm thinking, how the hell do they do it?"

"What d'you mean?"

Skinner explained about Hellgathen anatomy.

"Round the back...?" she asked.

He nodded, sagely.

Tynia had noticed it too. She hoped they got it out of their systems before Graham returned. She was tired of all the drama. Her mind strayed to hiffelfust and her glorious youth. Johnson and Hendraz had nothing on her.

Brash, Graham, and Newark sat in a bare, stone room. When the door opened, Brash stood. Allessa walked in, her head tilting, her grey eyes fixing him.

"Allessa," Brash said, taking her in. He'd missed those beautiful grey eyes, that long dark mane. "I need to speak to you," he insisted. "The man I was, I'm not him anymore. I don't think I... I mean, I haven't known who I was. I made mistakes... got onto this track and I was driven, but I realise now I... The way we were on that plantation, do you remember? That was me and you, and everything else, well, it's all been... confusing. Do you understand?"

Newark leaned in to Graham. "Confusing as hell. What the fuck's he talking about?"

"Lucas..." Allessa hesitated. She looked at Graham and Newark. "Could you leave us, please?"

They got up, Graham scowling at her as they walked out into the corridor. He leaned against the rough stone wall. "The cold-hearted cow's going to slam him down."

"Well," Newark said with a sniff, "he did fuck off with Trot."

"Whose side are *you* on?"

"Hers. Weeks I was stuck on that plantation."

"Newark, let it go."

"Me let it go? You've had a face like thunder for ages now. 'Bout time *you* let it go."

"It's different. You know what Daria and I were to each other."

Newark huffed. "You were with the Saffria for months."

"Because Daria dumped me!"

"Yeah, well, she was fucked-up."

"Thought you were my mate?" Graham accused.

"I am but you're turning into one miserable fucker."

Frowning, Graham fell silent.

They waited a long time, Newark miffed there was no coffee on the go. Did they even have coffee? They could at least have offered whatever herbal crap they did drink.

"D'you think they're screwing in there?" he asked.

"No, poor bastard will be on his knees, begging."

"Yeah, I never thought Brash would turn into a goddam pussy. Quite sad, really..." Newark felt glum, remembering the man he used to admire.

More time passed.

286

"I reckon they're screwing," Newark said.

"Like he'd be so lucky..."

The pair came out at last, Brash looking happy. He and Allessa walked off down the corridor.

"Told you," Newark said, cleverly. "Where are you going?" he called to Brash.

Brash glanced around. "I'm taking Allessa to the craft. I've written a song for her."

"Christ-sakes," Graham muttered, shaking his head.

When they returned to the ship, Newark and Graham headed to the bar. They were bored of Brash's piano playing.

Allessa, however, was star-struck. Tears welled in her eyes as she watched him. He played expertly, and with such soul. She could hardly believe he had all that inside him. Lucas had altered. He was finding himself, letting go of something heavy. She'd missed him so much. A deep desire arose in her.

When Brash took her to bed that night, he proved to be as virile as she remembered, yet an added sensitivity heightened the pleasure. As for Brash, he appreciated those tentacles in a way he never had before.

*

"So," Graham said to Brash the next morning. "You and her picking up where you left off?"

Brash stared at the lilac sky, taking in a deep breath. Grey mountains surrounded the old stone city, rising up majestically. *He* felt majestic. "I don't know yet. She's Head Sentier. I'm not sure what her decision will be."

"You don't look too worried?"

"I am worried but it has to be her decision." He glanced at Graham. "I'm going for a walk." He headed out over the land.

Newark emerged from the ship. "There you are. Are we going yet? I'm bored."

"We're waiting for Allessa to decide if she wants him or not."

"They've been screwing all night, haven't they? I thought it was a done deal."

"Apparently not."

Graham wandered off. Newark spotted Brash and followed after him. He seemed the better option.

Graham headed for the city, climbing worn, uneven steps. The old stone buildings stood on a mound of rock. A more formal entrance, with an arch, stood further around, but he took the back streets. The whole place was pedestrianised, and deafeningly quiet.

As he moved through ancient narrow walkways, Sentier bowed their heads graciously, knowing who he was. If it hadn't been for the crew, Olixder would still be their Head. The Sentier had lost their way under his leadership but Cornelius had got them back on track. In fact, the Sentier had been disappointed Cornelius wasn't with them this time. His talk on wisdom had been enlightening.

Turning onto a wider street, he arrived at the grand stone arch, staring at the castle-like building beyond it. Walking under the arch, he entered the building through an enormous doorway, and asked to see the Head Sentier. A grey-eyed, silver skinned beauty nodded graciously, and led him to that same stone room.

Graham looked around the bare walls then plonked himself down and waited.

"Graham?" Allessa asked when she walked in. "Is everything alright?"

He stood. "What's going on, Allessa?" he asked, bluntly. "Are you going to dump him or not?"

She tilted her head. "Dump him? We are not together yet. I have a lot of things to consider."

"Like Flint for instance?"

Allessa hesitated. "Flint?"

"I saw the way you sniffed around him. Jenna was preparing to fight a council of evil maniacs, and you were steaming in on Flint."

Her grey eyes probed him. "We believed Jenna and Lucas were together at the time, as you well know."

"Look, Brash has turned into a sop. If you screw around with him then dump him, he'll fucking fall apart."

She tilted her head. "I appreciate your concern for Lucas but you are not seeing clearly, Graham. Lucas dumped me. I may have developed some feelings for Flint but that would not have happened if Lucas had not rejected me in the first instance." She tilted her head to other side. "You seem... different, Graham? Why are you so angry with me?" She reached out and touched his arm. "Ah, you are projecting."

He stood back. "What?"

"You are projecting your troubles onto me. Things have changed between you and Johnson, and you are having difficulty accepting it."

"We were talking about you and Brash."

"We were never talking about Lucas and I, were we?"

Graham stared at her. The grey eyes remained on him. "Alright, I hate her," he spat.

"No. You're hurt. She cannot find happiness with you anymore. Don't punish her for that. Don't punish me. And stop punishing yourself. Things change."

The words fell out of him. "I thought we were meant to be together..."

"I know. Expectations often lead to disappointment. But you have to let her go, Graham."

"This is bullshit," he spat, striding out.

When he got to the craft, he made for the bar, dumping himself down with a bottle. He sunk his second drink when Newark and Brash walked in.

"There you are," Newark said.

Grabbing a couple of glasses, Brash and Newark joined Graham, pouring themselves a drink.

Brash eyed Graham, thoughtfully. "Newark tells me... Johnson wants Emilio."

"Tuning back in, are you?" Graham said, sourly.

Brash chewed his lip, gauging Graham. "You have to accept the way things are. Don't you want her to be happy?"

"Yes. With me."

"But what if she can't be? If you cling onto someone you strangle them. You kill the thing you love."

"You're a fine one to talk, coming all the way out here."

"Allessa loves me."

"Good for her. Now take your psycho-babble somewhere else."

"It isn't babble." Brash rubbed his forehead, staring at the table. This was hard to say but maybe it could help. "My mother had an affair. I found out and became... angry, hostile. I despised her, wanted to punish her. Hated her for it. Looking back, I can see she loved the other man, not my father. She stayed for us, and for my father, but she was deeply unhappy. Though I didn't choose to acknowledge it at the time, my father was not an affectionate man. And... he punished her every day for wanting someone else. Yet, still, he wanted to keep her. She became ill." He swallowed hard. "The spirit and heart want what they want, and denying it squeezes the life out of a person." He looked up. "If Allessa chooses not to be with me, I will go with grace. That is love."

Graham brought his eyes up to him. "You've changed..."

"I'm seeing things more clearly. I made life hard for my mother because I didn't allow myself to see the whole picture. When she died, I buried myself, buried the guilt. Don't let bitterness make you into someone you're not, Graham. You know who you are."

God, this was deep, Newark thought. He'd never have imagined the three of them sitting around talking about love. Yet, following his first relationship with the bunny boiler, he was coming to see that love was a complicated issue.

Dead Weight

Jenna and Vincent lay on a beach, staring up at the stars, both of them knowing their time was short. Vincent wished this moment could last forever. The thought made him contemplate time.

Jenna turned to him, sadly. "I wish... I wish we had a lifetime together."

He looked at her, his heart squeezing. "So do I." He turned back to the stars. He had a question he didn't want to remain unanswered. "Why did you choose Brash, Jenna?"

"I made a mistake," she said, awkwardly.

"Yes, but why?"

She let out a sigh. "He was my first boyfriend, I suppose. I got... confused, nostalgic. I'm sorry I hurt you. It's you I want."

"How do you know?"

"Because I'm more myself with you than I am with anyone. Does that make sense?"

He smiled, turning to her. "It makes perfect sense."

She took his hand, her heart breaking. "There's so much more to you I want to discover, and now I'm not going to have time."

Vincent came over her, brushing her cheek with his hand. "If this is our last night, let's make it count."

He leaned down and kissed her.

*

Hendraz was an excellent kisser but she broke it off.

He frowned. "You sad Graham still?"

She shook her head. She couldn't understand it. She was single. Why should she feel guilty? "I'm sorry, Hendraz," she said, getting off his bunk. "This has to stop."

"But you, me, enjoying selves."

"I know but..."

"You free, me free, so...?"

She stared at him, realising she wasn't free. Her heart belonged to someone else, and though the sentiment made her want to chuck, she couldn't deny the feeling.

She gave him an apologetic shrug then left, walking off the craft, glad, at least, the tears had stopped. Staring up at the stars, she wondered how Trot was getting on. She should be there with her, not here screwing around with Hendraz. She felt like dead weight. She considered the strong possibility she would never see her mate again. Tears welled in her eyes. *Oh, for fucks sake!*

*

The ominous feather floated to the ground. Vincent turned to her, taking in every detail. "I love you, Jenna."

She blinked. "I love you too, Vincent."

They looked ahead, readying themselves, waiting for the next portal.

The pressure intensified; the wind got up. The air ripped apart, and blinding light appeared. Yet, the light did not vanish, and nothing stepped through.

"What's going on?" Jenna asked.

Vincent had a bad feeling. "I'm not sure but I think we should move."

They took to the air, flying away, glancing around to see the portal racing after them like a ravenous mouth.

"It's coming for us," Jenna yelled.

"Move faster!"

They couldn't escape it. The light devoured them, dragging them through spacetime.

Spewed out, they landed heavily. The portal vanished. A drab, dim world surrounded them. They struggled to sit up, each movement strenuous and sluggish, gravity bearing down on them. Jenna turned to Vincent, the movement infuriatingly slow, her words warped and long. A strange-looking figure caught in the corner of her vision but her head couldn't turn to it fast enough. When it did, she stared at an indistinct, gelatinous blob. The thing gloated, enjoying their predicament. They fought to get to their feet, completely at the mercy of this vile creature, whose laughter sounded weird. A high-pitched, fast-forward squeal.

Jenna realised the problem. Gravity wasn't heavy. They were. She transferred a thought to Vincent. "Raise your vibration."

As they raised their vibrations, lights came on to reveal a vivid, intensely vibrant world... almost unreal. Plants and trees glowed as if lit from within. The sky shimmered with a multitude of colour. The creature's iridescent skin had more substance, contained sparkling hints of turquoise, blue, pink. It didn't make him any more attractive, though.

"Welcome to my world," the thing impressed on them, opening its short globby arms.

Jenna frowned. It was playing with them? "It's a beautiful world," she remarked. "You look out of place here."

"Your mouth is too smart for you, Jenna Trot."

"Your mouth is too big for *you*. Tell me, is it supposed to look like one featureless slit across your face, or have you had an accident?"

Vincent glanced at her. The creature's look turned hard. "Enough of the pleasantries."

She and Vincent shielded as the blob threw out its flabby arms, the ground around them torn to shreds in a series of mini explosions. Quickly, they took to the air, the creature flying up after them. Jenna threw out a raft of light arrows, which got deflected toward Vincent. Vincent dodged, throwing out a light spear that veered toward Jenna. Their useless weapons proved dangerous, the creature revelling in their predicament, its slit mouth stretched wide.

The blob closed in on Vincent, firing a light shaft back at Jenna. It took her off-guard, piercing her leg, causing her to plummet. Focusing quickly, she produced an energy cushion to break her fall, landing on the ground intact. Her leg burned. She couldn't stand. Above her, Vincent battled desperately, his light sword crashing against two swords, which worked independently as the blob reclined in the air with his hands behind his head. *Arrogant fucker!*

The swords speeded up exponentially, Vincent struggling to stay in the game. Jenna manifested a sword in the sky. As it crashed down, the blob swept it aside with a careless wave of his hand. Any minute now, he would go in for the kill. Jenna's mind raced, her injury causing her vibration to lower. She had to purposefully increase it and as she did, something occurred to her.

Ignoring the pain, she focused, raising her vibration high enough to make herself invisible. Shooting up in the sky, she lowered her vibration at once. The world dimmed. She dropped like a boulder, slamming into the blob, the immense force driving him into the ground.

Vincent stared down at the mammoth crater, the squashed alien, and Jenna unmoving on top of him.

Frantic, he dove down, checking her over. She was unconscious, her breathing faint, her arm twisted at an unnatural angle. The alien's body had taken most of the impact but God only knew the damage she'd done. Keeping a lid on his panic, he lowered his vibration. The world dimmed. He worked in quicksand, struggling to pick her up, everything happening far too slowly.

Holding onto her, he produced a portal, praying it wasn't too late.

Taking a Break

Vincent paced around Tynia's living room. She'd asked him to leave the bedroom, said worry wasn't conducive to a good healing environment. Johnson had been there when he arrived. She sat in a chair now, crying. He had no space to think about that.

Dumping himself down, he put his head in his hands, thinking what he could have done differently, wishing he had thought of that manoeuvre first.

The wait proved agonising.

When, at last, the bedroom door opened, he shot to his feet.

"She's back with us," the old woman said, smiling at him, fondly.

Relief flooded him. He ran into the bedroom.

"Vincent...?" Jenna asked, staring up at him.

"I'm here," he said, taking her hand. "You had me worried there."

Jenna's gaze transferred to Johnson, standing at the end of the bed. Had she been crying? "You OK, Johnson?" she asked, concerned.

Johnson nodded stiffly. "Yeah. Thought we'd lost you."

Jenna's gaze lingered on her. She tried to sit up but Tynia touched her shoulder. "Have a rest, dear. You've earned it." The woman smiled at her, gently. "You've been lucky. You had internal bleeding but we got to it in time."

Jenna looked at Vincent. He leaned down to kiss her. The softest, tenderest kiss she'd ever experienced. Tynia averted her gaze. Johnson stared at them, fighting back new tears.

The kiss went on and Tynia coughed.

Vincent straightened, giving Tynia a sheepish smile.

"Vincent told me what happened," Tynia said. "But, for future reference, had you remained in your lower state in that realm, his weapons would have felt like pinpricks."

Jenna frowned. "Why did he take us there then?"

"I couldn't say but it's obvious he expected you to raise your vibration." She smiled, mischievously. "Seems you managed to surprise him, anyway."

Jenna's eyes turned wondrous. "Did you *see* the place?" she said to Vincent. "Those colours were off the spectrum..."

He nodded. "It was... quite something."

"Yes, dear," Tynia said. "You might want to check your clocks. You'll have lost some time."

Jenna stared at her, her eyes widening. "They'll be coming for us again then," she flustered, trying to sit up.

Tynia touched her shoulder. "Don't worry, dear. You weren't there long, and I'm going to place a shield on you both, give you a break. In fact, I'd better get on with that."

As Tynia walked out, Jenna glanced at Johnson. The woman was unusually quiet. "Where is everyone?" she asked.

"Brash, Newark, and Graham have gone to Lixia," Johnson told her.

"Why?"

"Brash is stalking Allessa."

"Allessa left?"

"Yes. And Hendraz is here now. Been learning the language."

"Hendraz?"

"Yeah, and... brace yourself. Skinner's got a girlfriend."

Jenna's eyes widened. They transferred to Vincent.

Vincent scratched his neck. "Yeah, forgot to mention that."

"She was part of a terrorist group we tracked," Johnson explained.

"What?"

"It's a long story. I'll fill you in later."

Vincent grabbed a chair and sat beside Jenna. "For a while there, I thought I'd lost you," he said, taking her hand, holding it to his cheek.

Johnson quickly turned and left the room.

"Is Johnson OK?" Jenna asked.

Vincent glanced at the door. "I'm not sure."

He stayed with Jenna until she fell asleep. When he walked into the living room, Johnson was nowhere to be seen.

"Is she asleep?" Tynia asked.

He nodded, lowering into a chair. "They're getting too strong," he said heavily, rubbing his forehead.

The old woman sat opposite him. "I know. I've been watching." It hadn't been easy to watch, although certain moments had proved entertaining.

He looked at her. "Could you help us?"

She'd expected this but it wasn't her place to intervene. She had leeway, of course, and training them was acceptable, but she'd already helped more than she should by shielding Damensa. Becoming involved in the play wasn't her role. It was difficult to explain this to them, of course. In life, it was hard to see the bigger picture. "Like I said to Jenna, I will hide you for a while, give you a break, but it wouldn't be right for me to actively intervene."

His brow creased. "Why?"

"Jenna once asked me who I was. Well, my role is that of a guide."

"A guide?

Tynia smiled, gently. "Believe me, from another perspective, you do not want me to intervene. If I did it for you, you'd never get there yourself."

"Get there? We're going to get killed."

"That's the risk you took."

"I don't understand..."

"I know." She'd said too much already. She always did get drawn in. Touching his arm, she got up. "I'll make you a drink."

She walked across the room, Vincent's eyes following her.

*

Jenna walked into the living room.

"She be awake," Hendraz said, striding up to her, hugging her tightly.

"Careful, Hendraz," Tynia said. "She's still recovering."

He stood back. "Sorry. I be careless."

"You speak English," Jenna said, adjusting to how weird he sounded.

"Be learning. Be part of crew now."

"Wow. That's great."

Sophia stared at Jenna in awe. She stood. "I've heard so much about you," she gushed.

Jenna studied the girl. She was pretty, seemed normal... *Skinner...?* "Good to meet you," she said, her gaze moving to the man in question.

Skinner smiled at her. "Good to see you, Jenna," he said.

Jenna...? As he conversed with her, she eyed him oddly. Skinner had more... dimension. Johnson, on the other hand, sat quiet and withdrawn. Her arms wrapped around her middle as if she struggled to hold herself together.

When the crew left, Jenna had a chat with Tynia about her. The woman filled her in then got up, walked into the bedroom, and retrieved a teddy bear. "Daria made me this," she said with a fond smile.

Jenna stared at it, alarmed. Vincent took the teddy with a sad, reflective smile. "She's breaking out of that cupboard at last."

The next day, after gleaning more information from Sophia, Jenna sought Johnson out. She found her wandering aimlessly on the beach.

"You OK, Johnson?" she asked.

The woman turned to her. She nodded, a little too quickly.

Jenna came straight to the point. "Tynia told me what you've been going through."

297

Johnson stared at her, intently. "I'm a fucked-up mess. I can't stop crying."

Jenna looked at her, sadly. "It's hard being shaken up from within but... and you're going to hate me for saying this... it's a process. You won't always feel this way."

"How do you know?"

"Because I've been a fucked-up mess myself, remember? When I lost my memory on Draztis, I lost who I was. I became, in your words, the Admiral's daughter again. But that happened because I'd lost a part of myself, a part I needed to find. And the same's happening with you. You'll find the part you need, and then you'll be all of you."

"I don't *want* to be some soft sissy."

"Am I a sissy? You got Trot back, didn't you?"

Johnson stared at her. "Yes... You came back..."

"The new and improved version," Jenna said, stretching her arms wide.

"You are... And you're still alive..." Johnson bit her lip. "I've missed you, you know?"

"I've missed you too. How about we get legless like old times?"

As their craft and, consequently, the bar was gone, they took a jug of Tynia's punch to Graham's empty hut.

"He built this...?" Jenna asked, looking around.

"Yep. Tynia can't bring herself to move in."

"It's fantastic... He should be an architect."

"I know. I'm sure he'll get there one day." Her eyes turned watery.

Jenna had the good grace to ignore it. Instead, she poured the punch.

Johnson sniffed. "So, you going to tell me all about it?"

Handing her a glass, Jenna recounted the events of the last few months. Johnson hung on every word.

"How many of those scumbags are left?" Johnson asked.

"Not many but they're getting stronger." Jenna felt her mood slide. She was done talking about them. "So, tell me what's been happening with you."

Johnson told her about their time in Kelparz.

"A bunny-boiler's bitch?" Jenna asked.

Johnson shook her head. "It was pitiful to watch."

"Poor Newark..."

"Yeah, well, he's back on form now."

Jenna studied Johnson. "And what about Emilio?"

Johnson looked at her. "Who told you?"

"Does it matter?"

"No," Johnson said, shaking her head miserably.

"He asked you to marry him, didn't he?"

Biting her quivering lip, Johnson stared at the floor. "I blew it."

"Maybe you can patch things up with him."

"Patch things up? I skipped out on him. He'll never forgive me."

"You don't know that."

"It wouldn't work anyway. Can you see me as a CEO's wife?"

"No, but he doesn't sound like a typical CEO. Maybe he doesn't want a typical CEO wife. Maybe you don't even have to get married."

"Well, I guess I'll never know now..."

*

With the pressure off, Jenna and Vincent took time to fully connect. They made love for hours, completely relaxed, knowing no-one watched them. Between times, they'd go for long walks or swim in the sea. Jenna discovered the fun side of Vincent. He dragged her down beneath the waves then soared out of the water, kissing her mid-air.

Flying together, they explored a range of mountains further inland. They made full use of them, jumping off the summits, and gliding through the air.

"We need bigger mountains!" Jenna called out, and Vincent laughed. She smiled at him. She didn't feel alone anymore. Someone understood what it was like to do impossible things, someone just like her.

To Vincent, it all felt like a dream. He feared waking up to find her back with Brash. The bitter irony was; their time together was short. The days and weeks sped by, time a treacherous thing. It raced when you enjoyed yourself, slowed when you were miserable, one's perception of it changing, the moment stretching or condensing. If he could have stopped time, he would.

*

"It's been weeks," Tastari said, "and we can't locate them."

The depleted Council had gathered. Only Aktimar, Helmus, Tastari, and Vishigad remained.

"Could they be dead?" Vishigad asked, brushing a hand over her bald, cream head.

"The girl was badly injured," Tastari remarked.

"That move was a touch of genius," Helmus reflected.

"The man wasn't injured, was he?" Aktimar pointed out. "And we can't locate him."

Helmus nodded. "The only thing we can do is carry on searching. Worms come out of the ground eventually."

"We devote ourselves to it around the clock," Aktimar asserted. "We don't rest until we find them."

"Yes," Vishigad agreed, emphatically. She stood. "I'm taking a break."

As they got up to take a break, Helmus breathed in, satisfied. They had picked an excellent candidate for this game. A real challenge.

Aktimar, on the other hand, wished they had not picked Jenna Trot. The decision had cost him dearly. He whipped his head to the side. The sudden spark of hope turned to confusion. The image vanished. The weird creature had been vaguely familiar.

"Was it her?" Helmus asked him.

"No," Aktimar said, staring that spot.

The Bigger Picture

"You look deep in thought," Jenna remarked.

"Tynia's not going to help us," Vincent said, staring off over the wild land. They hadn't mentioned the game these past weeks, and Vincent had been putting off telling Jenna this. He didn't even know if Jenna expected Tynia's help.

"Why not?"

He looked at her. "Apparently, there's a bigger picture that goes beyond this life." Jenna stared at him. "That was my reaction too." He took a deep breath. "Yesterday, she said, let me know when you're ready to continue."

"She wants us to pick up again?"

Chewing his lip, he nodded. "Tynia's old. She told me her time was short."

"How does she *know* that?"

"How does she know anything?"

Jenna stared at the ground, taking in that Tynia might die soon. If they lived, Jenna would miss her. She rubbed her forehead. "How short is short?"

"I don't know."

She looked at him with watery eyes. "These past weeks have been the happiest of my life."

He pulled her into him and kissed her head. "For me too."

"We're going to die, aren't we, Vincent?"

His held onto her, tightly.

"You saying goodbye each other," Hendraz said lightly, and they turned to find him with Johnson.

Jenna wiped her eyes, plastering on a smile. "What are you two up to?"

"We're not up to anything," Johnson snapped.

"Just walking," Hendraz said with a gleam in his eye.

Jenna's gaze followed them as they moved past.

"I think they're doing it," she said.

"Really?"

"Yes, but *how* are they doing it?"

"What d'you mean?"

Jenna told Vincent about Hellgathen anatomy. Vincent's eyes widened.

She caught up with Johnson later on. Jenna couldn't let this one go. She smiled at the woman, meaningfully. "Hendraz?"

"What you talking about?"

"Oh, come on, you can't fool me. I'm not even going to ask you how, but how?"

Johnson let out a sigh. "You don't want to know."

"OK. When and why?"

"One drunken night. That answer both questions?"

"Is it serious?"

"God, no. I already ended it once but..." She shook her head. "That punch of Tynia's is strong stuff."

Jenna smiled. "You're single, he's single?"

"Yeah, well, I'm going to knock it on the head before Graham comes back."

"I thought you two were over?"

"Try telling Graham that. I don't want to pour salt in the wounds. Not to mention the fact he's fucking lost it."

Jenna nodded, thoughtfully. "Listen," she said, more seriously, "Tynia is going to drop our shield soon, so we'll be picking up again."

Johnson stared at her, confused. "Why?"

"Because we can't hide here forever. Tynia's time might be short. We'd only be putting it off."

"If she drops the shield, he'll find Damensa, won't he?"

"No, the shield covers people, not places."

"You're not leaving, are you?" Johnson asked.

"No. But none of you must try to help us."

"I might be a fucking mess but I can still fire a gun."

"That won't work. That's how Serza died. Believe me, no-one can help us."

Johnson rubbed her brow. "Don't go fucking dying on me, Trot."

Jenna smiled. "You know, that's the nicest thing you've ever said to me."

"Yeah. I need help."

*

After a few nights of love-making, Jenna and Vincent told Tynia they were ready to continue. The old woman looked at them with pride and sadness. "I have never known a braver pair than you."

"Give us half an hour to get away from here," Vincent said.

"Very well." She touched both their arms. "I'll be praying for a miracle."

"Great pep talk, Tynia," Jenna said.

Vincent looked at the woman. "I thought intervention wasn't your thing?"

"It isn't *my* thing," she said, enigmatically, and he stared at her, oddly.

Reluctantly, they walked out of the hut, and off through the trees, Tynia by their side.

"Oh," Jenna said, turning to her. "If we don't come back, make up lots of nice stuff we said about the crew."

"Will do, dear."

"And... err... thank you, Tynia."

Tynia chewed her lip. "You're not cross I'm not coming with you?"

"I have no idea why you can't help us *but* I know you have your reasons."

"You have changed, Jenna. I'm so proud of you."

Jenna smiled at her.

Emerging from the trees, Jenna and Vincent took to the air, heading out over the hills. Down below, Skinner and Sophia stared up in shock. "D-Do you see this...?" Sophia stuttered.

Skinner's mouth hung wide.

Tynia came up behind them, watching too.

"They're flying..." Sophia murmured.

Tynia turned to her. "Yes, dear. They're like superheroes, aren't they?"

Skinner dragged his pallid face to her.

Praying for a Miracle

As they came in to land, Jenna grabbled a handful of purple bata leaves, the hills packed with the stuff. Breaking them up, she handed some to Vincent.

"How long do you think?" she asked him.

"Soon." He looked at her. "Are you scared?"

"Yes."

"I am too." Wrapping her in his arms, he hugged her, possibly for the last time. "If we don't make it through this, I'll travel through time to find you," he said, vehemently.

Swallowing hard, her grip on him tightened.

The air became charged and they broke apart, looking at each other for a long moment.

"Go high," Vincent said.

She nodded and they flew up together. The air cracked, the blinding light appeared, and the feather floated down beneath them. Steeling themselves, they waited. The pressure built again. The second portal opened.

A lithe, bony creature appeared. It reminded Jenna of Gollum. Except this one had clothes on – a shiny, silver jumpsuit. It looked up immediately, fixing them with huge aubergine eyes. They rained down light spears. It threw out an arm, sending their weapons off target as it leapt up, twisting, rotating at incredible speed. The two of them stared at how fast it revolved, then they dodged as it assailed them with volley after volley of light balls... hundreds of them, firing out continually.

Darting and dodging, they shielded, having no chance to focus, let alone get anything through that intense wall of balls. The assault was relentless. Their shields got hammered. Vincent took a hit on the leg and dropped, taking more hits on the way down. Managing to steady himself, he landed on the ground in agony.

Jenna glanced down at him as she flew back, trying to get out of range. The alien moved with her, still whizzing, still spewing out balls. No matter how fast she flew, she couldn't escape its reach. And it anticipated her moves every time. She would have made a portal, but she had no space to focus.

Burning pain made Vincent sick. He watched, helpless, as Jenna tried to escape the spinning light volley. Pushing through the pain, he raised his consciousness to produce a portal. At the first hint of pressure, the alien whizzed away, driving Jenna back too. Vincent tried again but he couldn't get a fix. Giving up on that, he attempted to take to the air. Searing agony floored him. He launched feeble light spears, but even strong ones wouldn't get through that intense orb of balls. Heart beating wildly, he looked at Jenna. She was tiring fast. She couldn't attack, defend, or get away. Her situation was desperate, and he could do nothing to save her. His vision swam as pain took over. Out of options, he prayed for a miracle.

Exhausted from dodging continually, Jenna knew it was only a matter of time before she was struck. Another portal opened in the distance. Aktimar was coming to finish this? He wanted his family first. *Screw that.* Vincent lay lifeless on the ground beneath her. They were done. She wanted to be with him, lie beside him as she died. She would drop, take the bullets as she fell.

She let gravity take her but the balls didn't hit. She glanced up. Gollum had stopped firing, had turned to the portal.

Jenna landed beside Vincent. "Vincent," she said, shaking him. She wanted to say goodbye, look into his eyes one last time, but his eyes didn't open.

Kissing him softly, she bowed her head, knowing she had to end her own life.

Taking a breath, she knelt up, producing a sword, aiming it at her heart.

Her gaze shifted to the sky. She gaped, entranced. Was she hallucinating this...?

Desperately, she laid her hands over Vincent and focused, letting the power come through her, feeling it pour into him. She didn't stop until she felt it stream back.

She waited, tears forming in her eyes. Was it too late? The moments stretched unbearably.

"Vincent," she pleaded, hitting his chest. "Come back to me, damn you!"

His lungs sucked in breath. A sob escaped her. Tears fell on her cheeks. She wrapped her arms around him.

"Jenna...?" he asked, confused.

"Look," she said to him, turning skyward.

He followed her gaze, his eyes widening. Was that... Fraza...?

Fraza rotated, spewing out balls of light like Gollum. Only, Fraza had bigger balls. The alien flagged. With its focus on Fraza, the creature left its undercarriage exposed. Kicking into gear, Jenna lurched to her feet. Flying up beneath it, she took aim, launching a spear. It rocketed up, impaling the alien through the length of its body.

The balls stopped firing. The dead alien dropped, Jenna dodging out of its way. Slowly, she turned to Fraza. The Kaledian smiled down at her.

Shooting up, she threw her arms around him. "I've missed you. You were incredible!"

"I've missed you too," he said, hugging her tight.

"I can't believe you're here..."

"I'll always come when you need me."

Jenna didn't take her eyes off him as they came in to land.

"Hi, Fraza," Vincent said. "Really glad to see you."

Fraza smiled. "Hello, Mr Flint. I'm glad to see you too."

Vincent noted how erect the Kaledian stood, how sure he sounded. He wasn't the Fraza they'd parted company with on Draztis.

Jenna gave Fraza a wry smile. "I see you've been busy in our absence."

"It's been... an adventure."

"I want to hear everything but first, how the bloody hell did you *do* that...?"

One Moment

The crew gathered in Tynia's hut, staring at Fraza in shock.

Fraza's eyes widened when Johnson threw her arms around him. Remembering herself, she stepped back. "We thought you were dead," she said, rubbing her nose.

His eyes lingered on her until Hendraz slapped him on the back and he nearly choked. "Good to see you, Fraza."

Skinner smiled at him, introducing Sophia as his girlfriend. Gazing at Skinner, Fraza's eyes transferred to the girl. She started speaking Kaledian. Few humans bothered to learn it.

"How did you get here?" Johnson asked.

"Through a portal."

"You opened a portal...?" Skinner asked, staring at him in awe.

Fraza nodded.

The crew noticed the change in him. For one, there was someone behind those eyes, and for two, his shoulders weren't stooped.

Fraza had to adjust to the changes too. Jenna and Flint were a couple now. Hendraz talked to him in English. Skinner looked head-over-heels in love, and the girl seemed to love him back. Johnson kept gazing at him with moist eyes. It freaked him out.

The rest of the crew returned two days later. They emerged from their craft, their eyes flitting between Jenna, Flint, and Fraza. They'd been certain all three were dead. Newark's brain hung on the brink of exploding. He didn't know who to approach first.

"Hey, you little fucker," he said, striding over to Fraza. "Where the hell did *you* come from?"

Fraza's eyes widened when Newark lifted him into a bear hug. Dumping him down, Newark threw his arms around Jenna. "I've fucking missed you, Trot. God, I'm glad you're back."

Letting go of Jenna, he clasped Flint's arm. "Good to see you, man."

Graham and Brash followed suit, slapping Fraza on the back, and hugging Jenna. Graham clasped hands with Flint but Brash just gave him an acknowledging nod and an uncertain smile. Flint nodded back.

Allessa came forward to greet them. Jenna couldn't bring herself to make eye-contact with the woman.

"Is it over?" Graham asked, hopefully.

"No," Jenna replied.

A few moments of digestive silence followed.

Newark looked at Flint. "You've got the power too? I tell you, Flint, you're a bloody mystery. You're a fucking god, man!"

Graham's eyes flicked to Brash but Brash held it together.

Tynia walked over to them, smiling at the new arrivals. "I've made punch," she said. "Anyone care to join me?"

Congregating in Tynia's hut, Jenna told the rest of the crew all about the previous months.

"So," Newark asked, raising an eyebrow to her, "did you manage to have some fun?"

"I've got a funny little story for you, Newark," she said with a smile.

Jenna relayed the details.

"A garbage disposal system?" Newark laughed so hard, tears came in his eyes. "Bet that taught the fucker."

Skinner watched Sophia, her eyes widening in awe at these people. The awed eyes turned to him and his heart soared.

"So, Fraza," Brash said, "it seems you've been busy too."

Fraza told them of his adventures, omitting to mention Jabreen. He kept that humiliation to himself.

Newark didn't hear about Fraza's solitary adventures. He contemplated the horror of a Kaledian nudist colony. It made him lose his appetite, which was just as well because there was no stew on the go.

Tynia's punch went down well. She kept filling Fraza's glass. There was something about the Kaledian that made her want to mother him.

Newark clocked it, wondering why she didn't fill *his* glass.

"The blues still under lock and key?" Brash asked.

"Yes," Tynia replied. "Daria and Hendraz have been taking them out." The old woman's eyes strayed to them.

They talked into the night, the crew together again after all this time. As Tynia stretched and yawned, they took that as their cue to leave.

Gravitating to the bar on the ship, they started in on Hellgathen drinks. Jenna's eyes kept flicking to Brash and Allessa. They appeared very much in love, and she hoped the Sentier's infatuation with Vincent was over. By contrast, Graham and Johnson didn't look at each other at all, although Jenna caught Graham giving Johnson a snide glance. Hendraz glanced at Johnson often, and Jenna hoped that wasn't a crash waiting to happen. Her eyes settled on Fraza and she smiled.

A glow of contentment spread over Fraza. He was home.

Brash and Allessa left the group first. A short time later, the crew heard music. Jenna, Vincent, and Fraza looked around, confused.

"It's Brash," Graham told them.

"What...?" Jenna asked.

"He's a maestro."

"What...?"

"He's a fucking pianist," Newark said. "Freaked the fuck out of us too."

Standing in unison, Jenna, Vincent, and Fraza drifted to the lounge. They lingered in the doorway, staring at Brash, mystified.

"He never told me he could play..." Jenna murmured.

"He's good," Vincent said.

Fraza wondered if his portal had brought him to an alternate reality.

*

Jenna couldn't get her head around Lucas playing piano. He played incredibly. And she never knew? When she'd hear the music, she'd drift into the lounge and watch him. He seemed so different... so soulful. The Sentier would be there, watching him, absorbed. That should have made Jenna feel better but it didn't. She felt troubled.

"It's weird," Jenna said to Vincent as they walked over the land, "everyone's changed. The only one who seems the same is Newark."

"Good old Newark," Vincent remarked with a smile. "We just need to keep him away from unhinged, controlling women."

Jenna nodded. "At the moment, he seems like an anchor."

Vincent studied her. "Brash and Allessa look happy, don't they?" he remarked.

"Yes."

"Does it bother you?"

She looked at him. "Why should it bother me?"

He shrugged.

"I'm bored, Trot," Newark called out, and they turned. "Got any ideas to cheer me up?"

Jenna's eyes lit. "Ever been flying, Newark?"

"What?" he asked, brow creased.

She and Vincent shared a smile then walked forward, grabbing Newark's arms, lifting him into the air. After screaming for a couple of minutes, he began to enjoy the ride.

"Don't fucking drop me!"

Jenna thought she might try this with the blue children if their mother would allow it. Collecting Fraza, they took Damensa and her children to the beach. Jenna and Vincent did a demonstration on Newark. Damensa frowned, unconvinced, but her kids badgered her until she reluctantly agreed. Craning her head, she watched the amazing sight. Two humans and a strange creature with orange hair joining hands with her children, and flying through the air. As nervous as she felt, she couldn't help but smile. A sudden realisation struck her. She trusted this group of aliens more than her own husband.

"You should have a go," Newark said to her, "it's a fucking buzz."

"Fucking buzz?"

"You know, fun."

Damensa nodded, thoughtfully. "Fucking buzz..."

She watched the smiles on her children's faces as they came in to land. Her gaze transferred to Jenna. She walked over to her and asked if she could talk. Jenna nodded, leading her away from the group.

"Daria said you saved universe?" Damensa asked, her eyes roaming Jenna's face.

Though the woman's command of English wasn't bad, Jenna used thought transference for convenience. "We all played a part in that," Jenna said. "And, the universe is a big place. We saved a part of it."

"That was very noble of you. If my husband knew about you," she said bitterly, "he should have helped instead of saving you for his game."

Jenna nodded, quietly.

"What did my husband say to you?" she asked. "Every word you can remember."

Jenna repeated everything she recalled from that initial encounter.

Damensa looked down, her blue eyes filled with pain. "He doted on us. I always thought he used his powers for good. I never imagined..." She shook her head. "I never knew him..."

Jenna struggled for something to say. "It... sounds like he loves you and the children, though?"

The woman's face tightened. "A murderer loved us. Everything I believed was a lie. Nothing was real."

Jenna looked at the woman, seriously. "He'll probably kill me but if he doesn't, I will kill him."

Damensa looked at her with teary eyes. "I understand."

The Calibstra walked away with her head bowed.

Jenna watched her go, a well of compassion rising up in her. Her gaze shifted to Brash and Allessa. They walked over the dunes, hand in hand. She

312

studied them for a while then wandered along the beach in a world of her own.

Vincent's eyes followed her, his gaze shifting to Brash and Allessa.

"I'm going to see if I can get Tynia to rustle up a stew," Newark said. "The sea air's making me hungry."

"You might regret that," Vincent remarked, absently, a tight feeling pressing in his chest.

"Yes, but I've got an angle. Fraza's here. She fucking loves him. She'll be bursting out of her wrinkly old skin to feed him."

"I was thinking," Fraza said, "we should take the children for a walk, maybe over the hills? Let them stretch their legs. Perhaps Damensa will come with us."

"May as well," Vincent said, dragging his gaze away from Jenna.

Jenna struggled to know what this strange, disconcerted feeling was. She lowered onto the sand, staring at the sea, thinking back over the past three years. She found herself remembering Lucas's kiss. Nothing in it told her of the soulful man beneath. Yes, he could be sensitive but soulful? He played the piano as if the notes were wrenched from his soul. Where had that Lucas come from?

Further down the beach, Lucas stopped and turned to Allessa. "You're sure you've done the right thing, giving up your position?" he asked, his eyes searching hers.

She nodded, smiling gently. "If you remember, I did not ask for the position. And... I've changed. I do not know where I belong anymore, except I feel I belong with you."

She took in his intent dark brown eyes, the dark hair straggling his neck. Memories from their time on the plantation flooded her. When she met him, she didn't think she could fall in love with anyone. He had opened up a new dimension in her. They had talked a lot on Lixia. Talked about Jenna, about the crew planning to kill her, and she came to realise Lucas had been lost.

She touched his cheek. "I belong with you," she repeated.

Smiling, he took her hand, leading her back into the dunes.

Jenna looked along the beach to find it empty. She'd come further than she realised. How long had she sat here? Vincent must have taken the blues back. Sometimes, she thought he was too perfect.

Her eyes widened as the air became charged.

Jumping to her feet, she ran over the sand, scanning the distance for Vincent or Fraza, shouting their names in the vain hope they could hear. She crashed to a halt as a portal opened in front of her, a feather floating to the ground. Further down the beach, another portal was opening already.

She took to the air, tried to mind-link with Vincent. Her opponent jumped out beneath her, looking up. A second later, an almighty force slung her down. She bashed on the sand, her feeble energy cushion barely breaking her fall. Adrenaline powered her. She took to the air again but again he slammed her down. Sore and winded, she looked at the lizard-like creature.

"Going so soon?" he asked, his mouth unmoving, his yellow eyes fixed on her. "I thought we could play for a while."

Trying to remain calm, her mind opened a channel to Vincent. The lizard stood there, allowing her to do it?

In the distance, Allessa ran down the beach toward her. The lizard tossed out an arm as if shooing a fly, and the Sentier flew back, crashing on the sand. Jenna sprang into action, throwing out lightning balls, spears, arrows, which the creature deflected toward Allessa. The Sentier created an energy wall, the light crashing off it as Jenna searched for her next move. She manifested a light sword in the sky. As it shot down, the lizard thrust out an arm, deflecting it back to Allessa. He smiled grotesquely. "I've seen all your tricks, Jenna Trot."

She manifested a light whip but the creature became a blur, flying around her at phenomenal speed, wrapping her in invisible film that pressed on all sides. She performed a total body shot but she couldn't shift it. What the hell *was* this stuff...?

After he'd done with her, he wrapped Allessa, the Sentier's moves proving useless too.

The cocoon tightened. Jenna's breathing laboured. Relief flooded her when she spotted Vincent and Fraza flying toward them. The lizard flew up to engage them. Fraza's spinning balls carried no weight this time. The alien's shield was too strong, the balls barely distracting him as he flew circles around them, wrapping them like insects. The crew ran down the beach in the distance, firing upward, but nothing got through to the lizard. They were forced to retreat as lightning rained down on them.

Battling to breathe, Jenna watched Vincent and Fraza become invisible. Mentally kicking herself, she raised her vibration, the pressure dissipating at last.

The lizard didn't seem concerned they had slipped his net. He could still see them, his eyes following their movements.

Down below, the crew stared up in disbelief. Brash's gaze moved to Allessa. He ran over to her. She struggled to breathe and he had no idea how to help her.

"What can I do?" he pressed.

Allessa's bulging eyes gaped at him.

Jenna scrambled for her next move. She could do little in this state. The lizard hung in the air. What was he waiting for?

Vincent asked the same question. The answer presented itself when a new portal opened. A hooded being stepped out of the light. Vincent knew only something of mammoth proportion could help them now.

Jenna stared at the hooded being as it walked toward her.

"I can still see you, Jenna Trot," he teased, his face in shadow. "Tastari is good. He can raise his vibration too, take you in this state as much as the other."

"You said, one at a time," Jenna shot angrily.

As the being drew close, she finally saw his face. A human face...? She stared at the good-looking features, the dark hair, the intense green eyes.

"You're human," she said, startled.

The green eyes never left her. "I wanted to meet you in case you die today and, fortunately, Tastari, bless him, is patient. You have proved to be so much more entertaining than expected. It is a shame your time is nearly through."

"You're older than you look," she said, studying him closely.

"I'm a hundred years old. When you advance in your training, you learn to slow down ageing. It's a shame you'll never get to advance, though."

"Then stop this. You could train me. If I'm a worthy challenge, I might be a worthy student. Is there any need for this?"

Helmus smiled. "When the game starts, there is no stopping it until its conclusion. I regret you are going to die but that is the game."

"One hundred years makes you inflexible, I see. Still just an old git at heart."

His smile didn't falter. "You have been ruffling feathers, haven't you, Jenna Trot? I respect your bravery, your inventiveness, and your spirit. But," he said with a sigh, "it looks as if you'll die today. If not, then soon by my hand. I salute you, Jenna Trot. Die well."

He bowed his head and turned to leave. Jenna panicked. This was it. The brick wall they had been facing. The lizard was way out of their league.

In the brief respite, Vincent had raised his consciousness higher than he ever had before. He had moved beyond time and space. If space was malleable at a higher level, then so was time.

Keeping himself at that level, he engaged the power and his intent. His intent was to lock time itself. There was just one moment. The frozen moment was all there was...

He felt the shift, saw everything exist in a perfect state of abeyance. The hooded being captured mid-stride. The lizard hanging in the air. Jenna and

315

Fraza frozen in their ethereal forms. The crew below staring up, as if gazing into eternity. The world hung suspended, except for Tynia, standing on the sand dunes, a smile spreading on her face.

Lowering his vibration, Vincent came down and grabbed Newark's gun. He flew up to the lizard and shot him in the head. He moved over to the hooded figure, taking in the human face. Pointing the weapon at his forehead, he dropped the moment, catching the flash of confusion and fear in the green eyes before he fired.

Behind him, the lizard fell from the sky.

The crew stared at the dead aliens. Jenna looked at Vincent, bewildered.

Tynia approached Vincent and he turned.

"You left out that particular lesson, Tynia," he said. "Why?"

"That is one lesson I am not allowed to share. Time is a delicate thing, leading to all kinds of contradictions. Besides, you would have used it too early and it isn't something beings like this should learn. And learn they will, eventually. So, with that in mind, Aktimar absolutely must die."

*

Aktimar stared in horrified shock. One minute, Tastari and Helmus had control. The next, Tastari was dead and that man shot Helmus in the head. How had the man or the gun *got* near Helmus? It was like he'd missed frames in a film. For the first time, he had no idea what he was dealing with.

Dragging a hand over his face, he looked around the empty council chamber. Everything he thought he knew crumbled around him.

He whipped his head to the side. *Her.*

"You've got one day, Aktimar. We'll come for you, one at a time. You might want to find out what you do not know. You'll receive a white feather before we come. One day, Aktimar."

The Cruellest Game

Aktimar wandered around his empty house, wondering if his family was still alive. He picked up his son's book, staring at it, pain stabbing his heart. Dropping the book, he snatched a vase, and hurled it against the wall.

Raking his hands through his indigo hair, he stared at the floor.

Taking a deep, collecting breath, he walked outside, and waited. For the first time, fear crawled up his spine.

He didn't wait long. Pressure built. Wind got up. The air ripped apart, and blinding light appeared as the portal opened. A white feather floated to the ground. He stared at it for a moment then stood straight, his look taking on a hard aspect. The second portal opened. But what came through floored him. It wasn't Jenna Trot. It was his wife.

He stood frozen, staring at her. "Damensa...?"

As he moved forward, she held out an arm. "Stay back," she said.

"What have they done to you?"

"They treated me well."

"The children?"

"Safe."

His gaze narrowed. "Is this a mind trick?" he asked, uncertainly.

"Do you not recognise your own wife, Aktimar?" She tilted her head. "I can understand that. I do not recognise you, either."

"What do you mean? What has she been telling you? Whatever it is, it's lies."

"She was an innocent person caught in your game. How many games have there been? How many innocents have you slaughtered?"

"Damensa, she is lying!"

"I thought you to be a good man. An honourable man. The man standing before me is someone I do not know."

"You do know me. She is not innocent. She is a murderer we have been hunting."

"Yet, they treated me so well?"

"She is the one playing a game. This is part of *her* game. Don't you see that?" He stepped forward. "Will you trust her or will you trust me?"

"Please, Aktimar," she begged wearily, her eyes pleading with him, "if you love me at all, tell me the truth."

He hesitated, a moment of conflict in his eyes. The truth was there, yet he would not give it to her. She bowed her head.

"Do you not trust your husband?" he persisted.

She looked at him with watery eyes. "Yes," she whispered, walking forward.

Aktimar smiled, holding out his arms for her. She rushed into them, clinging on tight.

"I love you," Aktimar said.

"I loved you too," she whispered.

She pulled back and plunged a knife into his heart.

His horrified eyes fixed her, taking in the tears streaming down her cheeks.

He dropped, his life blood spilling from him. She fell down beside him. "You were everything to me but none of it was real..."

His eyes never left her but he couldn't speak.

Finally, she pulled herself up, staring down at her dying husband.

A third portal opened. Jenna Trot stepped through. Aktimar focused, trying desperately to heal himself, but his consciousness was slipping. The two figures walked through the portal. The light disappeared. The cruellest game of all, dying by his wife's hand.

Just You

The crew waited for them on the beach. When they came through, Damensa dropped on the sand, broken. *She* would have to be the liar now, tell her children their father had died, but not by her hand. Johnson went over and sat beside her.

Vincent grabbed Jenna in a fierce embrace. "We're free," he whispered into her hair.

She hugged him tightly.

The whole crew felt a huge weight lift. They had done virtually nothing but, at least, they had been here. Sure, they couldn't do mind-numbing stuff like Flint, Trot, or Fraza, but team's a team. And now they could fuck off and go somewhere better.

"Well, what now?" Graham asked.

"Cornelius has a baby," Fraza told them.

"That's right," Jenna said with a gleam in her eye. "A little Cornelius."

"They'll be tearing their hair out by now," Newark remarked, thinking of all the screaming and crying, and wondering if they should find their own gaff.

"Are you coming with us, Hendraz?" Jenna asked.

"I be part of crew now." Hendraz wanted to travel and explore. He also wanted to revisit Johnson.

Jenna looked around. "Where's Tynia?"

"I'm here, dear," the woman said, coming into form.

"What are you doing?"

"Just warming up, dear. It's my time to go."

"Go? Where?"

"Home, dear."

"Home?"

"It's my time to die."

The crew stared at her. "Don't you have to get ill first?" Newark asked, scratching his head.

"Most do, yes. Now, I'm going to be mushy and give you all hugs. I must say, as troublesome as most of you are, I've become quite attached to you. I'll leave Daria and Damensa," she decided. "Daria's doing a sterling job there, and Damensa *did* try to kill me."

Graham glanced at Daria. She was being... supportive?

319

Tynia hugged them all in turn, leaving Vincent for last. "I've enjoyed your company most of all," she said with a fond smile. "You amaze me. You're definitely the one to watch," she said with a wink.

Smiling at them one last time, she turned and walked away, her form becoming less substantial.

"Holy fuck..." Newark murmured.

"Tynia," Jenna shouted.

Rematerializing, the woman turned back.

"You're taking your body with you...?"

"That's just matter, dear."

"Were you actually born? Was Hiffelfust real?"

"Oh, yes, dear. Very real and very enjoyable. I remembered who I really was at a young age. It was a revelation, I can tell you. But then I was supposed to remember." She smiled at their staring faces. "I've got a little trick for you."

The crew's eyes widened as Tynia transformed into a stunning young human. "Maybe Cornelius would have liked this one," she said with a devilish grin.

"Fuck me," Newark spluttered.

"Please watch your language, Mr Newark."

"Is that a mind-trick?" Jenna asked, staring at her.

"No, dear. It's a matter trick. Well, mind over matter, to be precise." She smiled at them, gently. "Anyway, enjoy the rest of your lives."

She turned, the crew staring after the young and, quite frankly, sexy woman. They continued to stare after she'd disappeared. Then the men shuddered.

"I always thought there was something weird about her..." Newark murmured, freaked out. "An old woman in a young woman's body? Imagine if she'd been in a young body and one of us..." He shuddered again.

Jenna and Flint continued to stare, sadness tugging at their hearts.

"Is it me, or are we getting used to unreal, fucked-up shit?" Graham said, glancing at Johnson again.

"I haven't got a clue about anything..." Skinner uttered.

"I'm so glad I met you..." Sophia said to him.

As they dispersed, Jenna's eyes moved to Brash and Allessa. They walked away, hand in hand, gazing at each other. She didn't recognise Brash. He had a softness, a depth, that wasn't there before.

Vincent watched her, thoughtfully.

Johnson stayed with Damensa in her hut that night, hanging in the background as Damensa told the children that their father had been killed.

The children broke down, pitifully. Johnson held onto her own tears, knowing now that Tynia had been right. Staying strong when you felt so much was freaking hard. It took everything out of her.

The following day, Damensa and her children were returned to their home planet. They would live with her parents now. The children appeared devastated. The crew, not realising how attached they'd become to the blues, were sad to see them go.

Hendraz had no choice but to leave his craft on Cyntros. Trailing his hand over the side of it, he said a long goodbye.

The rest of the crew took time to say goodbye to the place that had been home these past months. As Jenna wandered into Tynia's hut, a wave of sadness overtook her.

Vincent followed her in, feeling the same way. "She was the closest to a mother I had," he said and Jenna turned to him, sadly. "I wish there had been more time to say goodbye."

"Yeah, she sprung her death on us, didn't she?"

"Where do you think she's gone?"

"I guess we'll find out one day."

He came over, wrapping his arms around her waist. "Not for a long time, I hope. We're finally free."

She reached up to kiss him.

*

Brash and Allessa were inseparable during the two-week trip to the Milky Way. Brash treated the crew to piano recitals, although Newark, Hendraz, and Graham preferred to spend time in the bar. Johnson was still an insular figure, and Jenna watched Hendraz get nowhere with her, which was probably for the best because Graham was always in a foul mood.

Jenna and Vincent split their time between the bedroom, the bar, the flight-deck, and the lounge. Brash mesmerised Jenna when he played. This was a Lucas she had never known.

Tonight, as he played, Allessa caught Jenna studying him. The Sentier's head tilted, her grey eyes probing. Allessa's eyes flicked to Flint, who walked away, Jenna unaware of it.

After the recital, Jenna found Vincent in the bar with Newark, Hendraz, and Graham. Vincent's eyes lifted to her, remaining on her as she sat down.

"He's an amazing pianist," she remarked.

"Yeah," Newark agreed.

"Why didn't he tell anyone? None of us knew."

"He started playing after he had his melt-down."

"He had a melt-down?"

"Yeah. When Flint opened the portal, and we found out he had the power, Brash flipped out. Held up in his room. We thought he'd topped himself."

"He was in there for ages," Graham remarked, throwing back his drink.

Newark nodded. "At least, there's something he can do better than Flint." He turned to Vincent. "You can't play an instrument, can you?"

Vincent shook his head. "No."

"Thank Christ for that." Newark sighed. "Him and Johnson are not the same... Brash is all mushy, and Johnson's not Johnson anymore. I miss her..."

"They just need time," Vincent said, thoughtfully.

"Allessa took weeks to decide if she wanted Brash," Graham remarked out of nowhere.

"And he waited patiently," Newark said. "When has Brash ever been patient? It's fucked-up."

Graham shook his head. "The mushy bastard's going to get his heart ripped out. She could still dump him," he said bitterly.

Jenna studied Graham. He wasn't dealing with Johnson's rejection at all. She wanted to help him. "You know, you can't help who you fall in love with, Graham," she said, softly. "When Johnson met Emilio, she was single. You have to move on. Stop punishing her."

Graham glared at her. "Have you decided who *you* want, yet? Or will you flip back to Brash and blow Flint off again?"

"That's enough, Graham," Vincent said.

"That's one-sided, isn't it?" Jenna asserted. "Brash blew Allessa off too. Are you going to turn bitter against all women because you're hurt? I thought you were better than that."

"*You* kissed Flint when you were still with Brash," Graham threw at her. "You'll do the same to Flint."

"Shut up, Graham," Vincent said.

"Maybe I did kiss Flint," Jenna countered, "but that's none of your god damn business. Maybe Johnson did dump you because she had issues with her mother, but *you* got yourself a girlfriend and decided to move in with her."

"That's right, stick up for her. Bitches first."

Jenna stood. "You call me a bitch again, I'll knock you out."

"Graham, you need to shut the fuck up," Vincent growled.

"I've seen her looking at Brash. She'll be back in his bed before you know it."

Vincent's fist smashed into Graham's face before Jenna's got the chance. Newark thought Graham lucky he only got the one shot.

Hendraz loved humans.

*

Graham kept his mouth shut after that, unless he got drunk, but the crew gave him a wide berth then. Graham's remarks had got to Vincent, though. Jenna did look at Brash a lot. He'd seen her talking to him when Allessa wasn't around. But then, he reasoned, he and Allessa had talked too.

"You and Brash seem happy?" he had said to the Sentier.

"Yes. I am glad we did not... Well, it might have complicated matters... for both of us."

He nodded. "He's different, isn't he?"

"He has revealed much to me about his life before he joined the space corps. I think he is finding himself. We are good together." Her grey eyes looked at him in earnest. "I hope we will always be friends, Flint."

"Me too."

Vincent's doubts about Jenna continued to grow, remaining with him as they arrived on Marios Prime.

Cornelius and Takeza were overjoyed to see them. The baby, which had orange hair, was mauled to death, and got landed with a host of aunties and uncles.

"You're a fucking dad!" Newark announced, slapping Cornelius on the back. "God man, you look shattered."

Cornelius and Takeza took advantage of their babysitters straight away. They disappeared upstairs for some much-needed sleep. Allessa picked up the baton, the Sentier having a soothing effect on the baby.

Cornelius caught up with events the next morning.

"Tynia's dead?" he asked, sadly.

"Well, she's dead but she isn't dead," Newark said, his brow creasing.

Cornelius's brow creased too. Jenna explained the manner of her death.

"And get this," Newark said, "she switched into a drop dead gorgeous young woman *who*, she said, you might like."

The old man's brow creased again. He scratched his temple, glancing at Takeza with a helpless shrug.

The crew made themselves at home in Cornelius's gaff. Jenna hadn't spoken to Graham since that night in the bar. She couldn't believe what an arsehole he'd turned into.

When Vincent came down one evening to see Jenna studying Brash again, he'd had enough. He asked her to come outside with him.

The green twilight glow pervaded the sky. Scrubby grassland stretched around them.

"This time of day is growing on me," Jenna said, taking a deep breath.

"What are you doing, Jenna?"

She turned to him. "Breathing in the air," she said, smiling.

"No. That's not what I mean. Have you made a mistake again?" he threw at her.

"What...?"

"What's going on with Brash?"

"What are you talking about...?"

"You're always looking at him. He's changed. Is he what you want now? He travelled to Lixia to get Allessa back. She's renounced her position for him. You'll break her heart."

Jenna stared at him. "Good to know where your priorities lie."

"Well?"

"Well, nothing," she said, walking off.

He grabbed her arm. She shook it off, glaring at him. "You're right, Vincent. I'm some frivolous homewrecker. Poor Allessa's going to get her heart broken again. Why don't you give her a shoulder to cry on?"

"Don't be stupid, Jenna."

If he'd punched her, it couldn't have hurt more. "On top of all that, you, of all people, are calling me stupid...?"

"This is ridiculous. I just asked why you're looking at Brash all the time."

"No, that's not what you were doing. You asked me what's going on with Brash, accused me of wrecking Allessa's relationship with him, showing more concern about her than anything else, and then to top it all, you call me stupid and ridiculous."

He stared at her. That was exactly what he had done. "I'm sorry," he mumbled. "Do you have feelings for Brash?"

"No. I have been trying to figure out how I could have a relationship with him all that time and not know him, not see him. I have been dissecting it, trying to remember hints or clues but there's nothing."

"Why should that bother you?"

"Because nothing I knew was real."

"It was real at the time."

"Was it? I spent a lot of my life being blind to everything. So, it bothers me, OK? I'm sorry if you thought... whatever you thought. I didn't realise what I was doing." She turned and walked away.

"Are we alright, Jenna?" he called after her.

She turned back to him. "No. You never call me stupid. Ever. You obviously have feelings for Allessa, possibly don't even realise it, and you don't trust me. So, no, we are not alright."

"You could have talked to me about this," he said.

"You could have asked."

"I... I was afraid..."

The look on his face pierced her anger, made her chest hurt.

He bowed his head. "I don't have feelings for Allessa. It was a smokescreen. I *was* accusing you. I'm sorry... And I'm even more sorry for calling you stupid. I know what that word means to you."

"I don't want Brash. I'm sorry if I gave you that impression."

He closed the distance and wrapped her in his arms. "I'm sorry," he whispered into her hair. "Guess I'm jealous."

She looked at him. "You're the best thing that ever happened to me. I want you. Just you."

He brushed a lock of hair from her face. "And I want you. Just you."

A New Place

As the weeks passed, they settled into life in Jakensk. Cornelius decided they needed an annex to house the crew. The huge house felt cramped now. Jenna and Fraza hit the casinos to pay for it, and Cornelius didn't raise any objections. The building work kept the crew busy, Graham taking centre stage. If he could make a good job of this, he would showcase the place.

Johnson got some of her old self back. "Newark, if you drop another brick on my foot, I'll fucking floor you."

Jenna felt a new lease of life. The game was over, the scumbags dead, and she and Vincent were all loved up. Brash and Allessa were loved up too. As were Skinner and Sophia, though Jenna had spotted Sophia flirting with Hendraz.

Brash was coming out of himself, laughing and joking in a way he never had before. This Brash was light-hearted, less serious, and could tell a decent bloody joke. He'd shed years.

Johnson joked more too, although even Graham could see she wasn't entirely happy. She'd often be seen wandering around on her own.

"You know," Jenna said to her, "if you want Emilio, you should go for it."

Johnson sniffed. "I've burned my bridges there."

"Well, you won't know if you don't try."

"And get trashed for my efforts? No, thanks."

Graham finally apologised to Jenna for the things he said. "I didn't mean all that shit."

"Welcome back, Graham," she said, smiling at him. She looked at him, awkwardly. "Are you... OK with Johnson now?"

He looked away and nodded. "I've accepted it's over."

Jenna didn't feel convinced. Nor was she convinced Emilio was done with Johnson.

The annex got finishing touches. All the crew applied themselves to it, except Jenna and Vincent, who had taken themselves off for a romantic weekend.

Hendraz worked bare-chested, showing off his tattoos. It was for Johnson's benefit but she barely noticed. Sophia, however, took in eyefuls. Johnson watched her from beneath her shades, knowing Sophia liked adventure. Glancing at Skinner, she hoped the girl didn't act on it.

Taking herself off for a well-earned break, Johnson sat under a tree and closed her eyes. The breeze caressed her face like lover's fingers. A well of sorrow heaved up in her chest but she rode it through, letting it return to the depths. She had come back to herself a little but she knew she had irrevocably changed, and wherever she was headed, she hadn't got there yet.

A shadow cut out the light. She opened her eyes, staring up in wonder. Emilio stood there in all his glory.

"You look as beautiful as the day I first saw you," the Spaniard said, his dark eyes fixed on her.

In a daze, Johnson rose, still staring at him, hardly believing him real. Her eyes absorbed every detail of his gorgeous, fascinating face.

Sudden life possessed her. She grabbed him into a passionate kiss. The Spaniard wrapped his arms around her, squeezing her to him. Her heart soared. This was happiness. Life had finally given it to her.

Jenna and Vincent looked at each other and smiled.

Hendraz sized Emilio up.

Graham felt sick.

***

Printed in Great Britain
by Amazon

25666723R00185